ASHES AND DIAMONDS

	DATE DUE	
JUL 25 1998		
AUG 0 1 1998	DEC 26 1999	
AUG 3 1 1998	FEB 0 1 2002	
	OCT 16 2003	
OCT 13 1998		
OCT 20 1998	DEC 14 2006	
JAN 06 1999	MAY 0 6 2010	
JAN 3 0 1999		
	JUN 19 2013	

ASHES AND DIAMONDS

Jerzy Andrzejewski

Translated by D. J. Welsh
Foreword by Barbara Niemczyk
Introduction by Heinrich Böll

NORTHWESTERN UNIVERSITY PRESS

Evanston, Illinois

Northwestern University Press
Evanston, Illinois 60208–4210

First published in Poland under the title *Popiól i Daiment* by Spoldizielnia
Wydawnicza Czytelnik, 1948. English translation first published in Great Britain
by Weidenfeld & Nicolson, 1962. Published by Penguin Books in Great Britain,
1965. Published in Penguin Books in the Writers from the Other Europe Series,
1980. Northwestern University Press edition published 1991 by arrangement with
Viking Penguin, a division of Penguin Books USA, Inc.

Printed in the United States of America

First printing 1991
First European Classics printing 1996

ISBN 0-8101-1519-0

Library of Congress Cataloging-in-Publication Data

Andrzejewski, Jerzy, 1909–
    [Popiól i diament. English]
    Ashes and diamonds / Jerzy Andrzejewski ; translated by D.J. Welsh ;
foreword by Barbara Niemczyk ; introduction by Heinrich Böll.
        p. cm. — (European classics)
    Originally published: Evanston, Ill.: Northwestern University Press, 1991.
    ISBN 0-8101-1519-0 (pbk. : alk. paper)
    I. Welsh, David J. II. Title. III. Series: European classics (Evanston, Ill.)
PG7158.A7P613 1996
891.8'537—dc20   96-38228
                                                                                        CIP

The paper used in this publication meets the minimum requirements of the
American National Standard for Information Sciences—Permanence of Paper
for Printed Library Materials, ANSI Z39.48-1984.

Contents

Foreword

Many of the questions that Heinrich Böll raised in his introduction to the 1980 Penguin edition of Jerzy Andrzejewski's *Ashes and Diamonds* have been answered by subsequent events of the past ten years in Poland, and, even more dramatically, in autumn 1989, when the "peoples' republics" of Central and Eastern Europe began to crumble with astonishing rapidity, revealing the decay and corruption within. Although Andrzejewski's novel presents a microcosm of Polish society at the end of World War II, his vision is relevant to all of that part of Europe divided between Eastern and Western "spheres of influence," whose peoples' fate hung in the balance in those chaotic days in May 1945.

The world Andrzejewski depicts is one of destruction and devastation, to be sure, but beneath the ashes lies a faint glimmer of life, of hope. From the destruction would come the creation of a new world, whose exact shape was not yet clear in 1945. For Andrzejewski's characters, choices were still possible—or so it seemed to them. Their world was poised on the brink of change: the old social and political order had already crumbled, but a new order had yet to be firmly established.

To a certain degree Andrzejewski's depictions of Polish social classes were determined by the exigencies of postwar politics in Poland. Contrary to Andrzejewski's characterization, the aristocracy was not a spineless, decadent lot who at worst collaborated with the Germans and at best spent their time plotting to get themselves and their possessions out of the country. Many fought courageously in the non-Communist resistance, the AK or Armia Krajowa, which could not even be referred to by name in 1948, when *Ashes and Diamonds* appeared. The Communists in Andrzejewski's book are, by and large, decent people who fought valiantly for Poland's freedom and want to see her reborn as an egalitarian state and society. In reality, such men were surely few in number. If the purges of the 1930s, in which much of the

Communist elite, including the Polish party leadership, perished, did not alert them to the reality of Stalin's tyranny, then postwar politics in the countries "liberated" by the Red Army must have destroyed any illusions of even "true believers" about the nature of the system imposed by the Soviet Union. Denial is a powerful human impulse, however, and, just as during wartime, almost any kind of behavior can be rationalized, even justified. The most important consideration is to survive.

Ideologues like Szczuka and Podgorski are dangerous because they can justify any wrong, any act of cruelty, any extremist measure if it is carried out in the name of a greater cause, as they define it. Personal loyalties and attachments are secondary considerations. As Szczuka's archfoe, Colonel Staniewicz, explains, in a battle to the death there can be no compromises. "We're not worried by careerists. When the time comes they'll leave the sinking ship like rats. . . . But when it's a question of ideas which bring us enslavement and death, then our reply can only be death. . . . History will be the final judge as to who was right" (p. 50).

More revealing, perhaps, is the conversation between Kalicki, the old Socialist, and Szczuka, the Communist. Kalicki, the more experienced and realistic of the two, is very aware of the Russian imperialist nature of the Soviet system—a point that Szczuka is unwilling to see or admit. It is clear to both men that they are now on opposing sides, despite their common ideological roots and youthful values. The Polish Communists of 1945 have strayed far from their origins in nineteenth-century struggles for social justice and equality.

Yet the Soviet system was imposed on Poland and the other countries of the former Soviet bloc (today even this reference is hard to define—the "former satellites"? the members of the "former Warsaw Pact"?) by an occupying army and maintained by careerists and opportunists who saw an easy path to career advancement and social acceptance. Although the ideologues and "true believers" were necessary for the Soviets to establish control, it was the Swieckis, the Drewnowskis, the Weycherts who ensured that the system functioned, however imperfectly, from day to day. It is possible that men like Szczuka and Podgorski may even have found themselves on the side of the reformers in 1956 and 1970. Being reasonably intelligent and decent men, disgusted by the abuses and excesses of the Stalinist regime of Bierut, they may very well have sided with the Gomułkas and Giereks. They would certainly be found among the Jaruzelskis, Rakowskis, and Kiszczaks—men who never lost faith in their cause, but who were willing to bend to the realities of their time.

Perhaps the most sinister and frightening characters of the novel are the young conspirators led by Julius Szretter. These would-be terrorists lie, steal, and even kill, not in the name of some ideology—no matter how misguided—but for no purpose and with no remorse. What is most disturbing is that they are all from "good" families. These young nihilists are the logical products of a war that devalued human life, but they are also prototypes of the younger generation in East Central Europe today. Trapped in a system that offers them no real opportunities, and, to a large extent, devoid of the traditional values and beliefs that sustained their parents' generation, these young people have nothing to lose and nothing positive to anticipate. This is an extremely unpredictable and potentially volatile group in Poland and elsewhere in Eastern Europe, and they are disturbing spiritual descendants of Andrzejewski's fictional creations.

The drunken polonaise near the conclusion of the book unites all of the characters in unlikely pairings. For the first—and perhaps the last—time, Communist and aristocrat, intellectual and peasant, unite. Not to save Poland, but rather in one last Romantic fling, echoing the conclusion of Stanisław Wyspianski's masterpiece, *The Wedding,* when the wedding guests, representing all social classes, lose themselves in the "charmed circle" of the dance, falling under the spell of the music, the feasting and drinking, and, of course, the wedding celebration itself, which literally and symbolically united all Polish social classes.[1] Although the off-key orchestra, thumping pianist, and

---

[1] The famous wedding, which took place on November 20, 1900, between Lucjan Rydel, a young poet, and Jadwiga Mikolajczykowna, a peasant girl, was planned as a deliberately symbolic and consciously theatrical event. Wyspianski, who was present at the wedding as a guest, based his play, which premiered in March 1901, on the actual characters and events.

drunken, mismatched partners staggering through the ballroom of the Hotel Monopole provide a grotesque parody of Wyspianski's dreamlike atmosphere and colorful imagery, the message is nevertheless the same: the tendency of all classes in Polish society to lose themselves in Romantic illusions, in vain dreams of valor and glory, results in a paralysis of will and an inability to act in any useful, constructive manner.

It is the spell of this dream that Michael Chelmicki attempts to break when reality intrudes into his life. In the end it is this conflict between dream and reality that destroys him. The futility of the cause for which the handful of resistance (Armia Krajowa) fighters is still fighting becomes more and more obvious. This is of no consequence for a Pole, however. It is the gesture, the stand, the Romantic sense of heroism, self-sacrificing when necessary, which has always been most important. It is as futile to assassinate Szczuka as it was to resist superior German forces on Westerplatte in September 1939, or for the inhabitants of Warsaw to make one final suicidal stand in 1944. The result is less important than the gesture. To resist means to be alive; as long as one Pole remains alive, the nation lives in him (to paraphrase the Polish national anthem: "Poland has not yet perished / As long as we are still alive"). This is the battle that Michael Chelmicki must wage with his colleagues and with himself: devotion to traditional ideals and loyalty to his comrades-in-arms, against the pragmatic will to live and the recognition that human relationships provide a better measure of life and immortality than do sacrifices made in the name of abstract concepts. Christine, the ultimate pragmatist and anti-Romantic, shuns even the suggestion of personal attachment for fear of losing it. She realizes that "one cannot found one's life on even the nearest and dearest of people" (p. 42). For Szczuka, whose wife's death becomes less of a personal loss and more of an abstraction in the course of the book, "it is unwise to give the dead too much feeling and thought. They have no need of them. They need nothing. They do not exist. There are only the living" (p. 42). For a generation that witnessed death on a mass scale, life remains poised in a precarious balance between daily dehumanization and a fierce, stubborn clinging even to this devalued life, which yet contains a spark of hope—however faint—of a better future.

A man like Kossecki, the ultimate survivor, who is a perfectly ordinary man, even decent and honorable in normal times, can therefore cooperate with his tormentors and torment others, then rationalize his own behavior because "there's one set of values for wartime, and another for peace." "Certain people broke down in one way or another during the war" because "they couldn't endure the nightmare" (pp. 235, 234). As he points out to Podgorski, the uncompromising moralist, little is to be gained by putting him on trial. Other people—even witnesses to his crimes—would just as soon not be reminded of the dark sides of their own natures.

History seems to have proved him right. This argument has been waged again and again in postwar history. The zeal with which Nazi war criminals were prosecuted at Nuremberg by the victorious Allies soon gave way to indifference or even to a deliberate disregard once the wartime alliance fell apart and Cold War hostilities began. Former allies now became enemies and defeated enemies were enthusiastically supported as friends and buffers against "Communist aggression." The people of Berlin who cheered the armies of the Third Reich became courageous defenders of freedom during the Berlin Airlift. As a Pole, commenting on the respective economic and political situations in Poland and West Germany in the 1970s, remarked, "It's difficult to believe *we* won the war." For forty-four years there existed a "good Germany" and "the other Germany." Which was which depended on one's perspective. From a Soviet point of view, the vestiges of Fascism remained only in West Germany, while from the Western viewpoint, the tendency toward totalitarianism and blind obedience to authority was retained only in East Germany. Events of the last year, and in particular the reunification of Germany, have shown the absurdity of this formula of dividing the world into "good" and "bad" countries and peoples. The problems and anxieties posed by German reunification are a direct result of the artificial postwar division of Europe and have little to do with which side won the war. History is written by the survivors, however, and wars interpreted by the victors.

It is safe to conclude that the overwhelming desire to survive and to lead the semblance of a "normal" life has been the dominant factor in shaping the subsequent lives of Andrzejewski's characters. The Puciatynskis and the Telezynskis undoubtedly left Poland. Perhaps the remnants of the AK partisans did too. All of the others probably remained and survived as best they could, taking refuge from an alien and often brutal regime in the comforts of family, tradition, religion. As in all societies, human nature tends to put aside past pain and disillusionment and to get on with life. In Poland, just as elsewhere in Europe, the need to rebuild a ruined country and to reconstruct a shattered society (minus six million of its citizens) was paramount. Particularly after 1956, when Władysław Gomułka came to power, it seemed possible for Poland to pursue its own course within the Soviet bloc. Most Poles accepted the status quo and concentrated on their own lives.

History has proved who was right—or, at least, who was wrong. This is why the resentment and hostility currently directed against former Communists is so fierce in Eastern Europe, even when those are the only people with any practical experience in running a government or managing an economy. It will take time for this backlash to subside. This resentment is understandably strongest in those countries which had the most repressive regimes. At the present time (1990), Poland, traditionally one of the most vehemently anti-Communist and anti-Soviet countries in Europe, finds itself in the curious situation of being one of the last former satellites with Communists still in power. This is precisely because Poland's revolution has been proceeding gradually since 1956, and the latest phase has evolved over the past ten years. The fragmented groups that rebelled in 1956, 1968, 1970, and 1976 finally managed to coalesce and to unite their efforts in August 1980. They found a common voice and were galvanized into acting as a unified movement.

The formation of Solidarity was a unique phenomenon in Polish history. For a brief moment all levels and classes of Polish society stood together—Communist and clergyman, Christian and Jew, worker and student, bureaucrat and artist—united in a common goal. Their aim at first was not to overthrow the Communist system as such (this hardly seemed possible in

1980), but simply to take a stand against tyranny, injustice, and oppression. Solidarity has necessarily evolved with changing times and demands. It has inevitably separated into distinctive threads and tendencies; whether or not these individual threads can be rewoven, even if more loosely, into some sort of workable fabric remains to be seen.

The bankruptcy of the system was apparent in 1980, and despite the repression following the imposition of martial law in December 1981, it was only a matter of time until it would collapse completely. Communism came to an end in Poland with a whimper, not a bang as in the other Soviet bloc countries. The elections of June 1989 forced the Polish Workers' party to acknowledge and accept the situation. The election results showed beyond any doubt that, in the eyes of the Polish people, the Communist government had no legitimacy. Party candidates were simply crossed off the ballot when running unopposed—the Communists failed to win even the seats in parliament guaranteed them. This not only marked the first time Communists had lost an election in a Soviet satellite state but also provided the catalyst to motivate reformers, opposition groups, and ordinary citizens in the other Soviet bloc countries. The extraordinary images of former prisoners Lech Walesa, Tadeusz Mazowiecki, Adam Michnik, and Jacek Kuron sitting in the Polish parliament beside General Jaruzelski, Mieczysław Rakowski, and General Kiszczak, their former jailers, seemed almost surreal, the creation of a political cartoonist. Yet this is the peculiar position in which Poland finds itself today. In many ways the present situation is similar to that of May 1945. The old order has collapsed, as the next elections will decisively demonstrate. The collapse of Communist regimes in neighboring countries, including the Soviet Union, has made even the pretense of sharing power with the Communists unnecessary. The shape of the new order is not yet visible, but for the time being, ideologues on all sides (for the issues are no longer simply Communist/anti-Communist) recognize the need to compromise if a new system is to be forged out of the ruins of the old regime.

The last chapter in Poland's postwar history has yet to be written. Was the glorious experiment called Solidarity—which captured the world's attention and sympathy for a brief while—

another example of the "charmed circle" of mismatched pairs dancing against their will, bewitched by the spell of their own Romantic illusions, drunk on dreams of past glory and future hopes? Or can the lessons and mistakes of the past guide the Poles—and the Czechs, Slovaks, Hungarians, Romanians, Bulgarians, and Germans—as they enter the next phase of post-war history? Now that the old order has been destroyed, what will be found at the bottom of the ashes? Diamonds? Or chaos and confusion, leading to an abyss?

BARBARA NIEMCZYK

1990

Errata

In the D. J. Welsh translation of *Ashes and Diamonds* several of the Polish names have been translated incorrectly into English and two lengthy passages have been omitted from the text. The corrections and missing texts are here provided.

The main character is Maciek (Matt) Chelmicki, not Michael; the young nihilist is Jerzy/Jurek (George/Georgie) Szretter, not Julius; Christine's (Krystyna's) father is Ksawery (Xavier), not Kaspar; Hanka/Haneczka is Hannah, not Helen; Tadek is Ted, not Tom. Other names have been translated as follows: Wilga (Willa); Antoni (Antony); Stefka (Sally); Loda (Lola); and Andrzej (Alek).

On page 153, the following line was deleted after "Life was continuing": "But what did it carry with it? Loss or hope?" On page 219, "army uniforms" should read: "police uniforms."

The following passage should be inserted on page 218, following the sentence that reads: "He stood gazing at this inscription and was about to say a prayer when an instinct of shame prevented him."

After a while he walked farther on among the graves. Along the way he read on the blackened metal plates the names, dates, and brief commentaries which summed up some obscure person's existence in ordinary, commonplace expressions. An undisturbed silence hung over everything. A small squirrel scurried noiselessly between the gravestones and quickly began climbing the nearest tree. As he passed by the tree, it crouched high up in the branches and gazed down at him with keen eyes.

The grave he was standing at was different from the others. From the gold letters engraved on a black marble slab he learned that here lay fusilier Juliusz Sadzewicz of the First Regiment of Legioneers, who was born in 1893 and died a soldier's death in

1915. He counted the years. The dead man was the same age as he was now when he died. Under the name and dates some verses were engraved. He began to read:

From you, as from burning chips of resin,
Fiery fragments circle far and near;
Ablaze, you don't know if you are to be free,
Or if all that is yours will disappear.

Will only ashes and confusion remain,
Leading into the abyss?—or will there be
In the depths of the ash a star-like diamond,
*The dawning of eternal victory!**

He immediately assumed that this had to be a quote from some famous poet, but didn't have any idea who could have written the poem. He read it through once more and repeated under his breath: "Will only ashes and confusion remain,/Leading into the abyss?" What remained of this young, unknown fellow? Only ashes and confusion?

He stood with his head bent, his frozen hands clenched in the pockets of his coat; it was a long time before he realized that in thinking about the man lying under the grave marker he was thinking about himself. "Will only ashes and confusion remain,/Leading into the abyss?" He couldn't shake off those words. Finally he walked away from the grave, and walking on among the crosses crowded together, he repeated the lines to himself. At last he came out onto another narrow pathway similar to the first one. At the end of it a red wall was visible. The cemetery ended here. There was more open, unwooded space. But the wind died down and it was as still as in the depths of a forest. The ground smelled strongly of fresh dampness after the nighttime rainfall. And the air, gray until now, slowly began to lighten up. The sky was still overcast, but here and there it was punctuated with brighter streaks.

He noticed a small bench off to the side and sat down. Just past the red cemetery wall three distinct clusters of enormous chestnut

---

*The lines are from Cyprian Norwid, "Prolog," *Tyrtej, Tragedia fantastyczna,* stanzas 15 and 16. Quoted from Norwid, *Pisma wszystkie,* edited by Juliusz W. Gomulicki. Vol. 4: *Dramaty* (Warsaw: Panstwowy Instytut Wydawniczy, 1971).

trees, which looked like green clouds, were silhouetted in the slightly hazy air. Crows cawed noisily in their branches. Someone must have startled them, for they suddenly flew up in an agitated flock. For a while they fluttered in the air in a clamoring black cloud and then descended on the farthest cluster of trees. In spite of his fatigue he couldn't sit on the bench for long. A sense of uneasiness roused him. He stood up and proceeded farther down the pathway. When he turned around near the wall it was almost noon. He quickened his pace. In a while he was on the main pathway. It was empty. He then crossed over to the other side of the cemetery. There he stopped. He wanted to repeat the lines of verse. But he could only recall a few isolated expressions. Ashes, confusion, abyss . . . He repeated them in a whisper, but couldn't put them together to make any sense. They floated around in his head, isolated and independent of any meter. He wanted to turn around, to go back to look for the gravestone, when he heard the muffled sounds of an orchestra in the distance. For the longest time he stood motionless, weighed down by the same heaviness in his body which had come over him yesterday when, as he was saying goodbye to Christine, he caught sight of Szczuka getting out of a car.

The following passage should be inserted on page 220 after the sentence, "And I asked him: Does it frighten you?' "

He spoke slowly, as though he was having trouble finding the right words. But he could be clearly heard in the dense crowd. It was impossible to imagine a more profound silence. Chelmicki, although he stood far away, saw the broad-shouldered silhouette clearly above the sea of heads. He knew that large, rough-hewn face with its heavy, half-closed eyelids, by heart. He could close his eyes and see that man. He bent his head. A small ladybug crawled along a thin stem of milkweed. At this moment he didn't feel the slightest anxiety. Only weariness. And a desire to sleep. Szczuka's sonorous voice penetrated his consciousness like a distant call awakening one from sleep.

"Comrades! Only one thing can definitively strip a man of human dignity and the right to respect. This is death in the name of false truths, which bring slavery, injustice, violence, and degradation. When such great words as heroism, solidarity, and brotherhood fall by the wayside, then we, who survived years of the most horrible crimes, immediately ask: In the name of what are you a hero? In the name of what are you united and what does your brotherhood mean? If we didn't ask such questions, we would then have to equate the heroism of Fascist soldiers and the heroism of people fighting for freedom. We acted differently. In the course of the last few years we have condemned all acts which served violence and force, which brought harm and humiliation. We condemned people in order to save mankind, which was being threatened with extermination. We condemned without mercy, having paid a price of millions of murdered victims, destroyed cities, burned villages, the suffering and torment of millions. And today"—he paused for a moment and then firmly concluded—"we have to act the same way. At this very moment our enemy is breathing his last. The enemy of mankind. The disgrace of mankind. The might of Hitler's Germany ceases to exist. The war is ending. But don't delude yourselves into thinking that for us the end of the war means the end of the struggle. The struggle for Poland has only just begun. And, for that matter, the struggle for the future shape of the world. Today, tomorrow, the day after tomorrow, every one of you may perish in this struggle. And in the name of historical right, in the name of righting wrong and injustice in the world, in the name of developing forms of social life which will allow the masses of people to participate in the formation of history, a united mass strengthened by the bonds of self-sacrificing solidarity, in the name of these rights, in defending and directing them along a difficult path, we must condemn all those who cannot or do not want to understand the great turning point of our time. And again, as in past years, even though we are faced with a different enemy, we must pay for our truth with victims. Don't let this frighten you, comrades! We are not alone in this struggle, and those who fall in battle are not alone either. Their faith is our faith, and we attribute to their deaths an ardent, life-affirming significance. For only those truly die who believe in isolation or who serve false truths which are illusory and incompatible with the one great truth of our time. Future generations will only

despise them and will blame them or condemn them to oblivion.
Those people, however, who have understood the forces of
history and who have been in solidarity with their comrades, will
discover in the future the praise of soldiers fighting for
humanity, for one's own fatherland and for mankind, for the
world order. In the name of faith in mankind and in the world, in
the name of human brotherhood, let us, comrades, honor in our
two murdered brothers precisely such soldiers of truth and
peace. Glory . . . and life to them!"

Introduction

Thirty years after its first appearance, *Ashes and Diamonds*, that grandly conceived action shot of Poland at the end of World War II, is still a rich source of information, perhaps even more so for us today than for non-Polish readers in the year of its publication; moreover, it throws valuable light on present-day Poland and on how that country has evolved since 1945. *Ashes and Diamonds* is more than an action shot, however; the cast encompasses all the tensions and conflicts typical not only of Poland but also of those other European countries that suffered directly from the war: disoriented, demoralized youth and exhausted and bewildered adults, few of whom know whether they desire the old or the new and who play a waiting and opportunistic game while the idealists on both sides are primed to do battle.

Ashes and Diamonds is set during the few days before and after May 8, 1945, when the common enemy, the Germans, had been defeated and driven out — 'the moment of peace' that signified the opening of the battle for either a socialist or a nationalist Poland. Between these two alternatives many nuances, many permutations and combinations, existed: There were, for instance, many Socialists and Communists among the Poles who were aware of the imperialist nature of the Soviet Union – despite its pretense of internationalism – yet did not want a nationalist Poland. Readers familiar with the centuries-old dream of an independent Poland can well imagine how much dynamite had, in fact, accumulated.

May 8, 1945, marked the end of the war, but peace was still a long way off. In the classic sense of peace treaties, there is still no peace in Europe; there is merely no more war, and conventions have proved as durable as treaties – the durability of which is known to depend entirely on the policy of the stronger. How little those solemnly concluded nonaggression pacts are to be trusted is something of which almost every European state has had ample evidence in both world wars.

The most haunting relic of this unconcluded peace – a peace that is not yet a war but bears many of the hallmarks of civil war – is the frontier between the Federal Republic of Germany and the German Democratic Republic, where the massive investment of mines and armed personnel is a clear indication of the immense latent tension in Europe, a tension that often enough – along the Berlin Wall, for example – becomes bloodily virulent for those victims who 'merely' want to move from East to West. I mention this because the word 'frontier' is probably one of the most important keys to the tensions of Europe. All Europe was not only involved in World War II; it was also the theatre of war. From Stalingrad to Calais, from Sicily to northern Norway, from Athens to Vienna, the German Army had to be defeated and driven back kilometer by kilometer; not a village, not a town, not a family could have remained untouched. At the end of that war even the conquerors – regardless of whether they were actual conquerors or had merely been declared such – were exhausted, and they were then confronted with the task of instituting a new order whose magnitude is still beyond our computation. In addition to the consequences of World War II, there were also the reemerging consequences of World War I to be rectified. Old reckonings fell due concerning domestic, foreign, territorial, and ethnic issues; political and historical scars and wounds broke open again, the entire heritage of a continent that for more than a thousand years has been disputing frontiers (which, generally speaking, were also frontiers of religious or philosophical outlook). This absurdly small, densely populated continent, which has brought forth so much devastating unrest, while no longer at war, was still far from peace.

Scarcely a country in Europe had suffered to the same extent as Poland from the death and destruction inflicted not only by two world wars but also by wars and power struggles of previous centuries (although in saying 'scarcely' I already have misgivings when I think of Czechoslovakia, of Hungary, Rumania, and present-day Yugoslavia!). In order to sketch even the merest outline of Poland's history and fate, one would have to look back beyond the Vienna Congress of 1815 at the preceding eight or nine centuries. Forever contested and disputed, forever coveted, Poland was never genuinely under Polish rule for more than brief periods. The key word for Poland's fate is 'partition': partitioned between Russia and Prussia, among Prussia, Russia, and Austria, partitioned — a fact so easily forgotten! — between Hitler's Germany and the Soviet Union by an agreement signed by Vyacheslav Molotov and Joachim von Ribbentrop, one on behalf of Stalin, the other on behalf of Hitler, on August 23, 1939, one week before the outbreak of World War II. I well recall the triumphant announcement of this (umpteenth) partition of Poland, a partition which, after Poland was conquered and occupied by the Germans, culminated in Red Army soldiers and German troops, united in brotherhood at the then German-Soviet frontier that ran right through the middle of Poland, despatching trainloads of wheat from the Soviet Union to a Germany at war.

In order to understand the conflicts set forth in *Ashes and Diamonds*, it must be remembered that the Red Army occupying large parts of Poland until the middle of 1941 (when Hitler declared war on the Soviet Union) was the same army that three years later liberated (or 'liberated') Poland. Needless to say, in a novel published in Poland in 1948 this could not be even faintly suggested, yet it remains an essential factor. To understand the point of departure of Jerzy Andrzejewski's novel, another fact must be pointed out, one which he (and every Polish reader) takes for granted but which is less obvious to the non-Polish reader: Apart from what were probably numerous splinter groups, there were two major effective resistance groups in Poland, both directed against the German rule of terror — the so-called National Army and the Communist People's Army. Moreover, it has been established, and denied by no historian, that while the bloody armed revolt was raging in Warsaw from August 1944 until early October, the Soviet Army made not the slightest move to come to the aid of the Poles; instead, it *halted* its advance a few kilometers outside Warsaw – strange behavior for liberators, friends, or allies. This very army, which only three years earlier had been occupying Poland, proved anything but helpful, and no one is likely to blame the Poles for regarding that liberation as a further conquest, no matter how ardently the Polish Communist resistance fighters may have believed in liberation and trusted in the 'internationalism' of the Soviets.

In Andrzejewski's novel this problematic situation is expressed in a conversation between the totally sincere Communist functionary Szczuka and his old Social Democrat friend Kalicki. Perhaps the allusion to this 'detail' – the halting of the Red Army outside Warsaw – explains some of the tensions, conflicts, and homicidal actions in *Ashes and Diamonds* at 'the moment of peace'. Comparable, indeed almost identical, events occur in all liberated countries, from Angola to Vietnam, prompting many a foreign observer to assume erroneously that the old status – occupation or colonization – may have been preferable, since occupiers and colonizers tend to leave behind a political, moral, and economic chaos for which they then seek to blame their successors.

Ashes and Diamonds opens with a very ordinary scene that immediately arouses suspense: Szczuka, the functionary so sincerely dedicated to the creation of a 'new Poland', a man marked by torture and personal loss (his wife perished in a German concentration camp), is on his way to a political meeting, one of the first in this recently liberated area, in a car driven by his adjutant, the young Podgorski. On the way Podgorski happens to recognize the wife of his mentor, Kossecki, whom he knows to have also been in a concentration camp. He stops, speaks to Mrs. Kossecki, inquires about her husband. This opening scene contains all the hope, all the euphoria, of the imminent final liberation; however, this euphoria does not last long, only a few minutes, covering only a few pages of the novel, before Szczuka and

Podgorski learn of the assassination of two workers by a reactionary group. Szczuka, that wise old resistance fighter and Communist, immediately perceives that this attack was meant for him, not for the two workers Smolarski and Gawlik who were the victims; the short delay caused by Podgorski's conversation with Mrs. Kossecki on the street has saved their lives — for the time being.

The first seven pages of the novel are enough to show how little this peace is to be trusted, and Kossecki, the recently released prisoner, a lawyer with a stainless reputation, remains in the reader's memory as a potential hero. Later it will turn out that, under the pseudonym Rybicki, he had been a fellow prison-camp inmate of Szczuka's, a miserable collaborator who, plagued by memories and nightmares, is more inclined to regard the liberation as a horror. The suspense continues: What kind of Poles are these who, at the moment of peace, kill other Poles when each is a patriot in his own way? The action moves between the homes of the families and the Hotel Monopole, where the reader can meet them all: a snobbish, carping, hedonistic aristocracy, their speculations vacillating between emigration and restoration; a banquet of Socialist functionaries; young Chelmicki, directed by an obscure group to kill Szczuka; black-market operators; hotel staff members working every available angle; and assorted gamblers on the uncertain political future. It is a scenario offering wide scope for those whom we call opportunists, people who, in such situations, simply place their bets on one or the other alternative. Hardly has the common enemy been defeated when older rivalries and tensions surface; tried and true functionaries of the various resistance movements turn up, Socialists, Communists as well as opportunists, outright parasites from every camp, wheeler-dealers who know that in such situations two 'articles' are in special demand: arms and foreign currency.

What Andrzejewski describes proves to be a model for many comparable if not identical situations from 1945 to this day. A cast of waverers, intent on pleasure and survival, is not yet quite sure which side to join while in fact the historical and political situation is indisputable: The Red Army has liberated and 'liberated' Poland, and it will be the one to decide. Idealists and 'idealists' are on both sides – the old and young Socialist and Communist functionaries, true believers with whom, the reader feels, Andrzejewski has a sense of kinship, faced on the other side by the young officers bent on political assassinations, probably former members of the National Army who refuse to regard themselves as 'liberated', well endowed with the spirit of adventure, not entirely convinced of their task, heedless both in their tactics and in their attitude to life.

Then there are the sober-minded, determined Szczuka and Podgorski and – one of the principal figures in this novel – the old Social Democrat Kalicki, who probably mistrusts both sides and who, as characterized in 1948 in *Ashes and Diamonds*, provides a clue to much that has since happened in Poland in the way of inner resistance up to the point of revolt, especially between 1956 and 1978 – a resistance not always obvious to non-Poles. When Poles embrace German politicians, be they called Ulbricht or Honnecker, or when Poles embrace Soviet politicians, be they called Khrushchev or Brezhnev, the affection is not all that heartfelt. Despite those brotherly hugs at airports or railway stations, that cheek-kissing, those phony smiles, the partitions have not been forgotten, and far from forgotten is that vast area of Poland which fell to the Soviet Union after 1945, significantly larger than the area allotted to Poland toward the west: a great nation, almost thirty million, that always wanted so much to be Polish.

Without a doubt, the obscure group of young officers carrying out political assassinations in 1945 was murdering for a hopeless cause. There was no returning to a Poland of 1939, much less a Poland of 1914; the major victors – the powerful ones with the larger armies – determine what is to be left over for the minor victors. Meanwhile, many of the Polish emigrants from the various groups have no doubt realized this too. What the young

Chelmicki, joined by a son of Kossecki and other friends, was doing in 1945 was, politically speaking, pointless, although not entirely incomprehensible in the context of Poland's history. After all, the Soviets were more Russian than Soviet, had behaved far more as Russians than as Soviets back in 1939 when they divided up Poland with Hitler, and in addition there was that ancient, essentially Polish pride and anguish that Andrzejewski does not even mention, probably because it is simply too obvious to a Pole: their religion. To be Polish and to be Catholic meant one and the same thing, squeezed between the Protestant Prussians and the Orthodox Russians, who both similarly despised Poland. Indeed, the Poles might be regarded as the Irish of Eastern Europe: Catholic, despised, welcome as farm laborers, the butt of highly contemptuous epithets.

Now the Prussians had come back as Nazis, the Russians as Bolsheviks, and the (umpteenth) partition of Poland toward the east occurred 'without a murmur', because the Poles were allotted a share in the partition of Prussia. No, the young nationalist officers murder for a totally hopeless cause, and in the end they do indeed manage to get that impressive figure Szczuka: After the funeral of the two 'mistakenly' murdered workers, the morbid young Chelmicki disposes of him just before he in turn is disposed of by others. For all that, the author does not begrudge him a last romantic fling with the bar girl Christina.

There is yet another group of killers, not young officers but those children who combine a confused political romanticism with lust for adventure and crime, and this is probably the most sinister group in *Ashes and Diamonds* because it is the hardest to 'understand'. These are the children of the war as they existed in every European country and exist in every non-European country; these are the children who did not lose their sense of orientation because they never had one. As often as not their cynicism is assumed and at times very close to tears; abandoned by the adults, who are preoccupied with sheer survival, they are an easy prey to the blandishments of a deluded superman-dream. In

Ashes and Diamonds their leader is the young Szretter, a product of humanistically inclined parents, whose father is one of the novel's most likable characters. The distinguishing mark of these young people is that they all come from decent families, 'decent' being also the word for the Kossecki family, which has one son among the political assassins and one in this group of murderous children. The young Szretter cold-bloodedly and deliberately involves these children in bloodguilt by shooting a 'deviant' in their presence and implicating his cohorts in the removal of the corpse. They are children of almost every social level, from families who might be one's neighbors. One would exchange friendly greetings with them, offer to buy them ice cream, which they would accept — nice boys all of them, murdering, cheating, stealing, left to their own devices by unsuspecting parents amid the total moral disintegration that a war entails and that is confirmed by a peace that cannot be trusted.

It is surely no coincidence that these boys also tend toward the 'right' and obtain money to buy weapons against an enemy they have never seen — 'those Russians', those Bolsheviks. This group of boys is the mirror image of the group of young officers; it is no mere coincidence that the Kossecki family has a son in each group, brothers who have no inkling of each other's parallel activities.

In *Ashes and Diamonds* there is a crucial scene in which the younger Kossecki, Andrew, stands at the window in the middle of the night and sees a young Russian soldier also standing at the window in the next house; Andrew feels the futility of thinking in terms of 'enemy' and wants to unburden himself to his brother, but the latter's response is one of irritation. There is a further key scene between the political assassin Chelmicki and his mistress, Christina, who says to him in the morning: 'I don't want any partings or any memories. Nothing that can be left behind. No luggage.' That means: no personal, no spiritual, and, above all, no ideological luggage, and this attitude, too, is characteristic of many who have survived a war. After the war there was a play by Jean Anouilh, *Traveller without Luggage*, that was very popular, probably because it expressed what Christina tells her lover that morning.

Looking at the cast of *Ashes and Diamonds* and its conflicts, this Polish and European 'arrangement' in 1945, one is tempted to ask: What has become of them, if indeed they have lived happily ever after? What has become of Podgorski, the sincere, incorruptible Socialist who won't let go, who even refuses to let the contemptible Kossecki/Rybicki escape? What has become of Kossecki, of the disoriented, senselessly homicidal young officers, and of the murderous offspring of unsuspecting parents, who by now must be men approaching fifty, functionaries, perhaps, or teachers or salesmen? Do they sometimes think of their terrorist past, or are they in turn merely the unsuspecting parents of offspring of whose activities they have no idea? What has become of the opportunists to whom the 'new age' offered prospects of a career: the Swieckis, Pieniazeks, Drewnowskis – elderly gentlemen, no doubt, glorying in their laurels and counting off the 'good old days' on their rosaries? One who is certainly no longer in the land of the living is old Mrs Jurgeluszka, the washroom attendant at the Hotel Monopole who had to take charge of the troublemakers, lock them up, and discreetly 'discharge' them again, she too with no inkling as to what her grandson Telek, a terrorist from the very first hour, is up to. The waiters and kitchen maids, the carping stragglers of a feudal class who look upon the Monopole as a kind of private preserve: What has become of these participants in the great banquet of Socialist-Communist functionaries?

HEINRICH BÖLL
TRANSLATED BY LEILA VENNEWITZ

Ashes and Diamonds

From you, as from burning chips of resin,
Fiery fragments circle far and near:
Ablaze, you don't know if you are to be free,
Or if all that is yours will disappear.

Will only ashes and confusion remain,
Leading into the abyss?—or will there be
In the depths of the ash a star-like diamond,
The dawning of eternal victory!

—From Cyprian Norwid, "Prolog,"
Tragedia fantastyczna

Chapter One

Catching sight of a woman as she walked down to the Sreniawa bridge, Podgorski swerved to the pavement and stopped the jeep abruptly. Two young militiamen, armed with tommy-guns, shifted watchfully in the back seat. Szczuka, Secretary of the Party Area Committee who was next to Podgorski, straightened up and lifted his heavy, sleeplessly puffy eyelids.

'Trouble?'

'No. Just a minute, comrade.'

He got out without switching off, his hob-nailed boots clattering noisily on the pavement as he ran down the hill. The woman he wanted to catch was nearing the bridge. The pavement had not been repaired and was cracked across with shell-holes, so she was walking in the road, slowly, her head bowed, shoulders a little bent, and with a big, heavily-laden bag in her left hand.

'Mrs Kossecki!' he shouted.

Mrs Kossecki was so preoccupied that when she turned to face the young man in high boots, army trousers, a dark jersey and an open leather jacket, she did not recognize her husband's former clerk. But Podgorski was in too much of a hurry and too pleased by this unexpected meeting to notice the hesitation in her eyes.

'How are you?' He took her hand. 'I'm so glad I spotted you from the jeep . . .'

Now she recognized his rather hoarse voice and the inclination of his long, narrow head. He hadn't shaved for several days and the shadow of a beard darkened his chin.

Putting her heavy bag down, she smiled pleasantly. In spite of her grey hair, the lines on her forehead and the great weariness in her eyes, her smile was still youthful.

'Frank! How are you?'

'Me? I'm fine.'

She had last seen Podgorski that winter just after the battle-line had passed swiftly but turbulently through the town. He had dropped in one evening for a minute or two, in as much of a rush as when he had visited her secretly during the Occupation. She had not seen him since, though she had heard that he was back in Ostrowiec as Secretary of the Party's local committee. Although animated, he looked wan and tired.

'You don't look well, Frank.'

He shrugged; the jeep's motor was still running noisily. Suddenly the horn sounded twice.

'That's for you, isn't it?'

Podgorski turned. Szczuka, big and heavy, was leaning out of the jeep and beckoning urgently to him. One of the militiamen was standing by the jeep with his tommy-gun.

'Coming!' he shouted, then said to Mrs Kossecki, 'I must go. We're expected at the Biala cement works to make speeches at a meeting. But is it true that your husband's come back?'

She nodded.

'When?'

'The day before yesterday.'

Podgorski looked pleased.

'How is he? Worn out? What sort of a mood is he in?'

The horn sounded again before she could reply. Podgorski glanced at his watch. It was twenty past five. The workers' meeting at Biala was fixed for five.

'Sorry, but they're quite right to be impatient. . . . All right, all right!' he shouted before turning to Mrs Kossecki again. 'I'll drop in later on, if I may? In two hours' time, right?'

He raised her hand to his lips and said warmly,

'I'm so glad Mr Kossecki's survived and back . . .'

Szczuka accepted Podgorski's return without words, but indicated his watch. Podgorski drove on fast.

'Sorry,' he said presently, 'but that was important to me. We'll be there within fifteen minutes.'

Szczuka laid his heavy hands on his knees and watched the road slipping by under the jeep. They were driving through the side-streets of Ostrowiec and could go much faster, though the road was bad and very uneven.

Both sides of the slightly sloping street were lined with

6

houses, single-storied for the most part, and poor, showing traces of the war in their walls pock-marked with shell-holes, dislodged and scattered tiles, and windows nailed over with cardboard and planks. Others stood dead without glass and, in several places, walls ripped apart by bombs rose in solitude above the grey rubble. This part of the town was deserted, silent, and uninhabited, except for a bent little old woman pushing a wheelbarrow full of potatoes. The shattered branches of withered acacia trees stood out black.

'Who was that woman you talked to?' Szczuka asked.

Podgorski swung into a turning, passing a huge covered lorry.

'Mrs Kossecki,' he replied, 'the magistrate's wife.'

'Local people?'

'Maybe you knew him?'

'No. Look out . . .'

They were driving into the market-place and there were people everywhere, civilians mingled with Polish and Soviet soldiers. Army trucks, big lorries and trailers with petrol-cans were packed into the wide square, between some temporary huts and around a wooden platform painted red and white and used a few days earlier for the May Day march-past. Although the battle-line had passed this area in January and was now at its last gasp several hundred miles away to the west, the atmosphere was deceptively like that of a front-line town.

On the far side of the market-place the shapes of burnt-out houses stood black against the blue spring sky. Huge banners rose red above the street. A loudspeaker roared across the square in a penetrating, masculine voice:

'*Yesterday, May 4th at 6 a.m., an agreement to surrender was signed at Field-Marshal Montgomery's HQ, which declares . . .*'

Podgorski had to slow down and drove through the crowd repeatedly sounding his horn. The announcer's words resounded very clearly overhead:

'*All German forces in north-west Germany, Holland, Denmark, Heligoland, the Frisians and elsewhere, as well as all warships in the area, are laying down their arms and surrendering unconditionally. Military operations are to cease on Saturday at 8 a.m.*'

Podgorski glanced at his companion.

'Let's get on!' said Szczuka.

As they passed the Party building, over which a red banner waved, the guard at the doorway caught sight of Podgorski and began to signal to him to stop.

'Let's get on!' Szczuka repeated. 'We haven't time.'

Podgorski made an expressive gesture to the guard to indicate they were very pressed for time. Soon he had got the jeep out of the crowds and turned into the first side-street.

'Comrade Szczuka, did you notice the faces of the people listening to the communiqué?'

Szczuka nodded.

'Not a bit of enthusiasm, don't you agree?'

'They've waited a long time.'

'You think that's all?'

'Of course not,' Szczuka replied briefly, staring at the road, then glancing at his watch.

'Can we make it in ten minutes?'

'We ought to. It isn't far now.'

They were again driving through empty, ruined streets.

'How about Kossecki?' said Szczuka reverting to their earlier conversation. 'Did you know him before the war?'

'I worked with him in the local Courts for two years – until the war. He's a decent, honest man. He's just got back from a prison camp.'

'Oswiecim?'

'Gross-Rosen.'

Szczuka showed more interest.

'So he was in Gross-Rosen, was he?'

'Four years.'

Then he remembered that Szczuka, who had been in several concentration camps in the past few years, had been in Gross-Rosen too.

'You were there too, weren't you?'

'Yes. Not at the end, though. I managed to get away during the first evacuation last February.'

'You must have met Kossecki.'

Szczuka considered.

'Don't think so. What's he like?'

'Fairly tall, thick-set, dark . . .'

For a moment Szczuka tried to remember.

'I don't recollect him. A magistrate from Ostrowiec?'

'Oh of course,' Podgorski interrupted. 'You wouldn't have known him as that. They arrested him under a false name. What was it? I used to know.'

But he couldn't remember, so finally he shook his head.

'It escapes me for the moment . . .'

'Was he arrested in Ostrowiec?'

'No, in Warsaw. He had to get away at the beginning of '40, after the first big round-up.'

'Did you work together?'

'At first. Later I managed to join up with our own people.'

'Look out!' Szczuka muttered.

Podgorski laughed.

'Don't worry. I know this road like the back of my hand.'

The bridge over the Sreniawa river had been cut on this side of Ostrowiec and the detour followed a steep country lane enclosed in a ravine. The road could scarcely have been worse. Though the jeep was adapted to tackling the toughest ground, it could only force its way down the rough track with difficulty.

At one point the ravine narrowed. Young alders covering the steep banks brushed the jeep. Podgorski thrust aside an extended branch covered in tiny sticky leaves and some of them stuck to his palm.

'Spring's here already, see?' he showed Szczuka.

The road suddenly twisted and just beyond the turn it opened out and led down to the river across a fertile meadow, direct to the temporary wooden bridge. A group of people had collected near this bridge.

Szczuka leaned forward.

'What's up now?'

Podgorski had spotted the crowd as soon as he came round the corner: about twenty people with several militiamen among them. Then a little apart, in the meadow, they saw another American jeep, overturned.

Two militiamen left the group and ran into the road to signal the approaching jeep to stop. One of the militiamen in the jeep leaned forward to Podgorski and said:

9

'They're our men from Ostrowiec.'

'So I see.'

By this time other people, including workers from Biala whom Podgorski knew, had run into the road. As soon as the jeep stopped they were surrounded. One of the workmen, who had been with Podgorski in the 'People's Party' underground group, pushed forward before he could get out.

'You've heard already?'

'No,' he said slowly, looking at the frowning, serious faces; 'what's happened?'

'They've killed two of our comrades,' a grey-haired workman at the rear called out, 'that's what!'

Podgorski went white.

'Who?'

'Smolarski and Gawlik.'

Szczuka eased his huge frame out of the jeep and stood by Podgorski. He leant on a stick, because he was lame. Podgorski looked at him.

'Hear that?'

He nodded.

'You've picked a bad time to come, comrade,' said one of the workers.

'When did it happen?' Szczuka asked.

One of the militiamen came closer.

'Less than an hour ago. Men working on the bridge heard shots over here. They ran over, but it was too late.'

'Have the killers been caught?'

'Not yet.'

Szczuka shrugged.

'You'll catch up with them soon enough. Where did it happen?'

'In the ravine. They must have been waiting. A few rounds did it. The jeep ran downhill on its own and turned over . . .'

'Anyone here from Security?'

'We're waiting for them. We've let them know.'

Silence fell on the group. Leaning heavily on his stick, Szczuka stared at the ground. Larks sang loudly high above the hillside, on the clear air.

'Well,' Szczuka broke the silence. 'Suppose we go and have a look at them.'

He went first, limping, with Podgorski following. The crowd made way, then came after them. The overturned jeep was several dozen yards away. The meadow was fertile and rich, the grass almost knee-high.

'Good grass, this!' muttered Szczuka.

The bodies lay near the jeep, side by side, on their backs. Unnaturally stiff in the thick grass, staring with glassy eyes at the sky, their working-clothes spattered with blood, they looked like dolls rather than the men they had been less than an hour earlier. Podgorski had known them both, but the faces he remembered were irrelevant. An ordinary white butterfly fluttered above their still faces.

Szczuka looked at the bodies for a long time with narrowed eyes. Finally he leaned more heavily on his stick, stretched out his hand and pointed to the nearest.

'Who's he?'

Podgorski swallowed to moisten the dryness in his gullet.

'Smolarski. He was on the Factory council. An old Party member. He lost his two sons, one in '39 and the other was executed here, in '44.'

He spoke clearly, but in an undertone, as people usually speak in a room where a dead man lies. Szczuka listened in silence.

'The other?'

'Gawlik. A young lad, not much over twenty . . .'

'Twenty-one,' said someone in the crowd.

Podgorski stared at the still face of the murdered man.

'He only got back from forced labour in Germany a few weeks ago.'

Szczuka came a step nearer and, with both hands on his stick, he leaned over the bodies, attentively watching the dancing flight of the butterfly from beneath lowered eyelids.

'It looks as though you and I were meant to be lying here, instead of them,' he said in an undertone to Podgorski.

The latter shivered.

'You think so?'

'I'm positive.'

The sudden pain of his finger-nails driven into his palms

made Podgorski now realize that since getting out of the jeep, his fists had been clenched hard all the time. He straightened his fingers and some crumpled alder leaves dropped from his right hand. His first, quite mechanical reaction, which he would have made on dropping something useful, was to catch and pick up the leaves. But he prevented himself in time. He felt his hands sweating and wiped them on his trousers.

Szczuka turned away.

'Let's go,' he muttered.

Some men in the crowd came after them for a little way, walking in silence. The rustle of the fresh grass sounded against their boots.

'Well?' Szczuka questioned the thoughtful Podgorski.

'I was thinking about what you said. It's obvious. If we hadn't been delayed . . .'

'We'd have been lying there now, in the field. And they'd be alive . . . Well, that's how it goes. But it can't be helped.'

And he walked on, limping in his own way. Then he stopped. The people following him stopped too.

'Brace up, Comrade Podgorski. Do your job, as long as you're alive to do it, that's what counts!'

One of the workmen came up, a small, short man, with a grey face scarred from small-pox.

'Excuse me, comrade . . .'

Szczuka turned to him.

'You know what this is all about, comrade. You're in politics, it's your job to know . . . I wanted to ask you . . . anyhow, all of us,' and he indicated his companions, who had come closer and stood in a close half-circle, 'we want you to tell us how much longer this is going on.'

Szczuka raised his tired eyelids and looked at the men surrounding him with his bloodshot eyes. The stares of them all, expectant and concentrated, were fixed upon him. He thought a little then pointed to the dead bodies lying not far away.

'Is it them you're concerned about?'

'Yes, them. How long are men like that going to have to die? They're not the first!'

'Nor the last, either,' Szczuka returned. 'Does that scare you?'

An old workman shrugged.

'Me? Everyone wants to live. But who's scared?'

'Well then?'

The other man did not reply at once but looked at Szczuka who towered over him, as if seeking the meaning of his words in his face. Suddenly he put out his hand.

'I get it. You're right, comrade.'

Szczuka gripped his outstretched hand.

'Unfortunately it's not easy.'

'We know that.'

And, looking Szczuka in the eye, he said with simple solemnity,

'May God keep you, comrade.'

Szczuka opened his mouth to speak but hesitated and shut it again.

'Thanks,' he said presently. 'May God watch over you, too.'

While they were waiting for the Security men, he went down to the river with Podgorski. It was a deep narrow stream, almost level with the low banks. Startled frogs began to hop out of the grass and splashes broke the silence.

Szczuka paused on the bank, closed his eyes and passed his big hand heavily over his forehead.

'Tired?' asked Podgorski.

He denied it and opened his eyes at once.

Then he noticed a large fish. It leaped out of the water in midstream and fell back with a splash. Wide circles began to move across the surface.

Unexpectedly Podgorski snapped his fingers.

'I've got it! I remember the name Kossecki was arrested under. Rybicki . . . it's been worrying me.'

Engrossed in his own thoughts, Szczuka did not at first realize who was meant.

'Kossecki? Kossecki? What made you think of that?' Then he remembered the earlier conversation.

'What was that name you said?'

'Ludwig? Leopold? No, Leon, maybe Rybicki. Did you know him?'

Szczuka turned back to the river.

'Not personally. He must have been in another block. I heard the name, that's all.'

Another fish, smaller this time but still large, leaped above the surface. Szczuka lifted his stick.

'Fine fish you have in the Sreniawa.'

Chapter Two

The Kosseckis' villa stood in pleasant surroundings on the left bank of the Sreniawa. This modern district was called New Ostrowiec or simply the Settlement, to distinguish it from the old, right-bank part of the town. The Settlement was extensive. A fifteen-minute walk at most from the market-place, building had not started seriously until after the First World War, when various State and private firms began building cheap houses for their employees on the hilly, unoccupied sites on the far side of the river. These buildings, mostly jerry-built and ugly, were already well on the way to premature decay. Fortunately the appearance of the Settlement did not depend on the early houses. The area began to develop rapidly and building enterprises were only halted by the outbreak of the second war. It had become smart to live in the Settlement. The richer families of Ostrowiec – tradesmen, industrialists, senior Civil Servants, and prosperous professional men – built their own villas in the Settlement. Those who couldn't afford a house of their own rented one. There they could live in a house, admittedly more expensive than those in the town, but at least modern and in a better neighbourhood than the crowded, dusty, ugly streets of Ostrowiec itself. Just before the war a new hospital and a modern church had been planned. Proposals for industrializing Ostrowiec had meant that the town was prosperous. Now there were huts for the homeless on the road to the Biala cement works, and still workers lived in damp cellars and dark houses in the oldest part of the town behind the Old Market.

The Kosseckis had moved into their villa a year before war broke out. During the three years before that they had lived in the town proper on May 3rd Boulevard, near the barracks in which the famous Ostrowiec Hussar regiment was stationed. Before that they had lived in Warsaw. The move to a home of their own was an important event in their flat and somewhat ineffectual lives. The building cost every penny Kossecki had saved during his career as a lawyer. He had had his own practice at first and later – until his appointment as magistrate at the Ostrowiec County Court – was legal adviser to a big cooperative firm. The move had not made any fundamental alterations to their lives, except that the magistrate had farther to go to his courtroom and his two sons to their secondary school. But the fact that they owned their roof and their garden, which Mrs Kossecki planted lovingly, and the feeling of stability which always goes with ownership showed that the values and solid worth, which were the basic principles of both husband and wife, had come into their own.

When the Second World War broke out, Antony Kossecki was no longer a young man. Although he did not look more than forty, he was nearer fifty.

He was not a man of exceptional talents, nor one of those lucky ones to whom Fate seems to lend a hand in achieving success. Nothing came easily to him and, when he reached the height of his powers, his own experience led him to mistrust a quick and brilliant career. His attitude towards more successful men, who forged ahead through useful contacts, was one of contemptuous disdain. He was honest, stubborn, and ambitious; it was on these traits of character that his slow but steadily improving career was built. No sudden flights, but no unexpected set-backs or collapses either. He expected a good deal from other people, but judged himself by the same yard-stick. Those who did not know him well thought him cold, but he improved on closer acquaintance. Even if he did not arouse warmth or affection his opponents usually respected him.

He was born in the last decade of the nineteenth century, to a modest middle-class family which had been connected for several generations with a sugar-manufacturing town in Central Poland. He was the youngest of a large family and the sight of his older sisters and brothers, who had no ambitions outside work in the sugar-factory and family life, had encouraged him to break away. He left the family home – a damp and gloomy house with a garden and bee-hives at the back – at the age of thirteen. When the time came to decide on the future of the last of his seven growing children, old Kossecki, who had been at the sugar-factory for forty years, remembered that one of his childhood friends was a prosperous shopkeeper in Warsaw. As a result of this distant acquaintance, Antony found himself in that capital in 1905 and started to learn about the grocery trade. In return for his work, he got food, clothes, and one pair of shoes a year, and an iron bed in an alcove in a poky little room, occupied by three shop-assistants, not far from what was then the Vienna Railway Station.

Life in Warsaw was hard. The other shop-assistants made him do the household chores, so he rose at dawn, in pitch-dark during the winter months. He cleaned and brushed the clothes and shoes of the three men, fetched water from the yard, made tea, swept, and tidied up while the others washed and dressed behind a screen. He had to run to be at the shop at six, and three times a week he worked until closing-time, around 11 p.m. On the other three days they let him off earlier to go to evening classes, but they were not up to much. On weekdays, the shop-assistants would not let him light the lamp to read at night. This left Sundays when one of the assistants, quiet, consumptive Joseph, visited his mother in Marymont and the other two, Edmund and Theo, brought girls in. Kossecki's alcove was screened by a grubby blanket and behind it, closing his ears with his fists, he was free to pore over a book.

Three long years of his life were spent like this. They taught him respect for money and time and a contemptuous attitude towards facile, romantic consolations. After three years he felt mature enough to start life on his own; an ambition which had already begun to crystallize. When Joseph died, he had a chance of being promoted to counter-hand, but he threw over the shop and his alcove in the attic, and, since he had saved a few roubles, rented a cheap room from a widow near the river. After a few months of persevering study he made up the gaps in his education and passed – not brilliantly but adequately – the exams for Class 5 of the secondary schools. Only after he heard the results did he tell his family about the changes that had affected his life. His father had been dead for a year, but his mother sent her blessing and ten roubles. This was the first and last money he got from home. Sometimes they sent him food: honey, home-baked bread, or butter, but as a rule he was hungry.

He was a clumsy boy with long arms and coarse hair, and his school uniform was outgrown and shabby. He never knew how to be frivolous, how to make himself agreeable or how to enjoy himself, so he had no friends. He found learning difficult but once he had learned anything, he remembered it. His mother died just before he took his matriculation and he had to decide whether to travel home for her funeral or have another look at his notes on trigonometry, which he was not very good at. He chose trigonometry and his family never saw him again. His brothers and sisters, married by this time and with children, were not concerned with him. If he ever thought about his childhood or youth it was only as a contrast to his present life and to confirm and strengthen his faith in his own capacities and in his future.

By the time he reached the sixth form he had decided to become a lawyer. He showed no particular talent for the law, but he did not change his mind. His memory was average but tenacious, his enunciation somewhat poor, but he recognized these inadequacies and put a great deal of hard work into overcoming his innate deficiencies. Fifteen years later when many of his University colleagues had become famous or reached high public office, Kossecki had a reputation as a reliable lawyer and, later, as an honest, reliable and respected magistrate. He valued this reputation highly. He was one of those rare men whose difficulties and inadequacies teach them to appreciate basic values. Other men with his ambitions might well have been disappointed or envious, but this would have been foreign to Kossecki's nature.

The First World War was in progress by the time he graduated; by gaining the confidence of a well-known Warsaw lawyer, he found work and got to know what went on behind the scenes in the law-courts. He was called up in the Kiev expeditionary force in 1919, went through the whole campaign and shared its varied fortunes with his random companions. He was slightly wounded, promoted from private to lance-corporal, acquired a minor decoration and went back to his law office when demobilized in 1921. Soon this brief episode was forgotten. Other events drove it from his mind.

Finally he left the lawyer's office and established a modest one of his own, which was as important a decision as his earlier one to leave the grocery business. He was now thirty-one and settled down by getting sensibly and practically married to a Miss Alicia Skorodynska. She was a young girl, repatriated to Poland from the Ukraine, where her parents owned a small estate. As she had lost her father during the war and been parted from her mother, a victim of typhoid, at the frontier repatriation camp, she was quite alone in Warsaw and had no means of earning a living. She was not excited about her marriage to a potential lawyer, nearly ten years older than she, and not really very attractive; however, she brought him a healthy body, youthful charm, common sense and goodwill, and a placid character, with that dash of resignation which helpless people who have been a little badly treated by fate develop. She had sometimes dreamed of a more exciting destiny, but she accepted the one that came her way. She was domesticated and family life took up enough of her time and energy to enable her to harden her heart towards temptations and desires. Her husband was more affectionate than she had expected; she bore him two healthy sons; he never deceived her, she was 'the magistrate's wife' and had a social position; she had a maid, a fur-coat and, eventually, they owned their villa . . . What more, after all, could she have expected?

But this belonged to the past.

In the last few months when Mrs Kossecki went down the familiar road to the Settlement she was a prey to contrasting and very complex thoughts. One day, as she paused on the bridge – it was early spring and a sunny day, the air mild and heady – she realized, suddenly and unexpectedly, that she would never again be able to go home calmly and peacefully as she had before the war.

It was in her memories of the Settlement in the year before the war that Mrs Kossecki had really grown to know it. She had now had almost five years in which to think of that brief period as one of profound domestic tranquillity.

The enforced flight of the magistrate coincided with the

deportation of Poles from the Settlement and Mrs Kossecki stayed on in Ostrowiec with old Rozalia, their servant from Warsaw, and her younger son, Alexander, who was called Alek by all the family. The older boy, sixteen-year-old Andrew, had been taken to Warsaw by his father for safety.

The deportation came suddenly and the inhabitants were only allowed three hours to pack their belongings. Now, nearly every time she returned to the villa, Mrs Kossecki remembered that day in late autumn when she had been forced to leave it. Dusk was near, it was drizzling, and a thick, damp mist descended with the darkness. On German orders the lights were on and lit within. The shouting of the gendarmes and soldiers arose on all sides, and the lights which glimmered through the mist from the brightly-lit and emptying villas, showed dark groups of people drooping under the weight of their belongings as they trudged in silence down to the river.

For the first few months Mrs Kossecki lived with some acquaintances. The news came that Antony had been arrested almost accidentally and Andrew did not come home. He had managed to find a home for himself in Warsaw and a job, and was supposed to be studying. Then Antony was taken to Gross-Rosen and since he was understandably afraid of betraying his real name, she had no further direct news of him. Later – the interval was not long but to those it tormented it seemed like years – Mrs Kossecki was allotted a former Jewish apartment as one outcome of the establishment of a ghetto in Ostrowiec. She used up the last of her savings to buy a small loom and make enough to keep herself alive. In those years advantages were gained by some at the expense of others. Wealth fed on poverty, privilege on injustice, and even life itself, in all its haphazardness, grew uncertainly and on frail roots out of the deaths of unknown men.

From time to time Rozalia helped the meagre budget by making expeditions to the countryside for provisions, but after being beaten up by gendarmes her health gave way and Mrs Kossecki undertook the 'smuggling' trips herself.

Meanwhile, the best villas in the Settlement were taken over by German dignitaries, Gestapo or Army officers and higher officials, while the remaining houses were given to bombed-out

German civilians, and Hitler Youth Groups were stationed in the old cooperative blocks. Mrs Kossecki did not visit the Settlement at all during the Occupation. Each new spring seemed to promise the end of the war and when it passed, the hopes it had disappointed switched to the spring after. It seemed easier, amidst sufferings too cruel to be borne, and in the face of a constant threat of destruction, for people to divide time into disappointments.

Antony was alive, but news of him was increasingly infrequent and laconic. Alek suddenly grew up from the eleven-year-old boy he had been when war broke out. Swallowed up in Warsaw, Andrew reappeared in the former Jewish house a few weeks after the collapse of the Insurrection. The years had changed him and he seemed shamefully alien to Mrs Kossecki. He was silent and said almost nothing about himself, but his long boots, his lean, dark face and his cynical smile conjured up the disturbance of that strange world in which he had spent several years and whose many hopes, escapes, and defeats he must certainly have known. He did not stay for long. When a new wave of raids and arrests started in Ostrowiec, at the beginning of November, Andrew disappeared into the woods.

The war came to Ostrowiec suddenly and unexpectedly. The Germans tried to make a stand on the Sreniawa river and the town came under artillery shelling for two days and nights. On the third day, guns roared at dawn and the Red army began to force the river from Biala and the Settlement. By midday the first Soviet tanks were entering Ostrowiec.

Mrs Kossecki ran straight from her cellar to the Settlement. The town, set on fire at the last moment by the retreating Germans, was in flames and smoke. The market-place was burning, so were the barracks, the gaol and Ogrodowa Street, where the Gestapo had their HQ. There was a strong, crackling frost and a sunny sparkling sky. At first no one tackled the flames. Water was short. But nearly everyone rushed out into the streets. Some burst into tears. Shops were broken into and looted. In front of a vodka shop, spirit flowed from shattered vats into the gutters, drenching the corpses of two naked German soldiers with a bluish stream. Drunken shouting mingled with the clatter of machine-guns and the dry bark of single shots. All the western horizon was shuddering with the monotonous and heavy rumble of artillery.

Various pictures of this day returned to Mrs Kossecki, as clearly and persistently as the memory of that other earlier autumn still lived in her. Whenever she crossed the Sreniawa bridge, she remembered the Soviet soldiers who banned her passage. An icy wind was blowing up from the frozen river. Tanks, motorized columns, motor-cycles, and artillery were driving without a break along the main road. Finally she succeeded – thanks to her good Russian accent – in getting to the Settlement. Amidst the rattle and crash of rolling iron, she climbed the hill with soldiers accosting and stopping her now and then. The snow crunched underfoot. Clouds of steam arose. In several places dead horses lay across the gutters. Farther on, the road had been cut across by empty anti-tank ditches. Glass crackled underfoot near the first houses, white clouds of feathers fluttered in the air. Not far away someone was playing a rhythmical march on a mouth organ. Then night came.

Mrs Kossecki barricaded herself in her villa but did not sleep. The window panes had gone and the wind whistled through the rooms despite the closed shutters. She was afraid to turn the lights on. Soldiers kept battering on the door, their shouting and singing echoing in the darkness. Time after time, bursts of gunfire ripped the uneasy night apart and a huge glow rose over Ostrowiec.

Chapter Three

Now it was spring again, the most beautiful time of the year. Fresh green leaves and white clouds of flowering trees concealed the destruction of the war. But Mrs Kossecki knew the mutilation of her home by heart. The water-pipes had burst during the heaviest frost, there was no glass for the windows, the unheated walls were spongy with damp and a number of little repairs needed attention. The roof leaked and two upstairs rooms were quite spoiled. This once carefully-tended house looked deplorable with its shell scars, its plank-covered windows and its gaping roof.

Mrs Kossecki spent all day weaving, but despite the demand for her products, she could not cope with all the shortages. Sometimes she was overcome with such weariness that she could summon up neither the strength nor, worse still, the desire to shake off her discouragement. She had survived so far by sheer nervous tension; now – no longer forced to spend days and nights fighting her fear of the ceaseless danger – she began to sink into a state of inner emptiness. At times she fought off this torpor and sought salvation in a feverish and uneasy multiplication of her various tasks and occupations. But she had so many of these that her hands lapsed into idleness amidst the flood of industry. What lay ahead, what sort of life, what future? The worst years had passed but now, at the beginning of a new day, it looked as if so much had been destroyed, so much laid waste, so much crushed down and afflicted, that the destructive force, as though yet unappeased, was encroaching upon the present, poisoning even the future, in which she had placed her hopes during the worst periods.

She walked to the back of the house and knocked at the kitchen door. The front-door bell did not work, and deaf Rozalia could not always hear distant knocking. Mrs Kossecki kept meaning to have more front-door keys made; there were only two and the boys had both.

After a long pause Rozalia opened the door. She was a thick-set, sixty-year-old woman, with a big red face, small eyes and smooth grey hair. Like all deaf people, she spoke very loudly.
'Anyone called?' Mrs Kossecki asked.

Mrs Staniewicz, the wife of an Army major and Mrs Kossecki's companion on expeditions to buy meat and eggs, had called.

'When?'

'About an hour ago,' Rozalia screamed, 'but she went away directly. The master wouldn't see her.'

Mrs Kossecki was disappointed by this. However, she felt obliged to defend her husband.

'He's very tired. He needs rest, you see.'

Rozalia shrugged her broad shoulders.

'Of course I see. Don't I know it? Of course he wants rest.'

Mrs Kossecki went into the hall. It was empty, dark and unfriendly. Rozalia hurried after her.

'Didn't anyone else come?'

'Fabianski brought some wool.'

'He's brought it?' Mrs Kossecki was glad. 'That's good! Where is it?'

'Where is what?'

'The wool, Rozalia? Where is the wool?'

'How should I know?' Rozalia said irritably. 'He took it.'

'What do you mean?'

'He said he couldn't leave it, as he had to have the money first.'

Mrs Kossecki wrung her hands.

'What a trying man he is. I always pay him at once.'

'I said we'd pay directly.'

'What did he say to that?'

'He said he couldn't leave it with you not being here, because he wanted the money at once.'

'Oh goodness,' Mrs Kossecki said crossly, 'and wool's so hard to come by now . . .'

'Then he said he's got another lot at home. Only it's dearer. It's three thousand zloty . . .'

Mrs Kossecki made up her mind.

'It can't be helped, we'll have to take the dearer lot. Immediately, too, it may be dearer still tomorrow.'

'Of course it may. He said it certainly would be.'

'Fabianski said that? He really is too bad.'

Suddenly she was seized with feverish activity. 'Rozalia, you'll have to go to see him at once. Hurry up now.'

'All right. Isn't it windy outdoors?'

'Windy? No, it's lovely and warm. I'll give you the money at once. Come along.'

They crossed the hall into the bedroom.

Before the war, the Kosseckis' bedroom had been upstairs, but as the roof leaked they had had to move downstairs along with all the alien furniture left by the Germans. This furniture was a nightmare to Mrs Kossecki. The director of the work-camp, who had occupied the Kossecki villa, had had the Nazi mania for changing everything and had rearranged the whole house to suit his own tastes, which were not very good. There was an alien look about it all. Mrs Kossecki, who could picture the earlier arrangements down to the smallest detail in her mind, could not get used to this new and alien order. She had moved the furniture round, of course, and rearranged everything in her own way, but she had not really put her heart into it, and she did not feel at home. Whenever she went into the bedroom, she was repelled by the loud luxury of the huge carpet, the wide cupboard, the soft chairs and the cut-glass chandelier. The whole place was reminiscent of the tedious conventionality of a comfortable hotel.

Rozalia stopped in the doorway.

'Have you enough money?'

'Why not?' Mrs Kossecki asked in surprise. 'I got four thousand yesterday for that grey suit-length . . .'

Rozalia's small eyes gazed discouragingly at her mistress.

'I don't know nothing about that. You never told me.'

'What do you mean? Didn't I tell you last night?'

The old woman was offended.

'I'm not as deaf as all that, so as not to hear what you say.'

At first Mrs Kossecki felt like arguing, but a glance at Rozalia made her change her mind.

'Oh, very well. Perhaps I forgot.'

She opened the 'German cupboard' as she called it and brought out her father's old wallet from its hiding-place between the cold, neatly folded sheets. She had kept money for current expenses in this wallet for years. 'Dear me,' she thought, emotionally, 'what it's been through!' Apart from some photographs, it was the only souvenir she had of her parents. She opened the wallet and stood petrified. It was empty.

For several seconds all she felt was that cold drops of sweat were bursting out on her forehead. She looked again but found nothing. 'Keep calm, keep calm . . .' she whispered to herself. She began to go over the way she had hidden the money the day before and how, that morning, before going into town, she had taken one five-hundred from the eight five-hundred-zloty notes, putting the other seven back afterwards. She couldn't be wrong but, to make quite certain she began to turn the sheets over and over with trembling hands. Then she started to ransack the whole shelf.

Meanwhile Rozalia grew impatient. She could not see what Mrs Kossecki was doing behind the cupboard door.

'If you please, mum, if you want me to go directly . . . It'll be dark in no time . . .'

'All right, Rozalia,' she said from behind the door in an unnaturally loud voice, 'go and put your coat on.'

'What about the money?'

Mrs Kossecki pressed her hands to her temples.

'Is Mr Andrew in?'

'Is Mr Andrew what?'

'Is he in?'

'Yes, to be sure he is. He came in just a little while back. Some gentleman came to see him.'

Mrs Kossecki hesitated.

'And Alek?'

'Alek? Is he ever in? He rushed off just as you got back.'

Silence reigned for a moment.

'What do you want me to do, then?' Rozalia exclaimed. 'I don't know where I am.'

'I told you to go and get your coat on. I'll bring you the money directly.'

When Rozalia had finally left the room, Mrs Kossecki shut the cupboard door. But as she moved away from it she decided to go back. Re-opening the door, she began to shift the sheets to and fro in vain. In the big mirror, as she closed the cupboard door, she caught sight of her pale, worn face and was horrified by the suffering she saw in her darkened eyes. Mechanically, she raised her hands and began to tidy her hair. The house was silent but the birds were chirruping in the garden outside.

She turned away from the mirror and was about to go out when her gaze fell on a photograph of Alek standing by the bed. It was an old picture, taken when he was three years old. He sat on stone steps, in the sunshine, wearing a light shirt and short little trousers, with his right hand clasping his childishly bent leg. He had been a charming child, with fair curly hair and the round face of an innocent little angel. She suddenly remembered that it was in the year the photograph was taken that Alek had experienced his first great sorrow; two young storks had fallen out of their nest. For hours she had been unable to calm his sobbing, at night he would wake with a loud cry and would sob pitifully in his dreams, and for long, long afterwards, even in the winter, he had often referred in his conversation to the poor 'little storkies'. Many years had passed since those days, yet she had to close her eyes to prevent hot tears from streaming down. For a moment she felt the warm little body of the child in her empty arms and the same shiver of love and helpless sorrow that she had felt then.

She controlled herself and went out of the room quickly. On the stairs she heard voices coming from Andrew's room. She hesitated but only for a moment, since she realized that Rozalia might find out that the money had disappeared.

The only habitable room upstairs in the house was occupied by Alek, who had been sharing it with Andrew since the latter's return from the woods in March. Young masculine voices were carrying on a noisy conversation, almost a quarrel.

'Michael started it. It was your fault, you idiot!'

'Idiot yourself!'

'Here, mind what you're saying . . .'

'Oh, Jeez, what am I supposed to do, confound it all? How was I to know? The time was right, the same kind of jeep . . .'

The raised voices silenced the speaker. Then a new voice spoke.

'Keep calm, fellows. Pipe down a bit. We're not in the woods . . .'

She realized it was her son's voice. He went on, in the silence: '. . . then again, none of you is guilty individually. We're all guilty, because we were in it together and we messed up the whole job together . . .'

When Mrs Kossecki knocked, silence fell in the room. Presently she heard the easy voice of Andrew stressing the last word.

'Come in!'

She preferred not to go in, however. She was on the point of calling out, when the door opened and Andrew in his long boots as always, but without his jacket, with his short-sleeved shirt open came out. He was tall, fair haired and strongly built like his father. The room behind him was grey with cigarette smoke.

'It's you, Mother,' he said, a little surprised. 'I've got some friends here.'

'I know,' she interrupted, 'I don't want to disturb you, only . . . Shut the door, will you?'

He obeyed.

'What's happened?'

'I want to ask you a favour,' she began shyly. 'I have to buy some wool, for my loom . . .'

'And you're short of cash?'

She reddened, but it was too dark on the stairs for Andrew to see her embarrassment.

'It so happens that I am. So if you could . . .'

'Of course. You shouldn't be so . . . How often have I told you to give up the work? I've got plenty of money, but you always make so much fuss about it.'

'Presently, presently,' she replied evasively, 'when your father starts earning . . .'

Andrew made a gesture of dismissal.

'What can father earn? But how much do you want, five thousand, ten thousand?'

She looked at him in alarm.

'How have you got so much money? I want much less . . .
three thousand.'

'Is that all? It's not worth mentioning. Here, Mother.'

He reached into his trouser pocket and carelessly pulled out a
thick bundle of five hundred-zloty notes. Holding it in his fist,
he glanced at his mother.

'Sure you don't need more?'

She was so startled and stunned by the number of notes in
her son's hand that she did not hear him. He had no regular job,
and anyhow it was impossible to earn so much in any job nowadays.

'My child . . .' she began uncertainly, 'surely that money
isn't all yours?'

'Not mine?' he grinned. 'Why not?'

Then, catching his mother's searching look, he reddened and
his eyes shifted.

'You think there's a lot of money here? There's not as much
as all that.'

Hurriedly he counted out six banknotes and gave them to her.

'Here you are, three thousand.'

'Thank you,' she whispered.

Full of doubts and fears she began again,

'My child . . .'

But he seemed so alien and inaccessible in his strangeness that
she stopped without finishing the phrase. For a moment she had
a faint hope that he might understand her and make some frank,
comforting gesture. But she was not really surprised by his dry
matter-of-fact tone:

'What?'

'Nothing, nothing,' she said hastily. 'Don't bother, I'm going.
Thank you.'

Andrew thrust both hands into his trouser pockets.

'Don't mention it! It's nothing.'

She began to go downstairs slowly, holding on to the banister,
so uncertain of her strength did she feel. Andrew remained
standing on the stairs for some time. Not until she reached the
hall did she hear his door slam.

Rozalia was waiting in the kitchen, dressed to go out and with
a large black bag under her arm. Her head was tightly wound

into a warm woollen scarf. She stowed the money into her bodice.

'Why do you dress so warmly?' Mrs Kossecki asked in surprise. 'It isn't winter, you know.'

The old woman shrugged.

'I'd sooner not take risks. It's warm now but it may turn frosty within the hour. The wind may come up and catch me . . .'

Rozalia was becoming increasingly careful of her health.

Soon the garden gate banged behind her.

Mrs Kossecki began fidgeting round the kitchen. She shut the cupboard door which kept opening, swept breadcrumbs off the table, turned the loose tap tighter, pushed the basket of vegetables farther under the table. Then, in the midst of this mechanical activity, she felt so exhausted that she had to pull up a chair and sit down. At once the kitchen became quite quiet, except for single drops of water splashing in the sink.

She had sunk so deeply into her inner emptiness that she did not hear the door squeak and Antony come quietly into the kitchen. Not until his footsteps sounded close to her did she shiver and rise in alarm, certain at first that a stranger had come in. Seeing Antony, she sighed with relief. But her heart was beating so hard that she sat down again.

'Goodness, how jumpy I am nowadays,' she excused herself, her voice trembling a little. 'I thought a stranger had come in . . .'

Kossecki looked round the kitchen quickly.

'Isn't Rozalia here?'

'She's just gone to town. Did you want her for something?'

'No, it doesn't matter.'

At first glance he looked very well. He was carefully dressed in his best dark-brown, pre-war suit, which Mrs Kossecki had kept carefully all through the Occupation. He wore a clean shirt, his tie was neatly tied and his pre-war shoes decent. Only the uneasiness in his eyes and an unhealthy puffiness in his face, emphasized by the bony outline of his close-cropped head, betrayed a man deprived of his freedom for a long period.

Mrs Kossecki suddenly jumped up from the stool and ran across to the sink.

'Bother that tap! It keeps on and on dripping . . .' and, as she tried to turn it, she asked: 'Aren't you hungry? Would you like something to eat?'

'No, thanks. I'd like some tea, if there is any . . .'

Mrs Kossecki was pleased to have something to do.

'Of course. I've just brought a little tea, it should be nice. I'll put the water on, it won't be long.'

'Thank you,' he said, in a colourless voice.

And he went out, closing the door quietly. This was so unexpected that, unable to conceal her disappointment, she let fall the hand in which she was holding the tea-pot

It was Antony's second day at home, but she had already noticed that he avoided being alone with her. He hardly left the house at all but after meals, mostly in silence, he withdrew to his study. Several times when she had been in there, she had left the room again with the humiliating feeling that her presence disturbed her husband. He did not want her to share in his experiences, he avoided confiding in her and disposed of her questions about the camp with meaningless generalizations. In the end, she was able to understand this. Antony had never been talkative and she had managed to get used to this. She hoped that after a time, when Antony became domesticated again, his camp experiences would lose their hold over him and he would be able to talk about them with greater freedom. Yet it was hard for her to reconcile herself to the completely incomprehensible indifference which Antony had shown towards her from the first day. Her own life had not been easy in the past years. But Antony did not seem to understand this, at any rate he did nothing to indicate that he noticed and appreciated her difficulties. She comforted herself again by thinking that it would soon pass and in defending and explaining Antony to herself; but she found bitterness and resentment filled her heart in spite of the plausible explanations. Her whole life was based on the belief that she was needed. In the worst times she had longed for Antony's return. Despite the sombre and almost incredibly depressing news from the camps, she had believed that Antony would survive and come back. Now that she was proved right, each meeting with her husband wounded painfully and humiliated her.

When she had to go into his study now, she was afraid that,

opening the door unexpectedly, she would startle Antony and see him for a moment as he was when he was alone in the room. But she avoided knocking at his door lest it underline their mutual strangeness. But she approached his room noisily so as to warn him in advance.

Taking him his tea, she banged the kitchen door after her and walked very slowly across the hall coughing several times. She was certain that when she went in Antony would be sitting at his desk, busy apparently, preoccupied, looking through his scattered papers. She was right.

She put the tea-cup on his desk, but could not make up her mind to go out again at once.

'Here's your tea,' she said in an undertone.

Kossecki nodded his oddly shaped shaven head.

'Thank you.'

She noticed that he had a newspaper open in front of him, at the page she had seen him reading when she had gone in that morning. She withdrew to the window, unable to endure the humiliating thought that Antony must be tortured by his inability to meet the uneasy glances she gave him. Antony was certainly calm, but the hidden tension was reflected in his eyes.

Apple blossom gleamed white outside the window that was only half glazed. Although it was still light outside, half-darkness pervaded the room.

She pushed the plant on the window-sill nearer to the centre.

'It's not too cold for you?'

'No,' he replied hastily.

She looked to see whether the plant needed watering but found the earth in the flower-pot moist. Finding nothing else that needed attention she was on the point of leaving the room when she felt heavy, warm tears gathering under her eyelids. She trembled at the thought of bursting into tears, bit her lips and instinctively pressed her hands to her breast, as if to calm her sorrow and helplessness. Then she heard the tea-cup clatter in the saucer. The fact that Antony had started to drink his tea without waiting for her to leave the room gave her some consolation. But she was not sufficiently sure of her voice to say anything yet.

'Is it all right?' she asked presently. 'Not too weak?'

'No, it is very nice.'

It seemed to her that he said this in a rather warmer tone of voice, and pleased, she turned to him. Crouched at his desk, Antony was drinking his tea slowly, both hands round the cup, as though he sought to warm them. She was silent, deeply moved by this frugal gesture, and after a long pause Antony noticed her looking at him. For a moment his eyes shifted uneasily, then he turned his face away and replaced the cup in the saucer.

'Very nice tea. I haven't had such nice tea for a long time.'

'We had a hard time with tea, too. We could get it, but it was terribly dear.'

As soon as Mrs Kossecki said this she regretted foolishly comparing her own fate with Antony's in the camp. As quickly as possible, to cover her clumsiness, she hurried on:

'I met Frank Podgorski on the way home.'

Kossecki showed no interest whatsoever.

'He was so pleased you're back. He knew you were.'

'Already?' Kossecki raised his head. 'Who from?'

'I don't know. Someone must have seen you. You know what it's like here.'

He reached for the cup as Mrs Kossecki approached the desk.

'He was in hiding all the time, you know . . .'

'Who was?'

'Podgorski. He very much wanted to see you.'

He did not answer but leaned over the newspaper and rested his head on his hand, concealing nearly all his face.

Mrs Kossecki hesitated.

'I think you ought to see him, if he comes.'

Kossecki rose, pushing his chair back violently.

'I've told you I don't want to see anyone!' Then he controlled himself and added, more calmly: 'For the time being, anyway.'

He walked to and fro several times behind his desk and again grew irritable.

'It's Mrs Staniewicz today, Podgorski tomorrow, someone else the day after, a crowd of inquisitive people within a day or two . . . After all I've been through, surely I have the right to peace and quiet, haven't I?'

Mrs Kossecki pressed her hands to her breast.

'It wasn't easy for me either. Don't think it was.'

Kossecki stopped.

'Do I think it was? What's that got to do with Podgorski?'

'You know it has. It has a lot to do with him. Only you don't see it . . . you seem to think . . . but I'm a human being too and deserve something . . . because I . . . I simply can't go on, I can't . . .'

With her hands still pressed defensively to her breast, she began quietly crying. Big tears flowed down her withered cheeks and her whole body shook with suppressed sobbing.

Antony did not try to calm her. He stood at the desk motionless, his eyelids lowered and his face a blank.

'Now, look here . . .' he began at last, 'why get so upset? There's no point.'

'Because it's more than I can stand,' she repeated in a broken voice. 'I'm so terribly sorry for everything . . .'

Kossecki shrugged.

'What does "everything" mean for God's sake? We're all alive, we've got our house back,' and he added with a touch of irony: 'What more do you want?'

Rubbing her reddened eyes with her hanky, she nodded.

'Well, what more?'

She began crying again. This time Antony made up his mind to leave the shelter of the desk. He came over to her.

'Stop it.' He put his hand on her arm. 'It's only your nerves.'

But he drew back at once and putting his hands behind him began to walk about the room. Mrs Kossecki watched him through her tears.

'I know it's nerves. But what can I do about it?'

Kossecki stopped.

'It'll pass of its own accord. So many things do. Everything will settle down gradually . . .'

But he spoke with such lack of conviction that she, expecting words of consolation, felt still more desolate. She thought of her sons, the house, the lost money . . .

'Sometimes I don't believe in anything,' she said apathetically. 'Sometimes, when I start to think of it all, I hardly want to go on living.'

'You say that,' he made a contemptuous gesture. 'But everyone wants to live.'

'But why! Who for?'

Antony said nothing.

'You try to judge everyone by your own standards. We weren't all in camps but sometimes life was difficult for us too.' Then, quite unexpectedly, in an unnaturally loud and unpleasant way, he began laughing. Mrs Kossecki shuddered. Instinctively she took her hanky away from her eyes. In the half-darkness that surrounded him she could not distinguish her husband's face, but only his outline. His laughter, not unlike the choking of a dry cough, sounded terrible to her.

'Antony!' she exclaimed in a terrified voice.

He stopped at once and silence fell in the darkening room. It lasted a long time. Finally, Mrs Kossecki managed with difficulty to control the trembling which came from the depths of her being and asked,

'Shall I get you some more tea?'

'No, thank you,' he replied from the darkness. 'I don't want anything just now.'

Chapter Four

It was dusk when Szczuka and Podgorski got back to town. The market-place looked different: it had emptied and a bluish half-light filled it. The bare outlines of burnt-out houses were still more sharply defined against a pea-green sky. As the spring evening fell, the crowds seeking fresh air moved in the direction of the Kosciuszko Park and May 3rd Boulevard. It was Saturday, the evening was warm and mild, though somewhat sultry. A few lorries were still in the centre of the market-place, but the soldiers moving about them were preparing to leave. The magnified sounds of a Chopin mazurka rose above the quiet square from the wireless loudspeaker. A patrol of four militiamen walked along the side of the market-place, taking up the whole width of the empty pavement. The shadows of the chestnut trees mingled with their long shadows. They stopped for a moment on the corner, then turned into the first darkening street.

Podgorski stopped the car in front of the Monopole. He got out first, with Szczuka levering himself after him. The two militiamen in the back seat got out after them. It was empty in front of the hotel but three droshkies stood a little farther away.

'At nine o'clock then, comrade?' said Podgorski.

Szczuka took his hat off.

'Yes, there's that banquet. I'd quite forgotten it. Can't it be put off? I must say I don't much want to go.'

'I don't suppose you do,' Podgorski agreed, 'but what can one do? It was Swiecki's idea.'

'Are many people coming?'

'About fifty.'

'Quite enough too! Well, it can't be helped.'

'Will you be staying in the hotel now?'

Szczuka reflected.

'I'll see; I may go out. I've got relations here, my wife's sister.'

'Really? I didn't know you were married.'

'I was. She's dead.'

Podgorski was embarrassed and Szczuka noticed this.

'As for my sister-in-law, you as a local man must know her husband, Staniewicz.'

'The major?'

'That's him. He was in the Ostrowiec Hussars. Now I gather he's a colonel.'

'Is he? The Staniewicz who was with General Anders?'

'Does it surprise you?'

Podgorski laughed.

'I was a bit startled by the association of you and Colonel Staniewicz.'

'Why? All kinds of things happen in Polish families. See you at nine o'clock, then.'

'Yes, and tomorrow I'll be here at seven sharp.'

On the Sunday and Monday, they were to visit all the Party organizations in the district.

'I'll remember,' Szczuka replied.

At the hotel entrance he turned back. Podgorski was standing by the car.

'I've just remembered. Are you going to see that man . . . the magistrate . . .?'

'Kossecki?'

'Yes,' Podgorski glanced at his watch. 'Nearly half past seven. I'll go over there now. Do you want to see him?'

'I'd like to. Mention to him if you get the chance that a comrade from the camp . . .'

'I'll tell him your name.'

'My surname probably won't mean anything. Just call me a comrade from the camp, from Gross-Rosen.'

'I see.'

'If he'd like to see me, he could call. On Tuesday, say.'

'Smolarski's and Gawlik's funeral is on Tuesday morning.'

'In the afternoon, then, between five and six.'

'Tuesday between five and six,' Podgorski repeated. 'What's your room number?'

'Seventeen.'

The short, bald porter, with a round, bespectacled face, who was talking to a young man in a light raincoat and brown hat leaning against the counter, reached for a key from the board.

'Number seventeen, sir.'

Szczuka leaned his stick against the desk.

'Any cigarettes?'

'Certainly. American or Hungarian?'

'May as well have American.'

He paid and at once opened the packet of Chesterfields. Before he could reach for a match, the man standing beside him obligingly produced a lighter from his raincoat pocket.

He was a young man, a little over twenty, dark with girlish eyelashes and blue eyes.

'Thanks,' Szczuka muttered.

He inhaled and offered the open packet to the young man and the porter. Both accepted. The young man, carelessly touching his hat-brim, lit his at once. The plump porter stuck his behind his ear.

'Should I reserve you a table in the restaurant, sir?'

Szczuka put his cigarettes away.

'No, thanks. But I'll have breakfast in my room tomorrow. At a quarter to seven.'

'Certainly. Number seventeen, breakfast at a quarter to seven,' the porter repeated. 'Will you be vacating your room then, sir?'

'No. I'll be away for a few days, but I'll keep the room on.'

He took the key and began limping up the red stair carpet. The young man leaned against the counter again.

'Nice bloke. Who is he?'

The porter shrugged. 'A visitor. What can you tell nowadays about people?'

'That's so,' said the other, indifferently, and with an equally uninterested movement he looked behind him.

Szczuka, leaning on his stick, had just reached the landing. Seen from below, he looked still more massive and broader in the shoulder.

The youth reverted to his previous position.

'How about a room, then?'

'What about it?' the porter looked at him discouragingly

from beneath his spectacles. 'There aren't any. I've told you already, they're all booked up.'

The other did not resent this refusal.

'Look here,' he began in a friendly manner, 'I've come here for a day or so. I'm staying with friends for the time being but I have personal reasons for wanting freedom, don't you see?'

The porter betrayed a certain slight interest.

'Is it a girl?'

The young man laughed, showing even, white and healthy teeth.

'That's it. But never mind, a single would do.'

He unfastened his raincoat and produced some crumpled banknotes from his jacket pocket.

'Give me a packet of cigarettes.'

'American?'

'No, Hungarian. I prefer them, they're stronger.'

He put a five-hundred-zloty note on the counter. The porter eyed it, tempted.

'I'll get your change directly,' he said, considering slowly.

'Never mind. Why bother?'

The porter muttered something indistinctly and put the banknote in his pocket, then leaned with a worried frown over the register.

'Well, look . . . this is booked, this one, no. Twelve was to be vacated, but wasn't . . . floor two is all booked . . . how long do you want it for?'

'A day or two – till Tuesday.'

'Tuesday? Well, perhaps something can be managed.'

'There you are, you see!'

'I thought it was for longer.'

'Why? I'm going to Warsaw on Tuesday.'

The porter looked up.

'You from Warsaw?'

'What do you think?'

'I'm from Warsaw myself. I worked at the Savoy.'

'In Nowy Swiat?'

'Fifteen years. A long time, eh?'

'Were you there during the Insurrection?'

'Certainly,' said the porter, proudly. 'To the very last day. Were you?'

'I was all over the place. First in the Old City, then the City centre.'

'You got through the sewers? My daughter was there. You may have known her? Basia Borkowska, her name was. I'll show you her picture . . .'

He reached for his wallet, rooted in it and finally produced a small, amateur, rather crumpled photo.

'That's the only photo I have left. Perhaps you knew her . . .'

The youth took the photo. It must have been taken on the beach, in sunshine, and showed the graceful figure of a young, smiling girl in a bathing dress.

'I don't think I did. She's pretty. Is she still alive?'

The porter made a gesture.

'Of course not. She was killed at the very beginning. And they took my son prisoner.'

'Where was that?'

'Somewhere near the Dutch frontier.'

'That's been liberated. Didn't you hear the news bulletin today?'

'Yes, but people don't feel like celebrating.'

Two people, an elderly peroxided woman and a young man in a tight coat, came in from the street, carrying on a lively conversation in raised, quarrelsome voices. They stopped it in the hall.

'Good afternoon, madam,' the porter greeted them. 'Number twenty-two, at your service.'

The man took the key. On the stairs they started quarrelling again.

The porter looked at the register again and rubbed his hands with satisfaction.

'You know something? I was going to give you a room on the third floor, but it's only a lousy hole, if you'll pardon the expression. You take number eighteen, on the first floor, you deserve it after Warsaw. I always keep a room or two reserved for my better, pre-war guests. A man has to live, eh?'

'I see,' the youth winked at him. 'All right. I knew we'd come to terms.'

The porter rubbed his hands again.

'We've got to stick together, us people from Warsaw, eh? Got any luggage?'

The other man indicated a brief-case on the desk.

'Nothing much.'

'Never mind! I had less than that.'

He took a German identity card out of his pocket. The porter straightened his glasses and set about writing down the entry. In spite of his glasses he crouched over the grey *Kennkarte*.

'Michael Chelmicki?'

'Yes.'

'Born Warsaw, 1921. Trade: labourer ...'

Chelmicki laughed.

'That's only for the benefit of the Germans! Trade – student.'

'A student,' the porter repeated.

Chelmicki settled his elbows comfortably on the desk and as he watched the porter writing he gave a careful look at the page of the nearby register. Although it was upside down he easily found the line with number seventeen.

'Single,' the porter deciphered.

Chelmicki nodded, then leaned over and read the name and surname: Stefan Szczuka, written in small pointed letters, looking odd upside down.

'Single,' he agreed. 'No special personal characteristics.'

It was very hot in the room. Szczuka threw his coat over a chair and went to the window without turning on the light. When he opened it, fresh air began flowing in at once.

The window overlooked a wide yard, closed at the far side by a low, wooden building which might have been a stable or garage. Behind it, almost black against the violet sky, were the fantastic shapes of a large garden. Lines of light from some of the hotel windows seemed with their frail brightness to shift that darkness deeper back into the thickening night. At one moment the wind rose and the dusk of the garden began to move. It looked beautiful and threatening.

Simultaneously, the sickening smell of fat rose from below, from the restaurant kitchen, and Szczuka closed the window and lay down on the bed. There was silence then, but the peculiar, uneasy silence of a hotel, in which the most varied and alien echoes arise from outside. There were footsteps deadened by the coconut matting of the corridor, a door slammed farther away, water ran into the hand-basin in the next room, more footsteps, the brief ringing of a bell, the splashing of water in the basin . . .

Presently he stopped paying attention to these sounds, placed his hands under his head and the eyelids closed of their own accord. Not until now did he feel real, great weariness. He knew, however, that he would not fall asleep. More and more often, when he needed rest sleep evaded him. Sometimes lying in the darkness during the long hours of the night, he would fall into a shallow doze, but when he emerged from its tormenting dreams, everything came back again. At times like these, he thought about the way in which the woman he loved had died. What had she thought about, then? How long had she had to suffer? And what pain had been her lot in those last moments? Any kind of suffering had seemed beyond her endurance. She had been strong and he knew she could be brave, but he also knew that neither strength of spirit nor courage are any defence against pain, nor do they temper the agony of a man dying alone and without dignity. He had already come to terms with the death of his wife. This was not the first time he had realized that one cannot found one's life on even the nearest and dearest of people. One hour, one moment, can turn a beloved woman or the closest friend into the past, and that can never remain the same. A man cannot live unless he pass with a certain cold indifference over death. It is unwise to give the dead too much feeling and thought. They have no need of them. They need nothing. They do not exist. There are only the living.

But he thought of his wife as living because he knew nothing yet of the circumstances in which she had died. Among the many women from the Ravensbruck camp he had met, only one had been able to tell him anything about Maria. She had been seen for the last time in autumn 1944, coming back to the barracks after digging potatoes, and already ill, and supported by two of her friends. How often had he summoned up this tormenting picture. He realized that Maria, coming back from digging potatoes, was no longer the woman whose face and figure were preserved in his memory, but after that, it was all darkness. He wondered about it at random and with helpless stubbornness, thinking about the deaths of executed women, driven into gas chambers, dying slowly in torture, finally cut down by a fatal injection or an ordinary blow. . . . What had Maria's death-agony been like? Until he had come into contact with the final misery of existence, he had always believed that conquering the fear of death is hardest to acquire where loved ones are concerned. In mourning the dead, whom do the living most often mourn, if not themselves? Those who cannot do otherwise can weep for themselves, but in the end, all suffering matters. It can be respected and even understood. But what meaning have all the torments of the living faced by those final human moments from which all hope has been cut off and to which only bitterness, misery of the body, cruelty, and contempt have been given?

He often talked to himself, when unable to sleep: 'Maria, my dearest, I have been spared and I can do something for the many people I meet, if they require it of me. Sometimes more, sometimes less. But for you alone I was unable to do anything, just when you most needed help. How calmly I should think of you if I could know that when you died you had at least one human being with you whose heart was filled with pity, and that you knew it . . .'

He sat up on the bed, his head in his hands. His temples were slightly damp. 'There's still fear in me,' he thought. He had to force himself to master his weariness and stand up. He turned on the light and stood for a while uncertain amidst these alien and indifferent surroundings. A high mirror at the far side of the room reflected his enormous and heavy figure with bent shoulders and long arms, now hanging loosely like those of a puppet.

Just then the key turned in the door of the next room and someone came in. The electric light switch snapped on. Then slightly deadened sounds of someone moving about the room came through the wall. Water flowed into the hand-basin, and the tune of a popular song, 'My heart's in my knapsack', being whistled by a man mingled with the splash of hands being washed.

Szczuka glanced at his watch. An hour and a half before the banquet at the Monopole and he felt incapable of spending it alone. He decided to go and see Mme Staniewicz. He knew he would never write to her, and she ought to be told of Maria's death. Once he had made up his mind, he felt better. He put on his coat and hat, then took his stick. His neighbour, walking about the other room, went on whistling.

Presently Szczuka found himself in the market-place. It was sultry and dark clouds were gathering in the east. It looked as though a storm was coming.

Mme Staniewicz lived in one of the streets crossing May 3rd Boulevard, not far from the Kosciuszko Park. Szczuka did not know Ostrowiec well and had to ask the way. It was not far. As he approached the Boulevard he saw a small bar on the corner and went in and drank two large vodkas at the counter.

As usual on Saturday evenings, Mme Staniewicz had people in. There were three of then: the two Puciatyckis who were living in Ostrowiec after having to leave their Chwaliboga estate and young Fred Telezynski, exiled from far-off Podlasie.

Mme Staniewicz, slender and graceful in a wine-coloured dress, was pouring coffee into cups on a tray. Adam Puciatycki looked round the room which was small and restful, strewn with carpets, full of tapestries, pictures and pretty ornaments, and although overcrowded (before the war, the Staniewiczes had had a much bigger flat), charmingly arranged.

'One has to admit, my dears,' said Puciatycki in his nasal voice, 'that in the Colonel's wife's home, one really can relax. One forgets all the ugliness out there . . .' and he indicated the window.

Mme Staniewicz smiled.

'I'm glad to hear it, but with one reservation, there's no Colonel's lady here!'

The Puciatyckis – he an elderly, lean man, with long limbs and a small, narrow head, she also tall with a long horse-like face – both laughed. Telezynski, big and powerful, with a short black moustache, was smoking a pipe with a look of boredom.

'Quite right,' said Puciatycki. 'I too prefer people not to use my title now. But, talking of titles, I must tell you of an amusing incident . . . A few days ago we were visited by our faithful Mroczek . . .'

'Who's Mroczek?' asked Telezynski.

44

'Don't you remember Mroczek? Our gardener at Chwali-
boga.'
'Oh, him! I had no idea he was called Mroczek.'
Puciatycki, displeased at being interrupted, shrugged.
'Never mind . . . Anyhow, Mroczek arrived, burdened with
all sorts of provisions, and said "Your Excellency . . ." and I
replied, "What Excellency? Don't you know, you fool, that we
now have democracy?"'
Telezynski burst into a loud, healthy laugh.
'And what did Mroczek say to that?' asked Mme Staniewicz.
'Mroczek? This is the best part! He said, in an offended tone
of voice, "But, Your Excellency, I'm not for democracy." Good,
don't you think? That's what Polish peasants are like!'
'Don't exaggerate,' Telezynski made a grimace. 'It isn't as
good as that. Go back to Chwaliboga and you'll find out.'
Puciatycki pouted.
'Of course I'll go back. You'll see in a year's time, they'll be
kissing my hand.'
Mme Staniewicz saw fit to revert to her role as hostess.
'Come along, the coffee is getting cold . . .'
Puciatycki reached for his cup. Before he took the first sip, he
inhaled the aroma of the coffee for a moment.
'Excellent!' he said more nasally than usual, inclining his
head at the same time in the direction of Mme Staniewicz beside
him. 'I congratulate you.'
He took her hand and kissed it. Then he stretched out his long
legs and settled himself, with a feeling of complete satisfaction,
more comfortably in the deep armchair.
'Isn't it too strong?' asked Mme Staniewicz.
'Not at all! Apropos of being too strong . . .' he glanced at
Telezynski, 'do you remember, Fred, what Tony Ustrzycki used
to say about coffee?'
Telezynski pondered.
'Tony?'
'Don't you remember? Coffee can never be too strong, nor a
pretty woman too weak.'
The other laughed. Telezynski took his pipe out of his mouth.
'I'm glad you reminded me of Tony. We've had news of him.'
'Really?' Puciatycki exclaimed. 'Where is he? Who's heard?'

'Rosa Wadolowska told me in Warsaw. He's written to Martha.'

'What about?'

'Nothing much. He's staying in London and apparently wondering whether to come back.'

'Come back? Where to?'

'Here.'

'Has he gone off his head?'

'Very likely. Rosa Wadolowska says he certainly has.'

Puciatycki was very excited.

'I never heard anything like it! He wants to come back here? What for, why? What's come over him? Such a sensible lad. Just think, my dear, Tony's wife Martha you know – the little Sulemirska . . .'

Mme Staniewicz had never heard of her, but she nodded with complete understanding.

'. . . is going quite off her head to get abroad, while he wants to come back! I'd never have expected this from Tony. But perhaps it's only gossip or some kind of misunderstanding?'

'Perhaps,' Telezynski replied indifferently. 'But I don't think so. If he wants to come back, let him.'

'It's madness!' Puciatycki muttered, and turning to Mme Staniewicz he lowered his voice confidentially. 'And how about our own business, my dear lady?'

'It's all going quite well.'

Mme Puciatycki leaned her horse-like face towards her too.

'My dearest, is it quite positive?'

'Positive?' Puciatycki made a grimace. 'You forget the times we're living in, my dear. Today nothing is positive.'

Mme Staniewicz disagreed with him.

'Forgive me, but why this pessimism? One's friends will remain friends . . .'

'Quite so,' Puciatycki nodded. 'I beg your pardon. But you're an exception. That is why we're confiding our destiny to your charming hands.'

Mme Staniewicz laughed. She had a pretty laugh and liked using it.

'In my husband's hands, rather. But we certainly shan't go wrong there. He'll use all his influence to get us out of here.'

46

Puciatycki turned towards the closed doors that led into the next room, and moved his head significantly. Mme Staniewicz placed her finger to her lips.

In the next room, also over coffee, Andrew Kossecki, leaning across a low table, was talking in an undertone to a middle-aged man, small and spare, with the bow legs of a cavalry officer. The light from a high, shaded lamp standing near-by, illuminated part of the floor, leaving the room and the two men in half-darkness.

Andrew straightened up.

'That's all!'

He crushed out a half-finished cigarette in an ash-tray and at once lit another. As he leaned across, his fair, fine hair drooped over his forehead and he tossed it back impatiently.

The colonel was smoking a cigarette silently and very slowly. In his other small, delicate, almost feminine hand, he was playing with a match-box. His head was well shaped, his brow convex and high, with a strongly drawn vertical line between his dark brows. When he had finished his cigarette, he crushed out the end precisely and retreated into the depths of his chair.

'Well, what about it?' he said in a concise voice. 'Admittedly I was expecting somewhat different results, but after hearing all this, I see no real reason for you to blame yourself. It was simply an accident, it can't be helped and I'd advise you not to worry, lieutenant.'

Andrew compressed his dark brows.

'I can't stand wasting work!'

'Who can? But that's not the point. As you certainly realize, many things we don't like happen to us. This has happened.'

'I know. But apart from that . . .'

'Apart from what?'

'Innocent people died unnecessarily.'

The colonel eyed Kossecki carefully and a slight smile appeared on his thin lips.

'Pangs of conscience, eh?'

'Do you think they're misplaced, colonel?'

'I don't know. I'm not your conscience. Who was killed, do you know?'

'Some men from the Biala cement works, apparently.'
'And how'd you know they were innocent?'
Andrew reddened.
'I suppose it.'
'Ah, you suppose it! You might just as well suppose that they
were, for instance, Party members. What then?'
The low, warm laugh of Mme Staniewicz, amidst the noise
of general conversation, came to them from the next room. The
colonel reached for a cigarette.
'But we're off the point again. How long is Szczuka staying in
Ostrowiec?'
'Until Wednesday, according to our information. He's leaving
early Wednesday morning.'
'So there are three days left.'
'One.'
'Why?'
'Sunday and Monday are out. He's going away.'
The colonel smiled.
'I see you're well informed. The Security police?'
Andrew nodded.
'Yes, we have a few of our own people there.'
'Are they reliable? They won't talk?'
'Out of the question.'
'Good. Let's consider what to do. The countryside isn't suit-
able for this operation.'
'Not really. There would be a lot of difficulties. Today was an
unusual opportunity.'
'I understand. What about Tuesday? What do you suggest?'
Andrew hesitated. A shadow crossed his lean swarthy face.
'Colonel, there's something I wanted to ask you . . .'
'Well?'
Andrew leaned across the little table and as he did so, his hair
again drooped over his forehead. He pushed it back.
'I don't know how to put it . . .'
The other man said nothing. It was evident from his expres-
sion that he had no intention of helping the young man out.
Andrew sat there gloomily, his brows knitted. Suddenly he
raised his head with a decisive movement.
'I'll be frank. Must Szczuka really be killed?'

The colonel showed no surprise. He reached for a match, lit a cigarette without haste, held it for a long time, then inhaled deeply. Andrew was looking at him tensely.

'Lieutenant,' he said at last, 'from what I know of your past, you're too experienced and good a soldier not to realize that as your superior officer I have the right to blame you for asking such a question. Isn't that so?'

Andrew reddened to the roots of his hair.

'I think . . .'

'I'm not asking what you think. I want a reply.'

For a while it looked as though Kossecki would argue. He controlled himself, however.

'Yes,' he replied, briefly.

The colonel nodded.

'I'm glad we think alike. Nevertheless, I'll answer your question. I understand your doubts. I'd even be surprised if you didn't have any. We're living and fighting under very difficult and complex circumstances. But the war years, which were the testing years for everyone, have taught us that things have to be regarded in their elementary, basic set-up. There's no time for subtle discrimination. If there had to be any discrimination, it must be simple and clear. Good is good, and evil evil. You agree?'

The colonel's calm, level voice supported and strengthened the truth of his words.

'So there's one thing we must get clear in the present situation. The Second World War is coming to an end. That's obvious. Another two or three days, perhaps a week – and it will be over. But we did not foresee an end like this. We thought that not only would Germany come out of the war defeated, but Russia too. Things have turned out rather differently. In today's set-up we Poles are divided into two categories: those who have betrayed the freedom of Poland and those who do not wish to do so. The first want to submit to Russia, we do not. They want Communism, we do not. They want to destroy us, we must destroy them. A battle is going on between us, a battle that has only just started? How old are you?'

'Twenty-one.'

'You started working in the underground . . .'

'In 1941.'

'You were seventeen then?'

'Yes.'

'And what were you fighting for? Wasn't it for the freedom of Poland? But did you imagine a Poland ruled by blind agents carrying out orders from the Kremlin and established by Russian bayonets? What about your colleagues, your contemporaries? How many of them died? What for? In the end how can people like you and me – alive and still at liberty – how can we show our solidarity with our friends if we draw back half-way?'

There was silence for a while and Puciatycki's nasal voice could be heard faintly through the door.

'Now, take Szczuka.' The colonel went on at last. 'Who's Szczuka? One of the intelligentsia, a trained engineer, a Communist. An excellent organizer into the bargain. And he's a man who knows what he wants. Now he's working for the Party in the provinces but tomorrow if nothing changes, he'll hold a responsible State job. He may be a Minister the day after tomorrow. Let's say he's an idealist. He was put on trial several times before the war and was sent to gaol. He was two years in a prison camp. He's the more dangerous. We're not worried by careerists. When the time comes they'll leave the sinking ship like rats. It's a waste to risk men like you – and bullets – on them. The cost is too high. But when it's a question of ideas which bring us enslavement and death, then our reply can only be death. The usual laws of battle. History will be the final judge as to who was right. We have already decided . . .' he inhaled his cigarette smoke and added with emphasis . . . 'because we have already chosen.'

Andrew sat with his head bowed, his strong, tanned hands clasped between his widely-set knees.

The colonel gave him a brief glance.

'Of course, you might ask me the fundamental question: whether we've made the right choice? Shouldn't one judge first, then choose? That's a problem, I admit.'

Andrew raised his head and looked questioningly at him.

'I'm not going to overcome you with clichés. You don't need them, do you? You're too intelligent for that . . .'

Kossecki shrugged.

'I'm not intelligent; I want to be honest, that's all.'

'Moral intelligence is precisely what I mean,' the colonel replied swiftly. 'You're not the only one bothered by doubts. But what answer can I give to them? Like you, I'm a soldier and carry out orders of my superior officers. Blindly? No, I believe they're right, because as a soldier I'm also a man and do not forgo the right to judge the world I live in. I assure you, lieutenant, that a man who does not want to be a judge does not want to be a man. And if one has the courage to judge, then loyalty towards oneself applies too. It's a matter, if you'll forgive me using such a big word, of conscience. That's all!'

He shifted in his armchair and reached for his cup.

'Meanwhile, our coffee has got cold . . .'

He drank his at a gulp and leaned over to place his small hand on Kossecki's broad shoulder.

'How about it then, lieutenant, can we get back to our interrupted discussion now?'

Andrew sat thinking. Finally he straightened up.

'Yes.'

'That's fine. And what was it I was asking you? Aha – what do you suggest? Have you a plan?'

'Yes. It's only a rough idea so far.'

'Well?'

Andrew moved nearer.

'According to our information, Szczuka is staying at the Monopole . . .'

The sharp sound of a doorbell came from the hall. Andrew stopped and looked at the colonel.

'Just a minute,' said the latter.

They heard Mme Staniewicz go into the hall.

When she opened the door and saw the massive figure of a man in the half light of the unlit stairs, she did not at first recognize her brother-in-law.

'Good evening, Kate.'

'Stefan!' She was startled and not enthusiastic. 'This is a surprise. Where have you sprung from? You here in Ostrowiec?'

'As you see.'

'But it's unheard of!'

She had changed little during the long years of war. She had always given the impression of being younger than she was and now she did not look forty; she was slim and had the skilfully preserved charm of a light blonde. Despite a certain family likeness, it was hard to imagine sisters more different from each other than Kate and Maria. As this thought struck him, Szczuka realized he had come here hoping to find at least a shadow of a likeness to Maria in Mme Staniewicz. He felt a pang of disappointment, but could not draw back now.

'You look very well,' he said.

Mme Staniewicz still could not get over her amazement.

'You know, I can't think of anyone I was less expecting to see. Come along, take your coat off. I'm so pleased to see you.'

As he took his overcoat off he noticed several coats hanging up.

'You have people in?'

'Oh, don't mind them! A few of my friends. The Puciatyckis . . .'

'I see you still like the aristocratic families.'

'Still?' she raised her thin pencilled eyebrows in feigned surprise. 'Do you think one's friends should be chosen because of their connexions?'

'Naturally.'

Mme Staniewicz was slightly confused. However, she smiled.

'I believe you wanted to tease me, didn't you? I see you haven't changed at all.'

He looked at her, this time without irony.

'On the contrary, my dear, I wanted to agree with you.'

'Excellent.' She pretended to take her brother-in-law's remark at its face value. 'I was afraid my visitors might alarm you. Come along. But of course!' – and she paused in the doorway – 'I see you've got back all right. You look very well. But what's the matter with your leg?'

'Nothing much.'

'Nothing serious?'

'Nothing at all,' he replied, though he had no doubt he would be limping for the rest of his life.

'What about Maria? She, poor dear, must have gone through some terrible things.'

'Everyone did in the prison-camps.'

'She's back now, of course.'

'No.'

Mme Staniewicz turned to him, her hand on the door-knob.

'Not back yet? Poor dear, it must be terrible for her. All the same, this is only the beginning, they'll start coming back from the camps now, for good. She kept well, didn't she?'

Szczuka nodded.

'There you are, then! If she kept well, that was the most important thing. You'll see, she'll be back very soon.'

He hesitated, but only for a moment.

'I expect she will,' he said calmly.

And he followed his sister-in-law into the room. The people sitting round the table turned in his direction.

'This is my brother-in-law, Mr Szczuka,' Mme Staniewicz said loudly, trying to hide the embarrassment she felt by an airy modulation of her voice.

She hated ambiguous social situations and all her earlier dislike of her sister's husband revived within her. She had never been able to understand what had persuaded a girl as pretty and intelligent as Maria to marry a man like him. Still more incomprehensible about it all had been the fact that they appeared to make an ideal couple. She recalled what her husband had once said about Szczuka. 'I can understand,' he had said after one of their very infrequent family gatherings, 'how a man may be a Communist. There are all sorts of deviations, after all. But why admit it? That's a bit too much for my taste and common sense.'

Meanwhile Szczuka, too big and heavy for the overcrowded interior, had taken one of the empty armchairs, next to Telezynski.

'Have some coffee?' Mme Staniewicz asked.

'Please,' he muttered in his own way.

'I beg your pardon,' Puciatycki asked from the other side of the table. 'Did I catch your name right? Mr Szczuka?'

'Yes.'

'I've heard your name somewhere,' Puciatycki drawled nasally. 'But where can I have come across it? Quite recently...'

'I can assist you,' Szczuka replied. 'You most likely saw my name in the newspaper, on the occasion of the Party congress.'

Mme Staniewicz stirred uneasily.

'That was it!' Puciatycki exclaimed. 'I don't of course read that sort of thing, but I remember it very well now – someone with the same name made a speech. I hope he was no relation of yours.'

'No.'

'I thought as much. But it must be disagreeable for you, all the same.'

Szczuka reached for his coffee.

'You think so? Apparently you've guessed wrong. I said he was no relation of mine, since he was myself.'

Mme Staniewicz, blushing slightly, tried to save the situation.

'What a delicious *quid pro quo!*' she laughed, somewhat too loudly. 'It might have been in a play. But it looks, Count, as if you've made a dreadful gaffe.'

'I think so, too,' Puciatycki said, entirely through his nose.

Roza Puciatycki was sitting stiffly upright, her face longer than usual, while Telezynski, with his leg crossed high and clutching his ankle, sucked at his pipe and gazed blinking at his cousin, then at Szczuka. Clearly he was entertained by the whole scene.

'I hope . . .' Puciatycki began.

Mme Staniewicz preferred to interrupt him.

'Of course, you don't know that my brother-in-law is an old pre-war Left-winger. He's had very radical views, ever since I can remember. Isn't that so, Stefan?'

'I see you are trying to justify me.'

'I beg your pardon,' Puciatycki protested, 'you are unjust, my dear sir. For myself, I've always placed a high value on people of character, on people of ideas, without considering whether I agreed with them or not. Surely this is the only possible attitude for a man with any pretensions to culture? You agree, I expect?'

Mme Staniewicz's eloquent look towards Szczuka seemed to say: you see how little you know about people. He was seized with profound distaste.

'Did you value the Nazis highly?'

Puciatycki snorted.

'I'm sorry, I don't understand . . .'

'It would be hard to deny them strength of character.'

'Quite so.'

'Or lack of ideology?'

Puciatycki folded his arms.

'If you're going to take that attitude, my dear man . . .'

Mme Staniewicz interrupted again.

'My dears, spare us! Haven't we anything else to talk about but the Germans?'

'We might talk about the Jews,' Telezynski put in, aside.

Mme Staniewicz made the face of a spoilt little girl.

'I don't want to know anything about that. I simply don't see why men, as soon as they meet, have to start talking about the war or politics. It's quite terribly boring.'

'It's my fault,' Puciatycki agreed. 'You're quite right. Faced with a lady's arguments, I am always defeated.'

She thanked him with a look and, pleasantly excited by her own skill, turned to Szczuka.

'More coffee?'

'No, thanks.'

In a way, though in a different way from Puciatycki, he too felt defeated. These people, in their way of living and thinking, seemed as transparent as the air. Yet anyone who opposed them with arguments, or wanted to preserve his own independence and difference from them, looked absurd in the end. In the silence which followed his brief and roughly uttered 'No, thanks' he felt his own absurdity very clearly. Why, after all, had he got into a conversation of that sort? So as to prove his own opinions or convince these people? Both had been mere clumsiness.

He looked at Mme Staniewicz and with her head slightly inclined and her shoulders turned to Puciatycki, she looked so like Maria that for a moment he was torn by the same feeling of utterly overpowering alarm and fear which seized him in his solitary nocturnal musings.

He lowered his eyelids and heard from a great distance, much feebler than the beating of his own heart, the voice of his sister-in-law talking to Puciatycki. He rose. Mme Staniewicz broke off in the middle of a phrase.

'Off already?'

'Yes. I'm sorry. I still have several things to do.'

'What a pity! I do hope you won't forget me while you're in Ostrowiec?'

He began to make his farewells.

'Of course not.'

She went into the hall with him and said, as he was putting his overcoat on,

'Give Maria a kiss from me when she comes back . . .'

'Of course.'

'I should so like to see her. We haven't met for ages.'

Now she was correct, almost cordial. She was erasing all her dislike of Szczuka, by nice manners, just as she erased the crows-feet round her eyes with maquillage. In the last resort, he decided, she was more surprising than deserving of condemnation.

'That's so,' he agreed; 'you haven't seen each other for a very long time.'

When he had gone, she tidied her hair at the mirror and went back to her visitors, still wearing the smile she had used to bid Szczuka good-bye. She was pleased to see they were enjoying themselves. Puciatycki had just finished telling a joke and Telezynski burst into his healthy laugh. Mme Staniewicz, though she didn't know what it was about, laughed too. As she had expected, no one said a word about Szczuka. On the contrary, the Puciatyckis and Telezynski did everything they could in mutual solidarity to show good humour and complete lack of care.

Presently, Puciatycki suggested having supper at the Monopole.

'It's nearly half past eight,' he glanced at his watch, 'just the right time. I think we should have at least one glass of good wine to drink to the success of our plans.'

'And to the end of the war,' Mme Staniewicz added.

Puciatycki grimaced.

'I suggest a glass of vodka will be quite enough for that. What do you think?'

'What about?' Telezynski asked. 'A glass of vodka? I'm always ready.'

'I know that. But in a general way . . . of the whole plan?'

Roza Puciatycki lit a cigarette.

'It doesn't seem too bad.'

'It's excellent!' Mme Staniewicz exclaimed. 'But how shall we get home again? This awful curfew . . . How late can one get about now?'

Puciatycki made a contemptuous gesture.

'Till ten, I believe. But that needn't concern us. We'll come back in a cab, if we don't stay till dawn. The Monopole goes on all night.'

At times Mme Staniewicz liked to give the impression of being helpless. She thought it smart.

'And you'll bring me home?'

'Whenever you like,' Telezynski bowed.

'How sweet of you! Don't laugh at me, but I'm terribly frightened nowadays of going out at night. . . .'

'Freddy,' Puciatycki turned to his cousin, 'have you been to the Monopole lately?'

'No later than yesterday.'

'How was it?'

'Quite amusing.'

Mme Staniewicz looked at her dress.

'Don't you want me to change?'

'On the contrary,' Puciatycki replied. 'We forbid it categorically. You look charming in that dress. Doesn't she, Roza?'

Mme Puciatycki put her arm round Mme Staniewicz in a motherly fashion.

'Dear Kate always looks charming.'

The latter blushed with pleasure. Puciatycki, pleased because everything had gone as he wanted, rubbed his hands.

'Let's be off, then! But we'll have to take those other two as well,' he indicated the next room. 'Young Kossecki seems a nice boy. And the other man . . .'

'You're right,' Mme Staniewicz recalled them, 'I'd forgotten all about them. They must have talked each other to death. How insufferable men are!'

She crossed the room and called through the door:

'Hullo there!'

Entering, she discreetly closed the door behind her.

'All this smoke! It's quite stifling!'

And in fact the small room was grey with cigarette smoke. The men rose to their feet.

'Am I interrupting? Haven't you finished?'

'More or less,' said the colonel. 'Did you have another visitor?'

'No one of any importance. A family call. Now we're going to take you with us to a debauch.'

'Whatever do you mean? Where to?'

'To the Monopole. After all, we must celebrate the end of the war somehow. And our plans, too, I hope they're going well?'

'Not too badly.'

'That's excellent. Let's be off then, shall we? I see you're trying to make up your minds.'

'Yes, I am. I still have an appointment to keep.'

'I'm sure it isn't important.'

'On the contrary.'

Mme Staniewicz sighed.

'What a bore you are with these everlasting appointments of yours! Very well, go along, I release you. But you'll join us later?'

'I'll try.'

'None of that. For sure?'

'Almost certainly.'

'You're unbearable. But I'll keep you to your word. And you, Andrew,' she glanced at the thoughtful Kossecki, 'have you an appointment too?'

'At the Monopole, as a matter of fact.'

'With a girl?'

'No, a man.'

'I hope you won't have to devote the whole evening to him?'

'Fifteen minutes at the outside.'

'Excellent! So we won't say good-bye. And, my dears, no serious conversations, I beg you. I want a gay evening . . .'

The colonel said good-bye to Andrew Kossecki immediately outside the gate. The side-street was short and secluded, with pink-painted houses and clumps of young chestnuts submerged in the rust-coloured dusk. Heavy clouds overhung the sky. It was very sultry and airless.

'There's going to be a storm,' he said. 'You going to the Monopole?'

'Yes.'

'I'm going the other way. Good luck to you.'

'Won't you be coming to the Monopole?'

'I doubt it. I'll see, anyway.'

They shook hands and separated. Andrew went towards May 3rd Boulevard.

The boulevard, bordering the Kosciuszko Park on one side, was full of people walking up and down. The curfew was still in force, so crowds of people were taking advantage of the brief May evening. Mostly young, they were strolling under the chestnut-trees in pairs, or in small groups holding hands, laughing and calling: the girls, with waved hair, in light dresses and high-heeled wooden-soled shoes, the youths with coats thrown over their shoulders, shirt-sleeves rolled up, some wearing leather shorts. All the benches under the chestnuts were tightly packed. There were many soldiers in the crowd. Several Soviet soldiers were standing round a bench in which some of their number were sitting. One was playing a mouth-organ.

Meanwhile it had become cloudier. The air was heavy and sultry, and the darkness was broken now and again by brief, still silent flashes of lightning. As military operations were still going on, the black-out was in force. The street-lamps were not lit, the premature dusk grew thicker. Now and then the headlamps of cars illuminated the gloom. Then the glow of long rays momentarily lit up the shadows of people among the trees, with a motionless branch of chestnut above and the long prospect of the boulevard in the depths. Then darkness fell over everything again.

Andrew walked along thoughtfully, paying no attention to the other people. The wireless loudspeakers were repeating the latest news bulletin. In the darkness a masculine voice recited:

'*Military operations are to cease on Saturday at eight a.m. . . .*'

The next loudspeaker, several yards farther on, took up the words as they faded:

'*This document sets out the terms for the final and total capitulation of Germany.*'

It must have been the dusk that made the announcer's voice sound louder than it had in the daytime. The unseen loudspeakers carried the words above the avenue and the waves of people, speaking evenly in an unnaturally loud voice. No one heard them now, crying out aloud in solitude. The victory they had waited six years for already belonged to yesterday.

Alek spent the afternoon by the river. He bathed and tried to get off with some girls from another town. When dusk was already approaching and he still had plenty of time, he went to the Baltic cinema to see a Soviet film about the partisans. Still later, in a small café not far from the market-place, he had an Italian ice. And he failed to notice that it was getting late.

Now he was late. Out of breath, without his cap, his coat thrown over his arm, he hurried along the boulevard so fast that, as he passed a group of youths and girls, he almost ran into Andrew. He caught sight of his brother's tall frame at the last moment, a few paces away, and although he stopped dead for a second, thinking himself lost, he managed to dart aside, towards a bench. In the obscurity he stumbled against someone's feet in long boots.

'What's up, blast you!' someone swore at him immediately.

He drew back hastily, but tripped over someone else. This time a woman squealed.

Meanwhile Andrew had gone by without seeing his brother. Alek set off again into the crowd but it took him a little while to get over the effect of the incident. He stopped, wiped the sweat from his forehead and smoothed his hair. He was ashamed of himself for giving way so easily and unreasonably to unnecessary panic. What, after all, would have happened, if Andrew had seen him? He was certain his brother knew nothing and never would. He trusted his mother as much as he abused her trust. If he had not been certain that this matter would remain a secret between himself and his mother, he would never have robbed her. He had found out today that to give pain to someone one loves requires a good deal of effort and strength, but runs no risk of consequences beyond the limits of love. Yet he did not feel courageous enough to take the burden of responsibility for what he had done upon himself. He did not, alas – he thought with shame – have the recklessness of Julius Szretter. How he envied his reckless courage and how he longed to be like him!

At the first turning Alek left the boulevard and began to cross the park. A few solitary couples were wandering along it. He hastened on passing yet another whispering couple in the shadow of a tree, then he was by himself. It was night. The tree-trunks, with their fantastic shapes and the mysterious thickets had wide expanses of silence and darkness between them. He came to the lake. Its dark, smooth surface lay soundless and still under clouds of weeping willows. For a moment a fresh, moist breath of air rose from the water. It was silent here and quite deserted. The light buzzing of mosquitoes hummed in the air, the gravel crunched underfoot and the farther he penetrated, the more wild and mysterious the park became.

Alek passed another lake and turned into a narrow path that led to a thicket of tall elms and beeches with lilac bushes, jasmine, and cherry beneath them. Alek knew where he was, despite the darkness, since he knew every corner of the park and all the secret paths by heart. Suddenly he stopped, holding his breath. Someone was following him. In the silence, he caught the almost inaudible crunch of gravel. Nimbly he left the path and hid in the thick lilac bushes. He did not have to wait more than thirty seconds with his heart beating violently. The footsteps drew near, then the outline of a man appeared in the dusk; he breathed deeply with relief as he recognized Felix Szymanski. He whistled softly, the other stopped and Alek sprang into the path.

Felix was shorter than Alek, strongly built, with a Mongolian face and dark, very thick, curly hair.

'Hullo. Were you scared?'

Felix shrugged.

'What of?'

'When I whistled?'

'No. I knew it was you.'

They walked on in silence for a time.

'Oh damn this sultriness,' Szymanski muttered.

The air was thick and clammy and the lightning was coming closer.

'What's the time?' Alek asked in an undertone.

Felix raised his wrist.

'I forgot my damn watch,' he replied, 'but it must be nearly eight-thirty, maybe later . . .'

The ground was uneven. It rose between small hillocks and dipped suddenly in narrow ravines.

'Got any cash?' Alek asked suddenly.

'Yes. Mind, we turn here.'

Felix grinned.

'You once came up on us that way from the rear. . . .'

'You remember?'

'Ah . . . But you got a thrashing then, all the same.'

'Who, me?' Alek was vexed. 'It was you who got beaten up. I was with Julius, and you with Janusz and Marcin. Don't you remember?'

'Aha, that's so,' Felix recalled.

Both had gone back for a moment to the far-off days when this wild, deserted part of the Kosciuszko Park had been the scene of their games.

Just behind the oak, a narrow pathway led into the depths of the undergrowth. Alek went first, Felix after him. The ground sloped downwards quite steeply. The park ended here and high above, on the edge of a cliff, barbed wire loomed. Farther on was a suburban street, now dark and deserted. Some feeble lights, which seemed to be suspended in the air, gleamed among the darkened houses. The window of one house must have been open, for the sounds of a piano came from it clearly. Someone was riding along the street on a bicycle, its little lamp looking like a glow-worm.

The undergrowth came to the foot of the cliff.

'Down there!' Alek whispered.

He turned left and penetrated into the depths unerringly, cautiously pushing back the branches heavy with fresh leaves. Soon he stopped.

'Here we are!'

Felix caught up with him.

'Good man! It really is a short cut.'

A yard away, and overgrown by thick grass and low shrubs, was a small cave. Cellar-like dampness wafted from it. Half-crouching, they began to ease themselves into its depths through a narrow passage. It was uneven and stony underfoot. Then a stifled voice was heard:

'Who goes there?'

'Freedom,' Alek loyally announced.

Felix had just tripped over a stone.

'Damn it! Show a light, Marcin, don't mess about.'

The gleam of a pocket-torch illuminated the passage. Somewhere below them, under the very low roof, slight little Marcin Bogucki was standing. Felix looked round.

'What's happened, has this hole got smaller or something?'

'You've grown up,' Alek grinned, 'but not much.'

'Enough for me.'

They said hullo to Marcin. His hand was cold and moist. He was not a healthy boy.

'Is Julius here?' asked Alek.

'He's been here for ages. He arrived first.'

He switched the torch off. A sharp turn in the passage opened out into a small cave with a high roof. The wavering light of a lamp on the wall illuminated the reddish walls and hard, uneven but well-trodden floor. The corners were in half darkness. Large stones gleamed here and there, brought in when they had been used as seats during ceremonial meetings of noble Indian chieftains.

Julius Szretter was standing with one foot on a stone. He was tall and slender, with a fair-haired, narrow, somewhat bird-like face, wearing sports clothes and a soft leather jacket. Not far from him, Janusz Kotowicz was leaning carelessly against the wall, elegant as always, a bit of a dandy, or at least pretending to be, in his faultlessly-pressed old flannel trousers and long, loosely-cut jacket.

'Oh God!' Felix muttered, looking round the cellar, 'nothing's changed here except that there's something funny about the size. It's smaller. Hullo, Julius!'

Szretter looked up.

'You're late!'

He had a calm and clear way of speaking and a slight undertone of superiority which he always used when he wanted to make his friends feel the distance between himself and them.

Alek blushed. Felix, who took Julius's leadership less seriously, merely shrugged.

'Are we? Not much, surely?'

Julius gazed at them with his narrow, deep-set eyes.

'I don't think I said whether it was much or not. You're late, that's all. Enough said.'

Janusz Kotowicz didn't even try to conceal his ironical half-smile. He brought a gold cigarette-case out of his pocket and lit a cigarette.

'You might at least offer me one, you rotter!' Felix exclaimed.

Kotowicz held out the case.

'Have one?'

Alek took one too. Marcin didn't smoke. Szretter refused.

'A new acquisition?' Felix eyed the cigarette-case.

'Like it?'

'Too fancy for me.'

'You ought to know!'

'Sit down, you,' Szretter interrupted; 'may I remind you this isn't a party or a saloon-bar.'

'That's too bad!' Janusz muttered, but so quietly that only Felix, standing next to him, heard.

They sat down on the stones in silence.

'God, how hard they are!' Felix grimaced and he leaned towards Janusz. 'Mind you don't freeze your bum . . .'

Marcin, with his wan, pale face, and his short, shabby jacket, looked frozen. He rubbed his hands together nervously. The silence lasted a short while. These walls, this obscurity full of moving shadows, these stones overgrown with mould – how many memories they held!

Alek couldn't resist saying:

'Julius, remember "Big Eagle"?'

Szretter, whose nickname this had been, frowned.

'Suppose we talk about that childish stuff some other time?'

'We used to have good times, all the same,' Felix interposed.

Szretter said nothing. He alone of those present was still standing with one foot on a stone, resting his chin in his hand. A wavering candle flame illuminated his dry, long face, and the shadow of his outline, magnified, was cast on the wall behind him and on the roof above. The silence was empty and shut off. The dull echo of a thunderclap rolled, somewhere very far off and as if from under the ground as well.

'The storm,' Marcin whispered.

It thundered again.

'Damn it!' muttered Felix, 'just like artillery fire.'

They all began listening. Then Szretter straightened his back.

'Listen, fellows,' he began in a clear but this time rather more cordial voice, 'I want to avoid any unnecessary misunderstandings . . .'

'Quite right,' Felix agreed.

Julius let this pass.

'We've known each other for years, from the time we were school-kids. We're old friends aren't we? But now I'm your leader. I give the orders, you carry them out. We're the first cell of our organization. We founded it ourselves and it'll be what we make of it. See what I'm getting at? This isn't friends playing a game.'

Felix spat a shred of tobacco through his teeth.

'Right, go on!'

'I don't want to have to talk about this any more. But it depends entirely on you. At least I know what it is I've got to do.'

Felix shifted on his stone and threw an oblique look towards Julius. But this time he said nothing.

'And now,' Szretter went on, 'let's get down to business. You got my order yesterday, my first order, by the way, saying that each of you was to bring five thousand zloty with you today. I hope the order has been carried out. But that's not all.'

'Not all?' Felix echoed uneasily.

'No. I also want to know where you got the cash.'

Alek blushed and looked down to hide it.

'I'll begin with myself,' said Szretter.

He brought the money out of his pocket and threw it down on the stone he was leaning against.

'Five thousand. It's part of my savings towards a motor-bike. Three-quarters of the total, in fact.'

No longer concerned with his own contribution he turned towards Kotowicz, who was seated nearest him.

'Janusz?'

The latter, looking bored, reached for his money, produced most of it and rapidly counted out several banknotes.

'Ten fivers. Nothing secret about it. Cash commonly called "private property", honestly made from currency exchanges. Anyhow, you know all about it.'

'Right,' Szretter said.

And he turned to Felix Szymanski.

'How about you?'

The latter laid his money on the stone.

'Where did you get it?'

Felix darkened.

'Oh Lord, what a bore! I flogged my watch. So what?'

Szretter was silent awhile.

'Right,' he said at last. 'Next! Alek?'

Alek, aware he was red to the roots of his hair, brought out his money and leaned over to put it with the remainder.

'Where did you get it?' asked Szretter, in an especially dry tone for he liked Kossecki more than any of the others.

'I had some of my own . . .'

'How much?'

'Fifteen hundred.'

'What about the rest?'

Alek said nothing.

'Where did you get the rest?'

It couldn't be helped. He forced himself to say:

'I stole it.'

Szymanski and Kotowicz stirred with sudden interest. Felix even uttered a prolonged whistle. Meanwhile Alek felt tremendously relieved.

'Who from?' Szretter inquired.

Very coolly he replied:

'My mother.'

He'd said it! It was over! And so easily! He felt in his bones that no one would blame him. Quite the contrary, in fact.

'Right,' Szretter said. 'Marcin?'

Marcin was sitting somewhat to one side, thoughtful, with his hands clasped between his knees. He raised his head at the sound of his own name and looked at Szretter calmly, with thoughtful eyes. A shadow crossed Julius's face.

'Your money?'

'I haven't got any,' he replied in an undertone.

Janusz Kotowicz made a movement as though to rise and say something, but Felix prevented him.

'Calm down, it's nothing to do with you.'

They all knew Marcin was poor, that he made a living by giving lessons, and that he supported his mother and younger sister. But Szretter said:

'My order was clear, wasn't it? Yet you didn't carry it out.'

The other didn't answer.

'Why not?'

Marcin's lips trembled a little.

'You know why. If I had five thousand I'd buy shoes for my sister . . .'

Janusz Kotowicz couldn't help exclaiming:

'That's your own affair! What's your sister got to do with us?'

Marcin turned to him.

'She's got a lot to do with me. Anyhow, don't worry,' he added with a touch of bitterness, 'I didn't buy shoes for my sister. I haven't got the five thousand zloty.'

'Then you should have stolen it, like Kossecki did.'

'Calm down, fellows,' Szretter exclaimed. 'This isn't your affair, Janusz. It's my job to make comments.'

Meanwhile Marcin had risen and was facing Szretter. He was very pale, his hands trembling.

'I'm sorry,' he said, barely able to control the shortness of his breath, 'but before you say anything, can I speak?'

Szretter eyed him attentively.

'Not just now. Later, just the two of us together.'

Marcin hesitated. The other touched his arm.

'Sit down.'

And when the other obediently did so, he himself drew back and leaned against the wall.

'Listen to me, this is how things are. I must have the whole amount by Sunday, that's to say, twenty-five thousand, not a penny less. I've got a very exceptional opportunity of buying guns, see? Leave the details to me, I'll handle them myself. And now,' he reflected a moment, 'we'll make up the rest of the cash like this: because Alek stole the money on my orders, I'll give it him back.'

Alek started up. The blood rushed to his head.

'I don't agree! Where I got it from is my business . . .'
Julius Szretter didn't even bother to reply.
'And Marcin's share will be paid by the one who has most money.'
'No!' Janusz Kotowicz jumped up, rage disfigured his handsome, doll-like features. 'Not likely! I'm not going to pay for him!'
'Yes you are! You'll pay up, and immediately too.'
Kotowicz drew back instinctively and looked round, as if to seek help from the others.
'Julius,' Marcin exclaimed from the side, 'you're humiliating me.'
'You?'
And again he turned towards Kotowicz.
'You've got thirty seconds to think it over,' he glanced at his watch. 'If you don't let me have ten fivers of your own accord, then you'll surrender every penny you've got on you as a punishment. Every penny of it. So make up your mind.'
'What a lark!' Felix muttered.
Alek's heart was in his throat. Marcin stood with his head bent, biting his lips. Meanwhile Kotowicz had gone white and now his face no longer showed rage, but panic and rat-like terror.
A deathly hush prevailed in the cellar. The monotonous, stifled thunder, like the roar of foaming water, penetrated from outside. The wind must have risen. The thunder sounded nearer than before.
Szretter glanced at his watch again.
'Seventeen seconds to go.'
Kotowicz withdrew another pace and cast a brief glance in the direction of the passage. Szretter nodded to Kossecki and Szymanski.
'You two – stand by the door.'
They obeyed, hypnotized.
'So that's the way it is, is it?' Kotowicz hissed. 'You're a fine lot, you are. You bandits . . .'
'Six seconds,' Szretter said.
Marcin sat down on a stone and hid his face in his hands.
'Two!' Julius's clear voice announced.
Suddenly Kotowicz leaped away from the wall. He had already

seized hold of the lamp – which flickered violently, rocking the cellar with shadows and streaks of light – when Szretter leaped across, seized him with both hands by the lapels of his jacket and hurled him into the corner opposite. Janusz went down but leaped up again at once and began mechanically to brush the dust off his trousers. Blood was flowing from his cut lip. Szretter pulled the sleeves of his pullover above his elbows and went across to him slowly. Kotowicz did not even have time to defend himself, but was reaching for his handkerchief to wipe his mouth, when he got the first blow in the face. He dropped the handkerchief, staggered and so astounded that he didn't even defend himself . . . Then Szretter began hitting him systematically, steadily, his fists clenched.

'Julius!' Felix shouted.

The weakly Janusz, who never played games, staggered like a puppet from one side to the other, shielding himself in vain from the well-aimed blows. Marcin sat motionless, his face still hidden in his hands.

'Oh God!' Felix muttered. 'I don't like this, it's a massacre. It makes me want to spew.'

Alek was silent. He stood frozen and staring, captivated by Julius's power. All Alek's heart and admiration were on Julius. He despised Janusz. Finally Kotowicz fell down. Szretter stood over him for a moment, then turned away, moved aside and unhurriedly rolled his sleeves down, then he produced a cigarette. He showed no sign of emotion. He was as controlled and cool as always. He merely smoothed down his hair and inhaled smoke.

Meanwhile Janusz was getting up slowly. On his hands and knees he began rubbing his cheeks with a hand covered in dust. He kneeled like this for a long time, as if wondering what to do. Finally he got up. In his dirtied, crumpled clothes, his face grey and bloody, his eyes puffy, he looked terrible. He snorted, spat out blood mixed with dirt and kept rubbing his face with his sleeve. However, his strength appeared to give way at this moment for he staggered and leaned against the wall. After a while he raised his head and gazed about with eyes that could scarcely see. An angry grin contorted his split lips. He reached into his trouser pocket and drew out a bundle of notes, which he threw down.

'There!'

He brought another bundle out of his other pocket, and said:

'Hope it chokes you!'

The centre of the cellar floor was strewn with banknotes. Szretter lit another cigarette in indifferent silence. The episode did not appear to interest him. Janusz reached into yet another pocket. Where he found a few paper dollars. He hesitated.

'No,' he said between his teeth, 'you won't have these, you swine!'

Furiously he ripped the notes in half, then across again, and again, and hurled the green fragments to the ground. They scattered like confetti.

'There! Wipe your noses on it!'

Felix Szymanski, who was a sensible and practical youth, could not help exclaiming:

'Oh Jeez, Janusz, you off your nut?'

The latter brought a few small, crumpled two- and five-zloty notes out of his pockets.

'Off my nut? You'll see soon enough. I'll show you, I'll give you something to remember me by . . .'

Szymanski and Kossecki at the entrance to the cave, looked at each other. Even Marcin looked up. Szretter was finishing his cigarette in silence.

'God!' Felix muttered.

Alek leaned towards him.

'He'll split on us.'

'Ssssh!'

Already certain of his superiority, Janusz pulled down his jacket, straightened his tie and wiped his face with his sleeve again.

'Have a good time!'

The scattered money rustled under his boots. However, he had not taken more than a couple of steps when Szretter straightened and reached into his trouser pocket. Marcin jumped up.

'Julius!'

Two shots, flat and stifled by the thick walls, crashed almost simultaneously, like the crack of a whip. Janusz reached up on tip-toe, remained for a second in this almost dancing position then swung to the left and, with his hands still raised above his head, slumped face downwards into the shadows.

Marcin was the first to rush over to turn him on his back. He was as heavy and inert as a sack of sand. Marcin started to rip his pink silk shirt off. Blood was seeping from his chest in a thin stream. In the heart of the silence the heavy rain continued to roar.

Marcin turned towards Szretter.

'Julius! What have we done?'

Szretter greedily inhaled the last of his cigarette and crushed out the stub underfoot.

'We? If you want some good advice, Marcin, I'll give it you: get up and stop carrying on like this.'

Meanwhile Felix Szymanski too, stepping carefully over the money, had gone to the recumbent figure.

'Oh God!' he muttered.

He eyed him a while, then looked obliquely at the kneeling Marcin.

'Get up, old man!' he said, with rough cordiality, 'why get worked up about a dead body?'

He gripped him by the shoulders and pulled him to his feet. Marcin did not resist. Felix gazed at the scattered money.

'He had plenty of cash, anyway.'

Alek was standing somewhat to one side. He was staring at the ground and biting his lower lip.

Felix suddenly grew impatient.

'Oh Jeez, why are you all so quiet, as if you'd been caught in the act? Well?' he looked at Szretter. 'What now?'

The other did not reply.

'What are you staring at?' Felix scowled; 'think I'm scared?'

'Aren't you?'

'Of course not. You off your nut? I've seen things like this before. Let's have a look at that revolver of yours.'

Szretter brought his revolver out and handed it to Felix. The latter examined it attentively.

'Not bad at all! Vickers?'

'Mm.'

He looked at his watch: it was nearly nine.

'Give it to me,' he reached for the revolver, 'we haven't time.'

He put the gun away and said:

'Well, fellows, that's enough. Leave him be,' and he indicated the body, 'for the time being, we'll have to pick up the money, then we'll decide what comes next.'

His controlled, clear voice brought some relaxation of the tension. The crime he had just committed was known to only the four of them, shut away in a cave, unknown to the rest of the world.

Kossecki and Szymanski dragged the dead body to the wall in the farthest corner of the cave where he looked smaller, in the obscurity and the solitude. Then they set about gathering the money with Szretter helping them.

'Look here,' Felix suddenly exclaimed, shifting the small scraps of banknote, 'twenty dollars!'

'Let's see!' Alek was interested.

'Look, a twenty-dollar bill! Good money, eh?'

'Hurry up,' Szretter reminded them, 'don't waste time.'

The paper money rustled in their hands. The shadows of their three figures moved slowly on the walls, like ponderous, shapeless animals.

'Julius!' Marcin suddenly exclaimed.

Szretter straightened up. Both his hands were full of banknotes. Marcin looked at him for a little while. His dark, always thoughtful and melancholy eyes seemed still more deeply set and as if overcast with mist. He looked pitiful in his tight, worn jacket with the sleeves too short.

'Julius,' he repeated imploringly, 'let me go home!'

Szretter frowned.

'Now?'

'Don't worry, I won't give you away.'

'That's not the point.'

Felix and Alek stopped work.

'If you trust me, then please . . . I can't help you at all.'

'That's too bad.'

'I just can't.'

'Yet they can?' Szretter indicated his comrades.

Marcin's lips trembled.

'Julius, please! I don't know how you feel. I don't want to know. This is all so awful. A dead man is lying there, one of our friends, but you're counting money and talking as if nothing had happened . . .'

'You off your nut?' Felix interrupted. 'What's that got to do with it? Do you expect us to leave the money here?'

Szretter motioned to him.

'Calm down!'

He stowed the money away in his pockets and went to Marcin, then put his hand on his arm.

'Do you think I did wrong?'

The other eyed him boldly.

'Yes.'

'Then suppose I hadn't shot him. What would have happened to us then?'

'I don't know, Julius, I just don't know. I know what's happened to him. Just look, how it all started . . . And what we've talked about so often. We were going to fight for Poland, for good and noble causes . . . Don't laugh, you yourself said so, often.'

'I know that. So what?'

'We believed if we were going to fight it would be for freedom and justice . . .'

Szretter scowled.

'Shut up, this isn't the time for speeches.'

'But what are we going to do now? With all this on our minds, with all this blood . . .'

'Don't exaggerate. Why talk about it? Blood! Blood doesn't mean much.'

'Julius, don't talk like that. You shouldn't!'

'Of course blood matters, but not the blood of our enemies. We're going to shoot them down like dogs. That's our purpose and our justification. And the fact that he went first was only an accident. Anyhow, I knew he'd end up like this.'

'You knew?'

'Surely you don't think I trusted him? Him? He was a ponce. I only took him on because he was in the currency racket. He might have been useful. I needed his money, not him. He gave himself away in no time luckily for us. He's cleared up the situation, that's all.'

Marcin hid his face in his hands.

'What you're saying is awful, Julius.'

'Don't exaggerate it.'

'Julius, after all, a person *must* count, any person. And a man ought to suffer if he really has to kill.'

'Don't make me laugh! Did you ever kill anyone?'

Marcin shuddered.

'No.'

'There, you see. I did. More than one as well.'

'They were Germans . . .'

'They were enemies. But there wasn't any suffering. I promise you.'

Marcin bowed his head.

'No, no . . .' he whispered.

'But that's the way it is. All right, go home if you want to. Have a good sleep. Tomorrow one of us will look you up. Mind you're in.'

'Yes,' he replied in a colourless tone.

He felt he was only preserving his useless freedom with something very fragile, lonely and terribly sad. Never in his life had he felt so deserted and so bitterly and cruelly disappointed. The world which had streamed with the blood of war for so long had again opened up its wounds and hatred, contempt and blind cruelty were still sickening human hearts. He knew that anything he said would sound false because the others derived their malevolent justification from events while he derived his from a belief in life and in the nobility of man.

Stooping, he slowly moved towards the dark passage. The other three watched him until he disappeared. He shuffled along the passage, stumbling now and again and groping at the cold walls. He had quite forgotten he had a torch. He stopped for a moment. There was silence behind him and in front. The rain-storm must have passed.

When he emerged from underground it was no longer raining. He was surrounded by the intoxicating scent of spring earth and moist vegetation. Fresh dew was falling on the undergrowth. The heavy clouds were rolling by: the sky, supported by clearing darkness, rose high and there, in its perfectly clear expanse, some young stars were gleaming like raindrops.

Chapter Five

Unfortunately the words were inaudible but the voices emerging from Antony's study were clearly distinguishable. Podgorski was talking nearly all the time. Antony's voice, stifled and low, spoke rarely.

From time to time Mrs Kossecki stopped working in the hope that if the monotonous rumble of her loom stopped, the silence in the dining-room would help Podgorski to understand that he ought not to extend his visit. She listened uneasily for the characteristic noise of a departure, but Podgorski's voice went on, and she returned to work. When Antony's voice sounded above the dry rattle of the loom she stopped again, trying to catch even a single word. She hoped that she would be able to reconstruct the exact meaning of Antony's conversation from a few phrases overheard by chance, but he was speaking too quietly, and anyhow he soon stopped and Podgorski's voice took over again.

She was unable to concentrate enough to give her work the necessary even and mechanical tempo. She stood up and, finding nothing to do at the moment, went into the kitchen. It was in semi-darkness. One window was half-open and the early evening chirruping of sparrows came through it.

Rozalia was washing up the supper-things. Mrs Kossecki was irritated at once.

'Why not put the light on, Rozalia? It's quite dark. Why wash up in the dark?'

She pressed the switch on, but the light which drove away the depressing gloom did not calm her.

'How often have I told you that it's silly to economize on such small things . . .'

The old woman said nothing, but the wet plates and spoons began to clatter noisily in her hands. Mrs Kossecki watched her silent fury in silence, but felt some relief.

'Rozalia,' she began in a conciliatory tone, 'what is Podgorski doing? He came in to say Hallo to Mr Kossecki and he's been in there for twenty minutes already. I don't know how he can.'

'Obviously he can,' said Rozalia loudly as she banged a freshly rinsed plate on the table.

Mrs Kossecki decided to go on expressing her views.

'I simply can't make it out. He ought to show a little tact ...'

Rozalia gave a brief laugh.

'Tact, indeed! Fancy expecting people to be tactful nowadays.'

And, with a view to depressing her mistress further, she added,

'Nowadays people don't respect anything at all in other people. They all think of nothing but themselves.'

'How can you say such a thing?' Mrs Kossecki exclaimed bitterly.

'Well, I can, so there! People now are allowed to behave like that.'

Mrs Kossecki gave up in despair. She thought she ought to leave the kitchen, but couldn't make up her mind to do so. She pulled up a stool, sat down and immediately lost herself in her interrupted thoughts. Meanwhile Rozalia went on drying up. The loud chirruping of the sparrows outside the window did not drown the noise of the dripping tap. Mrs Kossecki looked at it out of sheer force of habit.

'Rozalia, we simply must get the plumber in tomorrow ...'

'Tomorrow? But it's Sunday.'

'So it is. It'll have to be Monday, first thing in the morning. We must have that tap seen to. Have you put Alek's supper aside?'

'Of course. But if he was my son ...'

'You say that,' Mrs Kossecki interrupted hastily, 'because you haven't any children of your own.'

With a plate in one hand and the dish-cloth in the other, Rozalia turned her great body towards her employer.

'What's it got to do with having children? They're only a disappointment. For instance, here's you sitting at home and worrying. Mr Andrew's grown-up, but the other one ...'

'Rozalia, Alek isn't a child any longer, he's seventeen. He can't stay indoors all day.'

'I never said he could. But why does he go off wandering at night? And yet you stand up for him. First his supper, then he can't stay indoors, all this fuss and bother. It turns anyone up to see it.'

'What do you expect me to do?' Mrs Kossecki asked helplessly. 'Just tell me, Rozalia, what am I supposed to do? I should have to change completely never to worry about anything. But I can't do that at will. I know women who don't worry are better off, but I couldn't be like that. Even if I wanted to, I couldn't.'

Rozalia nodded her head.

'Of course you can't. It isn't easy to go against your own heart.'

'Rozalia, isn't the alarm-clock fast?'

'The alarm-clock?'

'How dreadful,' Mrs Kossecki wrung her hands, 'it's a quarter past eight. It looks as if Podgorski's never going. . . .'

Podgorski was standing by the window.

'Life isn't easy for any of us. After all, almost every Party member has been having to tackle jobs he'd never undertaken before. We've everything to learn. How to govern, to decide, to control men – new conditions of life, everything. Take me, for instance. I was trained as a lawyer, I've been a soldier for several years in the very peculiar conditions prevailing in the underground movement, and now I've got at least a hundred difficult problems to solve twenty-four hours a day, many of which have to be dealt with at once. Do you think that I and many of my friends never have doubts about our own capabilities? But we are straightening things up, because each of us knows he's not on his own: the Party stands behind everything we do and every decision we take. And we're in the right. That's most important.'

Kossecki listened attentively. He had forgotten the constraint he had felt when the conversation with Podgorski started. He had been sure that Podgorski would ask questions about the camp. But it had been different. Suddenly he realized that Podgorski himself must have gone through a great deal in the past few years, to pass over what had happened to others in silence. As soon as he realized this he felt safe; delivered from the thoughts which had tormented him so insistently in his solitude. He also found that no dark and troublesome fear of oneself can compare with the fear of other people. The burden of even the most painful loneliness may well be poisoned by this apprehension. What man can escape from himself? One escapes from other people. When you need no longer run away or fight back, you're safe. Admittedly, he wasn't sure whether he had always thought on these lines, but now he did.

'You've no idea,' Podgorski said, 'how glad we in Poland are of every man we get back. It looks as if with the war ending, we're beginning to grasp how much a man means and how much we need all of them, particularly worthwhile people. It's hard to put into words but you'll realize it for yourself in a few days. At the moment I dare say you feel a bit overwhelmed by our new Poland, eh?'

Kossecki reflected.

'Overwhelmed? I don't really know. The fact is I don't know what this new Poland is like, just yet.'

'What it's like?' Podgorski repeated. 'How can I put it in a few words? It's difficult, that's probably the best way to describe the tangle of conflicts and contrasts which we're faced with at every step and which we certainly shan't solve tomorrow or the day after. Anyhow, you'll soon find out how things are here. The war's coming to an end, but the fight here is only beginning. And it won't be a fight for just a year or even two . . . You might ask me, for instance, whether our Party has support from what is known as the broad masses of the Polish people? And the answer is that we haven't yet.'

'Even so . . .' Kossecki muttered.

'It's obvious! Some people hate us openly, others in secret, while still others simply don't trust us, don't know us, don't realize what the fight is about or why the revolution here must take this course instead of another. But this isn't the point at the moment, it isn't simply a question of numbers. During the war the Polish Workers' Party and units of the People's Army had no superiority in numbers either, but we represented a political line that was historically right and this turned out to be the most important and decisive thing. It's the same now. At the moment we haven't got much support among the people, but we have quality and right behind us. Unfortunately many people here don't understand, or don't want to. Hence the bitterness, disappointment, complaints, exhaustion, thousands of young people led astray, thousands of pitiful *émigrés*, the blind alleys . . .'

The silence lasted a moment.

'Before the war,' Kossecki remarked, 'you had quite Leftist views, yet you weren't a Communist.'

Podgorski paused in front of the desk.

'That's true. I wasn't a Communist but my wartime experiences taught me both Communism and patriotism.'

'Simultaneously?' Kossecki wondered.

Podgorski smiled and this young, pleasant smile relaxed the exhaustion in his face.

'How could it be otherwise?'

'I don't know,' Kossecki replied. 'I'm afraid there are still a lot of things I don't understand. You know more or less what my life has been like. You know it hasn't been easy. I reached a certain position in society without anyone's help, entirely by my own efforts. I tended to keep away from politics. I always tried to do my job honestly, according to my own conscience and the law. I might add that people respected me . . .'

'And do you know,' Podgorski interrupted briskly, 'why you gained my respect, for instance?'

Surprised by this question, Kossecki was silent.

'You must remember that my Left-wing views didn't win me many friends, particularly among the lawyers we used to know.'

'Yes. You were regarded as a dangerous Bolshevik.'

Podgorski shrugged.

'I wasn't liked anyway and you were the only person in that circle who was friendly and who tried to understand. That meant a lot in those days. Particularly for anyone just starting out in life.'

Kossecki bowed his head.

'I've always tried to understand everyone.'

'You know,' Podgorski said, 'I think that before the war many people had good qualities but were asleep, unable to shake off their torpor and speak out. Now, if you listen carefully, you'll see these sleeping forces beginning to wake in many people. You will probably find these new voices, new thoughts and new feelings in yourself too. Everything lies before us!'

He crushed out a cigarette in the ash-tray and, stooping a little, his hands deep in his trouser pockets, walked to the other end of the room.

Kossecki was sitting at the desk, leaning his head in one hand, fingering a paper-knife with the other. He listened to Podgorski carefully, but now his earlier uneasiness was returning. He shivered instinctively and realized that his eyes were shifting uneasily. He knew from his experience as a magistrate that it must look like the uneasiness of criminals and law-breakers fearing to be held responsible. As he caught himself behaving like them, he felt another kind of panic bordering on stupefaction and incredulity. The inescapable fear which a man has when he realizes that he has forfeited his life and everything he has worked for over a period of years and may be annihilated at any moment, without salvation and without a shadow of hope.

He reached out his hand and, after blindly groping for the lamp which stood on the desk, switched it on. Then he pushed his chair back, out of the light.

Podgorski blinked.

'Everything lies ahead of us and that's why it's so hard to come to terms with certain things. Today they shot two more of our friends . . .'

Kossecki went to the window and stood with his back to Podgorski. Presently he said:

'There's something I wanted to ask you . . .'

'Well?'

'Did you go through a lot these last years?'

The other shrugged.

'Like everyone else.'

'In a way that's not what matters,' Kossecki said, 'or rather it isn't what always matters. Anyhow, that's not the point. You found yourself in all kinds of situations. Were you ever in real danger?'

'All of us were.'

'Danger of death?'

'That too. It was hard to avoid.'

Kossecki reflected.

'That's so but it isn't what I meant. Were you ever in a position where, to save your own life, you . . . in order to save yourself, you couldn't help committing . . . a crime? Now, wait a minute. I'm interested in the necessity of choosing. On the one hand you're threatened with death, the absolute certainty that you'll have to die: on the other there's an open gateway . . . but at someone else's expense . . .'

Podgorski leaned against the stove, his head bowed, thinking. Kossecki glanced at him searchingly. He ought not to have started a conversation like this. It had come out unexpectedly, before he could control it, and now Podgorski's brief replies and his present silence showed how dangerous was the subject he had brought up. But he could not stop now. The conversation would have to be carried on to the end. Before he could decide what to say next Podgorski came to his assistance.

'No, I've never been in a situation like that. But I think if I had really had to choose . . .'

'Well?'

'I shouldn't be talking to you now.'

Silence fell again.

'I see,' Kossecki said at last. 'Are you positive?'

'No,' the other replied, shortly.

Kossecki had not expected this denial.

'No? I expected you to say Yes, without hesitation.'

'If anyone had asked me that question before the war I'd probably have said Yes. Any decent man would have in those days. People had confidence in themselves, in their courage and their morality. Certain things seemed impossible.'

Kossecki was listening tensely.

'Life then simply did not present such desperate alternatives. A man had a right to think of himself as decent and incapable of exceeding certain limits. Only criminals did so. But nowadays I've met so many people who broke down and failed this or that test that I don't attach much importance to what a man thinks of himself. I've seen men who thought they were brave turn out to be shameful cowards. Other people, who thought they were capable of the utmost self-sacrifice, proved to be hardened egotists. And the opposite, too – cowards doing things which needed toughness and unusual courage. . . . What does it all boil down to in the end? One must judge a man by what he does, and not by what he thinks he would do. Until a man faces the test, he can deceive himself endlessly.'

Kossecki waited impatiently for Podgorski to stop.

'I agree. It's all perfectly true in general. It's what I had in mind when I started this conversation. You must admit that my question startled you somewhat?'

'It did,' Podgorski replied frankly, 'I was really quite taken aback.'

'I didn't mean to be tactless.'

The other made a gesture dismissing any such supposition.

'But it might have looked like that. However, I was sure that you'd see it in that and in no other way. I am interested in the problem itself. I don't suppose the "either-or" problem occurred so often or so ferociously here in Poland, despite all the horrors of the Occupation, as it did in the camps. . . .'

Podgorski considered this.

'Possibly.'

'In the camps everything happened, almost every kind of daily situation, every feeling, every passion, and all unbelievably intensified and concentrated . . . whatever happened there took place only one step away from death. The only thing which gripped and vitalized people was a primitive longing to survive. Anyone who lost the will to live, died. Other people died too, but it was primarily these.'

Podgorski sat down on the edge of the desk.

'I see what you're getting at. The will to live at any price even at the expense of other people?'

'Yes, in any primitive struggle. The terror inherent in the camp system depended on this. To break people down, trample on them, deprive them of dignity, of human feelings, and to bring out the worst instincts in them.'

'But they didn't all give way to these instincts.'

'I know. But there were enough who did sooner or later, to make us think. It's a difficult problem. There's a limit to human endurance which is not the same for everyone. But here too there's a lower boundary-line, as you said. Below it, a man will do anything in order to live. I've seen people whose desire to save themselves became more violent the deeper they sank into degradation: the two things went together. Should we condemn them out of hand for that? Can we really condemn men because they could not resist the pressures of cruelty and degradation? As there's a limit to a man's physical endurance, so there's a limit to his moral endurance. Beaten and tortured for a long time, you finally lose consciousness. Mentally tortured you also lose consciousness, you fall into a complete stupor . . .'

Podgorski stirred violently.

'Just a minute, there's a flaw in this argument! Even if, as you say, a man comes to the point of losing his moral consciousness, he doesn't do so to the extent of not wanting to live.'

Kossecki blinked uneasily. He turned from Podgorski and leaned his elbow on the window-sill.

'That's so. But isn't this an instinct of self-preservation?'

Podgorski was silent.

'Mr Kossecki,' he said at last. 'Suppose you were to have a case in court . . .'

'I don't think I shall be going back to the courts.'

'Why not?'

'Anyhow, I don't know yet,' the other replied evasively. 'But suppose I were to?'

He turned back to Podgorski again.

'What then?'

'Suppose one of many trials is taking place. The accused, let's call him X, broke down in the camp and – to save himself – let the Germans make use of him for doing shameful things to his fellow-prisoners. One of the incidents you mentioned.'

'All right.'

'What sentence would you give apart from the existing laws. You yourself I mean, in accordance with your own feelings of justice? Would you clear him or sentence him?'

Kossecki was ready for the question.

'I'd sentence him,' he said calmly and unhesitatingly.

'And you wouldn't have doubts about what you'd done?'

'No, none at all.'

As he said this he felt his tense nerves relax. It was not fear, nor apprehension he felt now, but a tremendous, stifling weariness. He was indifferent to what Podgorski thought or what conclusions he might draw from their talk. Depressing and grotesque inanity was the meaningless truth left after the passing of all experience. His life seemed to have no more significance than a handful of dust. Once the hand was unclenched, nothing would remain.

He must have looked tired for Podgorski noticed the change in his appearance and glanced at his watch: it was a quarter to nine.

'I didn't think it was so late. Forgive me for talking so much. Have I tired you?'

Kossecki made a vague gesture.

'Never mind. It was very nice. I haven't had a chance to talk for a long time.'

Podgorski brightened and his face again looked younger.

'I'm glad. I hope this won't be our last talk. I've always respected you and still do.'

Kossecki smiled wanly.

At the door Podgorski remembered Szczuka.

'I nearly forgot . . .'

Kossecki wanted to be left alone but he managed to show signs of interest.

'I talked about you to someone today after I'd met your wife. He turned out to have been in the camp with you . . .'

Kossecki didn't even shiver.

'In Gross-Rosen?'

'Yes. I told him your name had been Rybicki, apparently he didn't know you personally but, all the same, he'd very much like to see you.'

'Who is he?'

'Comrade Szczuka, secretary of the Party's County Committee. A splendid man.'

'Szczuka, Szczuka?' Kossecki said mechanically.

'We're going to the country tomorrow morning for two days but we'll be back on Tuesday. Could you manage to call on him between five and six at the Monopole? Szczuka's staying there. Room seventeen.'

'All right,' Kossecki said calmly after a pause, 'Tuesday between five and six. I'll remember.'

He went into the hall with Podgorski and out on to the terrace.

Lightning flashed and a heavy roll of thunder sounded in the obscurity.

'It's going to rain,' said Kossecki, 'you'd better wait a bit.'

Podgorski shrugged.

'Never mind, I've a car.'

He ran down the steps quickly, the sound of a motor was heard, the headlights gleamed and the car moved off. The lightning flashed closer and closer and a strong gust of wind blew through the darkness.

Mrs Kossecki was waiting in the hall.

'Good gracious,' she exclaimed, 'what a time he took! I thought he was never going . . .'

He looked through her as though she were transparent and passed without a word. She wanted to call out but her voice died in her throat. After a moment she hurried after him but the door of his study was shut and he turned the key in the lock before she got there.

Mrs Kossecki started to knock on the door.

'Antony! Antony!'

He did not answer. She called his name again. He was lurking just inside the door, without moving, waiting for her to go away.

After a long pause she knocked again.

'Antony!' she whispered imploringly.

After Mrs Kossecki stopped knocking she waited for a long time without knowing why. Finally she walked away slowly. Antony didn't move, but stayed by the door. Presently he realized that he was shivering. He felt penetratingly, virulently cold. He was very familiar with the cold. It was fear.

Chapter Six

Drewnowski, Mayor Swiecki's secretary, turned up at the Monopole just after half past eight to make sure that everything was ready for the evening reception.

Drewnowski did not attach much importance to his job, though many people envied him. He treated it as a convenient though still low rung on the ladder of his career. He had ambitious and far-reaching plans for his future. He was ingenious and versatile, a pleasant companion, looked presentable and, in the past few months, had concentrated on gaining Swiecki's confidence.

The Mayor of Ostrowiec, a hack journalist before the war, was now a political figure and one of the country's new rulers. The fortunes of war had at first driven him to Lwow, then into the heart of the Soviet Union. He had returned with the First Polish Army. He worked in one of the Ministries during the Lublin period, and early in 1945 he took charge of propaganda in Ostrowiec. From this minor post he rose straight to the office of Mayor. Drewnowski had excellent reasons for linking his own career to Swiecki's. A new world was slowly emerging and taking shape from the narrow alleys, the ruins, the shattered fragments and chaos of the end of the war. There weren't enough men. The discontented did not take jobs. They were waiting. Meanwhile, jobs and positions were waiting for men to fill them. Anyone who wanted one – and knew how – took it. Fate favoured the bold. Drewnowski was sure that Swiecki came into the bold category. He backed him as though he were a horse and despised him because he needed him, but he had no difficulty in hiding these and other feelings. At twenty-two, he knew enough to have realized that people with excessive ambition are unwise to reveal that fact while they are still unimportant. All that was wanted – he often told himself – was a little deliberation and a little cold calculation. People could be manipulated like puppets and the game was diverting. But despite his principles, he was sometimes impatient and a prey to gnawing uneasiness. The last week had been a particularly trying time for him. Rumours had been going round Ostrowiec to the effect that Swiecki was to become a junior Minister in an important government department. Later another rumour said that Swiecki was destined for a post abroad. Drewnowski had not been able to get to the bottom of these fickle rumours, nor to check on their reliability. Swiecki himself said nothing and seemed unaware of what was said. Drewnowski hoped to find out something definite when tongues at the dinner-table loosened under the influence of drink.

As Swiecki had left the organization of the reception to his secretary, Drewnowski was particularly anxious that the banquet should go off as well as possible. He was rather excited, somewhat apprehensive and not really quite at the top of his form.

After leaving his hat and coat in the cloakroom he went to a mirror. His own reflection always cheered him. He was tall and well-built and knew he could make women like him and men trust him.

A number of guests were just leaving. Suddenly, as Drewnowski entered, the empty room filled with men and women, talking and laughing noisily. For a moment he was in the midst of them, surrounded by the smell of scent mingled with the sharp odour of alcohol. One woman kept saying, very loudly: 'Where shall we go now, Mr Krajewski, where shall we go now?' As he made for the far end of the hall, Drewnowski glanced at her companion. Seeing a thick-set man in horn-rimmed glasses, he turned away hastily. This was Krajewski, a well-known Ostrowiec lawyer. Drewnowski had known him for years; as a boy, he had sometimes called at Krajewski's luxurious villa in the Settlement. Drewnowski's mother had been a washerwoman.

Drawing back too hastily, he brushed the lawyer's companion lightly.

'Sorry,' he said, rather clumsily.

He gave himself a reassuring look in the mirror but he felt he was not quite as free and easy now as he'd have liked to be. He wasn't sure whether Krajewski had recognized him. He thought not, but as he was about to cross to the restaurant, he caught sight of Krajewski in the mirror whispering to the woman beside him. Immediately he knew they were talking about him and, in fact, the woman, a young platinum blonde, turned and gazed at him. The rest of the group joined them. He heard voices, not very tactfully lowered, and someone laughed out loud. Drewnowski went white and clenched his fists. He straightened his tie yet again. The mirror reflected several inquisitive faces, smiling mockingly and he was in no doubt whatsoever. They were very nearly pointing at him. This sobered him but he turned in a leisurely manner and glanced briefly, indifferently, at the amused group as he walked to the door. The whispering died down as he passed. He felt this was a victory for him. He no longer needed to despise these people. Contempt sufficed.

What was called the banqueting-hall of the Monopole was at the back of the premises. As it had no separate entrance, Drewnowski had to cross the restaurant, a low room with a platform for the band and a dance-floor in the centre, with boxes at the sides. It was full of people, noise, and cigarette smoke.

The band was just playing the 'Donkey Serenade', which had been popular before the war, so Drewnowski had to edge round the crowded dance-floor to reach the far side of the room. Someone caught him by the elbow; it was Pieniazek, a reporter on the *Ostrowiec Echo*, a small, swarthy man with a wrinkled, pimply face.

Drewnowski disliked Pieniazek. He did not know him well, but had heard about him from Swiecki who had known him before the war. They had worked together for a time in the editorial offices of a third-rate Warsaw newspaper. Swiecki had always talked of Pieniazek contemptuously, as a second-rate, drunken hack.

Pieniazek was drunk now. He staggered a little on his very short legs and his small, uneasily shifting eyes were clouded over.

'Good evening,' Drewnowski greeted him stiffly, 'enjoying yourself?'

Pieniazek made a grimace.

'This is a bawdy-house, that's what it is. A common or garden bawdy-house.'

He staggered and caught Drewnowski's elbow again. He

was grubby and slovenly. He had on a crumpled, dirty shirt, with a short and bedraggled jacket.

'Don't overdo it,' said Drewnowski and before the other could reply, added, 'Excuse me, I must go. I'm in a hurry.'

Pieniazek nodded.

'I see our respected Mayor isn't favourably disposed to the press. . . .'

'I don't know anything about that,' Drewnowski replied coolly.

'Don't you? No nice little invites to the banquet were sent, all the same.'

Drewnowski adopted an official tone at once.

'Your editor got one.'

'Him! And doesn't the name of Pieniazek mean anything?'

'I'm sorry, but the Mayor drew up the list of guests himself.'

'Did he now?' Pieniazek exclaimed. 'My colleague Swiecki!'

The reporter suddenly sobered up. He straightened his back and gave Drewnowski a curious, rather mocking glance.

'What are you looking at me for?' Drewnowski shifted impatiently.

'I'm wondering whether Swiecki will take you with him or not. That's an interesting question, isn't it?'

Drewnowski quivered.

'Take me? Where to? What do you mean?'

The other giggled and made as if to go away. Now it was Drewnowski's turn to prevent him.

'Do you know something? You ean tell me, surely!'

Pieniazek considered.

'Well?' Drewnowski insisted.

The other glanced in the direction of the bar, squeezed by Drewnowski and went off in that direction.

'Damn!' Drewnowski cursed.

He glanced at his watch: it was a quarter to nine. He could spare five minutes, though no more. He hurried after Pieniazek.

The bar was empty and secluded. The barmaid, a pretty girl with fair, soft hair was talking to a customer, Michael Chelmicki. She was not pleased by the arrival of more customers. Chelmicki grimaced too.

'Who's that?' he whispered, with a glance at Pieniazek.

Drewnowski reached the bar before she could reply.

'Two vodkas, miss.'

Pieniazek was already seated on a high stool at the bar.

'Make them doubles, Christina.'

The barmaid glanced inquiringly towards Drewnowski. It was all the same to him, providing he got it over with quickly.

'All right, doubles.'

'And a portion of mushrooms, Christina,' Pieniazek added; 'they have excellent mushrooms here, you'll see.'

Drewnowski's patience was rapidly ebbing away. The reporter clapped him cordially on the arm.

'Sit down. These high stools are very comfy.'

Drewnowski did so.

'What were you going to tell me?'

The barmaid served the vodka and mushrooms. Having done her duty, she went back to the other end of the bar where Chelmicki was sitting. Pieniazek rubbed his hands together.

'Here's to our colleague, Swiecki!'

Drewnowski gave up being the devoted secretary. They drank up and he glanced at his watch: the five minutes he had allocated were passing rapidly. Pieniazek pushed the plate of mushrooms towards him.

'Try 'em, they're good. Christina, the same again, please.'

Chelmicki leaned over the bar.

'Give it to them neat,' he whispered, 'it'll get them going sooner. It's our duty to help our fellow-men.'

The pretty barmaid smiled.

'I see you've a kind heart.'

Drewnowski had enjoyed his first glass and did not mind having another.

'You'll get screwed,' he said, taking his glass.

'We'll do that together,' Pieniazek retorted. 'Here's to you!'

They drank up again. Drewnowski reddened, his eyes filled with tears and for a moment he choked. When he began to get his breath back he said:

'Lord! What was that? What did you give us? That was neat spirit . . .'

Pieniazek sniggered with delight.

'For Heaven's sake, neat spirit! Just look what you've gone and done to this young gent . . .'

Christina was genuinely concerned.

'How could it have been? I can't have made a mistake . . .'

She began to search for the bottle she had poured the drinks from. Finding it, her face dropped.

'Well?' Pieniazek inquired.

'Yes, it was neat spirits. I'm most awfully sorry . . .'

'Never mind!' Pieniazek jumped up and down on his stool.

Drewnowski was sorry he hadn't been up to it.

'It's nothing,' he said carelessly, 'don't worry, anyone can make a mistake. You'd better give us another.'

'The same again?'

'Naturally! Neat spirits are better than vodka. Only you have to know what you're drinking.'

This time he swallowed the neat spirits easily.

'Well, now?' he leaned confidentially towards Pieniazek. 'What about Swiecki? Is he really going into the government?'

The reporter blinked his narrow and very befogged little eyes.

'Yes, he is!'

'Which department?'

'Propaganda.'

Drewnowski pondered.

'Not too bad. Though I'd sooner have had Foreign Affairs.'

'So would he.'

'You positive?'

'Muck always rises to the top.'

Drewnowski laughed and clapped Pieniazek on the knee.

'That's good!'

'Don't you worry, you'll finish up there too.'

Drewnowski laughed still louder.

'Of course I will, you'll see five years from now where I get to.'

Pieniazek hiccupped.

'Have a mushroom,' Drewnowski advised, amicably. 'I know what I want, see? That's most important.'

'Muck rises of its own accord,' Pieniazek hiccupped again, 'and what is it you want?'

Drewnowski made an expansive gesture.

'The lot! Plenty of money, first of all. I've had enough of being poor. Listen, didn't you know Swiecki before the war?'

'Yes.'

'What was he like?'

'A rotter.'

'That's good. He's the sort of man I need. You just watch me oust him. What're you laughing at? Think I won't do it?'

'Oh yes, you'll try it all right.' Pieniazek stabbed a mushroom with a toothpick. 'But that's only talk. You shake with fright in front of him.'

'Me? You don't know me. Me afraid of Swiecki?'

'Aren't you? I bet you wouldn't take me into the banquet with you.'

Drewnowski pondered.

'See what I mean?' Pieniazek rocked to and fro on his stool. 'You're afraid, as I said.'

At the other end of the bar Chelmicki glanced at his watch.

'In a hurry?' Christina asked.

'No. I've heaps of time.'

'Why did you look at your watch, then?'

'I've arranged to meet someone here.'

'A girl?'

'Could be . . . Disappointed?'

'Me? What's it got to do with me who you're going to meet?'

'Honestly? Suppose I didn't believe you?'

'Then don't believe it!'

'All right, then. So I don't believe it. How long are you on duty for?'

'Till the end. As long as there are customers, today it'll be right up to the end, I'm sure.'

'Does it have to be? Are you on your own here?'

'I am just now. Another girl comes on at ten but if there are a lot of customers, even the two of us can hardly cope.'

Drewnowski looked in their direction.

'Here, miss!'

'Confound him!' Chelmicki muttered.

Christina slowly went to the other end of the bar.

'How much?' Drewnowski demanded.

Andrew Kossecki was standing in the door that was draped

with a dark green curtain, and looking round the bar. Chelmicki caught sight of him at once.

'Hullo, there!'

The other came across to the counter.

'Hullo, Andrew. What's up?'

'Nothing. I'm hungry.'

'Me too. Let's order. Get a table.'

Chelmicki winked significantly.

'There's still something I want to see to here.'

Meanwhile Drewnowski was paying the bill and Pieniazek, not interested in the proceedings, was greedily finishing off the rest of the mushrooms.

'Shall we go?'

Drewnowski was entering an increasingly vague state but he liked it. He saw everything more clearly, more sharply and everything seemed incredibly easy. Life itself was in his grip and he was certain that he could shape it at will. The need for action made him swagger.

'I'm going,' he decided.

Pieniazek wanted to go on drinking, but seeing Drewnowski making firmly for the door, he hastily slid off his stool and followed, staggering a little.

Christina went back to Chelmicki.

'What can you let us have? My friend's sitting over there.'

'So I see. Not a girl, unfortunately for you.'

'What about you?'

'I've already told you it's nothing to do with me. What shall I get you? Something to drink?'

'We'll have that as well. And some *hors d'œuvres* to start with, we're terribly hungry.'

'There's cold meat, stuffed eggs, salad . . .'

'Anything. Whatever you like.'

'You trust me?'

He leaned over the counter.

'Shouldn't I?'

'You'll have to find out.'

'All right. I'll certainly do that.'

Andrew was sitting at a table at the far side of the bar. He was thoughtful and didn't notice Chelmicki come over.

'Here I am,' said the latter, sitting down next to him.

Andrew looked up.

'Have you ordered?'

'Yes. They'll bring it here. Have a look at that girl, Andrew...'

'Which one?'

'Behind the bar.'

'Not bad,' Andrew muttered indifferently.

Chelmicki glanced at him.

'You know what, Andrew?'

'What?'

'You ought to get tight to finish off this day ...'

'Think so?'

'It'll do you the world of good. I'd give you another bit of advice, only you'll get upset.'

Andrew shrugged.

'Don't bother, I know you and your good advice. It's not always effective.'

'I tell you, old man, it's always effective. Just stop thinking and let yourself go, that's all.'

'And afterwards?'

'What has "afterwards" got to do with me? "Afterwards" won't run away, don't you worry. It's the best way, I tell you. Just switch off. One snap and everything disappears. You remember nothing, nothing bothers you. A little vodka, then into the arms of a pretty girl, it always works. Is that such bad advice?'

'Possibly not.'

'Just tell me this – why the devil should you torment yourself? It doesn't help. You shouldn't take all this too seriously. Just push on through it all. Don't let it get you down. What else is there?'

Andrew did not reply. Perhaps Michael was right, he didn't know. He might think and live like this and find easy oblivion with the same carelessness, were it not for that contrariness which forced him to seek some consistent meaning in everything, even when life itself seemed to be crumbling away. What of it, though? Nothing was left of the enthusiasm of the past. Nothing left of that zeal, or of the desires and hopes either. The world of the victorious had again been divided into victors and vanquished. What had the dead died for, anyway? The war was dying, and no hope was dawning to justify the countless sacrifices, sufferings, injustices, violence, and the ruins which were left today. He remembered what the colonel had said an hour earlier about solidarity but he felt that it wasn't this but something quite different which concerned him. Thousands of people had been summoned to the battle in the name of the loftiest values and with great phrases: some had died for them, others had managed to save themselves, and once again life was mocking the tremendous words, humanity and justice, freedom and brotherhood. Only a huge muck-heap was left of the great and noble aims. This was the only meaning of that pitiful solidarity. . . .

Chelmicki nudged Kossecki.

'Andrew?'

'What is it?'

'What's got you down like this?'

'Shut up!'

Michael nodded.

'Oh, Andrew, Andrew . . .'

'Now what?'

'Nothing.'

'So much the better. I thought you were coming out with some more advice. . . .'

Mayor Swiecki arrived at the Monopole before nine o'clock. Rain was still falling heavily. When the driver jumped out of the car and opened the door, three men, splashing through the big puddles, ran one after the other across the space between the car and the restaurant door. Swiecki had not come alone. He had been in conference right up to the last minute and had come straight to the banquet, bringing his deputy, Weychert, and the chairman of the Town National Council, Kalicki, with him.

The manager of the Monopole, Slomka, was waiting for Swiecki in the hall. He had been a well-known restaurateur in Lwow before the war and was a fat man with white eyelashes, a round face, a pot belly and small puffy hands always flapping at chest level. Lewkowicz, previous owner of the Monopole and one of the wealthiest men in Ostrowiec, had died with the rest of his family at Treblinka.

Swiecki, a frequent visitor to the Monopole, greeted the restaurateur in a familiar manner.

'How are you, Slomka?'

'I'm always well, Mr Mayor.'

Swiecki smiled and turned to his companions.

'Look, gentlemen, at last someone who's not complaining and is satisfied with things. Don't you ever complain, Slomka?'

Slomka gesticulated with his plump hands.

'Heaven forbid! Why should I, Mr Mayor? If I'd an old wife, now, that might be something to complain about.'

'So she's young, is she?'

'On the contrary, Mr Mayor. I prefer not to get married. Why stick to one dish?'

Weychert, who was an architect by profession and a cheerful, sociable man, liked the phrase.

'Evidently you apply culinary ideas in life too.'

Slomka always liked to call his customers by their proper titles. Fortunately he knew Weychert and the position he occupied.

'That's very natural, Mr Deputy,' he bowed, 'seeing I'm a restaurateur.'

He almost sweated with apprehension lest the third man, about whom he knew nothing, should make a chance remark and force him to reply without calling him by his proper title. But Kalicki did not like large gatherings, detested the atmosphere of bars and had only been persuaded to come to the Monopole, because he wanted to meet Szczuka, so he showed no desire to join in the conversation. He was an elderly man, over sixty, tall and dry, with thick, grizzled hair and a long grizzled moustache which gave him a very old-fashioned look.

But although he was silent, Kalicki made Slomka uneasy. As he led the Mayor and his companions across the hall, he took advantage of the opportunity of approaching Swiecki.

'Mr Mayor, please pardon me . . .' he whispered, panting and waving his little hands briskly, as if swimming.

Swiecki was just replying to a greeting. People were bowing to him from all sides. He liked this. Nowadays he loved appearing in public. For a moment he pictured himself, followed by a large

96

suite, walking slowly through an Army guard of honour, all standing at attention.

'Excuse me?' he turned to little Slomka with a gesture as polite as if addressing a Prime Minister.

'I already have the honour of knowing Mr Deputy Weychert,' Slomka gushed, 'but the other gentleman . . .'

'Kalicki?'

'Precisely . . . I'm afraid I don't know his title or his position either. . . .'

Swiecki smiled benevolently.

'He's Chairman of the Town National Council. But you ought to know the town officials, Slomka, and besides' – here he took the fat man confidentially by the arm – 'if you really put such importance on titles.'

'But they're important, Mr Mayor,' Slomka panted, 'very important.'

Swiecki bowed to someone else.

'Oh, I don't deny it. So in view of this you can call me from today, from now, let's say, if it gives you pleasure . . .'

'What, Mr Mayor?' Slomka softly whispered.

'Alas, Minister, my dear Slomka.'

The restaurateur almost tripped up in his excitement.

'Mind where you're going,' Swiecki advised.

The other, as though moved by very great joy, had entirely altered into a beaming figure O. Everything about him now was beautifully round, his head, eyes, mouth, behind, little hands.

'What joy, Mr Mayor . . . excuse me, I should say Mr Minister! This is indeed a great day for me!'

At the moment there was no one in the banqueting hall, which was brightly lit with crystal chandeliers, except for two waiters in frock-coats who withdrew discreetly at the sight of people coming in.

Swiecki looked round.

'I see we're the first. That's good! By the way, Slomka, hasn't my secretary been here?'

Meanwhile the restaurateur was admiring the splendour of the table. Against its background of mirrors with gold frames and walls, somewhat faded admittedly but still smooth, the white table, decorated with roses and groaning under silver and *hors*

97

d'œuvres, had a magical effect upon him. Swiecki had to repeat his question.

'Mr Drewnowski?' Slomka woke up. 'No, Mr Minister, he hasn't been here.'

Swiecki smiled significantly to his companions.

'Hear that, gentlemen?' he said quietly. 'Minister already. You can't hide anything in a hot-bed of gossip like this town.'

'Do you want discretion?' Weychert smiled.

'In this case, perhaps not. But I shall have to get used to it.'

'Don't worry,' Weychert patted his arm, 'you won't find it difficult.'

'I don't suppose I will!'

Pleased, he turned to Slomka.

'Congratulations, Slomka. You've done very well. The table looks quite pre-war.'

Beaming with satisfaction, Slomka bowed in silence. He always accepted praise for his gastronomical arts in silence. He regarded it as his due.

Swiecki was offering cigarettes to Weychert and Kalicki.

'It's after nine already. I'm afraid our guests are going to be late. That wretched storm came at just the wrong moment.'

'Szczuka's staying in the Monopole,' Kalicki remarked.

Swiecki shrugged.

'What about it? We can't sit down to dinner with Comrade Szczuka on his own. I don't know about you gentlemen, but I must admit I'm hungry.'

'Me too,' Weychert said.

'But where has Drewnowski got to? I particularly told him to come early. What do you think of him?'

He turned to Weychert.

'I don't know, I'm sure. He gives the impression of being an enterprising young man.'

'I agree with you there! I think it would be worth taking him with me to Warsaw.'

'Talk of the devil . . .'

Drewnowski was standing in the doorway and, somewhat dazzled by the light of the chandeliers, was rubbing his hands foolishly, for he didn't know what to do with them. He felt quite drunk. The whole room, table, mirrors, and walls were going round and round before his eyes, breaking into a circle of lights, shadows, and weird shapes. But he had sense enough to force himself to sober up. Unnaturally upright and with unduly stiff gait he walked towards the others. Pieniazek followed him like a shadow and, tugging his shabby jacket down, came after his companion with his legs giving a little at the knees.

At first Swiecki could not believe his eyes.

'Who's that?' asked Weychert, curiously.

'Good God!' said the Minister.

Meanwhile Drewnowski had come up to them and managed to greet all three quite properly. Swiecki at once drew him aside.

'What's the meaning of this, Drewnowski? What's that scoundrel doing here?'

'Pieniazek?' Drewnowski said, in surprise, 'well ... I thought, Mr Mayor, that the Press ... that perhaps in a general way ...'

He became tongue-tied and broke off. Through the roaring that was going on inside his head he felt a wild desire to hit Swiecki in the face. When he realized this, he burst into a sweat all over.

'I thought,' he brought up a feeble shadow of his voice, 'that in view of various things ...'

Swiecki reddened.

'What nonsense is this? What's the matter with you?'

Pieniazek, smiling horribly, loomed up behind them.

'Con ... congratulations,' he hiccupped shamelessly, 'allow me, Min ... minister, on behalf of democratic journalists, to ...'

There was a noise in the doorway. More guests arrived.

The one-storied wooden building, under which Szczuka took shelter from the downpour on his way back to the hotel, had a narrow, low porch, opening into an almost rural yard with a well in the centre and a garden at the back. For the time being both the porch and yard were empty. Presently two more people ran into the gateway, a man and a woman. They looked like a man and wife coming back from a formal visit. He was tall and lean, with a bowler and dark coat, while she, also thin and over average height, wore a brown jacket and skirt. Like Szczuka, the sudden, fierce downpour must have caught them in an open section of the road. Before they could reach the nearest shelter they had been thoroughly soaked. The rain was falling fast. Thick streams of water poured down with a roar and thundered in the gutters, while now and then blinding flashes of lightning blazed in the half-darkness accompanied by deafening thunder-claps. It was a true spring storm, the first that year.

Szczuka, leaning on his stick as usual, had stopped almost in the entrance to the porch. He was tired by his walk in the heat. His leg, broken in the prison camp and set badly afterwards, bothered him whenever he walked far. Recently, too, his heart had been troubling him. Now he took a deep breath with genuine relief. The sultriness before the storm had gone, the air was freshening rapidly, and the invigorating smell of wet earth and leaves came from the far end of the yard and the garden.

The other two, still somewhat out of breath from their hasty flight from the rain, were shaking the water off their clothes. In the semi-obscurity of the gloomy porch, they reminded him of large birds fluttering their wings.

The woman said accusingly, 'I told you to bring an umbrella just in case. . . .'

The man was silently wiping his lapels. Lightning flashed at this moment and a thunderbolt crashed very close.

'Oh goodness,' the woman shivered, 'and just look at my hat. Just my luck, when I'm dressed nicely for once in a way. . . .'

'Don't make such a fuss,' the man muttered, 'your hat won't come to any harm.'

Fiery flashes cut across the darkness one after another. The downpour increased in strength.

'This rain'll do good, though,' the man remarked. 'The heat was unbearable.'

'How on earth are we going to get home?'

'We'll manage, don't worry. It'll pass directly. It was nice at the Gajewskis, wasn't it?'

They were talking in an undertone, but Szczuka could hear every word.

'I don't know,' she replied reluctantly, 'somehow one doesn't feel like talking to other people . . .'

'Don't exaggerate so.'

'You always think I'm exaggerating.'

'Well, do be honest . . .'

'It's all very well to talk like that. But all this is bad for me.'

'All what? Your hat?'

'Oh, stop it! You know perfectly well what I'm thinking of. Making our home into a refuge . . .'

Szczuka disliked overhearing other people's concerns. He brought out a cigarette and lit it to indicate his presence.

The man lowered his voice.

'My dear, how can we help it? I know it isn't convenient, but suppose you tell me . . .'

'You ought to talk it over sensibly with Irena and persuade her to go into hospital. It'd be better for her and for us too.'

'For us perhaps, but not for her. She's only been back a week from the camp, she hasn't anyone but us. . . . Don't you realize what it's like nowadays in hospitals?'

Szczuka began listening attentively.

'What about our house. What's it like at home?'

'At least it's not a hospital.'

The rain poured unceasingly, but the storm was passing and the thunder already farther away. Szczuka hesitated for a moment. He felt that if the matter wasn't cleared up at once, he would be troubled later, by letting a chance slip.

He went over to the couple on the other side of the porch and raised his hat.

'Excuse me, but you seemed to be talking about someone who's just come back from a camp . . .'

Both looked startled at first and somewhat apprehensive.

'Yes,' the man replied reluctantly, 'my sister.'

'Was she in Ravensbruck, by any chance?'

'Yes.'

Szczuka was silent a moment.

'Please forgive my intrusion . . .'

The man appeared to feel more confidence in him.

'Don't mention it,' he said cordially, 'how can we help?'

'I had someone very dear to me in Ravensbruck. My wife. She's dead, but that's all I know. I haven't any other details. One asks questions everywhere, but in vain. Was your sister in Ravensbruck till the end?'

'Yes, to the end. She was there four years.'

'That's a long time.'

'Since 1942. Now she's ill, poor dear, after what happened . . . But she'd certainly tell you anything you want to know; she may have met your wife. My name is Szretter, Professor Szretter.'

Szczuka introduced himself.

'If you'd allow me . . .'

'Please do,' the professor replied, 'we live at 7, Zielona Street, not far from the Batory secondary school.'

Szczuka recalled his trip next day.

'Unfortunately I can't manage it tomorrow. What about Tuesday afternoon?'

'Whenever you like. My sister is always in. She's ill, as I said. This is why we've been having a bit of bother,' he was clearly trying to erase the impression Szczuka might have gained from the conversation he had overheard. 'We have a tiny flat, with only two rooms, and there are we two and my son, who's almost grown-up, not to mention my wife's relations from Warsaw and now there's my sister as well. Under such conditions, you see . . .'

'My husband is a teacher at the secondary school,' Mrs Szretter said, 'but he also does research. And under such conditions he really hasn't a corner to himself any more.'

The teacher shrugged, looking very tired.

'Once, of course, I had all kinds of ambitions. Research, a university chair, that sort of thing . . . I'm a historian. But teaching in a secondary school also gives me a good deal of satisfaction.'

'But very little money,' Mrs Szretter remarked.

'My dear, one mustn't regard everything from that angle. Anyhow, there's no need to overdo it, we're not badly off, yet.'

'Not badly off! A cab-driver earns more than you do after fifteen years' hard work!'

Szczuka did not try to join in. He went on smoking in silence.

'Very likely,' the professor went on presently, 'you'll be able to learn something from my sister. I'd be very glad if you do. Nowadays everyone is searching for someone dear to them. But what can we do? People have died, have been separated . . . Ah, this wind!' – he breathed in deeply – 'A May shower makes all the difference. And it's clearing already.'

In fact the rain was falling much less fast. Szczuka threw away his cigarette and turned up his coat-collar.

'Till Tuesday, then.'

'Are you off already?' the professor said in surprise. 'It's still raining.'

'You'd better wait,' Mrs Szretter suggested. 'You'll get your coat wet.'

But Szczuka, explaining he was in a hurry, said 'Good-bye' and went into the street.

Parking his jeep at the County Committee offices and borrowing a mackintosh from one of the militiamen on duty, Podgorski made his way across the market-place, with its puddles, to the Monopole on the other side. Szczuka was just collecting his key from the flabby porter. Podgorski was pleased to see him.

'Thank goodness you're here! I thought you might have gone to the banquet.'

'We've time yet,' Szczuka muttered, 'don't worry.' He wanted to go to his room for a while, so they went upstairs together. It was as steamy as a bathroom and Szczuka opened the window immediately. The last drops of rain were mildly whispering in the obscurity. Stars had already started to shine.

Podgorski unfastened his overcoat and sat down on the edge of the sofa.

'I went to see Kossecki.'

Szczuka was taking off his wet coat and hat.

'Did you?'

'I told him you'd like to see him.'

'What did he say to that?'

'He promised he'd come. I got the idea he must either have met you or at least heard of you.'

'Very likely,' Szczuka muttered, taking his jacket off.

In his shirt-sleeves he looked still broader in the shoulders and chest. He pulled up his sleeves and began washing his hands. Presently, as he dried his hands, he turned to Podgorski.

'I must say all this is rather amusing, really.'

The other looked at him without understanding.

'When I was in the camp I promised myself many times that if I ever met this swine afterwards, I'd settle with him personally and pay him out for everything. But now . . . now it just doesn't matter. In fact I'd sooner not see him again.'

Podgorski sat very still and went pale. Szczuka regarded him attentively for a moment. Then he came nearer and heavily placed his still damp hand on Podgorski's shoulder.

'I suppose you know who I mean, Podgorski?'

Podgorski shook his head.

'No, it can't be . . . how can it be? Kossecki? He's a decent man, after all.'

'He's an absolute swine.'

'Kossecki?'

'To me, he's Rybicki, the camp orderly. Rybicki, Kossecki . . . But I'm afraid there's no mistake. There was only one Rybicki in Gross-Rosen.'

He clapped Podgorski on the shoulder.

'Head up, Podgorski! Such things happen.'

'What was he doing there?' Podgorski asked quietly.

'Rybicki, the orderly? Everything they told him to do and more.'

'Did he have a hand in beating people up?'

'You bet! He was very good at it.'

Podgorski passed a hand over his forehead.

'Did he kill . . . ?'

Szczuka shrugged.

'Not alone, he never had the chance. But he helped.'

'This is monstrous!'

'What do you expect? He was saving himself.'

'How could he? No, I simply can't imagine how such a man . . .'

'And yet he did. What surprises me is that he dare come back after all that. Of course, very few witnesses are still alive. And under a different name . . . you never know, he might have got away with it.'

Podgorski jumped up and went to the window.

'Now I understand . . . all our talk . . . like a fool I never suspected anything! It never even entered my head.'

He turned back suddenly.

'Why didn't you tell me this before?'

Szczuka pondered.

'I'm not sure. When I first heard his name it came as a shock to me too.'

'I'll bet it did.'

'People vary, you see, Podgorski.'

Slowly, absently, Podgorski rubbed his forehead.

'It's incredible that such a man . . . Oh God! And now what are you going to do? Do you want to wait till Tuesday?'

'Yes. There's no hurry.'

'Suppose he escapes? He knows what's in store for him.'

'That's not likely. He's a coward.'

'All the more likely.'

'No. A man like that couldn't run away.'

Podgorski wasn't quite convinced.

'Do you think he'll come here?'

'I'm sure of it. Let me handle it. I assure you this kind of man can be a criminal but he'll never take a risk. He's too attached to everything he's acquired. Our friend might easily forget, if circumstances were favourable, that he's committed crimes and could even come to believe he didn't. But he couldn't start a new life in new surroundings. He's not the type.'

Podgorski clenched his fists.

'How disgusting it all is!'

Szczuka glanced mockingly at him.

'No need to overdo it, Comrade Podgorski. This is nothing more or less than the bankruptcy of the petty bourgeois.'

They were drinking large vodkas. Christina had covered the table with plenty of *hors d'œuvres*: herrings, cold meat, egg mayonnaise, a mixed spring salad, fresh radishes, and two kinds of sauce for the meat – tartare and cumberland.

'Splendid,' Chelmicki said.

Both were ravenous and set about the food greedily. Then they ordered a steak for Kossecki and a *wiener-schnitzel* for Chelmicki, which he immediately cancelled for roast turkey.

'How about some wine to go with it, Andrew?'

Andrew didn't care. A slice of cold pork had assuaged his first hunger.

'As you like.'

So he ordered a bottle of Bordeaux. As Christina walked back to the counter his gaze accompanied her.

'Look,' he nudged Andrew, 'good legs, eh? Marvellous. Let's have another drink.'

The vodka was well chilled. The carafe in which Christina had brought it was clouded with a film of fine dew. Chelmicki filled up the empty glasses again.

He looked at Andrew sideways.

'Remember how we used to long for veal cutlets?'

Andrew smiled.

'Spring of forty-four? Yes, I remember. You got awfully tight.'

'So did you. We were all steamed up.'

Andrew grew livelier.

'Just a minute, that was the time we left Willa's at night and went to see Helen.'

'Remember how we marched through Zoliborz as if nothing was happening? That was your idea.'

'Was it?'

'Who else's? It was ours and Willa's. On the way we put on a whole opera in Wilson Square. We shouted our heads off. It was just our luck that a patrol didn't catch up with us. Remember, afterwards, when we came to her street, how Helen cursed us?'

Andrew pondered.

'Poor Helen.'

'She was nice.'

'Where was she killed? Mokotow, wasn't it?'

'No, somewhere in the city centre, I believe. Willa's dead, too. How many of us were there that night?'

'At Willa's? The two of us and Stasrik Kossobudzki . . .'

'And Krysztof.'

'That's it. There were five of us.'

'Now there's only us two left.'

'That's true.'

He poured more vodka.

'Here's to the two of us. You know what, Andrew?'

'What?'

'All kinds of things happened, yet they were good times.'

'Think so?'

'Weren't they, though? How we lived, then! Full steam ahead. And what good company it was! And the confidence we all had!'

'So what? Nearly all of them died.'

Andrew pushed his glass aside.

'We were different then. We knew what we wanted.'

'I suppose so.'

'And we knew what they wanted us to do.'

'Have you only just found that out? It's obvious. What could they want? They wanted us to die. Now they want the same again. All right. We ca. i do it, can't we?'

Andrew frowned.

'Don't be too sure.'

'You're a nice one, we'd better finish off this bottle.'

A large group of people appeared in the door. They were the people Drewnowski had met in the restaurant earlier. The downpour of rain must have made them change their minds about moving on. They had stayed at the Monopole. There were three men and two women. One of the latter, a young platinum blonde with fine brows and the upturned eyelashes of an American actress, wearing a squirrel coat over her bare shoulders, clapped her hands.

'Didn't I tell you? There's no one here, it's quite empty. And how nice it is! Come along, Mr Krajewski, this will do nicely.'

The group surrounded the counter and began to sit down on the high stools. Krajewski, the lawyer, sat next to the platinum blonde. Inclining his thick, red neck, he whispered something into her ear. She listened absently and presently glanced at the young handsome dark man standing at the other end of the bar.

'Doctor, come over here by me!'

Chelmicki scowled with evident distaste. The vodka had left its mark on him. He was excited, his eyes, shadowed with girlish lashes, had narrowed somewhat and now glittered.

'What the devil made that lot come in here?'

But the others were talking too noisily and were too concerned with themselves to hear him.

Meanwhile, Chelmicki was looking at Christina. She was pouring cognac into glasses but for a moment, as though she felt him looking at her, she cast a brief glance towards him. He nodded lightly. He wanted her to come to their table. She merely smiled and went on pouring cognac. The thick-set lawyer began to speak to her.

'Andrew, do you know who they are?'

'Who?'

'That lot over there by the bar.'

Andrew did not even glance in their direction.

'Is that all you're worrying about?'

'Do you know them? They look like local people.'

Andrew brushed his hair back and raised his head.

'Well?'

'I don't know. The only one I know is the one with the red neck.'

'Shall I bash his face in for him?'

'Do.'

Chelmicki rose swiftly but Andrew caught his arm.

'Are you off your nut?'

He hesitated a little, but sat down.

'Listen to me, Michael,' Andrew began, 'I want to talk to you seriously. I saw Florian an hour ago. We had a long talk.'

Michael turned to him briskly. The expression on his face became quite sober, tense, and vigilant.

'Was he furious with us?'

'No.'

'Honestly? He wasn't? I thought that must be why you were in this mood. Well? He agreed, then?'

'Yes.'

'To me as well?'

'Yes.'

'That's fine,' Michael said, pleased. 'I was a bit afraid he wouldn't agree. I've prepared the ground just in case. Guess where I've been living for the last few hours? Here.'

'You got a room?'

'Wait till you hear which room it is. Just imagine, we're next-door neighbours.'

'You and him?'

'Yes! Besides, I've seen him. We were standing next to each other, more or less like we are now. He's a pleasant man. He even gave me a fag. An American one. Can you imagine that?'

Andrew looked at him but said nothing. Michael stretched his arms.

'It's all right. Everything's working out very well. Don't you worry, I'll fix it, I'll make up for today's fiasco . . . I guarantee a first-class job, quick, accurate, elegant. Then we're away! That's decided, isn't it?'

'Into the forest? Yes, on Tuesday.'

'To join Szary's unit?'

'Not quite. Szary's been caught.'

'Oh Lord! Where?'

'I don't know the details. Florian didn't tell me. Anyhow, we can cross him out.'

'Too bad,' Michael said sadly. 'He must have been careless. Has anyone been given his job?'

Andrew hesitated. 'I have.'

For a moment Chelmicki was dumbfounded.

'Andrew, that's marvellous, Look, old man, we must celebrate this! Shall we order another bottle?'

Andrew shook his head.

'What's come over you?'

'Nothing. Don't bother me. I don't fancy it, that's all.'

Michael looked at him incredulously. There was still a little vodka in the bottom of the carafe. He poured it into his glass and drank it quickly. Clearly, however, his good humour had gone.

'Those swine are making a racket,' he muttered.

Only a part of the group enjoying themselves at the bar remained. The platinum blonde was dancing with the handsome doctor and the lawyer had changed places with one of his companions and was carrying on with the other woman. She was tall and dark, with a bird-like, exotic profile and a large, very red mouth. Christina, not busy for the moment, was doing her accounts at one end of the bar.

Chelmicki lit a cigarette and stood up.

'Where are you off to?' Andrew asked uneasily.

'Don't worry. I'll only be a minute or two.'

The curve of the gleaming, nickel-plated counter had only one exit at the rear, behind the Espresso machine. Chelmicki went straight to it and stood in the opening. He put his hands in his trouser pockets.

Christina did not notice him at first, then she blushed a little, put aside her accounts and came over to him. She looked slight and graceful in her dress of smooth, light material. As she smiled, her moist eyes narrowed a little and looked more oblique than usual.

'What can I get you?' she asked.

'You've forgotten us.'

She could not help noticing that he was staring insistently at her mouth. She pretended not to, however.

'I'm terribly sorry. I'll try harder next time.'

'What'll you have? More vodka?'

'Nothing for the moment.'

'No? I thought men in long boots liked drinking a lot.'

Michael blinked.

'From experience?'

'Possibly,' she answered casually. 'Not the nicest kind, though.'

Only now did Michael take his cigarette out of his mouth.

'When is the other girl coming? At ten?'

'Yes.'

'That's in half an hour. Can you get away at eleven?'

They were so close together that she felt his hot breath on her face.

'What about it? Will you get away?'

'Suppose I do? What then?'

'Can't you guess?'

'No. I'm bad at guessing.'

'Honestly? I'm staying here, in the Monopole.'

Christina leaned back a little and looked at him with amusement in her eyes.

'Are you? That's very nice for you.'

'Thank you. First floor, room eighteen. You can easily check. At eleven o'clock? Right?'

'I'm terribly sorry . . .'

'What now?'

'Christina!' Krajewski's voice came from behind the bar. She made a gesture as if to leave, but Chelmicki was in the way.

'Well?'

'Well?' she echoed.
'Room eighteen, at eleven.'
'I remember that. But . . .'
'More "buts"?'
After a moment she nodded her head.

Swiecki looked absent-mindedly at the people sitting round them. When they had started taking their places, confusion had arisen because Drewnowski had not put out the place cards. Swiecki had smiled, trying to charm everyone with smooth civility, but inwardly he had been livid. Seeing his secretary moving stiffly round the table, he clenched his fists furiously. 'I'll finish that idiot,' he decided firmly. He preferred not to look in Pieniazek's direction, but from time to time he heard the reporter's bellowing voice.

Pieniazek knew nearly everyone and felt on top of the world. Jettisoned by Swiecki as soon as more guests came in, he was not condemned to solitude, though Drewnowski had cleared off somewhere also. He accosted Major Wrona, head of the local Security forces. The latter was a man in his early twenties, small and slight, with a stormy, boyish face, somewhat contorted by a deep scar on one cheek. Wrona owned his present position to his recent and wholly admirable past in the underground movement. As he liked amusing himself and getting drunk, he did not dislike Pieniazek.

'I see you've managed to get plenty to drink already, Pieniazek.' He clapped him on the arm.

Pieniazek giggled.

'Naturally. So've you.'

'Pah!' Wrona grimaced, 'I don't fancy this sort of do, all right for the rotten bourgeoisie perhaps . . .'

Pieniazek rubbed his hands together.

'You'll get to like 'em . . . see if you don't!'

Unfortunately he was unable to finish, for Pawlicki, editor-in-chief of the *Ostrowiec Echo*, had been sent across by Swiecki and drew him aside. He was an unusually tall man, broad-shouldered, with a strong neck and the big head of a tapir. Little Pieniazek barely reached to his shoulder. The big man started.

'Get out of here immediately!'

'Me?' Pieniazek hiccupped. 'Why should I? Get out yourself!'

'You refuse?'

'I refuse! Is this a democracy or isn't it?'

'You won't go?'

Pieniazek stood with his head on one side and grinned insolently.

'I li-like it here.'

'Just you wait! You'll be sorry!'

'You th-threatening me? Who was it who toadied to the Fascists?'

Pawlicki went purple.

'Shut up, you swine!'

'It was you!'

Pawlicki glanced apprehensively towards the major standing nearby and talking to Weychert. Szczuka and Podgorski had just joined them. Swiecki, who was talking to Colonel Baginski, military commandant of the town, preferred not to come any closer and was watching Pawlicki's efforts from afar.

'Shut your trap,' the editor-in-chief snarled.

Pieniazek giggled faintly.

'Wasn't it you? Do you deny that you toadied to them . . . ?'

Pawlicki lost control.

'What about you?'

'Me?' Pieniazek puffed himself up proudly. 'Certainly I did.'

'Well, keep your trap shut, then.'

'I won't! Anyway, what'll you do to me? I always toady to our rulers. So do you.'

Pawlicki turned almost livid with rage. Wrona was quite obviously looking their way.

'You toadied to them!' Pieniazek squeaked.

Pawlicki clenched his fists and looked for a moment as if he were about to throw himself at Pieniazek. He controlled himself, however.

'Just you wait! We'll have a little talk tomorrow.'

And he turned his back.

'You toady!' Pieniazek shouted after him, triumphantly.

Seeing that Pawlicki had stopped talking to Pieniazek, Swiecki took the first opportunity of leaving the colonel.

'Well?' he whispered, taking Pawlicki's arm, 'did you succeed?'

Pawlicki threw up his hands.

'No use talking to him. He's tight.'

'Oh dear!'

'Best leave him alone, I'd say. Can't be helped.'

'Here? That's out of the question.'

'Suppose he starts a row?'

'If he does,' Swiecki muttered, 'there are ways of handling it. Perhaps you're right, though. It's really not worth while . . .'

'Of course it isn't. But what made you invite him in the first place?'

'As if I would! My dear man!'

'How did he get in, then?'

Now it was Swiecki's turn to throw up his hands.

'Never mind.'

He looked round.

'Everyone seems to be here. Shall we sit down?'

After the brief period of confusion, they began to take their places at table. Swiecki wondered whether to call first for a toast to Szczuka but soon decided that it was not the right moment. For the time being everyone was busy helping themselves and plates were passing from hand to hand. Swiecki himself was very hungry and besides he could not think of a single phrase with which to begin the first speech he was to make as a member of the government. Instead he took off his glasses and leaned across the table to Szczuka, saying confidentially,

'Here's to you, Comrade Szczuka!'

'Good vodka isn't bad!' said Colonel Baginski, jovially.

Swiecki was sitting between two Army men, Wrona and Baginski. Szczuka was opposite, with Weychert on one side and Kalicki, chairman of the Town National Council, on the other.

Drewnowski, still rigid and endeavouring by this rigidity to control the noisy roaring in his head, had taken his place at the end of the table. He could hardly swallow anything but attempted to join in the conversation which had started to be very lively at this end of the table. Unfortunately, only single words reached him, stifled as if wrapped in cotton-wool. Besides, the faces of his neighbours under the bright lights seemed to have been endowed with peculiar features and odd proportions. Pieniazek sat nearby. He was quiet for the time being, and modestly composed. He was clumsily dissecting carp in aspic with a fork, his expression meek, his befogged eyes wandering around in wonderment. A feeling of final defeat overwhelmed Drewnowski. Everything seemed hopeless and irrevocably lost. All his plans and ambitions, his whole career, his future. What rotten luck! He drained his glass and glanced towards Swiecki. The latter was busy talking to the sullen Wrona. The mood round the table was slowly becoming more animated. The silent and almost disembodied waiters were keeping watch to ensure no glasses stood empty. Those at the bottom of the table, whom the waiters did not have time to serve, helped themselves to vodka.

Szczuka was glad to have Kalicki next to him. They were old friends. They had known each other for many years, since before the First World War, which had caught them both in Geneva. Szczuka had been under twenty then. Kalicki, a good many years his senior, had outpaced him in experience, knowledge, and political maturity. In contrast to Szczuka, whose father was a tailor in a small town, Kalicki came from a wealthy landowning family in the Kiev district but while still at school in Warsaw he had met a group of young Socialists. As a result he became involved in some free-thinking incidents and had been expelled. Being well-to-do, he had little difficulty in moving from Tsarist Warsaw to liberal Cracow under the Hapsburgs. However, he could not rid his enthusiastic, aristocratic head of Socialism. He sacrificed his hurt and offended family for it. He also jettisoned the advantages deriving from the family estates. He turned his back on it all. He made himself independent and soon, full of an untroubled feeling of liberty, he began pacing the wretched Cracow gutters in the tattered boots most of his new friends wore. After matriculating, he paid a brief visit to England, then stayed for some time in Belgium, and finally moved to Switzerland, already thoroughly at home with chronic poverty. Community living absorbed him entirely. It was the idea to which he wanted to devote his life. For some time, during the war years, he and Szczuka had shared a room. Kalicki's influence on

114

Szczuka's development was very great at this time. Later, when both returned to Poland and each started working independently, their paths started to separate slowly. The Socialists' programme was not enough for Szczuka. He went farther and linked up with the Communist party. He married fairly young and in Maria found not only a wife but a loyal advocate of his ideas. Unfortunately he kept encountering unsurmountable difficulties in his profession. He was very good at it, but his political beliefs, which he never hid, and the conflicts he had as a result with his superiors, forced him to throw up one job after another. Later, in the thirties, a number of incidents with the police authorities made professional work impossible. Despite his excellent qualifications life slowly edged him outside normal society. Finally he was involved in a protracted and notorious trial which ended with a verdict of guilty. When he emerged from gaol three years later, the next war was rapidly approaching. Kalicki, on the other hand, true to his youthful ideals, had been closely connected throughout the inter-war period with the Polish Socialist Party and had played an important part both in its membership and in organizing the cooperative movement in Poland. He wrote a great deal, lectured and was a Deputy to the Sejm.

Apart from a few commonplace phrases on meeting, Szczuka had not yet had the opportunity of talking more freely to Kalicki. But presently Weychert broke off a long dissertation on the present situation in Europe and began seeking the best portion of eel in a dish. Szczuka took advantage of this and turned to Kalicki.

The latter was sitting silent and thoughtful, eating little and not drinking at all. He had last seen Szczuka just before the war, shortly after the latter had come out of gaol. Kalicki was one of the small group of Szczuka's non-Communist friends who visited him in those days. He had aged very much since then. His hair had turned grey, he was thinner and more stooping. With his fine, elevated brow and his aesthetic face to which long, old-fashioned moustaches gave an out-of-date appearance, he looked strangely alien and lost in thought.

Szczuka touched his thin, narrow hand.

'I'm glad to see you, old man,' he said, with rare cordiality.

Kalicki gazed at Szczuka with dark, deep-set eyes, which had lost their former sparkle and seemed extinguished and very weary.

'So am I,' he said quietly.

'We must meet, of course . . .'

'When are you leaving?'

'Early on Wednesday.'

Kalicki smiled slightly.

'So the war is over.'

'I should hope so,' Szczuka said. 'It sounds rather strange, doesn't it? The war is over . . . What about Tuesday evening? Are your family here with you?'

Kalicki shook his head.

'I'm alone.'

'How's your wife?'

'Mary? She was killed in the Uprising.'

'Killed?'

Finding nothing more appropriate to say, he began mechanically crumbling a piece of bread.

'Comrade Szczuka!' Swiecki called towards him, 'you have a full glass there!'

Szczuka nodded and drank his vodka. He went on crumbling the bread.

'My Maria died too,' he said presently.

Kalicki looked at him with weary eyes.

'In Ravensbruck,' Szczuka explained. He hesitated a moment. 'What about your sons?'

'They're dead too.'

Something stuck in Szczuka's throat.

'Both of them?'

'Yes. It was long ago. In forty-three. Let's meet on Tuesday.'

'Yes, Tuesday,' Szczuka repeated slowly.

The conversation broke off. On the other side of the table Wrona was talking in a loud voice:

'I know one thing. When we were in the forests, we imagined all this very differently. Some of our supporters are getting too tame and comfortable. If this goes on much longer, we shall lose the revolution. What's needed is to shake them up, like this.' He held up his clenched fists. 'Instead of doing away with the class

116

war, we ought to intensify it, catch our enemy by the throat, because if we don't kill them in time, they'll put a knife in our backs.'

Swiecki nodded with an understanding smile.

'That's all very well, major, but you're forgetting one thing. Politics isn't such a simple matter. At this stage we must first lessen various irritations.'

Wrona looked at him darkly.

'Whose? The kulaks? The landowners?'

'I'm speaking generally,' Swiecki replied evasively. 'We must draw them to us, unite them with us.'

'But who?'

'What do you mean "Who"?' Swiecki asked in surprise. 'The nation.'

Wrona's swarthy face darkened slightly.

'The nation? Comrade Swiecki, do you really know the Polish nation, do you know what it's like and what it wants? Who do you want to unite? Those who think of nothing but pushing the workers and peasants back into poverty and degradation? Or perhaps those who shoot from behind cover at our best men? Are they supposed to be the Polish nation?'

Swiecki opened his hands, 'I understand your indignation, I myself was very upset about many incidents . . .'

'But you'd like to inscribe " Love one another, brother Poles " on the standard of the revolution?'

'The country's destroyed, the people are exhausted, we must think realistically.'

'No!' He brought his fist down on the table. 'That isn't the way, that's not the Bolshevik way. It's true our country is destroyed and the people are exhausted, but it looks to me as if you, Comrade Swiecki, have no idea what great forces there are in this exhausted nation. These Communist forces will grow and wake up in other people . . .' His voice suddenly broke with almost boyish grief. 'It makes my heart ache to remember so many comrades who won't see this. . . .'

Swiecki took this opportunity to transfer his unnerving conversation to another plane.

'How's the investigation going into the case of those two murders?' he inquired.

Wrona eyed him in his own peculiar way.

'Don't you worry,' he muttered, 'the time will come. Even if we don't catch the bandits who committed these murders, sooner or later we'll lay our hands on all those who are behind this crime and others like it.'

'Don't you think, Comrade Wrona, that this may be the insane act of some individual?'

Wrona was silent for a while.

'After all, that likelihood must be considered,' Swiecki added.

The other drummed on the table.

'Can I ask you a question?'

'Do,' Swiecki said eagerly. 'What is it?'

'Do you believe in miracles?'

The Minister was slightly taken aback.

'I don't understand. Why should I?'

Wrona shrugged.

'How should I know, that's your affair. I'm simply replying to your question with another one.'

Meanwhile Szczuka had turned to Kalicki again:

'What plans have you for the future? Will you be staying in Ostrowiec?'

'I don't know yet,' Kalicki replied. 'They want me to go to Warsaw.'

'Rightly, I'm sure.'

'Think so? What is there for me there? What shall I do?'

Szczuka raised his heavy eyelids.

'I don't understand. What do you mean? Surely there's enough work?'

Kalicki made a gesture of dismissal.

'My dear man, why wrap things up in cotton-wool? People of my stamp are neither necessary nor in favour at present.'

'People of your stamp? I wouldn't recognize you, Jan. You, an old Socialist, talking like this!'

'Unfortunately, it's the truth.'

'Whose truth?'

'Whose? My own, I suppose. You say I'm an old Socialist. Obviously I'm a Socialist of the old school. My skin is too thin, I've too many scruples and doubts. I have my own views. And

I'm too fond of telling the truth bluntly, and people don't care for that nowadays.'

Szczuka leaned towards him.

'Besides, you yourself know it's as I say,' Kalicki went on. 'Why should we lie to each other?'

Szczuka stirred violently.

'It's not so,' he said in a hard voice. 'It's nothing like that. Have you really failed to realize that what is happening in Poland now is what we've been waiting for all our lives?'

Kalicki smiled bitterly.

'What has been, has been.' And he leaned towards Szczuka and lowered his voice. 'Now it's the Swieckis you need.'

Szczuka looked at him attentively.

'Come, come, old man! You've lagged behind somewhere on the way . . .'

'Me? Perhaps it's you who're not following the right road?'

'No, Jan,' Szczuka replied. 'The party is following the right road. We may make mistakes but the direction is the right one. You referred to the Swieckis. Of course there are such people with us. Now tomorrow they'll fall out.'

Kalicki was again silent for a while.

'I know that,' he said finally, 'and I'm not worried about them.' Kalicki raised his weary gaze to his old friend. For a moment, his dark eyes gleamed with their earlier glow. 'I'm worried about you,' he said, 'I'm worried about where you're taking Poland.'

At this moment Weychert leaned towards Szczuka.

'I'm afraid you're expected to make a speech,' he whispered with confidential irony.

In fact Swiecki considered that the appropriate moment had come for a toast, so he pulled himself together, his face bulging with importance and holding a knife in his right hand, he struck a glass but only those sitting nearest heard it and broke off their conversation. Swiecki was about to tap his glass again, when a very noisy ringing was heard from the far end of the table. It was Pieniazek, blinking his befogged eyes, banging a fork against his glass with all his might. The noise round the table died down at once and everyone began looking about curiously for the cause of this extraordinary din. Swiecki went red then turned pale again.

'Ssssh!' Pieniazek squeaked, 'the Minister wants to make a speech!'

Seeing Swiecki's confusion, Drewnowski very nearly burst out laughing. He hid his mouth with one hand.

'Do it again!' he urged Pieniazek.

But Swiecki soon had the situation under control. He rose and everyone's attention turned to him. Nevertheless, his voice trembled a little as he said his first words:

'Gentleman! Today is a great victory for re-born Poland. The sacrifices we made in the battle against Fascism have not been in vain. Fascism has capitulated....'

'Can you hold on?' Julius Szretter whispered.

Felix Szymanski was breathing hard.

'Yes.'

'Now then! One, two...'

They swayed to and fro then hurled their burden into the darkness. There was a splash, followed by the most profound silence. Drops of rain rustled among the trees. Lightning flashed far behind the town.

Felix rubbed his sweating forehead.

'Ouf! He was some weight!'

'Shut up,' Szretter hissed.

Alek was standing to one side, his hands trembling, the blood ebbing away swiftly from his head and his heart throbbing. For some time, while they had been struggling through the undergrowth dragging the limp body of Janusz along like a tree-trunk, he had been feeling sick. Now he opened his mouth and greedily inhaled the fresh, moist air but it brought no relief. Cold sweat stood out on his forehead, his guts were rising within him, he reached out instinctively and touched a bush, felt the moist, sticky leaves on his face and hands and crouched down and began vomiting.

Felix stirred in the darkness.

'What's up?'

Szretter stopped him.

'Leave him alone. Let him get it over.'

They were standing on the edge of the lake, amidst thick and wet grass, almost touching, though hardly visible to, each other. The foggy and soundless surface of the lake was almost invisible too, the darkness nearly impenetrable. Around them arose a thicket of weeping willow trees, full of mysterious rustlings.

'Julius?'

'What is it?'

'Let's clear out.'

He went over to Alek. The latter, bent double and clutching convulsively at the wet bush, was still choking and gasping. At last he stopped.

'Better now?' Szretter asked.

Alek shook his head feebly. Although the nausea had gone, he felt weak, exhausted, and indifferent to everything.

'Well?' Felix whispered impatiently in the gloom.

Szretter beckoned to him and he came across.

'Get going!'

Felix hesitated.

'How about you?'

'Don't worry, we'll manage. Anyhow, we can't go back together. See you tomorrow.'

Felix did not move.

'What's up?' Szretter asked impatiently. 'What are you waiting for? Get going, I said!'

Felix, still lingering, put out his hand.

'See you tomorrow. Shall I come round?'

'All right. And take care.'

'I know,' the other muttered.

He clapped Alek on the shoulder as he passed.

'Chin up,' he said.

He slipped away like a shadow into the undergrowth. Leaves rustled, branches creaked lightly on the earth. And silence fell again.

Alek didn't move. Szretter held him round the shoulders and felt him trembling.

'What is it? Do you still want to spew?'

Alek muttered something indistinctly. He straightened up, removing Julius's arm as he did so. For a little while he stood with bowed head, then he took a deep breath, just like a child after a fit of crying, and began to wipe his mouth with his hand-kerchief.

Szretter eyed him in silence. Alek, outlined near him, looked frail and lost in the darkness. He wiped his mouth slowly and lengthily. Finally he put the handkerchief away and breathed in again, this time without gasping.

'I'm all right.'

'Then be off home.'

Alek nodded.

'Felix and I'll come round tomorrow. Will you get back all right?'

'Of course.' Szretter clapped him on the shoulder. 'Have a drink of soda-water on the way home, it'll do you good.'

Presently he was alone. A tranquil calm prevailed all round. There was the smell of earth and trees and of the spring. A fine mist lay white across the lake. A startled bird called high up in the trees. It chirruped sleepily and fell silent again.

Despite the crowd in the hall and the shaded lights, Slomka's vigilant gaze caught sight of the tall figure of Puciatycki as soon as the latter entered the restaurant with his companions. The fat man grunted and caught hold of the first waiter who came to hand.

'Get a table for Count Puciatycki! The best there is!'

However, he had caught hold of a young lad who had only been working at the Monopole for a few days and could not cope with the Saturday crowd, nor did he realize the importance of the local customers.

'They're all taken, chief.'

Slomka could not stand being thwarted.

'When I say get a table, then get one, see? Instantly.'

And, leaving the waiter to his own devices, he began pushing his way between the closely packed tables. He reached Pucia-tycki as the latter was vainly looking round for a table.

'Ah, my dear Slomka!' he exclaimed, pleased to see the restaurateur, whom he had known before the war in Lwow, 'you're just the man we want. Can you find us a table some-where?'

'Directly, sir. Of course we can find a table for you, Count!

My respects, sir!' He bowed on catching sight of Telezynski with the ladies. 'The table's ready! Please be good enough to follow me.'

'That's fine!' Puciatycki drawled.

Leaving Telezynski to take care of the women, he started talking to Slomka on the way. He was very fond of talking to people of mediocre rank in the social hierarchy.

'You've plenty of customers, I see . . .'

Slomka was clearing the way round the dance-floor with almost imperceptible movements of his pot belly. The lights were turned down low to provide the proper atmosphere, and the crowd of dancers was lazily moving round and round to the melody of a tango, in a yellow and bluish half-light.

'The war's over, Count. Everyone wants to enjoy themselves.'

'Quite right, too. A sort of intermezzo, as it were!'

'Pardon?'

'A sort of intermezzo, I said. An entracte.'

'Oh yes, of course.'

Only now did he realize what Puciatycki meant. He blinked one round eye at him.

'You think so, Count?'

'Never mind!' He clapped Slomka benevolently on the shoulder. 'Don't worry your head about it, my good man. Everything's going to be all right. We've seen all kinds of things and survived.'

'You're quite right there, Count. That's what I always say. The main thing is to survive.'

The orchestra stopped playing and the lights came on.

The young waiter Slomka had ordered to find an empty table was talking to one of his older colleagues. Slomka swooped down on them.

'Where's that table for the Count?'

The other waiter, who had had years of practice at this sort of thing, saw fit to take the initiative.

'One moment, chief, a foursome is just leaving, I've given them their bill.'

Slomka gave the young waiter a withering look but turned a smiling face towards Puciatycki.

'A moment's patience, Count.'

Puciatycki made a grimace.

'What, isn't there one? This is a fine thing!'

He ostentatiously turned his back on Slomka and went irritably across to the women who were coming up with Fred Telezynski.

'Just imagine, all the tables are taken.'

Slomka, hastily clutching his hands together, teetered after him.

'One moment, Count, literally a moment. A table is being vacated now.'

'Don't bother me!' Puciatycki said crossly. 'Being vacated, indeed? Where? Do you expect us to stand about waiting here for an hour? Forgive me, my dear,' he gave his wife an appeasing gesture, 'but I can't allow you to be treated like this. It smacks of impertinence. Let's leave. I shall never set foot in this establishment again.'

Mme Staniewicz did not in the least want to forgo her amusement. They had wasted an hour as it was because of the rain.

'Oh dear, what a tyrant you are! Don't we women count at all?'

'Let's go to the bar,' Telezynski suggested. 'We're sure to find a free table there. Adam, d'you know who's working in the bar?'

'No, who?'

'Christina Rozbicka.'

'Rozbicka? Fancy that! Which branch of the family is she from? The Krzynowlogi?'

'No, that's her uncle. Her side are Poznan. You know, she's the daughter of Kaspar Rozbicki.'

'Good God!' Puciatycki said, amazed. 'Whoever shall we come across next? Did you hear that, Roza? Fred says the little Rozbicka girl, Kaspar's daughter, is working in the bar here. I ought to explain,' he added to Mme Staniewicz, 'that once, long long ago, Kaspar Rozbicki was terribly in love with my wife. . . .'

Slomka now saw that people were starting to get up at one of the tables on the far side of the room. He breathed a sigh of relief and wiped his sweating brow.

'There's a table now, Count.'

'We don't want a table,' Puciatycki snapped. 'We'll do without. We're going to the bar.'

Slomka wanted to say something else, but Puciatycki's decisive gesture shut him up. After a moment he edged across the room, turned back and again moved among the tables. But the young waiter who had upset everything by his inefficiency was nowhere to be found. Finally Slomka came upon him in a narrow corridor leading to the kitchen. The boy was carrying several dishes and wanted to get past, but Slomka cut off his retreat with his pot belly.

'So there you are! From tomorrow you can find yourself another job. Service in the Monopole isn't for giving practice to amateurs, d'you hear?'

The waiter looked sideways at him.

'Who d'you think you're talking to? You can give yourself the sack tomorrow, Jack.'

Slomka gasped with indignation. He reddened, and his little hands stopped fluttering.

'What was that you said? Insolence . . .'

'Come off it!' the youth drawled in a Warsaw accent. 'Mind the Union don't have something to say about this. Now move over, before I get mad. I've customers waiting.'

Slomka quite forgot he had a tongue in his head. He stood open-mouthed, his eyes popping, the blood mounting to his face. The other pushed him impatiently aside with his elbow and disappeared through the door into the restaurant.

Slomka felt terribly sorry for himself. Who, after all, would follow his coffin to the cemetery? No one. Not even a dog. His solitary corpse would be borne away in a hearse and shovelled underground like a useless lump. Tiny tears trickled from his eyes. 'I'd better go fishing tomorrow,' he thought dolefully, 'it'll do me good. And I'll get rid of that young scamp into the bargain.'

Slomka, himself again, went into the corridor. Old Mrs Jurgeluszka, widow of a Monopole doorman who had died many years earlier, was sitting stiffly upright on a low stool at the lavatory door, knitting a pullover for her grandson.

Slomka stopped and grunted.

'How's it going, Mrs Jurgeluszka?'

She raised her little, rabbity face with faded, senile eyes.

'The speeches is on.'

'Are they?' Swiecki's carrying and voluble voice came from behind the closed door. 'Ah, that's the Minister himself speaking now.'

Mrs Jurgeluszka accepted this information indifferently and went on knitting. Slomka glanced sideways at the lavatory. It gleamed perfectly white. Old Mrs Jurgeluszka was good at her job.

'Anyone been sick yet?' he hummed.

'So soon?' Mrs Jurgeluszka asked calmly, without stopping her work. 'It's too early for that. All in good time. Now there's the speeches. Later on they'll start running out here, see if they don't. . . .'

'You should do nicely tonight.'

'Just what I've been thinking. But you never know, sir. They had all kinds of banquets here before the war. Once there was even a minister.'

'Was there?' Slomka asked with interest. 'Who was he? What was his name?'

'Oh, I don't remember that. He was a-well set-up gent, though. He must have ate something that disagreed with him, or perhaps his innards was weak, for he kept coming out here all the time. And all the seat, if you'll excuse me mentioning it, sir, got nasty. But he never tipped me a penny.'

'Oh, shame! And him a minister?'

'But he was in a terrible state. I was afraid he was going to pass out altogether.'

'What a scandal that would have been, to be sure!'

'But he never left me a tip and that was that. You never can tell, sir, how God makes 'em. Some do, and others don't.'

Slomka stepped neatly aside as the door suddenly opened for one of the tail-coated waiters. Slomka beckoned to him.

'How's it going, Joe?' he asked in a friendly way, flapping his little hands.

The handsome waiter smiled tolerantly.

'All right.'

'They drinking?'

'So-so.'

Slomka rubbed his hands.

'Good! Don't forget the French wines. And liqueurs with the coffee. Mrs Jurgeluszka, I'll say good night to you now.'

In the kitchen he came face to face with the young scoundrel. They rubbed shoulders in the entrance and for a moment their eyes met. The waiter whistled insolently and turned his back just as the offended Puciatycki had done earlier.

'Hey, there!' he shouted in the direction of the chef, 'veal cutlet twice! Stewed fruit and cream once!'

Slomka's insides contracted. He felt he must console himself somehow for his humiliating defeat. The fishing trip he had planned for the next day was not quite what he needed. He glared at the dish-washers from beneath lowered eyelids. The first of them was a healthy, stout girl with a broad bottom.

He retreated from the kitchen and in the passage he caught a page-boy by the ear.

'What's your name?'

'Tom, sir.'

'Good! Now, you listen to me, Tom.'

'Yes, sir?'

'Just nip into the kitchen and send Sally to me. Do you know which one she is?'

'I know, sir.'

'Be quick about it, then.'

Presently she appeared, hot and very red in the face, her hands still wet, smelling of sweat and washing-up water. Slomka pranced round her.

'Sally.'

'What?' she muttered reluctantly.

'Come to my room for ten minutes. Upstairs.'

'Not again! I've had enough of that caper. Everyone in the hotel's laughing at me as it is.'

'Don't be silly. They're jealous. I'll give you a pair of stockings. Real French ones, too. Come up for ten minutes.'

'Silk ones?'

'Of course.'

She reflected for a moment.

'All right,' she replied slowly, 'but if my fiancé ever finds out . . .'

Sally's boy friend had returned only a few weeks earlier from forced labour in Germany and was now working in the Biala cement factory.

'Don't be silly,' he muttered, 'how could he?'

He watched the girl's generous bottom with relish as she walked away, then glanced into what was known as the artistes' room.

This was a little cell used by the soloists appearing in the cabaret. Today's programme was entirely new and had been billed as a great sensation. Hannah Lewicka was appearing, with the well-known dancers Seiffert and Kochanska.

As no one answered his knock, Slomka pushed open the door and peeped in. The light was on but the room empty. It contained only a few sticks of furniture: a plain table, with a large mirror propped up against the wall, a battered green sofa, some chairs and a red screen in one corner. An open suitcase lay on one of the chairs, full of disordered rags and tatters, a pair of bright blue trousers with narrow legs was hanging down to the floor, while a yellow dress with frills lay across the lid of the case, and a black Spanish hat lay on the floor. The tiny room had no windows and was as hot and stuffy as a greenhouse.

Slomka was about to withdraw when a man's voice came from behind the screen.

'That you, Lola?'

Slomka grunted, but before he could reply Seiffert came out from behind the screen, quite naked. He was of medium height but despite his compact, powerful, and still youthful build, his body was somewhat too heavy for that of a dancer. He did not seem in the least disconcerted at being naked.

'Ah, it's you, good evening. Seen Lola anywhere?'

Slomka guessed Seiffert meant his partner Kochanska.

'No, I haven't. Hasn't she got here yet?'

The dancer did not reply. He went to the suitcase and began rooting about among the costumes. Presently most of them were on the floor.

Slomka was slightly uneasy.

'Surely Miss Kochanska won't be late? You're starting at ten precisely. The place is packed. And Miss Lewicka isn't here yet either . . .'

Seiffert shrugged.

'What's that got to do with me? I can't think what you've got hold of that Lewicka woman for. She sings like a cat, has a face like the back of a bus and bandy legs into the bargain.'

He went back to turning the contents of the suitcase upside down.

'What's become of my yellow scarf? That half-wit must have forgotten it. Damnation! What am I supposed to dance my bolero in? It's the best number.'

Suddenly he calmed down and drew the scarf out from the very bottom of the suitcase.

'Here we are! All my gear is pre-war. The only trouble is, quite frankly, that these costumes don't fit her any longer. Kochanska, I mean. They've had to be let out. She's getting thick round the waist, see? She won't last much longer, you'll see.'

The door squeaked. Both men looked round quickly. Lola Kochanska was standing on the threshold. She was small and fair-haired. Under her fur coat she was wearing a long, dark evening dress sewn with sequins. Her pretty, though rather waxen face was now distorted with fury. The faded features of an ageing outraged woman stood out under a thick layer of rouge and powder.

'You here?' Seiffert muttered indifferently and began looking through his own photographs as calmly as you please.

Kochanska slammed the door shut behind her.

'You thought I hadn't heard, did you? You swine! Who won't last much longer? You'd better watch out for yourself.'

He glanced at her with unconcealed contempt.

'Don't bellow. You're hysterical.'

'And what about you? I only dance with you out of pity!'

'Is that so? Then shut up, for goodness' sake.'

'If only you knew! Any other girl in my place would just spit on you, you broken-down old object!'

'Girl, eh? You're nothing but a painted old hag.'

Slomka slipped tactfully away, as the dancer's laugh echoed down the corridor.

At the door into the bar he met the local impresario, Kotowicz. 'Good evening, director,' he greeted Slomka cordially.

'Hannah Lewicka's here already, she's in the bar. What a charming girl she is, to be sure!'

'And the others are quarrelling,' Slomka informed him.

'Oh, Seiffert and Kochanska!'

'Can't you hear them?'

The dancer's hysterical laugh penetrated this far and Kotowicz smiled tolerantly.

'It's nothing, don't worry, my dear man. They've been quarrelling like this for twenty years, everyone knows it. They'll dance the better for it. She gets over her hysteria, he . . . and that's that. It makes them younger. By the way, have you seen my son?'

Of late, Janusz Kotowicz had been a frequent visitor to the Monopole, but Slomka had not seen him this evening.

'Naughty boy! He was to bring me some cash. We work in cash as far as possible, you see. One has to make a living somehow. A man can't live by art alone these days. If there's anything you ever need in this line, I recommend him. You've no idea what a head for business that boy's got . . . See you later. I must say hallo to our artistes.'

When he had borne his magnificent head away, Slomka glanced at his watch. He saw he only had five minutes before the arrival of Sally. However, he looked in at the bar.

The small room, almost empty a quarter of an hour earlier, was now full of people. Customers from the large room, mostly youths and girls, who came in here for vodka between dances, were crowding noisily round the bar. Most of them knew each other well, but those who had not yet met soon did so as the glasses went round and helped establish a single friendly crowd. The girls were mostly plain and clumsy, badly dressed, with curls and fringes arranged high over their foreheads. Healthy and well-developed with prematurely adult and blasé faces, the youths were dressed in a queer mixture of civilian and military clothing of German, Soviet or American origin, and were being very gallant to the girls. Some were already quite drunk.

The lawyer and his group had changed their seats at the bar for a more comfortable small table. Several other people had joined them, some men and the petite Hannah Lewicka, with her charming and innocently childish face, who was in Ostrowiec for the first time. Her appearance at the Monopole had been preceded by a noisy advertising campaign organized by the ingenious Kotowicz. In any case, the name Hannah Lewicka was now quite well known and popular. Before the war she had appeared in suburban Warsaw cinemas in 'live' interludes, but her singing in cafés and fashionable night-clubs during the occupation had brought her wider fame. Her thin, girlish little voice played on sentimental feelings, while the sentimental ditties she sang intensified them.

Near this large, noisy group, the Puciatyckis were sitting with Kate Staniewicz and Fred Telezynski. People unknown to Slomka were sitting all round. These were the people staying at the Monopole in transit.

Christina could hardly attend to all her customers. They were calling for vodka from all sides, here for three small ones, there for five, and yet again for three, then two more, unceasingly. One of the youths, quite drunk and with one arm stretched across the top of the bar, was urging her to have a drink. Seeing Slomka, he turned towards him.

'Come on, fatty! Have a drink! It's on me! Miss, two double vodkas for this citizen here and me.'

'Christina,' Slomka grunted, 'send up a bottle of brandy to my room. At once!'

And he quickly slipped away.

Meanwhile, Telezynski had been signalling in vain for Christina to come over to their table. She had seen him, but could not get away from the bar even for a second. Mme Staniewicz felt hurt because Andrew Kossecki, a few tables away, had merely nodded instead of coming over at once. She wanted to enjoy herself, to dance, to feel young and be with young people, whereas the evening had gone badly right from the start, not at all as she had planned it. Puciatycki looked tired and was sitting silent and moping in his low, soft chair. His wife was eyeing Christina Rozbicka through an old-fashioned lorgnette. Presently she leaned across and said:

'She's a pretty little thing.'

Sunk in depression, Puciatycki did not at first realize who was meant.

'What little thing?'

'The Rozbicka girl.'

'Oh, her. Let's have a look. Yes, not bad in the least. Like Kaspar.'

'Kaspar? I don't think she is, at all.'

'I tell you she is! Fred, ask her to come over, we must meet her.'

'Can't you see what's going on over there?' Telezynski replied.

Mme Puciatycki directed her lorgnette upon the young people round the bar.

'What extraordinary creatures! Where on earth do they all come from? It's terrible work for such a young girl. I can just imagine what she must be going through, poor child.'

Fred smiled cheerfully.

'Don't worry about her, my dear. She's very good at it. I assure you women of our class do very well at that sort of job.'

'You're hateful!' Mme Puciatycki exclaimed, vexed. 'I don't think you'd like it very much if your sister had to earn a living like that.'

'Why not? If she made a good thing of it.'

'Fred!'

'I'm serious. There's too much talk about this sort of thing. The old days are over. I'm beginning to wonder seriously whether to leave the country at all.'

'Are you mad?' Puciatycki livened up.

'Not at all. I've had a good offer here. I could start as a driver to the Presidium of the National Council any day.'

Puciatycki laughed softly.

'Excellent! A brilliant joke, Fred.'

Telezynski shrugged.

'It's not a joke at all. I met Dominic Poninski not long ago. He's simply waiting for the foreign embassies to get back to Warsaw, then he's going to apply straight away for a job as driver in either the British or American embassy. It's an excellent idea. Dominic's a very good driver. So am I, for that matter!'

Puciatycki's lower lip protruded.

'My dear man, forgive me . . . but there's a difference between driving for the British ambassador and – a Party member. Don't overdo things! Let's be sensible!'

Mme Staniewicz decided to treat the whole thing as a joke.

'You're impossible!' She smacked Fred's hand. 'You talk like a capricious child. But I'm going to try and get you to leave in spite of everything, instead of becoming – what would one call it? – a chauffeur-in-charge, I suppose?'

'Do you think that it would be more profitable to drive a cab in Paris or London?'

'For Heaven's sake!' Puciatycki said crossly, 'can't a Telezynski be anything but a chauffeur?'

'That's the only job I can do,' said Fred shortly. 'Except that I suppose I could be a gigolo, but I'm afraid that's all. That's how I was brought up.'

He rose, said 'Excuse me' – and left the table. Mme Staniewicz lifted her eyebrows.

'What's come over him?'

'He's mad!' Puciatycki shrugged. 'All the Telezynskis are.'

Meanwhile Fred had gone to the bar from the back. Christina caught sight of him and nodded. Presently she hurried over.

'How are you, Fred? Back in the Monopole? And still sober?'

'As you see.'

'Why so sulky?'

'I've had enough of all this.'

'Of what, Fred? Drinking?'

'No. I mean all this absurd waiting about for no one knows what . . .'

She eyed him searchingly and with some surprise.

'Listen, Christina, you're a sensible girl . . .'

'Thank you.'

'That was no compliment.'

'So much the better.'

'Would it be absolutely idiotic if I were to take a job as a chauffeur?'

'Why should it be idiotic? You drive very well.'

Fred brightened.

'Someone talking sense at last! You're an angel.'

'Fred!' She shook one finger at him. 'I warn you, you'll get terribly tight again. Like last night.'

'Could be. But you're still an angel.'

The uproar round the bar suddenly intensified.

'I must get back, Fred – I'm afraid.'

'Just a minute. I'm with the old Puciatyckis.'

'Are you?'

'You know, they used to live at Chwaliboga.'

'I guessed as much. I'm still *au fait* with the upper classes. What about it?'

'They simply must meet you. Do them a favour. They're bores, but . . .'

'Of course, only a little later.'

'Whenever you like.'

'When Lily Hanska comes on duty.'

'Fine! Are you working all night?'

Christina hesitated.

'I don't know yet. I may get away earlier.'

'Come over anyhow.'

'Andrew, who's that booby?' Chelmicki asked. 'The one walking across the room now.'

Andrew had seen Telezynski at Mme Staniewicz's that day for the first time and did not remember his name.

'I don't know.'

'Of course you do. He's sitting with those people you bowed to.'

'I know, but I've no idea what his name is.'

He pushed away his plate with the steak unfinished, drank his wine and stood up. Michael looked at him sulkily.

'Leaving?'

'Yes. I've had enough of all this. You staying?'

'Yes. Good-bye.'

It was crowded and noisy in the entrance hall. The people who did not want to stay at the Monopole all night were hurrying to get home before curfew. Andrew had to wait before he could get his overcoat from the cloakroom. Overheated people, surfeited with smoke and alcohol, were crowding round. He put his coat on and was about to make for the exit when he heard the low-pitched voice of a woman behind him.

'Leaving already?'

He turned. It was Mme Staniewicz. He was slightly embarrassed.

'Yes.'

'I'm sorry. You didn't even come over to say hullo.'

Mme Staniewicz turned towards the cloakroom.

'What a frightful crush! I left my cigarette-case in my coat pocket. But I'm keeping you and you're probably in a hurry?'

'No, I'll make it.'

Mme Staniewicz looked round.

'It's really not at all amusing here in the Monopole. If I weren't with my friends . . .'

For a moment she waited for some decisive gesture from Andrew. When he failed to make one, she managed to cover a light shadow of disappointment with a warm, low-pitched laugh.

'I won't keep you. Run along.' She gave him her hand. 'I don't want to have you on my conscience and you must get home before curfew. Please call on me some day, but not only when the colonel is there, won't you?'

He wanted to say he was leaving Ostrowiec in three days' time, but changed his mind at the last moment and, leaving her question unanswered, bowed and kissed her hand in silence.

When he was outside, he was not sure whether he had done the right thing and walked on, lost in thought. The night had become fine, warm, and starry. The pavements had dried after the downpour and only shallow puddles remained. A long line of military cars stood in front of the Monopole. Their drivers were idling about. Several were drinking vodka inside one of the cars. Some militiamen were standing beside it, drinking with them.

The people leaving the Monopole separated slowly. They were still reluctant to go home. So their farewells were prolonged, they crowded into groups, laughing and calling loudly to one another. Loud, drunken singing came from the far side of the market-place. Droshkies taking people home rattled over the cobblestones. A brief volley of shots came from a distant part of the town, towards the May 3rd Boulevard.

But, above all these sounds, a voice from a loudspeaker was echoing in the depths of the obscurity:

'. . . *military operations are to cease today, Saturday, at eight a.m.*'

Alek set off in the direction of home, walking fast. Rounding a corner into a narrow side-street, he came face to face with an Army patrol. Although he carried no arms and his identity papers were in order, he nevertheless felt that same disagreeable chill which had always come upon him whenever he had had to pass a German patrol during the occupation. A sensation of humiliating shame added to this chill.

Alek had a front-door key but when he put it into the lock, it would not go in. The door must be bolted. He thought for a moment. He was sure his mother had not gone to bed, but he lacked the courage to knock. He retreated and walked round the house.

Light was shining through the gaps in the black-out curtains over the kitchen window. He knocked and the shuffling steps of Rozalia were audible sooner than he expected. She came over to the door, then stopped.

'Who's that?'

'Me,' he replied, in a low voice.

Inside, she slammed the door noisily. He jumped.

'Couldn't you shut the door quietly, Rozalia? You'll wake the whole house.'

'It's only them with bad consciences as want to come home quietly. I've no need to be afraid of making a noise, thank goodness.'

He shrugged and put a good face on things as he walked past the old woman. The house was silent, he stopped undecided in the middle of the kitchen.

'I'm off to bed. Good night.'

'What about your supper? I'm not going to serve it in the dining-room at this time of night. You'll have to eat it here. I'll warm it up.'

'I'm not hungry.'

'Not hungry, indeed! Your mother specially told me to put your supper by. And now you're not hungry. . . .'

'Why should I be?' he said crossly. 'Good night.'

Mrs Kossecki was waiting for him in the hall. She had seen him long ago from the dining-room window. When at last she saw her son's slender shadow, first at the garden gate, then slowly approaching the house, the terrible weight of anxiety left her. He'd come home. This was all she wanted. He was back. Then, however, everything else surged insistently back. She had to make a great effort of will to prevent herself from hurrying into the kitchen. She began praying fervently, her thoughts formless and confused, with all her suffering body and her despair and pain.

Alek walked across the hall with his head bent and did not notice his mother until he reached the stairs. He stopped and smiled shyly.

'Hullo,' he said quietly.

At first she was unable to utter a word.

He looked pale and wan to her, bedraggled, his hair tangled, dark shadows under his eyes. Where had he been? What had he been up to all these hours? And why had he needed that stolen money? He stood within arm's reach of her, yet she knew nothing about him: this son of hers, little Alek, whom she still always thought of as a pure, innocent child, was a dark and irritating secret to her. All the sleepless nights she had had on his account, all the tears and joys associated with him, now quivered in her constricted heart as if they wanted once more to bring to life the burden of her unwanted and bitter love before finally and irrevocably withdrawing it into the lost past.

Alek stood staring at the floor, and, as the silence persisted, a dark flush spread over his forehead, cheeks and ears, giving a blood-red shade to his neck. He saw his muddy boots through downcast eyelashes.

'Alek!'

'What is it, Mother?'

'Haven't you anything to say to me?'

'Such as what?' he stammered. 'We went to the pictures.'

'Alek? What about it?'

'What do you mean?'

'How could you do it? To think it was you, my child, my son, whom I trusted and believed in so! Stealing in secret . . .'

'What on earth . . .?' he began angrily.

'You know what I mean.'

'I've no idea!'

'So you haven't even got the courage to admit it? Alek, aren't you ashamed of yourself?'

He began going through his pockets feverishly and found the money crumpled in his trousers.

'Here!' he thrust the banknotes into his mother's hand. 'I haven't stolen anything. You'd better count it.'

'What's this?' she whispered.

'It's the money, that three thousand zloty I borrowed.'

'Borrowed?'

'It wasn't for me at all. Julius Szretter needed three thousand to send to someone, and his father wasn't getting home till evening, he'd forgotten to leave it. So I wanted to borrow it from you, but you weren't in . . . Perhaps I shouldn't have helped myself, but I wanted to do Julius a favour. He gave it back straight away. Then we went to the pictures, the last performance.'

She was looking at him all the time, and, in his breaking voice, in his face across which all his emotions passed like lights and shadows, she found all the beauty of her love for him, all the unlimited and incomparable joy of finding her son again.

'My little boy . . .' she whispered through her tears.

And for the first time in many, many years, she wept for joy. She put her arms round Alek and drew him against her as though he were a small, helpless child. Confused by this sudden outbreak and by her tears, he stayed motionless in her arms, scarcely breathing, trembling slightly. She felt this.

'My child,' she began stroking his face and tangled hair, 'I did you a terrible injustice. You must forgive me for thinking of you in that way. I'll never do it again. You'll forgive your old mother, won't you?'

'Mother, don't . . .'

'No, it's all right now. Don't say anything. Don't think of it. My little one. . . .'

Sally was fifteen minutes late. She arrived with her eyes puffy from crying, but Slomka, irritated by waiting, did not notice.

'What have you been up to, you fool! I told you to come in ten minutes, didn't I?'

The girl stopped in the centre of the floor and burst into loud, vulgar tears. Slomka had not expected this. 'She's afraid of me,' he thought with relish. And his anger died down.

'All right, all right. Stop snivelling.'

'Oh my God!' she began still more loudly. 'Oh, my God . . .!'
'Shut up, you fool! I'm not angry with you any more.'
'As if I cared! You don't know nothing. Oh my God . . .!'
Slomka was somewhat discountenanced.
'What are you carrying on like this for? Have they been talking in the kitchen?'
She shook her head.
'What's up, then?'
'They've murdered Stasiek! The swine have shot him.'
Slomka blinked.
'Who is Stasiek? Who shot him?'
'My Stasiek. My fiancé. You know! Oh, the swine! I hope God punishes them, that's all.'
Slomka waddled round her and she put her head in her big red hands.
'Oh Jesus, Jesus!' she began rocking to and fro.
'Why did they kill him?'
'How should I know?'
'It can't be true. You must have got it all muddled up.'
'No, never. "Listen," the policeman said, "they shot two blokes from the cement works this afternoon, down by the river." Something came over me directly. Then Felka asked, "Who was it they shot?" – she's always the first to ask questions and he said, "Smolarski and Stasiek Gawlik." Oh my, something hurt so inside of me I thought I'd drop down dead there and then. And he said, "They must have wanted to shoot someone else and killed them two by mistake".'
Slomka poured out some brandy.
'Have a drink,' he said, giving her a glass.
She was still rocking to and fro and groaning, her hands to her head. All she had was a vigorous, young body. And it was only through her body that she could express the pain she felt. Warm indolent heat came from her. Her skirt had risen above her knees, revealing generous white thighs. Slomka shifted from one foot to the other.
'Drink up. Good stuff, this. And don't take on so. What's happened can't be undone.'
She raised her head, blew her nose noisily and took the glass. She drank it.

'Sit down on the bed. You'll be more comfy.'

However, she yielded passively and heavily to his advice. The wide bed sank slightly under her weight.

'Oh, the shame of it,' she suddenly exclaimed, 'to think that anything like this . . .'

'What do you mean?'

'That I had to find out about it all from someone I don't even know. Here they've murdered my fiancé and nobody of his family even comes to let me know what's happened. They know where I work. But not them!'

'Perhaps they haven't had time?'

'They'd plenty of time to say nasty things about me to Stasiek, when he got back from Germany. Sally's this, that, and the other they said. What did it have to do with them anyway? Now, mind!' she jerked away from him, 'in a hurry, eh?'

'What if I am?' he grunted.

'Sssh!'

Presently a smile brightened her tear-reddened, puffy face.

'Show us them stockings. I'll wear them at the funeral and Stasiek's sister'll die of envy. She ought to have minded her own business, the bitch. . . .'

'It's nice, dancing with you.'

'Sweet of you to say so.'

'I mean it. People say I've got very bad manners.'

'Do they? I haven't had a chance to find out yet. This is a nice tango, don't you think? It reminds me of pre-war days. You were sitting with Andrew Kossecki just now, weren't you? Is he a friend of yours?'

'Yes.'

'Yet he went off leaving you on your own?'

'Why shouldn't he? I'm not a girl.'

'I guess not. Do you know that even though I didn't know you I was a bit cross with you?'

'With me?'

'Andrew promised to keep us company tonight.'

'He could have done.'

'The pair of you were supposed to have so many things to talk about. Anyhow, never mind. Don't let's talk of the absent.'

'Who's that young man at your table?'

'Fred Telezynski. He's a count.'

'Is he the cousin of the girl working at the bar?'

'Christina Rozbicka?'

'Is that her name?'

'Didn't you know? But why don't you tell me about your-self?'

'Aren't I doing so?'

'In that case, I'm afraid you were right about your bad manners.'

'See what I mean! So she's his cousin, is she?'

'Don't be a bore. Why did you ask me to dance if you only wanted to find out about Telezynski's family tree?'

'Miss Rozbicka's, rather.'

'In that case, you've picked the wrong person.'

'That's a pity. Are you cross?'

'I'd like to go back to my table right away. You needn't come with me.'

'This is a very nice tango, don't you think?'

'Didn't I make it clear that . . .?'

'Won't you introduce me to your friends?'

Drozdowski, a young doctor who had been working in the local hospital since the Warsaw uprising, was listening to Krajewski's words with a tolerant smile on his face.

'No, my dear sir,' he interrupted, 'this sounds all very fine, but I'm not going to let myself be taken in by any ideology.'

Krajewski was indignant.

'Taken in! What an odd expression to use! And in this con-text, I might add, thoroughly inappropriate.'

'In my view it's perfectly appropriate. You talk about London, the Anglo-Saxon world, the West, Christian civilization, and the defence of genuine democracy . . .'

'Surely there's no question of being "taken in"? These con-stitute lasting, eternal values.'

'They're merely words, my dear sir. The very same values are proclaimed in the East.'

'Not at all, not at all! That's just my point.'

'Or at least values equally lasting.'

'One side must be right . . .'

'Right? Do you expect to find the truth anywhere in all this muddle? What for?'

'My dear man, one has to believe in something.'

The platinum blonde was admiring the handsome doctor with her wide, glassy eyes. His well-shaped, round head was covered in gleaming black hair like a helmet, his olive complexion and strongly-formed jaw, and his hands, covered from the wrists with thick hair, struck her tipsy, excited imagination like the embodiment of a new man.

The rest of the group, gathered round the childishly chirping Hannah Lewicka, was not interested in what they were saying. Krajewski looked tired. He took off his thick, horn-rimmed spectacles and rubbed them slowly with a handkerchief as he looked straight ahead with the protruding, lifeless eyes of an astigmatic.

Drozdowski gazed at him with unconcealed pity.

'Yes, yes, my dear Krajewski. There's an end to all truth now that the war's over. We've seen too much. The conjurers and cardsharpers have given away their tricks. It's the end of blackmail.'

Krajewski went on rubbing his spectacles.

'And what is left, then?'

'A great deal. There's still life.'

'You said that beautifully,' the platinum blonde exclaimed.

Krajewski briskly put on his spectacles again.

'Now let me tell you what this is,' he said, tapping on the table.

'It's death. No, don't laugh. It's not a disease. It's death.'

'Oh, Mr Krajewski!' the blonde protested.

Krajewski shifted impatiently.

'It's death, death,' he repeated emphatically, leaning right across the table as if he sought to emphasize the final truth and irrevocability of his judgement by doing so.

Drozdowski was not at all impressed.

'I'm very sorry, my dear Krajewski, but I don't feel as if I were dead.' Before the lawyer had time to reply, Kotowicz came up to their table. They made room for him at once.

'Whew!' he exclaimed, dabbing his finely chiselled forehead.

'You'd never believe the way Seiffert and Kochanska carry on! It's incredible!'

He poured a little wine into a glass, added soda-water and began drinking slowly. The others leaned forward, curious.

'What happened? Have they murdered one another?'

'Not quite. But they've been having a tremendous scene. He as naked as God made him, she in an evening dress. . . .'

Hannah Lewicka opened her naïve blue eyes very wide.

'Naked? Whatever do you mean?'

'What I said,' Kotowicz laughed and everyone else began laughing too. Hannah pouted.

'Whatever are you all laughing at? I haven't said anything silly. My dear,' and she turned to Kotowicz, 'why are they all laughing at me?'

'You're so charming!' he replied. 'Delightful!'

'But they're all laughing at me and don't think so at all . . .'

The platinum blonde leaned towards her neighbour.

'Just look at her playing up.'

Drozdowski shrugged carelessly. He did not answer, but moved closer to her. She felt his hot breath, permeated with nicotine and drink.

'Be careful,' she whispered.

'Do you care what people think?'

'Are you really leaving next week? And you're leaving the hospital too?'

'Of course. There's nothing for me here.'

'Where are you going?'

'West to Silesia, Breslau . . . I'll see what turns up when I get there. Now is the best time. Everything's in confusion, the land doesn't belong to anyone. A man can take what he wants.'

'I envy you,' she sighed.

He caught her leg between his and pressed it hard.

'We could fix that.'

Kotowicz had turned to Krajewski.

'Well?' the lawyer asked, 'have you got it?'

Kotowicz made an expansive gesture.

'I'm desperate. The money was to be here at half past nine precisely. You know me, Mr Krajewski, I've never yet let you down. If I fix a time, then if an earthquake . . .'

'There's been no earthquake to my knowledge.'

The impresario made another gesture.

'Let's call it a higher force! I'll bring you the cash myself to-morrow, before noon. You can count on me.'

Mme Staniewicz, accompanied by Chelmicki, went past them smiling, on the way to her table. Kotowicz jumped up and bowed to her.

'See the young man our colonel's wife has hooked for herself?'

'So she's on her own here?'

'With the Puciatyckis.'

'High society, eh?'

He glanced tactfully behind him. Mme Staniewicz was introducing Michael Chelmicki to her friends.

Lily Hanska appeared just before ten o'clock. She hurried through the bar, smiled at Christina and disappeared into the corridor. Presently Christina joined her. Lily was taking off her light raincoat.

'How are you, dear? Lots to do?'

'Awful. I was beginning to be afraid you weren't coming.'

'I overslept,' Lily smiled. 'I slept like a log all afternoon. Isn't my face puffy?'

'Not a bit. You look lovely.'

Lily brought out a comb and began combing her thick, black, curly hair, which was cut like a boy's.

'Listen . . .' Christina said. 'Would you mind terribly if I got away at eleven tonight?'

'Are you crazy? On a Saturday? What's happened? Are you sick?' Lily eyed her attentively. 'What is it?'

'Nothing, I just want to go early.'

'A boy?'

Christina put her arms round Lily and kissed her.

'Lily, how clever you are?'

'So it's a boy? Handsome, at least?'

'Amusing. Terribly sure of himself. But don't worry, I'm not going to fall in love.'

'I should hope not. Do I know him?'

'I don't think so. I'll pay you back next Saturday.'

'Oh, all right,' Lily muttered, reaching for her powder-puff. 'You're crazy though. What about the boss?'

When she got back to the bar she was at once beseiged by an impatient crowd. However, she found a moment to look for Chelmicki. He was not at his table. Where could he have disappeared to? For a moment she was slightly apprehensive, but just then she caught sight of him at the Puciatyckis' table, with his back towards the bar. He was talking to Fred.

During the Occupation all Weychert's contacts had been with London. Since he had not realized in time which party would be most advantageous, he was a member of the Democratic Party. The fact that he was on good terms with Swiecki had certainly provided him with a convenient and reasonably well-established position on the Town Council, but he was not at all sure how things were going to turn out when the new mayor was appointed. Consequently he had been trying for some time past to get better acquainted with people in the Polish Workers' Party. He knew Podgorski, who was next to him at the table, very slightly. But even though Podgorski, like everyone else, had drunk a good deal, the alcohol had not made him more talkative. He sat dejectedly, closed in on himself and Weychert's frequent attempts to draw him into more active conversation were defeated by his gruffness.

Weychert was not touchy, but he could not help wondering whether Podgorski hadn't got something against him personally. He hastily thrust this idea aside, but doubts remained, poisoning the hitherto pleasant atmosphere. In order to wash away the unpleasant thought, he drank his vodka out of turn.

The atmosphere in the room was growing freer. At either end of the table, in particular, noisy conversations, loud laughter and gesticulations were growing more excited, for drink had loosened their tongues.

Red in the face, his hair disordered, Drewnowski had just drunk a toast with his neighbour, Matusiak, secretary of the works council in the Biala cement factory. Drewnowski leaned over to him with drunken cordiality.

'My life's been as hard as hell. Yours too, I dare say?'

'What of it?' the other muttered, 'no harm done. I'm strong.'

'That's it! Me too! And now all that's over. Now it's our turn. We're on top now.'

Matusiak eyed him from beneath black, well-defined brows.

'Think so? There's still a lot to be done. Did you ever know Stasiek Gawlik? They shot him today.'

'Don't worry about that! We're on top all the same. You'll be a director yet, just you wait and see.'

He turned to Pieniazek and clapped him on the back. 'This lad'll be a director. So will I. All of us will be. And you'll be president. Where are you going?'

The reporter, blinking his glassy eyes, was making slow, ponderous gestures with his arms and legs, apparently aimed at getting up.

'Nowhere,' Pieniazek muttered, 'I'm going to make a speech.'

Swiecki pushed his chair back a little and called to Pawlicki, who was sitting a few paces away:

'Pawlicki!'

His brief and expressive gesture behind Wrona's back at once indicated to Pawlicki what was going on. He hesitated.

'About time, eh?'

Swiecki nodded.

'Immediately. It's high time.'

'What's up?' Wrona inquired.

'A mere detail,' Swiecki replied airily.

Meanwhile Pieniazek, supported on one side by the amused Drewnowski, had finally managed to get up. But he was so preoccupied with the effort that he did not notice the massive figure of Pawlicki loom beside him. Pawlicki seized Pieniazek under the arm and, before the latter knew what was happening, propelled him swiftly from the room. Not until they were in the corridor did Pieniazek try to resist. But Pawlicki no longer needed to use restraint. Before old Mrs Jurgeluszka could open the lavatory door, he had shoved it open and pushed Pieniazek, scuttling like a spider, into the interior. The old lady hastily shut the door and was about to return to her chair and go on knitting when Pawlicki reappeared.

'A towel, please, and some soap,' he said.

She provided them hastily and gazed round the lavatory in vain. The other man was nowhere to be seen.

'That's that! You in charge here, Missus?'

'Yes, sir.'

'Good! Now mind you don't let anyone let that scoundrel out. I've locked him in there' – and he indicated one of the w.c.s – 'and he's to stay there till I come for him. The Minister said so. Get me?'

'Yes, sir. But supposing . . .'

'Supposing what? There's no supposing about it. He's to stay in there and that's that.'

'Yes, sir.'

'Don't forget, now!'

He brought a crumpled hundred-zloty note out of his pocket and gave it her. She bowed low.

'Oh, thank you, Your Excellency.'

On his way back to his seat, Pawlicki paused by Swiecki.

'That's seen to him, Mr Minister.'

Without turning, Swiecki gripped Pawlicki's hand in a friendly manner.

'Thank you, I'll remember. . . .'

The vision of an editorial office in Warsaw appeared in Pawlicki's imagination as he took his place at table again. 'Sometimes even someone like Pieniazek serves his purpose,' he thought fleetingly.

Meanwhile, Weychert had decided to have another attempt at making contact with Podgorski. He turned to him in a friendly way.

'You don't seem to be in the best of spirits today.'

'I'm tired,' Podgorski replied shortly.

'So am I,' said Weychert, snatching at this slender topic. 'We've had an unusually busy day, in connexion with Swiecki's departure. However, I must say that a gathering like this is relaxing. I remember during the war . . .'

Podgorski did not even attempt to grasp what the other man was saying. He was entirely absorbed in irritating and persistent thoughts of what he had learned about Kossecki from Szczuka. He was not concerned with Kossecki himself, but the peace that was about to start had not brought what he expected. Amidst the dying fall of cannon, the days now free of fear and nights no longer torn apart by bombs nor lit by fires, he had believed that springtime was fulfilling the hopes of the dead and the living alike. But mankind was deathly sick and weary unto death. There was no corner of earth in Europe not drenched in blood and many millions had been murdered. Their monstrous deaths now seemed simple in comparison with the fate of those whose lives had been spared, but whose hearts and spirits had died. The defeated guilty lived on in their victims. So what did the triumph of victory signify? He suddenly seemed to himself a weak man, incapable of the difficult task and sacrifices the world demanded. He doubted himself bitterly, painfully. . . .

Kalicki meanwhile, as though needing to justify himself to Szczuka, had reverted to their interrupted conversation:

'Listen, Stefan,' he began in an undertone, 'you've known me long enough to know what my life's been like, so I'd like you to understand. . . .'

'I think I do,' muttered Szczuka.

'Just a minute! I've been fighting against Russia ever since I was a boy. . . .'

'Tsarist Russia.'

'I was sixteen when I first went to gaol.'

'So what?'

'The harm lasts a lifetime.'

'What harm?' Szczuka demanded. 'I was in a Polish gaol first of all. Does this mean I have to nurse a grievance against Poland to the end of my days without ever considering what Poland really is?'

Kalicki shook his head.

'That's different. A man doesn't choose his own country.'

'Nor history either. But a man lives in order to shape both his own country and history. No, I simply can't believe you've gone so far astray in your ideas. How did it happen? You, an old fighter, a great name in Socialism, are beginning, if you don't mind my saying so, to make use of the arguments our enemies use. What will you become tomorrow?'

Kalicki was looking at the table, crumbling bread.

'Tomorrow? Fortunately I'm too old to worry about what I'll be tomorrow.'

'Do you honestly see no difference between the Soviet Union and Tsarist Russia?'

'Of course I do. It's a different system. I don't deny there are differences. But Russian imperialism and Russian aggression are the same. No, no!' he gesticulated, 'I know what you're going to say, but please spare me your propaganda. I know where I stand. The East will always be the East. That never changes. Anyhow, you'll see in a year or two. Poland won't exist any longer. Our country, our culture will all be lost, all of it . . .'

At this moment his voice broke painfully. He stopped. Szczuka also said nothing for a time.

Kalicki shivered and sat up.

'I'm sorry for you, Jan,' he whispered at length. 'Life has beaten you.'

'Perhaps so,' he said in a controlled voice, 'but my life concerns me and me alone, whereas you're losing Poland.'

'It's hard to argue with you,' Szczuka said.

'Not worth while, either,' Kalicki said shortly.

Hearing footsteps in the hall, Mrs Kossecki opened the dining-room door.

'That you, Andrew?'

He stopped by the stairs. 'Yes.'

She asked him to wait a moment, went into her room and emerged again, holding the money.

'What's this?' he asked, surprised.

'Don't you remember?' Mrs Kossecki reddened. 'I borrowed it from you earlier today.'

'Oh, that! What are you giving it back to me for, mother? I told you it didn't matter. Keep it.'

'No, no, please! You must take it.'

Her tone was such that he did not try to persuade her.

'If you say so,' he muttered, putting the money in his pocket.

She felt she was hurting his feelings, but could not explain why she did not want this wretched money and could not keep it.

'Tomorrow is Sunday. You'll be home for dinner, won't you?'

He hesitated.

'I'll see. Perhaps.'

'Do try. Your father would like it. We never really see you.'

'All right,' he forced himself to say, 'I'll try. Good night, Mother.'

'Good night,' she whispered.

It was dark in the room upstairs but he caught sight of his brother outlined against the faint starlight.

Alek was sitting on the window-sill, both arms round his knees, his head bowed. He had undressed and wore only his underpants.

'Not in bed yet?' Andrew muttered reluctantly.

Alek looked up but said nothing. His swarthy, sunburned body gleamed like bronze in the darkness. Andrew withdrew to the far side of the room. On the way he stumbled against a chair on which Alek's clothes lay in disorder. He pushed it crossly out of the way and went to the light switch.

'Mind,' he said brusquely, 'I'm going to turn the light on.'

Alek slipped silently from the window-sill. He closed the window and let the blinds down. As soon as Andrew switched the light on the room became crowded and stuffy. Alek was standing by the window, blinking in the light. He was lean and was at the stage of development when his over-long arms and legs made him look clumsy, even ludicrous. Andrew cast him a disparaging look, turned away and began to undress.

Both beds were ready for the night. He threw his jacket over Alek's and sat down on the bed to take his boots off. The right one came off easily enough but he always had trouble with the other. As he tugged at it, he felt Alek watching him. He glanced across. The other immediately averted his eyes.

'What the devil are you hanging about for? Go to bed.'

Finally he managed to pull his boot off. He threw it under the table, rose and went into the bathroom in his slippers. The bulb in there was broken and would not light, so he opened the narrow window.

The neighbouring villa looked very near in the darkness. Its first-floor windows were half-open and faintly illuminated by a light inside the house, in one of the other rooms. Soviet officers had been stationed in this house for some weeks past. Their voices were clearly audible in the surrounding silence. At some moments they seemed only an arm's length away, with their alien, singsong voices, loud laughter, or the tinkling of a balalaika. A fresh, pure tenor voice was humming a plaintive tune.

Then one of the Russians appeared in the doorway. He looked young. His bright, open shirt clearly outlined his tall and motionless shape.

Andrew stared at him tensely. So that was the enemy! One of what the colonel called the barbaric invaders, who were setting off in their millions to conquer Europe. But despite the thought, he was more stirred and moved at this moment by a sudden fellow-feeling, which made this alien and unknown man into someone almost close to him. What was the young Russian thinking about, far away from his own country, home and family, in an alien and unfriendly place? Why had he left his friends and sought solitude? Everything separated him from this man, but at the same time everything seemed to link them. He was suddenly overcome with a deathly weariness. What do such moments mean? Impulses of the heart have no meaning.

When he went back to the bedroom, Alek was lying with his face to the wall. He turned out the light and got into bed too. For a long time he lay on his back, eyes open, his hands under his head. Then Alek stirred.

'Andrew!' he whispered.

There was silence for a time. Alek sat up.

'Andrew, you asleep?'

The other turned over furiously.

'Let me alone, confound you!'

He turned to the wall and pulled the eiderdown over his ears. Alek said no more. So he closed his eyes. However, he knew he would not get to sleep for a long time. Fifteen minutes or more passed like this. A shallow doze was beginning to take hold of him when the sound of quiet, stifled sobbing reached him from the other side of the room. At first he thought he was dreaming. He raised his head. Presently he threw off the eiderdown and went over barefoot to his brother's bed, carefully avoiding the table on the way.

'Alek!' he said gently.

Alek's sobbing stopped. He was lying with his face pressed into the pillow and his legs drawn up. The eiderdown had slipped off to the floor and Andrew replaced it. Finally he sat down on the edge of the bed and leaned over his brother.

'What's up, Alek?'

He put one arm round him, and as he held him, was permeated through and through by the shivering of the slender boyish body. He felt his brother's face, feverish and moist with tears, close to his own. Emotion caught him by the throat.

'Alek, kid . . .'

He wanted to draw the boy closer but the other broke away violently and started pushing him away.

'Get away!'

'Alek!'

'Get away!'

He retreated to the far side of the bed, against the wall and curled up there like a wild creature. His eyes glittered, he was breathing rapidly. Andrew put his hand out.

'Alek?'

The other repulsed him.

'Get away, d'you hear!' he exclaimed in a stifled voice, 'I hate you, I hate you!'

Hannah Lewicka pushed her way with difficulty through the crowded room to the dance-floor. Kotowicz preceded her. Finally she reached the spotlight and noisy cries of 'Bravo!' came from all sides. She thanked her audience with a girlish, rather shy and surprised smile. The room, plunged in half-darkness and tightly packed with people, with a heavy cloud of smoke suspended over the closely-packed heads and with only this circle of brightness in the centre, now seemed larger than when fully lit. The applause died away and Hannah stood for a moment motionless, arms hanging limply at the sides of her long, bright dress. When complete silence prevailed she nodded towards the band and the violins took up the first refrain.

Enchantment fell upon the room. In the silence, undisturbed by the slightest breath, the frail and childish voice of Hannah Lewicka resounded with moving simplicity and purity.

She sang:

> *Willows, sigh no more*
> *with a sorrow that tears at my heart,*

> *don't cry, my dearest love,*
> *things aren't so bad for the partisans . . .*

Her long evening dress did not matter, nor did the artificial setting of the dance-floor and spotlight. She was a simple, ordinary girl like thousands of other Polish girls. Girls just like her had carried messages, delivered underground newspapers and orders, smuggled arms and money, loved their boys, fallen in the ranks of the executed, or on the Warsaw barricades. The words had been arranged for these fair-haired, graceful girls, they had been young wives and sweethearts, their immature bodies had been loved by boys who had learned life from love and death. Out of the woods and as if from the very heart of these bygone years, came the simple words:

> *They're playing a dance tune,*
> *and a bullet rips the bunker,*
> *death mows us down like a scythe*
> *but it's not so bad for the partisans . . .*

A heavy, indolent fever settled on the crowd like a dream. All around, in the smoke and half-light, frozen figures stood petrified, heads bowed, with listening faces, staring eyes, some full of tears, others glassy and unseeing. People who had been drunk a little earlier now looked sober. The song, carried on the little childish voice, had pushed back time, had opened up the past now tragically lost in fear and platitudes, in lies and stupidity, in the fumes of alcohol, in easy love and easy money, in cloudy illusions and vain, blind griefs, in all this confused life which was leading to what? Remembrance seized them all. The shadows of the voices of the dead, of houses that no longer existed. The shadows of landscapes, or of their own fates. But no joy had emerged from those years. Life was continuing.

The song ended, the band stopped, but the enchantment did not dissolve immediately. The silence lasted a long while and no one stirred. Only then did the applause break out, feeble and scattered at first, until it surged into a deafening uproar. The lights came on.

Chapter Seven

He awoke from a heavy sleep drenched in sweat, his heart in his throat. At first he could not make out where he was in the darkness. The room was silent, but within himself a stifled, choking shriek was boiling up. He heard it as clearly as though a man had shrieked close to him, in the dark. He sat up and clutched at his head, which was full of the suppurating uproar, but the shriek did not die down. It whined on under his skull. A penetrating shudder shook him from within. Automatically he reached for the bed-clothes and his fingers came into contact with the stiffness of the clean sheet, then with the silk eiderdown. He was at home, in his own bedroom, on the once German bed which he shared with his wife.

Mrs Kossecki was asleep next to him breathing steadily and quietly. He leaned over her but then she sighed a little and stirred. He drew back but she did not wake.

For a time he was overcome with amazement. Could any peace be more profound than this? It was night, the house was asleep, his wife was sleeping beside him and a clock ticked. He stopped shivering. He was not thinking. He leaned his head against his knees. Calm. Quiet.

Then he shivered again. Someone had cried out in the darkness. He sat up and listened intently. Had the voice been outside the house, in the street? A moment or two later he realized that that shriek had again been within himself. He could hear it all round him, in his breast, his throat, his temples. It was the shriek of a man being beaten. He moved convulsively and stiffened, as if to stifle this voice by the immobility of his body. 'It'll pass . . .' he thought. He clenched his fists so hard that his nails cut into the flesh. But the shriek was growing in strength, it was mounting, reaching along his arms. He felt that in another second all the surrounding darkness, the night in whose unseen claws he was held as in a huge cavern, would resound with this appalling shrieking. He could not bear it. He jumped off the bed and uttered the shriek out loud.

Mrs Kossecki awoke instantly. She sat up blindly and, still wrapped in sleep, reached with trembling hands for the light switch. At last she found it and the light came on.

Antony was kneeling on the floor near the bed. He looked heavy, massive and bony. His face was pallid and altered. In his striped pyjamas, with his unshapely, shaven head, he looked like a criminal out of prison. When he turned the gaze of his glassy eyes upon her, with their dead and unnaturally extended pupils, she drew back instinctively.

'Turn out the light!' he muttered indistinctly.

She obeyed at once but Antony did not stir. Crouched by her pillow, she saw the massive outline of his body, like the trunk of a tree, looming beside her out of the darkness.

'Antony! What's the matter?'

'Nothing.'

She made a great effort to control the trembling of her voice.

'Why don't you lie down?'

He did so. Silence again descended.

'Were you dreaming?'

'Perhaps. I don't remember.'

'You cried out.'

'Did I?'

'Your shout woke me.'

'I'm sorry.'

He spoke calmly and distinctly. He no longer felt afraid. Calm had returned. He lay flat on his back, eyes closed, trying to give the rhythm of sleep to his breathing. But he knew he would not fall asleep. His wife's nearness weighed upon him increasingly. Suddenly he felt he could hate her simply for being so good, faithful, mild, and devoted.

'Antony!'

'What is it?'

'I wanted to ask you something . . .'

'What is it?'

She hesitated. In the daytime she would not have had the courage to start a conversation like this. Now the darkness emboldened her.

'I keep on thinking about the way you're keeping everything to yourself, Antony. After all, I know . . .'

'What do you mean by "everything"?'

'Everything you've been through . . . I know it must have been hard, Antony, you must have lived through terrible things. But if only you'd . . .'

'If only I'd what?'

'Before, when you were worried or anxious, you always used to talk it over with me. Don't you remember?' Her voice trembled slightly. 'Am I so foreign to you, now? Can't I help at all?'

'How, for instance?'

She stopped again. 'She's going to burst into tears,' he thought. But she did not.

'Ours used to be a happy marriage, Antony,' she said quietly.

So that was it! Used to be, a long time ago . . . The past tense in all its variations. For her, life still had some sort of continuity, some single meaning flowing along in a simple stream.

'We were happy together. Twenty-two years, Antony.'

He said nothing. Twenty-two years? She might as well have said ten, thirty, even forty years. She did not understand that life could fall apart like a mouldy piece of rag. His hatred suddenly flowed away leaving not a trace behind. Nothing had any meaning, not even hatred. He had barely two days left before the end. On Tuesday afternoon he was to see Szczuka and from that moment his name would no longer be Kossecki. Everything he had done under this name over a long period of years had proved to be like so much thistledown compared to the weight the man called Rybicki could place on the other side of the scale. He imagined a courtroom and himself in the dock, listening to the long list of crimes he had committed, then sentence being pronounced. It would be in the large, high room in which he himself had judged human guilt for several years. What could he say in his defence? Everything and nothing. How rigid the paragraphs of the legal code now seemed to him, when faced with life. 'There are blemishes on a man's honour,' he imagined himself saying calmly and loudly, 'and offences which, in the name of justice, can only be left to the judgement of man's own conscience.'

Mrs Kossecki moved closer to him.

'Antony? Aren't you asleep?'

'No.'

'Don't be angry . . .'

'Of course I'm not,' he said almost kindly.

'If only you weren't so secretive, so shut up inside yourself, it would be so much easier for you. And for me too,' she added in a lower voice.

'Think so?'

'I know it. I try so hard to leave you in peace, so you can have a real rest. But I can see you're torturing yourself. I'd like to help you somehow, Antony. But sometimes I think I only bother you and you don't need me at all.'

'Why? I want to be alone for a while. For five years I was hardly ever alone.'

'Did you get beaten?' she whispered.

'Like everyone else,' he replied, after a long pause. 'Particularly in the beginning.'

'Was it better later on?'

'A little. In a manner of speaking.'

The darkness and silence seemed to remove the importance from his words. For a moment he had the impression no one was listening to what he was saying.

'Afterwards there were others to be beaten,' he said.

At first she failed to understand.

'Others? Germans?'

'Of course not! Other prisoners, Poles, Frenchmen, Italians, Russians, all kinds. Don't you see?'

'No. How could there have been others to be beaten?'

Only goodness could be so stupid, he thought. 'As usual,' he replied coolly, 'good intentions and fortunate circumstances made it possible for me to become an orderly eventually. Do you know what that means?'

'Yes, I heard about it.'

'There you are, then! One got many advantages from the Germans then. And in exchange . . . isn't it obvious? Many people did it. They managed to survive.'

Silence fell. He lay down again. The silence persisted.

'Well?' he asked at length.

'It's terrible, Antony! I simply can't believe it.'

'Believe what?'

'Just think, Antony, what must have happened to such people, even if they're never caught and punished.'

She had guessed nothing. Not even a shadow of suspicion had reached her. So much the better. He was overcome with weariness and sleep. He felt he could sleep now. But first he wanted to make sure.

'I thought you'd taken what I said literally.'

'Literally?' she wondered.

'That I did the same things myself.'

'Antony, how could you think so?'

'Why not? The camps changed people.'

'You see what I mean?' she exclaimed in an emotional voice, 'you can be proud that you lived through all those horrors and remained yourself.'

Kossecki turned over towards the wall without a word. He wanted to go to sleep.

'Good night, Antony,' she said after a long pause.

'Good night,' he answered sleepily.

Pieniazek, locked in the w.c., gave old Mrs Jurgeluszka no peace. For a long time he was quiet, then suddenly he started a violent scuffling in the w.c., shouting and banging on the door. It was not pleasant, but what could she do about it? He was bawling indistinctly, scrabbling at the door like a rat, hurling himself against the narrow partition, then he quietened down and began his scrabbling again. But she was afraid to open the door. Sighing deeply, she went back into the passage.

The noise in the banqueting-hall was increasing. Weychert, who had become discouraged by Podgorski's silence, had decided to make a very long speech. He was followed by several others and after each speech the noise of chairs being pushed back and the clink of glasses could be heard. The banquet was coming to an end with black coffee. When the waiters pushed open the door, Mrs Jurgeluszka had a glimpse of the whole room. It was very smoky and hardly any of the guests were still in their original places.

Pawlicki was just dragging Drewnowski out of the room. He

could scarcely keep on his feet and seeing Mrs Jurgeluszka, Pawlicki beckoned to her.

'Here's another customer. When he sobers up a bit, send him home. He's finished here.'

He himself was slightly tipsy but still quite conscious. As he pushed Drewnowski towards the lavatory, the latter stumbled and fell heavily against the wall. He was very pale indeed, his dank hair falling over his brow, his head sinking.

Mrs Jurgeluszka recognized him at once. She had lived near old Mrs Drewnowski for many years and remembered Frank, who was a little older than her own Felix, as a young lad. Of course, now that he had started making a career for himself and had moved into a different world, he no longer lived with his mother and only rarely called at the house in Gabarska.

'How about the other one?' Pawlicki inquired. 'He seems quiet. No bother?'

'I think he's asleep now, sir,' Mrs Jurgeluszka replied.

Pawlicki rubbed his hands together with satisfaction.

'That's the idea! He can sleep it off.'

He went up to Drewnowski and poked his fist under the latter's chin without further ado.

'Well?'

Drewnowski looked at him with befuddled eyes.

'The game's up. You can say good-bye to that career of yours, now . . .'

'Clear off!' Drewnowski mumbled.

Pawlicki laughed out loud.

'You wait, you'll be singing a different tune tomorrow. Adieu!'

Drewnowski didn't answer. His head had sunk on his chest again and he looked as though his bones had gone soft and lacked the strength to support his body.

Mrs Jurgeluszka went up to him.

'Mr Frank!'

He did not recognize her at first but she stroked his head maternally.

'Whatever made you drink so much, Mr Frank? It's bad for you.'

Drewnowski made a gesture.

'Nothing's bad for me. This is the end.'

'Whatever do you mean? The end?'

'It's the end. I went up to Swiecki and began saying something to him, but he looked at me . . . You know what he said? "I'm afraid," says he, "we shan't have the pleasure of working together any longer." Shan't have the pleasure! See what I mean, Mrs Jurgeluszka? It's all gone down the drain. I'm right back where I started.'

'Of course not. Everything will work out all right tomorrow, you'll see.'

Drewnowski shook his head.

'Nothing will work out. I know him. He's a vindictive beast. He'll do everything he can to destroy me. But don't tell my mum. Promise you won't tell, Mrs Jurgeluszka?'

'Of course I wouldn't.'

'It's all because of that Pieniazek. Bloody fool! If it hadn't been for him I'd never have got so tight.'

When he left he insisted that she take a five-hundred-zloty note. She sat down on her cane chair and took up her knitting, then started thinking. The unexpected money was a windfall, she hadn't wanted to take it, but this was how things had to go in this world: one man's meat was another man's poison. Anyhow, could anyone foresee what lay ahead? It had looked as if Frank Drewnowski would go far. He'd been lucky lately, more than most. Then all at once . . . And Felix had been longing for a new shirt for ages. He wanted a yellow one . . .

In the banqueting-room, Swiecki was rising to his feet. The noise of chairs being pushed back mingled with the general uproar. Groups talking noisily formed round the sides. No one was leaving yet.

Weychert and Pawlicki went across to the Vice-Minister.

'You leaving?' Weychert asked.

Swiecki yawned.

'I've had enough. I'm bored.'

'Me too,' Weychert agreed. 'What's happened to Podgorski, by the way? He hasn't said a word all evening . . .'

Swiecki shrugged.

'No idea. Maybe he has a pain? Anyhow, that man on my left talked far too much.'

'Wrona?'

'Yes. Still, what do you think' – and he took Weychert's arm – 'how did it all go off?'

'Very well indeed!'

'Wasn't there a little too much about me in the speeches?'

'Does that worry you? Who else could they have talked about?' Swiecki smiled.

'Don't overdo it, after all Szczuka's someone too.'

'So they say. But the future belongs to the new men.'

'That's another matter. Where is he now?'

'Szczuka? Talking to old Kalicki.'

Kalicki and Szczuka were standing at the far end of the room, smoking cigarettes in silence. The meeting they had looked forward to with some emotion had brought them nothing but disappointment. Both felt this and both knew that the evening had separated them for ever, placing an unbridgable abyss between them. They no longer had anything to talk about.

Szczuka glanced at his watch. The other man noticed.

'What's the time?'

'Nearly midnight. Time to go. Do you live far away?'

'No. Anyhow, I'll get a lift in a car.'

'Good-bye then. Look after yourself.'

They shook hands rather clumsily, instinctively avoiding one another's eyes. Kalicki stood there a moment or two longer, as if wanting to say something. However, he said nothing, merely straightened his back and nodded, then slowly went towards the exit. Szczuka watched him go. Not until then did he realize that as they were saying good-bye both had passed in silence over the meeting arranged for Tuesday. So much the better, he thought.

Christina stirred and Michael felt her hair against his cheek.

'I thought you were asleep,' he said quietly.

'No.'

He raised himself on one elbow. Her eyes were open. They looked bigger than they did in the light and moist and warm. The fine, golden gleam of her hair brightened the darkness. She lay as quietly as though she were not breathing at all.

Michael did not stir either. For a moment all this seemed almost unreal to him. This darkness, beyond time and space: the silence: the tranquillity which held the spaciousness and the terrifying transparency of sleep, this sky be-starred in its depths. And, more than anything else, this body he held in his arms whose frail shape he could distinguish in the obscurity. He had possessed it before he learned to know it, but it was not alien to him. The perfection of this moment permeated him with greater peace than he had ever felt before, or even been able to imagine. He had lain with many girls like this before but those facile episodes had been hastily snatched between other and more important matters. They had lasted only briefly leaving behind hardly any recollections. Primitive, violent, and impatient, they had ended in saturation but there was no ending here. Yesterday did not exist, nor tomorrow. He felt Christina's heart beating steadily against his chest and listened to this imperceptible movement with all his might. Finally he was not sure whether it was her heart or his own. Suddenly he was seized by a vast tenderness, an unknown emotion which made him catch his breath. He thought for a moment that he should express, even confess, everything he was now feeling and experiencing but he couldn't find the words. He simply leaned over Christina and slowly, very tenderly, as if he feared to trouble the peace and quiet, began kissing her hair, temples, and cheeks. He had never kissed a girl like this before: he had not even known it was possible. Suddenly he had the strange impression that in these kisses and in his own lips which he wanted to make lighter than air, he was finding not only Christina in the darkness but himself as well. He wanted to whisper: darling, my dearest . . . but an instinct of shame prevented him.

Christina was silent too. Her eyes were open and she seemed lost in her thoughts. What could she be thinking of? What did she feel just then?

Michael drew her closer.

'Tired?'

He hesitated. No, he could not tell her what he was feeling just then.

'It just occurred to me . . . We've only known each other a few hours, and yet it seems to me we've known each other for ages . . .'

She was silent for a moment.

'I don't know,' she said at length, 'I hadn't thought about it.'

She'd been sure he would reply to this cynically, in the way he had been talking to her hitherto. However, he said nothing. She waited a little longer but nothing happened. She merely felt his arm tremble slightly as if a brief shudder had run through it. Leaning over, he was not looking at her now. She saw the outline of his face and neck immediately above her and for a moment she wanted to kiss him and draw him close. She stifled this longing and for the first time since coming in here, she was apprehensive. She had agreed to go to his room only because she had looked on it as a meaningless adventure. She had wanted to spend the night with a nice-looking, unknown youth, that was all. He had seemed an excellent choice! She thought he would be cynical, self-assured and rather coarse. She had expected him to treat her rather like a prostitute. Yet he had proved shy in his youthful passion, delicate and tender. The silence began irritating her. She knew that silence, at times, can be more eloquent than words so she decided to break it immediately.

'I wonder whether you really thought I'd come?'

He leaned over her so closely that she felt his breath on her face.

'No, I wasn't at all sure.'

'Do you want to know why I did?'

'Yes, why?'

'It's easy! Because I couldn't fall in love with you.'

He said nothing.

'You still there?' she exclaimed presently. 'Can I have a cigarette?'

The bedside table was near him with a packet of cigarettes lying on the edge. He put a cigarette into her mouth and took one for himself. Then he reached for the matches. However, he had to remove his arm from Christina to light them. She took advantage of this to shift into the depths of the bed. The match flared in the darkness but they did not look at one another in the brief instant of light. Michael groped for an ash-tray and put it on the bed between himself and Christina. It separated them like a suddenly erected barrier and they went on smoking for some time in silence. The two cigarette ends glowed in the darkness. Suddenly he asked, 'Don't you want to fall in love, then?'

'With you?'

There was a clear touch of irony in her voice. But he did not answer as she expected and wanted him to.

'No, it isn't myself I'm thinking of. In general.'

'I don't think I do.'

'On principle?'

'Possibly. Why make life more complicated?'

'It gets that way of its own accord.'

'All the more reason, then. Why drag in more complications?'

The cigarette glow revealed the outline of her hands and arms.

'Tell me about yourself,' he asked unexpectedly.

'Myself? What for? What an extraordinary idea!'

He did not answer.

'Well, if you want me to . . .' she said presently, 'though it won't interest you. Before the war I used to live in the country. Near Mogilna.'

'And then?'

'Then we moved to Warsaw, mother and I. The Germans arrested my father right at the beginning.'

'Did he die?'

'Yes, in Dachau. What else is there to tell? That's all.'

'Is your mother still alive?'

'No, she died during the uprising.'

'So did mine. Haven't you any family?'

'No, thank goodness.'

'Why thank goodness?'

'Well, at least fewer of my close relations died.'

'I see,' he muttered, 'that's true enough. I had a brother who died in action, back in forty-three.'

'There, you see!'

'My father's in England. But I don't suppose he'll be coming back here now.'

'No other family?'

'No one close. Are you staying in Ostrowiec?'

'I don't know. For the time being, I suppose.'

'And then what?'

'I don't think about that.'

She put her cigarette out. He inhaled deeply and followed suit. He put the ash-tray back on the table. They lay in silence for a

164

long time. Finally he turned towards her and put his hand under his head.

'Sleepy?'

'No.'

Once again he felt almost painfully aware of the feeling which had seized him for the first time a few minutes earlier, when he had been holding her in his arms.

'I wasn't at all sure whether you'd come, really,' he said quietly.

Her voice came to him as if from very far away.

'You've told me that already.'

'Don't you believe me?'

'Why shouldn't I?'

'You don't know me at all.'

'Nor you me.'

'Yes, I do!'

'How can you?'

'But I do.'

It seemed to him that her body shivered a little. He drew nearer.

'Cold?'

'A bit.'

He put his arms round her and drew her to him.

'Better now?'

'Warmer, anyhow.'

She lay there in his arms and again he felt the beating of her heart against his chest. Suddenly she raised her head.

'Tell me something . . .'

'What?'

'What are you really like?'

'How do you mean?'

'You're quite different now from before.'

'Different?'

'Haven't you noticed?'

He pondered an instant.

'Well, perhaps so . . . Is that bad?'

'Good heavens,' she said quietly, 'it doesn't matter.'

But her eyes, now very wide and intent upon him, seemed to think otherwise.

'Doesn't it matter, really?'

She made no reply.

'Tell me . . .'

'I don't know!' she whispered. 'Hold me closer.'

He did so. Now she felt good. That was all. He kissed her half-closed eyes with slightly parted lips.

'You know something?' he whispered, 'I never even suspected . . .'

'Suspected what?'

'No, nothing.'

He stopped as though breathless. Then, still more quietly, he said,

'It's because of you that I'm different.'

'Is that what you were going to say?'

'No. But that too.'

'And what besides?'

Suddenly the sound of heavy footsteps, deadened by carpet, came from the passage. Michael raised his head and began listening. The key grated in the next door and a man came into the next room. He closed the door behind him and turned on the light. In the silence the sounds were as clear as if there had been no walls. Even the creaking of the floor-boards was audible.

Christina raised her head.

'What's the matter?'

'Our neighbour has come back.'

'Do you know him?'

'No.'

He lay down again but could not stop listening to the sounds from the next room. Only now did he realize that ever since Christina had come in an hour before, he had not once thought of why he was in this alien hotel room. That hour seemed to lie outside the rest of his life, cut off from everything that had been and was going to be. Now it had all come back. Szczuka could be heard opening the window.

'Everything's terribly audible,' Christina whispered.

'Yes. What are you doing tomorrow?'

'Tomorrow?'

'I mean today. It's tomorrow already.'

'I'll be in the bar as usual in the evening.'

'And in the day?'

'Nothing much. The Puciatyckis have asked me to lunch.'

'Oh, them! Are they relations?'

'Very distant ones, according to Fred Telezynski. Anyhow, I only met them today. And you too, officially, at the same time.'

'Was I silly?'

'A little. But I was the only one who noticed. Why did you join them?'

'Can't you guess?'

'You fool,' she whispered.

Szczuka was walking about on the other side of the wall, backwards and forwards along the same line, more or less in the centre of the room, with the floor creaking continually under his heavy footsteps. Michael tried not to hear. He closed his eyes tight and held Christina more closely, so as to concentrate on the caress of her fingers. Her hand suddenly stopped. On his left side, under his ribs, was a long, rough scar.

'What's that?'

'Nothing much. A scar.'

'Were you wounded? When?'

'Before the uprising. In an incident.'

'What did they call you at home?'

'At home? It varied. My father called me Mike and my mother and brother Michael.'

'And your friends?'

'Michael.'

He felt she was smiling.

'What are you smiling at?'

'I was remembering – when I was little my father used to call me Tina.'

'Tina,' he echoed softly, 'nice.'

He touched her mouth with his lips. They parted at once, moist and full of warmth. He kissed her violently as if he wanted to express not only everything he was feeling, but also to find escape and his only safe refuge. But through the roaring of blood which began pulsing within him, he continued to hear the footfalls going backwards and forwards. Beneath his eyelids in the darkness the outline of Szczuka formed, like a figure in a dream just as he remembered it when the other, bent and leaning heavily on a stick, had been going up the stairs. What harm had this man done him? Why did he have to kill him? To kill him! For the first time, the phrase sounded threatening and alarming. He had killed so often and it was so simple. Life and death moved on side by side and enemies died as did friends. The lives of both were suspended above a precipice. The death of one and the other cleared away like smoke. But this alien man who, before going to bed, was making a solitary journey between his four walls, this unknown man who was at the same time so well known, was still alive. He continued to move about, form plans, have longings, hopes and hold on to his own life. Had he a family? Did he value his life? Who needed him? Who loved him – a woman, perhaps, or a friend?

A shudder of apprehension seized him and he raised his head. His lips which had been full of Christina's mouth now felt dry and stiff.

'Are you going to lunch with them?' he asked in a stifled whisper.

At first she did not realize what he meant.

'What lunch?'

'At the . . .'

'Oh, that! What put that into your head?'

'Aren't you?'

'I don't know yet.'

'Don't go!' he whispered imploringly.

She said nothing.

'Don't go! Let's spend the day together. With you . . .'

'What?'

'You know what I mean.'

His eyes gleamed, his dark hair fell across his brow.

'Christina!'

She drew back suddenly.

'No, no!'

'No?'

'I don't want to. It's no use.'

He wanted to kiss her but she resisted.

'I don't want to, I don't . . .'

Her voice trembled and broke.

'Why not?'

'Why not? Don't you see? You'll be going away . . .'
He could not deny it.
'Yes. I've got to.'
'What's it all for, then? Tomorrow we'll say good-bye . . .'
'I'm not leaving at once.'
She shook her head.
'It comes to the same thing in the end. I don't want any part-
ings or any memories. Nothing that can be left behind. No
luggage.'
'Not even pleasant memories?'
'Not if they can be nothing but memories!'
Szczuka was still walking about in his room. When he stopped
silence fell and Michael lay down. Presently Christina leaned
over him and began stroking his hair.
'When are you leaving?'
He wanted to say 'in a week's time', but could not bring him-
self to lie.
'On Tuesday.'
'Will you be coming back?'
'I don't know. But perhaps I could still change my plans.'
'Your plans?'
'Various things. One in particular, the most important.'
'Could you?'
'Perhaps . . .'
'Why, though?'
She lay down beside him and went on stroking his hair. The
touch of her fingers had all the delicacy of kisses.
'Look,' she said, gazing into the darkness overhead, 'I've my
life, you've yours. We've met accidentally. It's been nice. What
more can we want?'
'Nothing.'
The bed creaked behind the wall. First one shoe then the
other dropped to the floor.
'Hold me close,' she whispered.
Her heart was beating very fast. Suddenly he felt her lips hot
on his throat. Just beyond the wall, water flowed into the hand-
basin.
'Dearest.'
And suddenly he felt relief, tremendous happiness, complete

and astounding delight, just as if he had expressed, with this one little word, not only his own thoughts but had also shielded himself by this oath against everything that was dangerous, painful and tangled with problematical contradictions.

'Dearest,' he repeated as tenderly as he knew how.

It was dawn and the last visitors were leaving the Monopole. The lights were being turned out in the rooms, the waiters tidying up the tables. Slomka, grunting and waving his little hands as always, was urging them to hurry. Dusk still lurked in the corners, but daylight timidly peered in through the blinds. The band were putting away their instruments. The young pianist strummed out the 'Storm company' march with one finger.

They were singing 'For he's a jolly good fellow' in the bar. The discordant voices of men and women mingled in a howling uproar. 'For he's a jolly good fellow, and so say all of us . . .'

'Enjoying themselves,' the red-haired saxophonist muttered.

Presently Kotowicz stumbled out of the bar, uncertain on his feet and waving his arms as if snatching at the air. His head had lost none of its magnificence, however, and with his hair tangled above that elevated brow, he looked like inspiration personified.

'Just a minute, gentlemen? Are you artists, or are you not?'

'At this time of night?' the violinist muttered.

'Time doesn't exist for artists, my good man. I demand wholehearted obedience. Whole-hearted!'

Kotowicz's superb appearance and the power in his voice were so suggestive that Slomka speechlessly retreated among the tables. Meanwhile the yelling in the bar had stopped. Instead there was the typical hullabaloo of drunkards starting to leave a night-club.

Kotowicz was proposing something to the musicians in a secretive whisper. They eyed each other, undecided. Kotowicz drew back and looked at them as if to judge the effect of his words.

'Well? Gentlemen!'

The young pianist who had remained in the background until now came over to his colleagues. 'What does he want us to play?'

'Chopin's Polonaise.'

'Which one?'

'Heaven knows! How can we play it?'

The pianist went up to Kotowicz.

'Which polonaise do you want us to play?'

The other eyed him contemptuously.

'In A flat, young man, A flat.'

'All right.' The pianist rubbed his hands. 'The one that goes Tam-ta-tam, ta-ra-tata-tata-tatam ... Is that it?'

Kotowicz beamed.

'That's it! Excellent! Delighted to meet you, young man. Thank you. Do you hear that, gentlemen? You have a great artist in your midst. Well now! Off we go! Not another word! No more explanations. This is a historical moment!'

Meanwhile the pianist was taking counsel with his colleagues. The fat violinist protested a good deal at first, but finally they must all have given in, for, still arguing among themselves, they began going back to the platform and taking out their instruments.

Kotowicz had withdrawn to the middle of the dance-floor when a crowd of people started to pour in from the bar. He turned towards the dozen or so people. Hannah Lewicka, who had been dancing the can-can on a table, was laughing tipsily and imitating a Negro dance with the skirt of her evening dress pulled well up. The men surrounding her – Swiecki, Puciatycki, and Pawlicki – were clapping their hands in time to the movements of her legs and haunches. Weychert, a cigar in his mouth, was shouting something to Roza Puciatycki. She, with brick-red patches on her long, horse-like face, was listening attentively, breaking out now and again into a brief, broken laugh. Mme Staniewicz and Kochanska were cuddled up to the handsome Dr Drozdowski, while the platinum blonde, now quite neglected and already thoroughly tight, was being looked after by Krajewski the lawyer. Seiffert was embracing curly-haired Lily Hanska. He was wearing light, well-pressed trousers and a loosely cut jacket, also light in colour.

Kotowicz, standing in the centre of the dance-floor, threw back his thick head of hair and flung out his arms with an expansive gesture.

'Ladies and gentlemen!'

They all stopped, startled and a little apprehensive. Even Hannah Lewicka stopped, with her dress up. Then whispers started. The extraordinary Kotowicz silenced them immediately.

'Not another word!' He made superb gestures with both arms. 'Come closer, if you please.'

Crowding together, obedient and already quite silent, they moved out on to the dance-floor. It was gloomy in this part of the room, so that when they came to a halt amidst the shadows and froze into immobility, they gave the impression of one body with many strange and confused limbs. Outside the windows the dawn chirping of birds was audible. Frail rays of light entered the depths of the room through cracks in the blinds.

Emboldened, the dish-washers moved out of the kitchen corridor one after the other. The chef peered in too, wearing his white hat. Old Mrs Jurgeluszka looked on behind him. A little page-boy clambered up on the table.

For a long time Kotowicz had been preoccupied with conjuring up a mood. He now felt it was perfect. Excitement resounded within him like an organ. He straightened himself and grew bigger, and then, with a gesture he had not used before, he stretched out his arms before him.

'Marvellous! Splendid! And now – a great discovery! The dazzling finale. A greeting to the new day! Ladies and gentlemen! Let us dance the polonaise!'

Movement started amidst the crowding people. The idea pleased them.

Kotowicz raised his voice, 'Not another word. A polonaise in couples. A gigantic procession. Our national epic!'

'Hoorah! Hoorah!' everyone applauded except Hannah Lewicka who wasn't at all sure what was happening. She wanted to go on dancing. With her skirt up, she kept moving her legs uneasily and shifting her haunches. Her girlish little face was tense with the desire to dance.

'Now – let's begin,' Kotowicz exclaimed. 'Ring up the curtain. Fine, excellent! Now, Master of Ceremonies, Mr Seiffert, come here please!'

The latter, not entirely surefooted, hastened on to the floor and more applause broke out.

'The Master of Ceremonies and I,' Kotowicz raised his voice, 'will lead the polonaise. Master, over here please. And the first pair – Minister Swiecki and Countess Roza Puciatycki!'

'Of Chwaliborg,' Weychert shouted.

When the pair emerged on to the floor, the rest of the company greeted them with cheers. Slomka clapped fervently too. Swiecki gave Mme Puciatycki a courtly bow.

'Madame, I am honoured. . . .'

'The next couple!' Kotowicz shouted, 'Count Puciatycki and the Queen of Song, Miss Hannah Lewicka!'

'It should have been Lola,' Seiffert exclaimed.

'The third couple – Deputy Mayor Weychert, and the finest of all dancers, Lola Kochanska.'

These emerged giggling and stumbling on to the dance-floor amidst the cheers of those waiting their turn.

'Next – Major Wrona . . .'

'Count him out!' voices cried. 'He's stayed behind.'

In fact, Wrona and Telezynski were the only people who had remained in the bar.

Wrona lifted his glass.

'Here's to you. My name's Edek.'

'Mine's Fred. Here's to you.'

Wrona put one arm round Telezynski.

'You're the only one of that lot who's a decent chap. You're an aristocrat, that can't be helped, but you're straight, you are.'

'You know what you can do with the aristocracy.'

'Good for you! Pity you weren't with us in the woods.'

'I was, though not with you.'

'Pity you weren't with us, though. Still, never mind. There's time for you to be one of us. But that lot in there's nothing but muck,' and he pointed to the other room.

Kotowicz was calling upon further couples. For a moment he wanted to pair off Pawlicki and Mme Staniewicz, but seeing how she was cuddling up to Dr Drozdowski, he changed his mind. Pawlicki got Lily Hanska. They were followed on to the floor by Krajewski the lawyer, with the platinum blonde who was by now in a state of mumbling stupefaction and finally came Drozdowski and Mme Staniewicz. Excitement seized Kotowicz. What grand names they all had! What a polonaise it would be!

'Zig-zag and lightning flash!' he roared. 'Strike up the band!
En avant! Hail to the day!'

To the boisterous sounds of the polonaise, in half-light and
following closely upon the gesticulating Kotowicz and Seiffert,
the couples now moved off between the tables in the direction of
the exit. The waiters and the excited, giggling dish-washers
crowded after them at a little distance. Slomka followed too.

All the instruments of the band were playing off-key. Only the
pianist thumped unerringly at the pianoforte as forcefully as
though trying to shatter it. The rhythm worked upon them all.
The couples drew out into a long procession and stiffly, rather
like puppets bowing and scraping, they moved one after the
other, identical in their movements, staring ahead with glassy,
unseeing eyes.

Slowly, as the polonaise and the crowd following behind approached the exit, the room grew emptier. When it was quite
deserted, Pieniazek suddenly loomed among the tables,
crumpled and bedraggled, still quite drunk despite several
hours' sleep. He staggered across the deserted dance-floor on
wavering legs, waving his arms about to the beat of the polonaise, bowing and scraping like the rest and moved on after them.

They were in the hall. The full light of day was shining. The
old cloak-room attendant, hardly able to stand up, hurriedly
opened the door wide. The dancing procession began to emerge
into the street stiffly and drowsily, to the music of the now
distant band.

The day promised fair. The sky was transparent and blue,
with a faint, pink glow on the horizon. The air was pure and
cool. The market-place was deserted. Kotowicz was still in
ecstasy.

'Marvellous,' he mumbled, 'splendid!'

Suddenly he roared at the top of his voice,

'Long live Poland!'

A silence followed. A few doves fluttered up from the roof of
the hotel. Then, very far away, somewhere amidst the burned-
out ruins, a wandering echo dully called back: 'Poland!'

Chapter Eight

On Sunday 6th May, Julius Szretter wrote in his diary:

'*I have long known the theory of leadership and how to acquire the traits of character necessary to a leader. But it was not until yesterday evening that I was able to apply this knowledge to myself. Previously I had only supposed, whereas today I know for sure. Yesterday evening was a decisive test for me. I passed the test and no longer have doubts.*

'*Note: I cannot count on all the boys to the same extent. Marcin B is no use. Anything can be done with Alek K. He is as soft as clay. This is both good and bad. The worst of it is that his courage derives from cowardice. But his type is necessary. He worships me infinitely and blindly which diverts and amuses me. How I relish shaping men to my will! As for Felix S, however, I am rather afraid of his independence . . .*'

He stopped writing, wanting to cross out the last phrase. He changed his mind about doing so, however. After considering for a while, he started a new paragraph:

'*Note: I should not have used the words "I am afraid." It should read: I mistrust his independence. I shall punish myself for failing to control my mental reactions. I shall not smoke a cigarette until midday. Betrayal of oneself in the face of others means stupidity. Betrayal of oneself to oneself is weakness and lack of discipline. One must be clad in iron to fetter others. Certain thoughts, feelings and reactions must be ruthlessly and mercilessly killed in oneself. One must be able to rely on oneself as on a precision tool.*

'*To revert to Felix S – I am not sure whether he and I will one day come into serious conflict. So much the worse for him. I can . . .*'

The sound of the doorbell interrupted him with the phrase

half-finished. He glanced at his watch. It was early, just after eight o'clock. He listened for a while. No one answered. His parents were staying in bed later than usual, as always on a holiday, in the room they had been sharing lately with his sick Aunt Irena. However, his mother's cousins, the two old maids, the Misses Dabrowski from Warsaw, were up already and could be heard noisily pottering about in the kitchen. But neither could be relied upon. So he put his diary away in his school satchel and went into the hall.

It was dark and so crowded with various bits and pieces of furniture that it was difficult to move. A huge cupboard occupied most of the space and boxes, baskets, and suitcases of various sizes were piled round it. An iron bed, still unmade, stood against the other wall. The Misses Dabrowski slept in it.

One of them, Aunt Fela, a small fat woman, put her head, still in curling pins, through the door. She seemed very apprehensive. Seeing Julius, she started signalling to him not to open the door. Both the Misses Dabrowski still had the feeling of living in the years of occupation and every time the doorbell rang their reaction was one of panic. He pretended not to notice those eloquent gestures. The older woman, seeing Julius pushing his way between the cupboard and bed straight for the door, whispered in a terrified voice:

'For goodness' sake, don't open it, Julius!'

'Why not?' he countered sharply.

Aunt Fela retreated hastily in confusion into the kitchen.

The early bird proved to be Kotowicz. He wore a light suit and light hat, with equally light chamois-leather gloves. In his right hand he was holding an old-fashioned cane with an ivory handle.

'Oh, I'm so glad it's you, my dear Julius,' he exclaimed. 'It's just a small matter, so forgive my calling so early. . . .'

Szretter smiled politely.

'Don't mention it, please come in. Father's still in bed, but I'll tell him you're here.'

Kotowicz removed his hat and came in cautiously.

'For goodness' sake,' he interrupted, 'I'd never venture to disturb your father at this time of day. My business is, as it were, with you, and is personal, my dear boy.'

'Oh, is it?' Szretter asked cheerfully. 'Please allow me to go first, it's terribly crowded in here.'

In his room he politely gave Kotowicz a chair.

'Take a seat, please.'

Kotowicz looked round for somewhere to place his hat. Finally he put it on the edge of the table, placed his gloves next to it and, still holding his cane, began looking round again. The unassuming, typically bourgeois furniture indicated that the room was used as a dining-room. But a bed, still unmade, stood against one wall, with an ordinary table and bookcase in the corner.

Kotowicz summoned a benevolent smile to his splendid, though rather pallid, face.

'So this is where you reside, so to speak?'

'I'm afraid so. As you can see, our flat is very crowded.'

'I know,' Kotowicz nodded. 'Janusz once mentioned it to me. It's very sad. How many rooms have you, if I might inquire?'

'Two.'

'But that's terrible! And how many people live here?'

'Six just now.'

'How dreadful,' Kotowicz exclaimed indignantly. 'To think that a man like your father, an eminent scholar . . . it's unbelievable. This must be looked into. It simply must.'

He brought out his silver cigarette-case and offered it to Julius, who declined.

'Don't you smoke?'

'Yes, I do. But I won't have one just now.'

He gave Kotowicz a light and brought him an ash-tray. Kotowicz inhaled.

'This visit is about Janusz. That's really why I've come. You're friends, aren't you? You needn't tell me, I know and am very glad of it. Janusz couldn't have chosen a better friend. No, don't deny it, please! You're too modest. I know a good deal about people, you can trust my judgement. Anyhow . . .' – he put aside his cigarette and sat upright in the chair – 'now I'm going to tell you quite frankly what has brought me here so unexpectedly. Uneasiness, my dear young man. A father's uneasiness. But why don't you sit down, my dear boy? That's right! Now, please tell me, as man to man . . .'

He broke off, leaned towards Szretter with a gesture of friendly confidence and placed one hand on his knee.

'My dear young friend, I know all about it. I flatter myself I'm the most understanding of fathers and I always treat my son as though he were a grown man. He goes off on the loose, has a good time, gets tight . . . that's his affair. I don't interfere and I don't pry. When I was his age I was up to all kinds of things too. But, my dear Julius, please try to understand my uneasiness now; the lad had a great deal of money on him. Well, perhaps not a great deal – but quite a lot, anyhow. And, what's more important, it wasn't his. It was a deposit! Do you see my point? He agreed to meet me last night at nine-thirty in the Monopole. He didn't turn up at nine-thirty, or at ten. He simply didn't come. Very well, anything might have happened, I quite understand that. I got home rather late myself last night. But he still hasn't come home, my dear boy. He simply hasn't come back. You see?'

Szretter, who had been listening attentively, made a helpless gesture.

'I don't know what to say. He must have gone off somewhere.'

'Yes, I know that. But where? Who with? A woman?'

Szretter smiled.

'I couldn't say. Possibly. Janusz never mentioned anything to me. As a rule, of course, we tell each other most things but I've no idea where he can have got to this time. I saw him last night . . .'

'Did you?' Kotowicz exclaimed.

'Certainly.'

'What time was that?'

Szretter thought for a moment.

'Before nine, I think. Yes, it must have been before nine because it was just before the storm.'

'And what did he say? Where did you meet him?'

'In May 3rd Boulevard. I was with Kossecki and Szymanski, friends of mine!'

Kotowicz made an impatient gesture.

'Never mind about them. What did he say?'

'Nothing. We didn't speak. He was with some strangers.'

'Women?'

'No, they were men. I think there were two of them and I don't know whether he even saw us. I don't believe he did. You know what the boulevard is like in the evenings, crowded and dark. . . .'

Kotowicz was eyeing him with a searching, inquiring look. He believed in the strength and eloquence of his own gaze. He was convinced no lie or evasion could hide from it. This lad was undoubtedly speaking the truth. With his frank, likeable face, his fair hair, all charming freshness and simplicity, he was the embodiment of the upright and sincere youth.

He sighed deeply and leaned on his cane.

'Where's he got to, the young fiend? He's been away for hours. It's all very well but with that money on him!'

'Don't worry,' Szretter said cordially, 'he'll turn up.'

'I should hope so. But when – that's the point? I've promised to repay the money by midday. It's the word of a Kotowicz, my dear boy! See what I mean? And what am I to do now?'

'Yes, I see.' The other frowned. 'He oughtn't to have done it.'

'No, indeed!'

'I'll mention it to him if I have a chance.'

Kotowicz gazed at him touched and warmly clasped his hand.

'Thank you from the bottom of my heart.'

Szretter smiled, revealing his even, white teeth.

'Don't mention it! We often tell each other home truths.'

'Ah, youth, youth!' Kotowicz sighed again, and rose. 'Still, you've encouraged me, my dear young friend. You've worried me but encouraged me too. And now I must be off. Remember me to your parents and please apologize to them for such an early call. And tell Janusz off properly when you see him for going off with all that money . . .'

Hardly had the door closed on Kotowicz than Aunt Fela peeped out of the kitchen.

'What is it, Julius?' she whispered, 'who came?'

'Someone to see me,' he replied gruffly.

Back in his room he took a cigarette mechanically. However, he put it down again directly. He could see Kotowicz crossing the yard from his window. He was walking slowly, stooping and leaning on his cane. When he had disappeared through the gate, Szretter brought his notebook out of the satchel, thought a moment and then began writing under the previous, unfinished phrase:

'An expected visit from that old Fool K. went off well. One reservation: at the very beginning I quite unnecessarily mentioned that we only have a small flat. I even said I was "afraid so". That was unnecessary, I am not ashamed and I don't give a damn. But I gave the old fool the opportunity of saying something sympathetic. Disgusting. It is below my dignity to allow anyone to show pity.'

Felix Szymanski lived near the market-place, on the third floor of an old block of flats. Szretter did not want to climb the twisting, steep stairs, so he went into the yard first. It was gloomy and close, full of the heavy stench of uncleared dustbins. Presently Felix leaned out of a window on the top floor, naked to the waist and holding a towel.

'Hullo!' he shouted. 'I'll be down directly.'

Szretter went back into the empty street. A low brick wall stood on the far side. Beyond it, chestnuts were in flower. Four ragged little urchins were playing beneath them and squabbling noisily over their game. The lively tune of a country-dance came from the loudspeakers in the market-place.

In three minutes Felix came down. He had two ham sandwiches.

'Hullo,' he said, 'had breakfast?'

'No.'

'Here, then,' he gave him a sandwich, 'it's lovely ham, my grandmother brought it from the Monopole.'

They walked in silence for some time, eating.

'Good, eh?' Felix asked presently, his mouth full.

Szretter nodded. Soon the other glanced sideways at him.

'Sleep all right?'

Szretter shrugged.

'Any reason why I shouldn't?'

'I was only asking. I slept all right. How about Alek? Did he get home?'

It was not far to Marcin Bogucki's. He lived in the lower part of Ostrowiec, in Rzeczna, near the river. Not until they were in the market-place did Szretter suddenly say:

'You know what, I've been talking to old Kotowicz.'

Felix blushed and halted.

'When?'

'Half an hour ago. He came to see me.'

'Honest? And what happened?'

'Nothing. It's all right.'

'Was he looking for Janusz?'

'He was more worried about the money Janusz had on him. He thought I'd know where he spent the night.'

'And what did you say?'

'Nothing much. I said we'd seen him yesterday evening. You, Alek...'

'You mad, Julius? You said we'd seen him?'

Szretter smiled tolerantly.

'You're a fool. You don't understand at all. That's what had to be said. We met Janusz on the boulevard some time before nine. He was with two unknown men. One was in his forties, tall and thin, in a dark suit... Don't you get me?'

'All right,' Felix muttered, 'so you didn't blurt anything out?'

'Me? You may have noticed, yesterday, that I'm not in the habit of blurting things out.'

The other made no reply. They turned in silence out of the market-place into a long, narrow street. Szretter was whistling between his teeth.

'Oh hell!' Felix suddenly cursed. 'You know what?'

'Well?'

'I never wanted to get mixed up in this.'

'Bah!' Szretter replied indifferently.

Bogucki lived at the far end of the street, in a one-storied wooden house. A thick, young alder tree stood green in a yard full of sunshine. The river, gleaming between the trees, flowed below.

The wooden house was as long as a barrack hut, with a dark, moss-covered roof, sinking a little with age. A narrow balcony on thin columns ran right along the first floor. A big ginger cat was sunning itself on the balustrade. Coloured garments were hanging up to dry and it was as quiet and peaceful as in the country.

Steep, creaking stairs, with a shaky banister, led to the first floor. Half-way up, Szretter stopped and looked back at Felix.

'Look here, you! Don't talk too much.'

'What do you take me for?'

Szretter smoothed his hair and knocked at the first door. A brass plate was nailed to it, bearing the almost indecipherable inscription: Stephanie Bogucki: Dressmaker.

No one answered for some time.

'Perhaps there's no one in?' Felix whispered, wiping his sweating hands on his trousers.

Szretter knocked louder. This time a door creaked inside the house and Marcin's mother opened the door: she was a small, frail woman, whom both had known for several years.

'Good morning, Mrs Bogucki,' Szretter said, 'is Marcin in?'

'Yes,' she whispered, 'good morning. Come in. Oh, and Felix too,' she said, only now catching sight of Szymanski in the background. 'I'm so glad you've come.'

They went into the hall.

'Is he still asleep?' Szretter asked.

Mrs Bogucki shook her head.

'No, he isn't asleep . . .'

She wanted to say something else, but her voice suddenly broke and she burst quietly into tears. The lads glanced at each other swiftly.

'What's happened?' Szretter asked uneasily.

Mrs Bogucki could not answer for a while. When she finally quietened down a little, she began to speak in a broken voice:

'A terrible thing, my dears . . . Marcin's been taken ill. Yesterday he had a haemorrhage. I just don't know what to do. . . .'

'A haemorrhage?' Szretter whispered.

Mrs Bogucki wiped away her tears.

'Come into the kitchen and I'll tell you all about it.'

The kitchen was bright, large and very clean. A table covered with oilcloth stood in the middle. Against one wall was a bed with a plush bedspread. A fair-haired, thin, frail little girl of perhaps eight was sitting on a low stool by the window, clutching a large doll.

Mrs Bogucki closed the door to the hall.

'Please sit down.'

Szretter went over to the little girl.

'How are you, Halina? I haven't seen you for ages.'

Her pale little face went slightly pink. She looked down and sat as quiet as a mouse.

'Halina!' Mrs Bogucki exclaimed. 'Say good morning to the young gentlemen. You know Mr Szretter and Mr Szymanski.'

Felix had gone over to her too and knelt down.

'Got a new doll, eh?'

'Ah,' she whispered shyly.

'Who bought it for you? Did Mummy?'

'Marcin.'

'And what's its name?'

The little girl smiled faintly.

'Barbara.'

When they turned back to Mrs Bogucki she began talking. Apparently Marcin had come home late the night befoie, terribly tired, had refused anything to eat and gone straight to bed.

'You know how frail he is and overworked with those lessons he gives. First of all I thought it was just that he was tired. I went out of the room for a minute or two to make him some tea and when I went back he was sitting at the table with his head down. Something told me there and then. I called to him but he didn't move, just as if he hadn't heard. So I ran over and then I saw his eyes were shut and blood was pouring out of his mouth . . .'

She started crying again. Halina, by the window, was whispering to her doll. Both boys sat with their heads bowed.

'Did the doctor come?' Szretter asked.

'At that time of day? No one would. I begged and prayed but as soon as they found out it was so far, they didn't even listen to me. It wasn't till this morning that one came.'

'What did he say?'

'What do you expect? He comforted me, like any doctor. But I know what it is. If only we were rich. . . . But as things are . . .'

She got up suddenly.

'Excuse me a minute, I think I heard him calling.'

When she had gone out of the kitchen, Felix gave Julius an

oblique look. The latter was sitting there thoughtfully. Through the half-open window they could hear the impatient tapping of pigeons picking up crumbs on the window-sill.

Presently Mrs Bogucki came back. They both stood up.

'What was it?' Szretter asked.

'Marcin would like to see you. He says he must see you. But don't let him talk a lot, there's good boys. The doctor said he wasn't to.'

In the other room the blinds had been pulled down at both windows almost to the bottom. Only narrow beams of light glimmered beneath them. Religious pictures in narrow gilt frames were hanging on the walls and a table with a sewing-machine stood by one window, with a larger table holding books and writing materials under the other.

Marcin was in bed, supported on high pillows. His face was as pale as the sheets, his cheeks and temples sunken. His nose had grown sharper and longer and his eyes glittered with an uneasy, feverish light. When he saw them coming in he tried to raise his head.

'Don't move!' Szretter called from the doorway, 'Hullo! What have you been up to?'

Marcin gazed at his friends in silence.

'Sit down,' he whispered at last.

'It's all right,' Felix muttered, 'we'll stand.'

His hands were still sweating so he kept rubbing them on his trousers. Szretter drew a chair up to the bed.

'Sit down,' and without concerning himself with Felix any more, he turned to Marcin:

'Don't you worry, old man,' he said cordially in his light voice, 'a haemorrhage isn't all that bad. Just stay in bed and rest and it'll be all right. You'll be better again by summer.'

Marcin gazed at him with glittering eyes, then his lips moved. Julius leaned towards him.

'Better not talk. You mustn't get tired.'

The sick boy shook his head.

'What did you do with him?' he whispered.

Felix shifted uneasily on his chair. The silence lasted a little while.

'Don't think about that,' Szretter finally said calmly. 'That's up to us. It's all been fixed.'

Marcin closed his eyes. With his eyes shut he looked like a corpse. He was scarcely breathing. Although the blinds were down, the pigeons tapping on the veranda were clearly audible. A large engraving of Saint Christopher with an infant Jesus in his arms was hanging over Marcin's bed. Szretter eyed it although it was a shoddy specimen of quite exceptional ugliness and incompetence.

'He's gone to sleep,' said Felix in an undertone.

But Marcin was not sleeping. He opened his eyes and looked first at Julius then at Felix.

'I want to know. What did you do with him?'

Szretter shrugged.

'Why do you want to know? I've told you it's up to us.'

'And to me.'

He clutched at the eiderdown impatiently and tried to rise but lacked strength. He fell back on the pillows. He lay still for a time.

'I want to know,' he said in a scarcely audible whisper, 'that's all.'

Felix said: 'Tell him, Julius! What difference does it make? If he wants to know . . .'

Szretter sat there thoughtfully.

'Julius!'

The latter suddenly straightened up.

'No,' he said in a hard voice and rose to his feet. 'Let's go. Chin up, Marcin, everything's going to be all right. We'll come and see you again in a day or two.'

Marcin's eyes closed again. Felix leaned over him and clumsily clasped the powerless hand lying on the eiderdown.

'Cheerio, Marcin!'

'Don't come again,' the sick boy whispered.

He said this to Felix but Julius, standing at the side, overheard.

'Have it your own way,' he said coldly. 'Chin up.'

Mrs Bogucki was waiting for them at the kitchen door. She looked at them apprehensively and searchingly as soon as they came out.

'Well? How do you think he is?'

'Don't worry,' said Szretter. 'He's very weak, but that's always the way after a haemorrhage. He'll buck up.'

She stood with her hands pressed against her breast, gazing with weary eyes at Szretter, as if to draw comfort from the sight of his healthy, youthful, attractive face.

'You think so? May God grant it. If I should ever lose him . . .'

'Don't think of that.'

Her tears were choking her and she only shook her head.

'Shall we go?' Felix stammered.

Szretter suddenly put one hand in his pocket and brought out two five-hundred-zloty bills, which he gave to Mrs Bogucki.

'Here,' he said cordially, 'take this from us. It's for medicine and for a doctor.'

She eyed it in alarm.

'What is it?'

'Money. Take it, please. Marcin and I had various things to settle.'

'I don't know whether I should, really.'

'Of course you should. Only don't mention it to Marcin just yet. We'll have a reckoning when he gets better. There's no need to bother him now.'

She was very touched.

'May Heaven reward you, my dears.'

At this moment, the feeble voice of Marcin came from the other room. Szretter wanted to go in but she prevented him.

'Wait a moment, I'll just peep in and see what he wants.'

She returned almost at once.

'He's asking for you again,' she beckoned to Julius.

'For me?'

'Just for a moment.'

On the threshold his eyes met those of Marcin's. He went over to the bed.

'What is it?'

The other made a gesture for him to come closer.

'Did you give my mother money?'

Julius hesitated.

'Yes. So what? Stop acting like a hysterical fool.'

Marcin did not answer. He suddenly raised his head and called out:

'Mummy!'

She hurried in at once.

'Mummy, that money . . . you know . . .'

Mrs Bogucki was embarrassed.

'What money, son?'

'You know. Please give it . . . put it on the table. . . .'

She stood there helpless, not knowing what to do. Marcin raised his head.

'Mummy!'

She looked at Szretter, as if to seek help from him.

He was staring at the floor. She hesitated a moment, then produced the money and placed it on the table. Marcin, who had been watching her tensely all the time, lay back on the pillows.

'Thank you, Mummy. And now please leave us alone.'

When she had gone out, Szretter exclaimed,

'What on earth do you think you're doing? You've got to have money to get better.'

'I don't want that money.'

His forehead was moist with sweat and his eyes sunken into his face. He looked even paler than before.

'Take it . . .'

'If you say so . . .'

He put the money into his pocket and had turned to go when Marcin whispered:

'Julius!'

'What is it?'

He guessed rather than heard that the other wanted him to lean over. Controlling his distaste he did so.

'Don't be angry with me, Julius. I can't help it. But I believed in you so much, you were my best friend . . .'

Out of breath, he closed his eyes. Presently he reopened them.

'Julius!'

The other stood motionless, an indifferent expression on his face.

'What now?'

'I don't want you to feel badly on my account. . . .'

'Me? Don't worry about that.'

'Believe me, nothing matters in life now.'

'Is that so! Well, it's up to you. Is that all you wanted to tell me?'

'Yes.'

'Look after yourself, then. Cheerio.'

He turned and went out. When they were on the stairs again a little later, after saying good-bye somewhat too hastily to Mrs Bogucki, Felix asked in an undertone:

'What did he want you for?'

'Nothing much.'

Quickly, without looking back at Felix, he went down the stairs. The other caught up with him in the street.

'Oh Jeez,' he muttered, wiping his face and neck with a handkerchief, 'what a business! I'm sweating like a pig.'

Szretter walked on in silence, taking long strides, his hands in his trouser pockets, whistling. They were following a path between alder trees, which crossed uneven, wild land by the river-bank. It was shady here and smelled moist. The path was still muddy from the previous night's rain and birds were chirping loudly in the thickets. Some naked lads were bathing at the other bank. Shouting and pushing, they scrambled up an overhanging willow and jumped off it into the water.

'Julius!' Felix exclaimed.

Szretter was in front, still whistling through his teeth.

'Well?'

'Think he's going to kick the bucket?'

'Don't know.'

'Too bad about him. But it's got him.'

He broke off a twig and pulled off the leaves, then began hitting low branches along the path.

'Admit it, Julius,' he exclaimed presently, 'it got you too, didn't it? You were a bit scared, eh?'

Szretter suddenly stopped and turned round.

'What was that you said?'

Felix gazed in amazement at his altered face.

'What do you . . .'

'Say that again!'

He came closer to him. He was almost a head taller. Fear

passed across Felix's slanting eyes. However, he tried to put a bold face on it.

'Don't be silly. What's come over you all of a sudden? Think I'm afraid of you?'

Szretter stared at him for a little while with narrowed eyes. Suddenly he stepped back, took off his jacket, threw it to the ground, straightened up and smoothed his hair.

'Well?'

Felix glanced at him sideways.

'Want a fight?'

'Come on! Less talk.'

Felix thought a little. Finally he began slowly taking his jacket off. He considered for a moment or two what to do with it. It was his only good holiday coat. Finally he put it down carefully on the nearest bush. Then he started turning up his sleeves phlegmatically. Szretter watched him coolly.

'Ready?'

'Hold on! What's the hurry?'

And he went on rolling up his sleeves. His arms were strong and thick, taut with muscles. He was ready, then suddenly rolled his shirt-sleeves down again with a violent gesture.

'No! I'm not going to fight you.'

'Afraid?'

'No, I'm not afraid. But I don't want to.'

He picked his jacket off the bush and put it on again.

'Funk!' said Szretter, in his light voice.

'I'm not.'

'What then?'

'I don't want to fight you, see? I'd fight anyone else but not you.'

'Why not me?'

'Because I won't.'

'Have you thought about what happened yesterday?'

'What do you mean!' Felix protested. 'You crazy?'

'What is it, then?'

'Oh, Jeez, Julius, are you off your nut altogether? Shut up, and listen to me. Are you our leader or aren't you? If not I'll fight you at once. . . .'

'You don't want to beat me, is that what it is? You're so certain you'd win?'

Felix kicked at a stone lying in the path.

'It isn't that. I don't want to try, that's all. Do you mind?'

He stood sulkily, sideways to Julius, stubbornly kicking at the damp earth with his heel. Szretter suddenly brightened up.

'Felix?'

'Well?'

'Give me your hand. I see your point. You're right.'

Felix turned briskly, his eyes laughing.

'And I'm sorry,' said Szretter, simply.

'Don't mention it,' the other stammered. 'Let's go.'

Presently, by taking short cuts, they reached the high road leading to the Settlement. Alek was waiting for them and when they called he came out into the garden. He was paler than usual but in good spirits.

'Hey, look at that!' Felix looked at him with admiration. 'New trousers?'

'Like 'em?'

'Not bad at all. But I'd like 'em better on me. Hey, a new shirt too?' and he touched the fine, flaxen material.

'Ah!'

'It's all right for you,' Felix sighed, 'you have a fine time of it, you do. But I'm going to get a new shirt too. I'm going to buy it tomorrow. It'll be a smasher, I tell you.'

Although it was still morning, the sun was warm. Crowds of people were thronging the bathing-beach which stretched along a good distance of the sandy river-bank below the bridge. There was no shade, and it was hot. The veranda café, built just before the war, was now only black and burned-out ruins. The changing-cabins had been burned down too. Several Soviet soldiers were lying on the thin grass which covered the hillocks leading to the beach. Lorries and Army trucks kept passing along the road. Clouds of white dust were blown by the wind straight on to the beach.

Leaning over the balustrade of the bridge, they looked for a time at the people sun-bathing and swimming.

'Look there!' Felix suddenly exclaimed, 'nice girls, eh? Suppose we stay here?'

'Don't worry,' Alek said, 'you'll find girls on our beach too. Only last night, I met two . . .'

'All right, let's get going,' Felix decided.

They bought three ices from a street hawker and crossed over to the old town. The place they had used before the war for bathing and sunning themselves was outside the town, near the meadows bordering the Kosciuszko park.

On the way Szretter began telling Alek about Kotowicz and their call on Marcin. He listened indifferently, without a trace of surprise or emotion, without interrupting or asking questions. A sunny half-smile played on his lips, his head was bent back and his absent gaze wandered across the tall riverside poplars.

Szretter was not sure how much of what he was saying got through to Alek.

'Hey, you!' he exclaimed at last, with a touch of impatience.

Alek was watching a small fluffy cloud slowly move across the sky.

'What?'

'Mind you don't get muddled up. We've all got to say the same thing.'

Alek laughed carelessly.

'Don't worry! But d'you know something?'

'Well?'

'It's not a bad idea to say we met Janusz. It's pretty good in fact. But I'm not so keen on those two geezers. Listen, it's all very well saying he was with two men, only we can't describe them too well. Their height, or what they were wearing and so forth. That'll look fishy. As if we'd agreed on it. It was too dark at the time. And what concern was it of ours, anyway? He was going somewhere, that's all. If it had been in the daytime then it would have been different, see?'

The other was silent. Alek glanced at him with a rather pitying half-smile.

'Surely you didn't describe them to his old man?'

'No,' Szretter muttered, 'I said there were two of them, that's all.'

Only now did he realize he was justifying himself to Alek. He bit his lip.

'That's all right, then,' Alek praised him. 'In my opinion it's best to say as little as possible in cases like this. Nothing definite, either. It could be, perhaps, and so forth.'

Felix clapped him admiringly on the shoulder.

'That's the idea! He's right, Julius, isn't he? I don't like saying too much either. But you were lucky not to be with us at Marcin's. He's a goner, I tell you.'

'It's his own fault,' Alek shrugged. 'Why doesn't he stick to his own affairs? He's not suited to this sort of thing and he's paying for it.'

'That's so,' Felix muttered, 'but it's too bad, all the same. He was a decent kid.'

Szretter had not uttered a word. He was walking along the embankment, thinking, his dark brows frowning and hands behind him.

'What's eating you?' Alek suddenly asked him.

'Me?'

'There's something, isn't there?'

'You're imagining things.'

The other did not regard the matter as closed and turned to Felix.

'Don't you think he looks worried?'

'Wasn't it here somewhere?' Felix looked round at the river.

'A bit farther on,' Alek replied. 'Don't say you've forgotten already.'

They were now following the low bank, at the water's edge. A thick osier bed grew on the far side. It was deserted and quiet and the air above the undergrowth buzzed with flies. Frogs were jumping about in the grass and now and again the water splashed. The red roofs of the last houses in the Settlement stood out clearly on the opposite slope.

The only person they met on the way was an elderly man, fishing. He was sitting on a small folding stool, all the vigilance of his plump body concentrated on his rod, of which the float was peacefully rocking on the water not far from the bank. His jacket lay carefully folded beside him. On it was the Sunday issue of the *Ostrowiec Echo*. On the other side was a small bottle of water.

As Felix passed, he peeped into his basket. The fat man, intent on his float, did not even stir.

'Well,' asked Alek, when they had gone a little way, 'had he caught anything?'

Felix made a pitying grimace.

'Two measly sprats. Fancy a fat old bloke like that bothering! Just look' – and he turned round - 'how he's keeping his belly up on his knees. Looks funny, eh?'

Alek turned and burst out laughing. From a distance the fat man looked very ludicrous. Only Szretter showed no interest. He was still silent, a few steps ahead of his friends. Suddenly he halted. He looked clearly disappointed.

'Now what?' asked Felix.

'Don't you see? Some other lot's got our place.'

And in fact, two people – a man and a woman – were sunbathing a dozen or so paces away, in a spot where the fresh grass seemed from a distance denser than elsewhere and which, on the very brink of the river, was shaded by a thick clump of willows.

'Confound them!' Felix exclaimed. 'But why bother about them, lads? Let's get down there and get undressed.'

Alek stopped him.

'Hold on a bit, what's the hurry?'

'I want to get my things off and have a nice lay down.'

'Let's go farther. It's nice along there, beyond that turn.'

'Why should we? Honestly, you're a funny lot, you are! Afraid of other people. . . .'

'And you're a fool! With that lot near we shan't even be able to talk freely.'

'All right, so we won't talk. I want to get sunburned.'

Szretter interrupted the squabble briefly and decisively.

'Don't talk so much, let's go.'

'But I'm going to our place,' Felix insisted.

'That's up to you. I'm going farther.'

Felix sighed.

'Honestly, you're a funny lot, you are . . .'

They walked on together in silence. Then Felix halted.

'Look, she's nice, that girl. Not bad, eh? You can do as you like, but I'm staying here.'

Pretending to tie up his shoe-lace, he dropped behind them. Not until he set off again after his companions and noticed Alek nod to the couple as he passed did he change his mind. He walked past them both quite slowly, in order to have a good look. Both were young, she a fair blonde, sun-tanned to a fine gold, and he well-built and swarthy. A feeling of envy seized Felix.

'Oh hell!' he muttered to himself, 'It's all right for them.'

And he caught up with his companions.

'Here, Alek! Do you know them? Who are they?'

'He's a friend of my brother's.'

'Is he? And who's she?'

Alek shrugged.

'I don't know. Some tart or other.'

'Come off it! She doesn't look like a tart.'

'Should she?'

'Why not? They're easy to recognize.'

'Oh dry up,' Alek laughed mockingly, 'and what do we look like?'

Felix reddened a little.

'Us! What about us?'

The other clapped him protectively on the arm.

'You know, Felix, you're a decent chap, only sometimes you're a bit dense. Suppose Julius tells you what we look like?'

He left the path and looked round the river-bank.

'Come on,' he beckoned to his companions, 'this place is all right.'

Alek started undressing quickly and soon straightened up in his red bathing-trunks. The others were still on the path. He beckoned to them again, but when this had no effect, he shrugged, turned on his heel and ran lightly down to the bank and jumped into the water. For some seconds he was out of sight. Finally he surfaced in the middle of the river, shook his head, pushed his wet hair back and started off in a rapid crawl towards the opposite bank.

'He swims nicely,' Felix muttered admiringly, 'let's get undressed, eh?'

Szretter agreed in silence. Felix was ready first. He hid his torn, sweaty, socks in his shoes and pulling off his loose, woolly underpants, he glanced uncertainly at Szretter, who was slowly unfastening his shoes.

'Going in, Julius?'

'You go. I'll sun-bathe a bit.'

Felix was still hesitating. He shifted from one foot to the other and rubbed his hairy chest with both hands.

'Go on, then!' Szretter exclaimed impatiently. 'You want a nurse or something?'

Alek meanwhile had landed on the other bank and was shaking the water off himself.

'Felix!' he shouted, 'Come on in, it's lovely and warm.'

When the other finally had plunged in, Szretter stripped and stretched out on the grass with his hands under his head. The sun was shining from behind, so he could keep his eyes open. The sky stretched above, very high, perfectly blue, still and cloudless. He thought of nothing. Suddenly he was overcome with weariness and sleep. Swallows were darting about overhead with shrill cries. A cricket chirped somewhere nearby. Blackbirds were whistling in the osiers. Suddenly it all quietened down and the silence grew profound and motionless, just as the sky overhead was vast and motionless. He closed his eyes and waited tensely for some sound to break this all-pervading tranquillity. It lasted a long time, or so it seemed to him. He was about to sit up when the grass rustled very near him. He opened his eyes. Alek was standing there. Drops of water glistened on his dark skin. His wet hair hung forward over his forehead. He pushed it back, but it fell down again. So he left it alone and stretched out his arms indolently.

'Aren't you going in?'

'Not yet. Where's Felix?'

'On the other side, the sun's hotter over there. Better for getting sunburned.'

'What did you come back for?'

'Me? I wanted to talk to you.'

Szretter was silent for a long time. He gazed indifferently and somewhat sleepily at the unchanging blue and cloudless sky. The blackbirds in the osier-beds were whistling very loudly.

'Well?' he said at last.

Alek sat down beside him and rested his chin on his knees, which he clasped with both hands.

'When are you going to see that man?'

'What man?'

'You know, the one with the guns.'
'Oh, that! Never you mind. I'll handle it.'
'Think so?'
'Quite sure.'
'Then you're wrong, because we're going to handle this business together.'
'You and me?'
'Yes.'
'All right. You can pretend what you like. Now let's pack this up, see?'
'Certainly, providing you agree. But . . .'
'More "buts"?'
'From now on you needn't count on me any more. I'm telling you this straight. So as to avoid any misunderstanding.'
'Thanks for putting it so straight.'
'Don't mention it. You'd do better to congratulate yourself on being efficient. Losing three people out of four within twenty-four hours isn't doing too badly at all.'

Szretter jumped up violently, pale, his face altered. Alek eyed him with a mocking smile.

'Cut it out, Julius. Keep that for the others. It looks all right, but it doesn't impress me.'

It looked for a moment as though Julius was about to explode. He controlled himself, however, and lay down again on the grass.

'What is it you want, really?'
'I don't want anything. I'm telling you that's what!'
'All right, then. So what is it you demand?'
'Listen to me. Since yesterday our position has altered. There were five of us, now there's three. That's not enough. We've got to change it right away. Now that we've got some cash, guns . . .'
'Not yet.'
'But we're going to have. There must be more of us.'
'Supposing there must? What then?'
'You organize one group of five, I'll organize another. With equal rights.'
'Suppose we do. What then?'
'Then? We'll coordinate everything we do. We two will be the administrative centre. The others will carry out the orders.

As for our campaign, we must first of all get a lot of money. It doesn't matter how. Anyhow. We've got to have money. We'll organize two straightforward secret military units. That's how big things start. You'll see!'

Szretter turned over and rested his head on one hand.

'This isn't a new idea. You're repeating my own plans.'

'All right, what if I am? But you wanted to direct it all by yourself. And that doesn't suit me.'

'Since when?'

'Since now.'

'And I suppose you want me to give you an answer at once?'

Alek rose and lazily stretched his arms.

'No, not at once. I'll wait. I'll give you fifteen minutes. I'll swim over to Felix and be back in fifteen minutes. Think it over.'

Szretter watched him go. He walked lightly, stepping like a boy. His over-long legs looked even longer and thinner from behind.

He looked back at Julius from the bank and grinned defiantly. 'Don't get sore!' he called, 'it might spoil your looks!'

Szretter stretched out on his back. Again he had the calm, soundless sky overhead. But the sun had risen somewhat higher and its blinding glow began hurting his eyes so he closed them. The hot air resounded with the thin buzzing of flies. A blackbird whistled briefly in the osier-bed. It stopped. Another answered from a distance.

On holiday afternoons in spring and summer, crowds of people made it a habit to go to the Balabanowicz café which had long been famous for its iced coffee and ice-cream. During the occupation it had been open, like the Monopole, for Germans only, and only now that the summer balcony had been open for a few days had it reverted to its pre-war look.

Michael Chelmicki and Christina were sitting at the far end of the terrace, up against the freshly painted railings. The latest news was being broadcast from the loudspeakers in the square: the German forces were collapsing; twenty salvos from 124 cannon had been fired in Moscow to celebrate the victories of the II Belorussian Front; units of the British IInd Corps had occupied

Denmark; Danish resistance forces had seized Copenhagen; since the Allied armies landed in Normandy, the number of German prisoners amounted to five millions; the mass surrender of German forces in the north had been followed by the surrender of the Austrian and Bavarian group; three German armies had surrendered to the American and French VIIth army; General Patton had launched an attack in Czechoslovakia; an uprising had started in Prague on Saturday afternoon, by evening most of the city was in the hands of the insurgents. Soldiers of the VIIth American army had captured Frank, the former Governor-General, near Berchtesgarten.

The last piece of information was followed by loud whisperings on the balcony. People stirred energetically at their tables.

Michael leaned towards Christina.

'Hear that?'

At the sound of his voice close to her, she awoke from her daydream.

'What?'

'They've caught Frank.'

'Have they?'

'Do you think they'll hang him?'

'I suppose so.'

He eyed her attentively, with affectionate uneasiness.

'What were you thinking about? Don't you want to tell me?'

'Why shouldn't I?' she smiled rather sadly. 'I was thinking about something I really oughtn't to be thinking about but I've stopped now. Don't look so reproachful.'

'I'm not.'

'What is it, then?'

'Don't you know even yet?' he asked quietly.

They gazed at one another for a while. Warm sunbeams illuminated Christina. Sometimes, as the wind stirred the chestnuts, light, soundless shadows crossed her face, hair and arms.

'You've got us sunburned,' Michael said in a stifled voice.

'Have I?'

She looked rather absently round at the people crowding on all sides, then at the crowd filling the pavement and at the chestnuts in the sunlight.

'What is it?' he asked.

'You know, sometimes it all seems unreal . . . the whole day. But sometimes it seems too real.'

'But tell me, though' – he leaned his elbow on the table – 'wasn't it nice?'

'Too nice.'

She glanced secretly at her watch. He noticed and said: 'You've time yet.'

'Not much. I'll have to go home first and change.'

'I'll come with you, shall I?'

She nodded: 'But don't come to the bar.'

'Don't you want me to? Why not?'

'No, I'd sooner not see you there. Have dinner somewhere else, will you?'

'But you'll come up later?' he asked uneasily.

Lights and shadows were continually crossing her face, her eyes were permeated with the same warmth and moisture as at night.

'Of course! Are you still uncertain?'

'More than yesterday.'

'Silly!'

'Well, you see . . .'

'What?'

'If one wants something very much, how can one be sure?'

She did not reply.

Suddenly a loud voice addressed them: 'Hullo there, Christina!'

Both looked round. Not far off, by the railings, was curly-headed Lily Hanska, in a white sports skirt, with a tennis racket under one arm. She was waving her other hand gaily to Christina.

'Who's that?' he asked in an undertone.

Before she could answer Lily Hanska had squeezed into their corner.

'I've found you!'

Christina smiled.

'We're not hiding. You haven't met, have you? Mr Chelmicki – this is Lily Hanska.'

Lily gave Chelmicki her hand gazing at him with intense and unconcealed curiosity.

'I know you by sight. You were in the bar last night, weren't you?'

'Yes, I was.'

'But you're not a local?'

'No.'

'He's leaving in a day or two,' Christina put in.

'Are you? So soon? But you'll be back?'

'Most likely.'

'Aren't you sure?'

'Really, Lily!' Christina protested.

The other girl laughed, leaned over the railings, put her arm round Christina and kissed her cheek.

'Don't be cross, dear. I congratulate you,' she whispered, 'he's a nice-looking boy.'

And she looked at Chelmicki again.

'I'm talking about you, so don't listen.'

'Been playing tennis?' Christina asked.

'Mm. But I played like nothing on earth. You were lucky to get away early last night. Guess how long it went on?'

'Till morning, I dare say.'

'But you'll never guess what happened.'

And she began telling them about the previous night. That Weychert had kneeled before Roza Puciatycki, Hannah Lewicka had taught Swiecki to swing, Seiffert had been slapped in the lavatory by a young man, how Puciatycki had invited everyone to Chwaliborg in a year, the platinum blonde had made a hysterical scene about Dr Drozdowski, while Mme Staniewicz and he . . . in a few minutes she had described everything and everyone.

Chelmicki and Christina listened without being at all sure who the people were, nor what situations she was describing.

'What about Fred?' Christina asked.

'Fred? Let's see . . . Oh yes, he got drunk too. He quarrelled with old Puciatycki, then made friends with Wrona, you know, the Security man . . . Well, have a good time, I must rush. Good-bye' – she gave Chelmicki her hand – 'we're bound to meet again. You're nice. Bye-bye, dear . . .'

She kissed Christina's cheek and whispered:

'You can be ill again today. Don't worry, I'll stand in for you.'

'Will you really?' Christina gazed at her in surprise, 'you're joking!'

Lily shook her curly head.

'Not at all! Bye-bye.'

'Just a minute. How can I thank you?'

Lily rolled her eyes comically.

'What won't we do for love? Bye-bye!'

Michael sighed with relief when she had gone.

'Didn't you like her?' Christina asked.

'I don't know. A bit . . . crazy, isn't she?'

'A bit. But she's very brave. She supports her entire family and you'll never guess what she said at the end.'

He shook his head.

'Well . . . we've got the whole evening free. I needn't go to work. Lily will stand in for me.'

'Really? That's marvellous!'

She was watching him chin in both hands.

'Guess what else? I'm very glad.'

'My dearest . . .' he whispered fervently and leaned across and kissed her mouth hard.

'Yum-yum!' shouted a youth going past.

Both laughed but all at once Michael grew grave.

'What is it?' she asked anxiously.

'Listen . . . I want to tell you something . . .'

'Nothing sad?'

'No. Well, I don't know. I was thinking of it last night. And today. Only you mustn't laugh at me.'

'Tell me what it is first.'

'I'd like to change certain things. Arrange my life differently. It's hard to put into words. . . .'

'You don't need to,' she said quietly, 'I can guess.'

'Can you?'

'Is it so hard, then?'

'You see I haven't ever made up my mind before about things, they've worked out by themselves. Get me?'

'Yes.'

'But now it all seems somehow different. I want to live like other people. To study. I've got my matric. I could enrol at the Polytechnic. Listen . . .'

She was listening intently, as though considering herself.

'Well?'

'And how about you?'

'Now look,' she eyed him reproachfully, 'you weren't to talk about anything sad.'

'Is it sad?'

'Perhaps none of it will come off. You're not entirely independent.'

'I know that. But I can try. I'll do anything I can. I have a friend here whom a lot depends on.'

'The man you were with yesterday?'

'Yes. I'll explain it all to him, he's bound to understand.'

She suddenly recalled his conversation with Andrew the previous evening.

'My dearest,' he said unhappily, 'if only I'd known yesterday what I know now!'

'I shouldn't have come to you, then,' she whispered.

'Tell me,' he exclaimed presently, 'would you come away from here?'

She nodded.

'Honestly?'

'Why not? There's nothing to keep me here.'

He hesitated a moment. Then he put one hand uncertainly upon hers.

'To think,' his voice trembled, as if hope and apprehension together were flowing through him, 'to think that I never knew before what love was . . .'

'And now?'

'It's you,' he whispered fervently, 'you are love.'

'Is he here?' asked Alek.

Szretter looked round the balcony attentively.

'I can't see him.'

'Perhaps he's over on that side by the square?'

'Could be. Come on.'

As they were walking round the railings to the café, Chelmicki and Christina left the balcony.

'There's young Kossecki,' Michael said, pleased to see him, 'just a minute, darling.'

He left Christina and quickly caught up with them.

'Alek!'

The latter turned hastily.

'How are you?' Chelmicki greeted him, 'listen, will you tell Andrew I've got something important to see him about and I'll call tomorrow evening. Don't forget, will you? Before eight o'clock tomorrow.'

'Right,' Alek replied, 'I'll tell him.'

'Thanks. How was it by the river?'

Alek smiled.

'Lovely!'

Szretter was waiting for him. When Alek joined him, he gave him a questioning look.

'Nothing important,' said the other. 'How about him, is he here?'

'Yes. At the last table. That fair-haired bloke. He's with someone else.'

Alek looked that way.

'Just a minute. I've seen him somewhere before.'

'I dare say,' Szretter muttered.

Alek tried to remember and finally said:

'He's Klimczak, isn't he? He was in our class. He took his matric just before the war and your old man used to say he was the best historian in the class. Isn't that him?'

'That's it.'

'So that's how I know him! And who's the other man?'

'I don't know. Never saw him before.'

'Let's get going.'

'Hold on.' Szretter prevented him. 'There's no telling who the other one is.'

'So what? If your man's one of ours . . .'

'He's all right. He's too involved in various things not to be.'

'Well then?'

The other, however, had caught sight of them and was beckoning. He was a young man of medium height, small and slight, with a lively, ingenious face, and smooth, fair hair. His companion looked about the same age. He was a well-built blond and handsome in a simple way. A carafe of vodka stood on their table, with soda-water in tall glasses.

'Hullo there,' Klimczak greeted Szretter cordially. For a moment he eyed Kossecki sharply.

'Don't I know you?'

'Of course,' Alek replied easily.

'At school?'

'That's it.'

'Good! Sit down, then. This is a friend of mine' – and he indicated his companion – 'you can talk freely. He's one of us. Hasn't been long, of course, only recruited today, but never mind that. There's rejoicing in the land for every conversion. He's been exposed, by the way, to higher authority . . .'

'Shut up, Edek,' the other muttered, 'what are you going on about?'

'Well, you ashamed of it or something? These chaps are all right, nice fellows, I used to go to school with 'em. He's a decent chap too, I tell you, but he hasn't found the right way yet. He wanted to make a career for himself in the Communists' offices. Frank, I tell you you'd have been wasted if you hadn't got yourself tight and made that muck-up of it all. Your better instincts awoke in you. You sorry?'

The other shrugged.

'Why should I be? But don't talk so much.'

'Right! Just a minute, we want some more glasses for these lads. Don't worry even if anyone sees you. You're with an old school-mate, see? Why not? Waiter!' he called to a waiter standing in the café door, 'two glasses! And two sodas.'

Presently he poured the vodka out dexterously.

'Here's to us! Drink up! When it's hot, soda-water goes down best on vodka.'

'That's fine!' He rubbed his hands when they had drunk. 'Now to business. Got the cash?'

'Yes,' said Alek.

'How much?'

'Ten tenners. The rest on delivery.'

'O.K. The goods'll be ready tomorrow. Where d'you want them?'

This time Alek loyally left the reply to Julius.

'In the park,' said Szretter. 'Six p.m. By the second pond.'

'That's a hell of a way!' Klimczak complained. 'Can I get an ice-cream cart that far?'

'Of course you can,' Alek assured him.

The other reflected briefly.

'O.K.!' he decided at last. 'They're bright lads, eh, Frank? Thought it all out very neatly. That's what I like to see.' And he sipped a little soda-water. 'Let's get this business over and we can get away the day after tomorrow. The two of us are going up to the coast to look around. We need a change of air. The climate here doesn't suit you, does it, Frank?'

'You talk too much,' the other replied stormily.

'All right, I've finished. Now there's only the cash and I'll see you tomorrow.'

Szretter reached into his pocket for the envelope of money but Alek nudged him under the table.

'Mind!' he muttered, 'the old geezer's coming.'

Szretter glanced into the street and straightened up.

'Just a minute, fellows,' he said coolly.

Kotowicz, in the light suit he had been wearing that morning, youthfully erect and cane in hand, was walking along the pavement. Casting brief glances round he was obviously making for the balcony. Szretter got up quickly. They met at the balcony entrance.

'Ah!' Kotowicz exclaimed, pleased. 'Good evening, my dear boy!'

He shook him by the hand fervently.

'Is Janusz back?' asked Szretter.

Kotowicz frowned.

'And he'd better not come back, either! My dear boy, do you know what he's exposed me to? The shame of it? The unpleasantness?'

'Of course I do. But I don't see . . .'

'There's nothing to see. It's obvious. Only too obvious, alas. The rotter!'

'But suppose something's happened to him?'

Kotowicz raised his bushy brows in surprise.

'Him? My dear man, you don't know him. No use talking about it. The scoundrel has either cleared off with the cash or with some tart. I know my own son. Unfortunately he's cast in a different mould from you. That can't be helped. The Lord doesn't bless all of us with good children. A cuckoo can turn up in the best of nests. So what? No, you'd better write off your friend, he's not worth bothering about, I, his father, say so.'

Bidding good-bye to Szretter, he moved on to the balcony, raising his hat now and then with a cheerful smile in response to greetings. He knew all the locals and was himself a widely known figure.

Mme Kate Staniewicz was sitting with Dr Drozdowski and caught sight of his splendid outline. She started waving and distributing salutations on the way, he reached their table.

'How are you, my dear lady? And you, doctor? How very nice to see you. And how are you?'

'Fine!' Mme Staniewicz smiled, 'after the good time you arranged for us!'

In her broad-brimmed straw hat and flowery spring dress she did not look much more than thirty. Drozdowski, in a light linen suit, with his black hair and olive skin looked more than ever like a Spaniard or Italian.

Kotowicz glanced at the empty chair.

'May I?'

'But of course, please do! I've been longing to see you.'

'Dear lady!'

'Do you know why? There's a favour I very much want to ask of you.'

'At your service,' he placed one hand on his heart, 'for you—everything.'

'But this is a very materialistic business, alas.'

'Never mind. Man doesn't live by the spirit alone.'

'Quite right,' Drozdowski interposed, 'as a doctor, I know something about that. Do you mind if I put the proposal to our friend?'

'Oh do,' she exclaimed, 'I don't know how to discuss such things. I simply don't know the first thing about them.'

Drozdowski pulled his chair up to Kotowicz.

'Mme Staniewicz has some savings in the form of gold and jewellery . . .'

'I see,' Kotowicz nodded.

'She'd like to turn them into cash.'

'Quite right, too! I entirely approve. Money ought to live, circulate and move. I quite understand. No sooner said than done! I'll give you all the help I can. When should I call on you, dear lady?'

Mme Staniewicz glanced at Drozdowski.

'What about tomorrow?'

'Yes, that would be best,' he agreed with a charming smile, 'tomorrow afternoon, say.'

'Good!' Kotowicz nodded. 'A quick decision is half the battle. I'll report to you tomorrow afternoon.'

He leaned his great shoulders against the frail back of the chair and sighed deeply.

'What a superb day! Just look at the sunlight in those chest-nut trees. So delicate, so much life and beauty! And to think that even the greatest genius couldn't reproduce that little miracle of nature . . .'

It was late at night when, after several sleepless hours, Julius arose, lit the small lamp, brought the notebook out of his satchel and wrote:

'I have lost. The blow came from the least expected quarter. It can't be helped. To conquer, one must learn how to lose. Alek K. hates me. But I hate him more. We'll see!'

Chapter Nine

On weekdays the floor show at the Monopole started at eight because of the curfew. Christina had to be in the bar by seven. Chelmicki went as far as the restaurant with her.

It was a warm day, but the weather was not as perfect and spring-like as the day before. Faded clouds were moving across the sky, the wind was rising and it looked as though rain might fall during the night. A speech of some kind was being broadcast by the loudspeakers.

They had to separate for the first time in two days. Christina wanted to say good-bye at the entrance.

'Not yet,' he held her back.

'It's late.'

'A minute or two. Do you think it will be late today?'

'I don't know. There's not much doing on Mondays as a rule.'

'By ten o'clock?'

'Could be.'

Three men, talking loudly, went into the hotel. Michael was still holding Christina by the hand.

'I'll be waiting.'

'Are you going to your room now?'

'For a little while.'

'And then what?'

'There's this talk. When I get back I'll look in and tell you about it, shall I?'

She nodded.

'But only for a minute.'

'All right. And don't you worry. It'll all work out.'

'Think so?'

An army jeep, white with dust, was passing. It drew to a stop with a screech of brakes a few yards farther on, in front of the hotel. Both glanced at it automatically. Chelmicki shivered. It was Szczuka, in his dusty travelling coat, slowly getting out of the jeep, leaning on his stick. The driver, a tall young man in a leather jacket and long boots, was already standing on the pavement. Two militiamen, youths of twenty, were sitting with sub-machine-guns in the back of the vehicle.

Michael suddenly felt Christina tug his sleeve.

'Why are you staring so?'

He turned back slowly with a heavy and entirely unnatural movement and she noticed that he was terribly pale.

'Michael!' she exclaimed, alarmed.

He tried to smile, but a grimace contorted his lips. He could hear Szczuka's low, stifled voice and the noise of his companion's hob-nailed boots as they went into the hotel.

'Michael!' she whispered again. 'What's wrong?'

This time he managed to smile naturally.

'Nothing. Nothing serious. Honestly!' He pressed her hand. 'I was imagining things.'

She eyed him inquiringly once again, still with a trace of uneasiness.

'Who were those men?'

He feigned surprise.

'What men?'

'Those two who got out of that car just now.'

He looked round. Szczuka and the other man had gone into the hotel. Only the two militiamen remained by the jeep. They were smoking cigarettes on the pavement.

'No idea; visitors, I suppose.'

'You don't know them?'

'Why should I?'

He said this with such indifference that she believed him.

'See you later, then,' she smiled.

He watched her until she had disappeared through the restaurant door.

Chelmicki moved away from the hotel entrance and walked on slowly. After several steps he realized that instead of going towards the other entrance he was walking in the opposite direction. He turned back and caught sight of Andrew coming towards him. Startled by this unexpected encounter, he halted.

'Hullo,' Andrew greeted him, 'where are you off to?'

209

'Me? I was just coming over to see you. Did your brother tell you?'

'Yes. Didn't you get my letter?.'

'What letter?'

Andrew eyed him attentively.

'I left it with the porter. I called three times today and you weren't in. What have you been up to?'

'I've just told you I was coming to see you.'

Andrew grew impatient.

'I don't know what's wrong with you. I specially wrote asking you not to come since I'd come to you at seven. It's that now.'

'Something happened?'

'No. I've left home that's all. I'm staying with Sroka.'

'Why?' Michael asked anxiously.

'Nothing much. But come on, we can't stand here in the street. Where shall we go? To the Monopole Bar.'

'No, for goodness' sake!'

He was aware that he was blushing. Andrew noticed and grinned ironically.

'The band'll disturb us. Come up to my room.'

'All right. Evidently you've been for a long walk.'

'How do you know?'

'By your shoes.'

Following Michael into his room he took off his jacket, sat down on the bed and indicated the wall.

'In there?'

Michael nodded.

'Is he in?'

'Yes. He's just come back.'

'Nice neighbour.'

Chelmicki said nothing.

'Why have you left home?' he asked presently. 'Did you have a row?'

'Something of the sort.'

'What was it about?'

'No use talking about it. A family conference about my future, my studies and so forth, can't you guess? As far as my father's concerned, the world stopped in thirty-nine. He simply doesn't understand a thing, even though he spent years in a concentration camp. He keeps on about position, future, respectability and so forth. Whereas I'm in an awkward position when it comes to this sort of thing. I can't put it to them frankly and openly.'

'Do they know you're leaving?'

'Yes. That's how it all started. Of course they don't know why or where I'm going. Anyhow, let's forget it.'

Chelmicki stood there thoughtfully.

'Oh Lord,' he said suddenly, 'I can't imagine having a family and rowing with them. If my mother or father were here . . .'

'You?' Andrew said in surprise. 'What's all this about? You don't give a damn. Besides you're right. A man shouldn't get attached to anything. What's the use? You've only got to break away afterwards. But that's not the point just now. Listen . . .'

'Well?'

'Sit down! I'm not going to shout at you across the room. What's the matter? You look as if you'd been hit on the head.'

'Well?' Michael asked, sitting down.

'It's about tomorrow. Before he left, Florian . . .'

'He's left?'

'Yes, he went into the country yesterday. Here's a postcard he sent with some instructions. First of all, I'm to report in Kalinowka tomorrow morning. The lads'll be waiting for me. So I'll have to get away by the first bus in the morning. You listening?'

Michael was sitting hunched up, elbows on his widely parted knees.

'Yes, I'm listening.'

'In principle, Florian wants Sroka, Swider and Tadeusz to leave early, as you've decided to get tomorrow's business over on your own. All the same, I don't know how you plan to do it, or where or when. D'you want me to leave you a couple of the lads to help, or not? Make up your mind. Anyhow, fix it so you can get to Kalinowka by tomorrow evening. I've got papers for you with a fine-sounding name!' He tossed a new card on to the table, 'Stanislaw Cieszkowski. And tomorrow's your new birthday too. But joking apart – I must say I don't like your staying here at all, nor your wandering round the town. You must have met dozens of people and every second passer-by must know you by sight. Have you been on the drink?'

Michael shook his head.

'No? Then what have you been doing? Chasing women?'

Chelmicki rose suddenly and started walking about. Finally he halted in front of Kossecki.

'Look, Andrew, I want to talk to you seriously. . . .'

The latter leaned back comfortably against the wall.

'That's just what I've been waiting for.'

'Try and understand, that's all. I want to get out of all this. I want to arrange my life differently. You know I'm no coward, that's not the point. Surely you believe that?'

Andrew was eyeing him searchingly. He didn't seem in the least surprised.

'Go on, I'm listening.'

'I just can't go on like this and I don't want to either. It's all so hopeless. How much longer can we live like this? And what's ahead? After all, I've got to start a normal existence some time. I know you'll think it a bit odd for me to talk like this, but . . .'

He sat down and put one hand on Andrew's knee.

'Look, Andrew, I'm going to be absolutely frank with you. I've met a girl and fallen in love with her. She loves me too and we want to start our lives together. Try to understand, Andrew, I just don't want to go on killing, destroying, shooting and hiding. I want a simple, ordinary life, that's all. You've got to understand.'

Andrew straightened up and frowned.

'Sorry, but I haven't got to understand at all. Can you tell me where you stand in telling me all this? Are you my friend or my subordinate?'

Chelmicki, embarrassed, reddened slightly.

'I don't get you. . . .'

'Isn't it clear? As far as I'm concerned, I must make it clear that in this case I can only be your superior officer. That's all. What now?'

Michael looked at him helplessly.

'I don't know what to say. I was talking to you as my closest friend. I thought that you of all people would understand.'

212

'Enough of this sentimentality,' Andrew interrupted brusquely.

He got up and went to the window.

'Anyway, who said I wouldn't understand, you idiot? But what's the point? Consider it all soberly. You've fallen in love, all right, that's your business. And the girl loves you, that's your business too. Yours and hers I suppose. But if you want to throw off your obligations from one day to the next, then – I'm sorry to have to say this – but it's no longer your own private business. Don't you know what it's called?'

A warm flush covered Chelmicki's face.

'Andrew, I'm not deserting, you know. I've come to you with my problem.'

'With what? With the fact that you want to desert! And you're asking me to shake hands in a friendly way, give you my blessing and say: that's fine, my dear fellow, you're in love, do whatever you like. Look here! How many times have you and I been in action together? Suppose you'd fallen in love then, would you have come to me and said: "Look, Andrew, I've fallen in love, I want to start living peacefully, so you can't count on me any longer." Would you have ever said that then? And when we were in the Old City uprising, would you have said it then?'

'That was different.'

'No, that's where you're wrong. You're a soldier now just as you were then.'

Chelmicki turned towards him violently.

'But what is it I'm supposed to sacrifice everything for? I knew, in those days. But now? You tell me! What do I have to kill that man for? And others? And go on killing? What for?'

'Don't get worked up. You've known all along what for and you knew last Saturday, when we talked over the whole business.'

Chelmicki said nothing.

'No,' he said at last, 'I never considered it.'

'That's no justification.'

'I'm not trying to justify myself, Andrew. But consider my position.'

'And once I've done that, you expect to go on with your loving, eh?'

Chelmicki bowed his head.

'Andrew,' he said presently in a low voice, 'don't you see that a man can change?'

'I know that. But something remains which does not change and which you've completely forgotten.'

'Discipline?'

'More than that – honour; but don't let's be absurd. Let's do without fine words. We're not romantics after all. Honour isn't loyalty to oneself. What are you, after all – the third, the tenth? Just consider! Who are you? You say you've changed. In a week's time you may be yet another man. To whom do you expect to be loyal? To each one in turn? No, old man, it isn't like that. Loyalty is outside of us. You're forgetting that for many years you've been and still are one of us. That's what really matters. You're loyal to yourself if you're loyal to solidarity. That's what honour is, d'you see? But no one is concerned whether you change or whether you don't.'

Chelmicki was listening, still hunched up, his hands clasped between his knees.

'What am I to do, then?' he asked finally, in a dull, heavy tone.

'In the first place, pull yourself together and don't give way. Then . . .'

'I know. Are you so concerned about this one man?'

'It isn't him, you fool! It's a question of orders. Either you carry it out or I do it for you.'

Michael straightened his back.

'You?'

'Of course, that's obvious. What d'you think? I've wanted to tackle this business myself right from the start. Don't you remember? Didn't you ask me to let you do it and put the whole matter to Florian in this light?'

Someone came out of the next room into the corridor. The door slammed and the key turned in the lock.

Andrew listened for a while.

'That him?'

'Sounds like it.'

'Has he gone out?'

'I suppose so.'

'Are you keeping an eye on him?'

'I don't know. He only came in a little while ago, as I told you.'

'What's he going to do tomorrow?'

Michael's hand crossed his forehead slowly and wearily.

'The funeral's at ten . . . you know, those two . . .'

'Which two?'

'Them! You know!'

'Oh, yes. Right. And then what?'

'I don't know.'

Andrew burst out:

'How on earth do you expect to do it at all? Where and when? Look, Michael, I don't want to put this into words but what made you tackle this job in the first place? Have you seen Kaspar?'

For a moment Chelmicki could not remember who he meant.

'Kaspar? Oh yes. The little man from Security? No, I haven't seen him.'

'I suppose you haven't even tried to?'

He took his hands out of his trouser pockets and began walking restlessly about.

'Who's this girl?' he asked suddenly.

'Never mind.'

Andrew shrugged.

'You might at least answer like a man.'

'Why should I? You said it was my business.'

They said nothing for a time. Andrew started to walk about again and Chelmicki rose.

'Very well, then. I'll do it.'

'Tomorrow?'

'Yes.'

'How, though?'

'That's my affair. You needn't leave me anyone, I'll do it by myself. Don't worry. I shan't do anything foolish. My own life is too precious so you can be easy on that score. But that'll be the end of it.'

Andrew glanced at him searchingly and suddenly, turning without a word, went to the window again. He stood there for a long time. Finally he asked:

'So I'm not to wait for you at Kalinowka?'

'No.'

'Well,' he said calmly, 'our ways part. You're going over to the other side. I don't suppose we'll ever meet again as only one of us can be right.'

He stood for a time thoughtfully. Finally he straightened his back, came over to Michael and put out his hand.

'Good-bye.'

Chelmicki managed to say, 'Good-bye,' in a strangled voice. All the past, full of the shadows of dead friends, reminded him of that terrible glow of hope and brotherhood.

'Andrew!' he exclaimed, as the other went out.

Kossecki paused in the doorway. He was pale, his lips drawn.

'What?'

'Tell me . . . do you yourself . . . believe you're in the right?'

'Me?' he echoed with a touch of surprise. 'No. But that isn't what matters. Good-bye.'

Fifteen minutes later Chelmicki came downstairs. He bought some writing paper from the plump porter and there in the hall, at the counter, he hastily scribbled a note in pencil:

'*My dearest,*

I'm free though not till tomorrow evening. I couldn't do what I have to otherwise. Don't come today. I'll explain it all to you later and please don't worry. Tomorrow I have to go to Warsaw. The train gets in at ten p.m. If you can come with me, then write me a note and we'll meet at the station. If you can't, I'll try and reach you before I leave or I'll write to you from Warsaw, and let you have my address.

My dearest, keep cheerful. It's only till tomorrow. Only one day more. Don't worry!'

He put the sheet into an envelope without re-reading it, fastened it down and gave it to a page, telling him where and to whom the letter was to be delivered. Then he sat down in an armchair.

The page boy came back with the reply sooner than Chelmicki had expected. His hands trembled as he began tearing the envelope open. Inside was a small page torn out of a notebook, with the words 'Yes. I love you' written on it.

'Good news?' the porter asked confidingly.

He nodded.

'Excellent.'

He read the three words once again but he felt no joy, not even **relief.**

Chapter Ten

After the heavy rain which had been falling all night, it was cooler and the day was cloudy and windy. Chelmicki reached the cemetery far too early. After a number of speeches in the market-place, the funeral procession was not likely to leave the Party building before eleven, and the journey to the cemetery, via Red Army Square and the May 3rd Boulevard, would take at least an hour. Judging from the crowd which had started to gather in the market-place by ten, the funeral of the murdered workmen promised to be a great manifestation. It was only a quarter past eleven. He had plenty of time.

The cemetery was old and very neglected. Mossy gravestones lined both sides of the path, with crosses covered in reddish rust, others of wood, blackened and drooping to the ground. The thick grass, yellow here and there with dandelions, had over-grown many of the graves. This must be the oldest part of the cemetery. But when he turned into one of the narrow side-paths, the solitude and neglect of the graves oppressed him still more. Here the graves were poor, plain wooden crosses for the most part, packed close together, in the cool shadow of rustling trees and covered with thick undergrowth. He halted for a while. A flat tombstone, which had fallen over, attracted his attention. He went up to it. It bore no cross and was marked only with a large and clumsily engraved headstone, with an indistinct, worn inscription. He had to crouch over to read it.

> *Passer-by*
> *I was what you are*
> *You shall be what I am,*
> *Let us pray for one another.*

The stone bore no name or date. He stood gazing at this in-scription and was about to say a prayer when an instinct of shame prevented him. Soon he could distinguish the slow and solemn melody of a funeral march. With an effort, his frozen legs giving a little at the knees, he walked slowly towards the main alley. At its crossing, by the cemetery gate, people were gathering. At once he caught sight of army uniforms among them.

He leaned against a tree and took off his hat. He felt cold sweat under his fingers. The band was drawing nearer and in the silence which prevailed in the cemetery the rhythm of the march poured out with greater force. He shut his eyes and yielded to the insistent and nagging thought which he had tried to force into forgetfulness. He had killed these two men with his own hands. It was not they that he had wanted to kill. He had meant to kill another man. But the lack of meaning, the accidental character of the crime made it still more horrible. He could find no justification for it. Everything cried out against him. As for the blind solidarity Andrew spoke of, for honour and loyalty to oneself right to the bitter end, even against oneself – he felt there was a truth in man still more sensitive and lastingly just than all these other truths and bonds. How could he have held Christina's body in his arms for two nights without a shock of horror? Or look her straight in the eye in the daytime, talk to her and be happy? How had he dared to tell her that he loved her? His life had hitherto moved in separate ways. In one he had killed, in another he had been a friend, in yet another the lover of girls met by chance. A new life, indeed! For the first time, he realized that there is only one life. There is no 'old' and 'new' life. Nothing in life sinks into oblivion and no act can be undone. Even in the moments of uneasiness he had had so often in the past few days, Christina had not seemed as distant and unattainable as she now became. Had he fallen in love in order to lose – thanks to love – everything he owed to love? He felt he had gone astray in all these complexities, that some important, vitally important, bond which might reconcile these contradictions was evading him; and that the inner voice on which he had relied was not clear enough nor strong enough within him.

Chelmicki withdrew among the graves. He took his hat off automatically. The procession moved very slowly along the alley. The steady tramp of many feet was audible and at last came the two heavy wooden coffins borne by workmen. A small group of men and women followed the coffins, the families of the dead men. Behind them came a huge crowd.

Although some distance away, Michael at once caught sight of the broad, massive outline of Szczuka among these strange, unknown people. He was in the first rank, stooping somewhat, his eyelids down, leaning heavily on his stick. He was about to mingle with the crowd when he caught the attentive gaze of a militiaman standing near. He hesitated and then went over to him.

'Whose funeral is it?' he asked in an undertone.

The other, who looked like a simple young workman, evidently took him for a passer-by and replied in a somewhat hoarse voice,

'Victims of Fascist criminals.'

Chelmicki nodded and moved across to the crowd. These were nearly all workmen, heavy, bony, poorly dressed. Their simple faces, grey despite sunburn and hard-working, resembled one another in the mass so much that it was as if life itself had endowed them through the years with the same strength and resistance. Standing side by side, they formed one compact, huge mass.

Some of the workmen looked at Chelmicki. Although he did not read in their eyes that he was intruding, he felt he was. He withdrew several steps backwards. The wind had died down completely and in the undisturbed silence he caught sight of Szczuka once again.

He must have mounted the earth dug out of the grave, for he was head and shoulders above the crowd. He stood motionless for a while, heavy and enormous. Finally he raised his head.

'Comrades!' he shouted.

His voice rose above the crowded heads strongly and clearly.

'Three days ago,' he began in his hard, rather ponderous but nevertheless very penetrating voice, 'by the bodies of these murdered comrades, one of you asked me: how much longer will such men die in Poland? I could not give him a precise answer. And I asked him: Does it frighten you?'

When he stopped half an hour later, his voice continued to vibrate for a moment in the air. Then silence fell upon the motionless crowd. Chelmicki realized that nothing that had been said had penetrated his awareness. He had merely heard the voice and thought . . . he could not even recall what he had been thinking about. He raised his head and gazed through a haze at the red banners being lowered.

Swiecki, who was in a hurry and had already complained about the funeral taking so long, left the cemetery first, taking Weychert and Pawlicki with him. Soon more cars set off after them: those of Kalicki, Colonel Baginski and other local dignitaries. A couple of militia controlled the traffic at the gate. The workmen left the cemetery in groups and finally only one vehicle was left – Podgorski's jeep. He, Szczuka and Wrona were almost the last. Szczuka was lost in thought, Wrona looked very tired and they moved very slowly in silence. Not until they reached the gate did Podgorski turn to Szczuka:

'Where shall I take you? The hotel?'

Szczuka halted.

'No. Where's Zielona Street? Is it far?'

'A good way. It's the last crossing before Red Army Square. Just beyond the Batory school. Have you something to do there?'

'Yes.'

'We're going the same way, then. You going home?' he asked Wrona.

'Yes,' he replied.

They all got into the jeep. Wrona got in first. Szczuka had just put one foot on the running-board when he suddenly drew back. Podgorski glanced at him inquiringly.

'You go ahead,' Szczuka said.

'How about you?'

'I'll walk back.'

'You can't! You're tired after all this.'

'That's why. I'd sooner walk. Anyhow, please forgive me both of you, but I'd like to be alone for a while.'

Podgorski was hurt.

'Sure?'

The other smiled almost benevolently and clapped Podgorski on the shoulder cordially.

'Your jeep is fine, but I like relying on my own legs occasionally, even if I am lame. See you later!'

As he got into the jeep, Podgorski remembered Kossecki.
'Don't forget this afternoon!'

'Of course not.'

Presently he found himself at the end of the May 3rd Boulevard. As he turned into it, Podgorski and Wrona passed in the jeep. He waved to them and went walking on slowly, thinking. Following him a dozen yards behind was Chelmicki.

The house in Zielona was a three-storied building with shallow shell marks on the façade and a long yard inside. As there was no list of tenants at the gate, Szczuka had to find the caretaker. A dishevelled ruffian, blinking drink-reddened eyes, told him Professor Szretter lived on the second floor back. The centre part of the house was in ruins, bombed.

The stairs were wooden, dirty and gloomy, the windows on the landings without glass and the walls bare of plaster. A thick odour of cabbage mingled with the sharp smell of washing filled the staircase and one of the Professor's visiting-cards had been pinned to the door of the flat.

He rang once, then again. No one came. The flat seemed empty. Not until he rang a third time did he hear muffled and uneasy whispers inside. Finally the apprehensive voice of a woman called out:

'Who's there?'

'I'd like to see Professor Szretter,' he replied.

More whispering came from behind the door.

'Is he in?' he asked, somewhat impatiently.

Apparently he was not.

'Or Mrs Szretter?'

'She's out,' replied the same terrified voice, 'there's no one in.'

'Is the professor's sister in?'

This time the whispering went on longer. The incident began to amuse him.

'Well?' he asked in a friendly way, 'is she?'

'Yes,' came the reply at last, 'but she's lying down.'

'I know,' he nodded, as though carrying on an ordinary conversation face to face, 'it's the professor's sister I want to see. Please tell her it is someone who is anxious to get certain information about Ravensbruck. The camp at Ravensbruck.'

His explanation must have aroused a certain amount of confidence, for after a short whispering council, one of the women shuffled away into the depths of the flat. Familiar with these domestic habits, he waited patiently for them to open the door. However, he was ready for yet another disappointment. In fact the key grated once then again in the lock, the chain clanked and finally the door opened.

The entrance hall in which he found himself was gloomy and full of bits and pieces. A small fat woman, in a padded blue dressing gown, began apologizing because he had had to wait so long. He let her run on for a moment or two about the need for being as careful as possible and finally interrupted:

'Can I see the professor's sister?'

She broke off half-way through an involved phrase, her square face with its flaccid cheeks flushed with offence, and pointed to the door at the end of the passage.

The room was gloomy and so crowded with furniture that Szczuka halted somewhat uncertainly on the threshold. Two large beds, side by side, a cupboard, a chest of drawers, an old-fashioned dressing-table with a mirror. . . .

'This way,' came a faint voice from the depths.

Now he noticed a narrow sofa under the wall parallel to the door. A thin, very worn woman was sitting on it, her grey hair drawn smoothly back. At first he took her for an old woman. However, as he came nearer he realized she could not be over forty. The mild gaze of her once fine eyes rested on Szczuka in a friendly way.

'Good day,' she said, giving him her thin, almost transparent hand, 'I'm glad you've come.'

Her cordiality startled him a little.

'Please forgive this intrusion,' he said. 'Did your brother mention me? We met by chance on Saturday. . . .'

'I know. Won't you sit down?'

He looked round for the chair. It was by the dressing-table, so he pulled it closer to the sofa and sat down heavily. What, after all, had he come here for? The attentive and friendly gaze of this alien, unknown woman began to irritate him. He could not stand sentiment and was afraid that this unnecessary visit would proceed in that sort of mood.

'You are just as I imagined you,' the woman said suddenly.
He raised his painfully heavy eyelids.
'I don't understand . . .'
'Maria talked a great deal about you. Isn't it a strange coincidence you should have found me here?'
He said nothing for a long time.
'You knew my wife?' he asked finally, in a low voice.
She nodded.
'We were in the same block for nearly two years.'
'I see . . .'
He still found it difficult to believe that, when he had finally given up hope, an ordinary coincidence should enable him to meet just the person he had so longed to find. This woman had seen Maria later than he himself had, had shared that life with her, heard her voice, been with her?
She must have guessed what he was thinking, for she asked:
'You never expected a meeting like this when you came here . . .?'
'No. So you were with my wife?'
He felt he ought to ask her some questions. But although he had asked himself so many in solitude, he could not think of any now. What should he ask about first: how she had lived: or how she had died?
'Maria was very brave,' said the woman.
Once again he found no words.
'Really?' he said.
He had to make a great effort to understand what the woman on the sofa was saying. He saw her weary, childishly little face, saw her mild, kindly eyes, heard her voice and for a long time failed to catch a single word. He listened without interrupting, his eyes closed and his big heavy hands resting on his knees. So he had not been mistaken. It had all been just as he supposed. But what he had supposed was now a certainty. Out of a very distant world, out of the depths of his lost past, the woman he had loved and whose courage had so often supported him in difficult times was coming back to him and reviving in him his enfeebled belief in man. She was coming back unaltered, just as on the day when he had said good-bye to her for ever. She had been a blessing to her fellow-prisoners. She had supported them

spiritually and her calm, her goodness and sacrifice, her belief in victory, had saved many women from breaking down. She had been loved.

He wanted to ask about her death, but then decided not to. She was dead. What did it matter how she had died? She lived on in the minds of those with whom she had shared a most difficult fate. She lived on in the women she had saved from doubts and despair. This had a meaning, not the way she had died and what she had lived through in her last solitary moments. Suddenly he felt a long forgotten calm.

Leaning against the banisters, Michael decided to count to sixty slowly. He tried to accentuate each number in his mind clearly and precisely . . . five, six, seven . . . eleven, twelve, thirteen . . . He realized he was automatically speeding up the counting and at once slowed down again. There was black coal-dust on the stairs. A spider was creeping up the wall on the edge of a crack in the plaster . . . twenty-four, twenty-five . . . In his right hand he could feel the cold, smooth metal of his revolver. The spider suddenly stopped at a point where the plaster had broken away completely. Once again he caught himself counting too fast and not pronouncing the unspoken numbers clearly enough . . . thirty-one, thirty-two . . . A gramophone was playing on the far side of the yard . . . forty-three, forty-four . . . It was a familiar waltz . . . forty-eight . . . The spider had disappeared, and he could not see where it had gone. 'This won't work unless I find it,' he thought . . . fifty-two, fifty-three . . . His gaze moved attentively over the wall. It was not there. Where could it have got to? . . . fifty-eight, fifty-nine . . . Suddenly he caught sight of the spider. It was creeping down the wall again . . . sixty!

He moistened his dried lips and began going upstairs. He counted seven stairs. The seven days of the week. But he could not remember what else came in sevens. He rang the doorbell. Of course! The seven lean years and the seven years of plenty. The seven deadly sins and the seven sacraments.

Footsteps sounded behind the door.

'Who's there?' asked a woman's voice.

'From the electricity company,' he replied.

Listening to Szczuka negotiating before the door opened, he was prepared for a similar incident. But it looked as though his explanation was satisfactory. The face of an old woman appeared in the half-open door, still fastened by a chain.

'The electricity company again? They brought the bill on Friday.'

Chelmicki smiled politely.

'It's only to check the meter, Missus.'

His appearance must have given her confidence, for she took the chain off. Chelmicki looked round slowly. It was a gloomy, crowded passage, with cupboard, suitcases, and the kitchen door open to the right of the front door. The other woman was at the sink, holding a large saucepan lid. Calm now! That was all that was needed providing none of the other tenants of the flat came in.

'There's the meter,' said the woman.

Suddenly her broad face with its straight fringe of hair turned greyish-yellow.

'Not a sound, now,' he muttered in an undertone.

He signalled to her to go back into the kitchen. But before she moved, the other woman – also small and plump – put the lid on a saucepan and was standing in the door.

'What are you . . .' she began, then broke off.

'Be quick!' he insisted.

Both retreated in panic. Terror had deprived them of speech. With their greyish faces, blinking eyes and similar gait, they looked so funny that Chelmicki smiled.

'Don't be afraid,' he said politely, 'nothing's going to happen to you. It's the man who came in a little while ago. That's all.'

He looked round the kitchen. There was a door in one wall, he opened it and saw the larder.

'In here, please, Hurry!'

They bustled in obediently. He pushed first one, then the other inside, shut the door and locked it. It was quiet. He had nothing more to do in the kitchen and went into the hall. Suitcases, trunks, a cupboard. Where had they got such a huge object from? A door, then another. Beyond the latter could be heard a woman's voice. He opened the first door but the room inside was empty. Right! All set thanks to that spider, he thought.

Not until he was crossing the yard did he hear the feeble cry of a woman behind him. He guessed rather than heard 'Help! Help!' The yard was deserted, the gate empty. He went out into the street and set off at a steady, but unhurried pace towards May 3rd Boulevard. A droshky was rattling along, it was getting warmer and the sun shone. Sparrows chirped loudly in the roadway round some horse droppings and a young woman was walking along with a pram. A van with furniture stood in front of the corner house and he caught sight of his own boots in an oval mirror leaning against the wall. May 3rd Boulevard was crowded with schoolchildren. He looked at his watch. It was six minutes past two.

Presently he found himself in Red Army Square. Only a few people sat on the balcony of the Balabanowicz café. He crossed the square and turned into a side-street. He passed one house, then another and a third. They were respectable blocks of flats. Then came an open site. Beyond it was a long, wooden building. He looked in at the gate. It opened into a wide yard with a garden on one side and factory buildings on the other. He soon found a wooden, white-washed urinal in the yard, went into it, shut the door on the hook, relieved himself, then took the revolver out of his jacket pocket and threw it down the lavatory.

Back in the street, he felt thirsty so he went back to Red Army Square and gulped down a beer in the bar on the corner. Then he took the quickest way to the market-place. When he got there, he found a crowd filling most of it.

He went between the booths and said to the first passer-by: 'What's happened?'

The elderly gentleman, with a beard and straw hat, shrugged his shoulders and didn't know. He'd stopped because other people had. But a youth on a bicycle overheard Chelmicki's question.

'They're going to make a special announcement,' he explained, 'the war must be over.'

The man in the straw hat made a contemptuous gesture and walked away.

'It'll be on directly,' the youth told Chelmicki.

The crowd was growing. More passers-by stopped. Suddenly the loudspeakers rumbled:

'*Attention, please!*' [the announcer's penetrating voice rose above the crowd], '*this is Radio Warsaw and all Polish regions. We are now broadcasting a special communiqué. Today, May 8th, the unconditional surrender of Germany has been signed in the ruins of Berlin, capital of Germany, by the German High Command. The document was signed on behalf of the German High Command by Keital, Friedeburg and Stumpf.*

'*Zhukov, Marshal of the Soviet Union, signed on behalf of the High Command of the Red Army. Air Marshal Tedder signed on behalf of the Headquarters of the Allied Expeditionary Forces. The following were present as witnesses: General Spaats, Commander in Chief of the United States Strategic Air Force, and General Delattre de Tassigny, Commander in Chief of the French army . . .*'

The crowd listened in silence. No one moved. Every passer-by was standing in the place where the first words of the announcement had reached him. Passing cars also stopped. A car horn blew briefly in the silence.

'*Tomorrow*' [the announcer went on] '*will be the first day of peace in Europe. Poland and all the nations of the world will solemnly celebrate the destruction of the Nazi forces, the collapse of the cruellest tyranny the world has ever known, the victorious termination of the most terrible of all wars and the start of a new era of peace, freedom and happiness. In order to commemorate for all time the victory of the Polish nation and her great allies over the Germanic aggressors, of democracy over Naziism and Fascism, of freedom and justice over enslavement and lawlessness, the Council of Ministers has today issued a decree fixing May 9th 1945 as a national holiday of victory and freedom.*'

Scarcely had the announcer's voice died away into the silence which prevailed across the square than the sounds of the national anthem rang out. People uncovered their heads. When the anthem came to an end, no one moved for some time. Finally, everyone began moving away slowly and still in silence.

The plump porter was standing in the doorway of the Monopole.

'Well?' Chelmicki asked him, 'so the war's over.'

The other blew his nose loudly. Behind his spectacles his eyes were red.

'It'd be different if you could have said that in Warsaw before they destroyed it . . .'

'Hm,' said Chelmicki.

He took the key to his room and went upstairs. First he went into the lavatory and took the forged papers in the name of Cieszkowski out of his jacket pocket, tore them up and pulled the chain on them. Not all the scraps of paper disappeared so he waited a little and pulled the chain again. This time all the paper was sucked away by the rush of water.

In his room, he locked the door. He took off his coat and hat, threw himself on the bed and fell asleep instantly.

Before going out, Kossecki looked into the kitchen.

'Rozalia,' he asked in the doorway, 'where's your mistress?'

'I'm here,' she called from the other side of the room.

He retreated into the hall. Mrs Kossecki, looking very worried, came out after him. Seeing Antony in his overcoat and hat she said:

'Going out?'

'Yes,' he replied mildly, 'enough of this staying indoors. I need a bit of fresh air.'

'About time, too!' she said, pleased. 'It'll do you good, but you'll be back for supper won't you?'

'Of course. What's the time now? It's only just on five.'

She went to the door with him.

'You've no idea of what's been happening . . . I told the plumber to come yesterday to see to the tap that kept dripping. And he charged me a hundred zloty, everything was supposed to be fixed and now as soon as I go into the kitchen, there's the tap dripping again! You can't trust anyone nowadays.'

'Tell him to come again.'

'The plumber? And have him charge another hundred zloty?'

'We'll see. I'll speak to him.'

She was seized with such amazement that she could not utter a word. Meanwhile Kossecki opened the front door and went out. After the clouds of early morning, the sky had cleared completely and the sun lit the earth with delicate brightness. The air was clear and fresh.

'What a lovely day! And look – the lilac has started to come out.'

He turned and eyed the villa's damaged walls. Mrs Kossecki noticed him doing so.

'Just look what they did to our house. . . .'

'Don't worry. Everything will be put right gradually.'

She could not make out what had come over him and changed him so unexpectedly. Suddenly she was overcome with melancholy.

'I keep thinking about Andrew . . .'

'Hm,' and Kossecki made a disparaging gesture.

'Did we do the right thing in letting him go?'

'My dear, he's not a child. He's a grown man. He knows what he's doing. When I was his age, I'd been independent for a long time and worked hard. If he hasn't learned to respect work at his age, I'm afraid we'll never teach him to.'

'But you mustn't forget,' she tried to defend Andrew, 'the abnormal conditions he grew up in. . . .'

'All the more reason. It's just these conditions which ought to have taught him firmness and responsibility. My childhood wasn't easy either. Anyhow, there's no need to exaggerate things. What was is past, and we shouldn't revert to it. If he wants to make money easily, doubtfully, and prefers a gay life to study and work, there's nothing we can do. He has his own powers of discernment.'

'Has he?' she whispered. 'He's been so odd lately.'

He pressed her hand, 'Every man who has something on his conscience is a bit odd.'

He stopped at the gate and turned back.

'Don't forget to send Rozalia for the plumber.'

Erect and with his former springy gait, he went down the street. So the war was over! The world was getting back to normal. People had regained the right to a normal life. As for the past – from today it would have to be left to its own devices, along with everything else, with human suffering and human blunders. The first day of peace had automatically erased all these past days. What's important is not what a man used to be then, but what he is today. War has one set of criteria – peace another. It was in this frame of mind that he intended to talk to Szczuka. He was certain that if the latter were sensible and had a genuine feeling for reality, he would agree.

He met several acquaintances on the way. He felt that most of them would probably not have recognized him if they had seen him in the street two days earlier. Today they greeted him with the same respect as of old. He was not surprised. He had stood in front of a mirror before leaving home, in his hat and overcoat and had seen himself for the first time as he had been before the camp: well set-up, erect, middle aged, with a high forehead, a masculine face and a frank look in his eyes. 'Who knows whether attachment to life isn't the basis of morality?' he had thought then.

The market-place, which he had not set eyes on for some years, surprised him with its traffic, the number of people about and the cars. The difference, when compared with the pre-war years, was startling. People looked shabby and drab, the houses neglected for the war had left many traces on them, the cars were all Army, well used and covered in dust, the pavements strewn with rubbish but despite all this slovenliness and poverty, vital, energetic life was effervescing all round. Red and white banners were waving above the roof-tops. The old 'Starry banner' march resounded from the wireless loudspeakers.

A large banner was hanging over the Monopole too. The plump little porter looked over his spectacles at the visitor entering. A pre-war customer, he at once realized.

'I'm looking for Mr Szczuka,' said Kossecki, 'which is his room? Eighteen isn't it?'

Disappointment was evident on the porter's face.

'It was,' he muttered.

'What? Has he left?'

The other made an eloquent gesture.

'What?' said Kossecki, not understanding.

'They've got rid of him.'

And, regarding the matter as closed, he started sorting out a pile of letters on the counter. For some time Kossecki eyed the envelopes of varying size and colour.

'When?' he asked.

The porter adjusted his spectacles.

'Today.'

Kossecki stood thoughtful for a time, finally turned and began walking slowly towards the exit. Suddenly he recognized Podgorski rising from a chair on the far side of the hall. He went over to him quickly.

'What's happened? Is it true?'

'Yes, it's true,' said Podgorski.

'But who was it? Where?'

'Who! It's always the same.'

And eyeing Kossecki attentively, he said:

'I was waiting for you.'

'Me?'

'Yes. I want to talk to you.'

'Certainly. Where, here?'

'No. Let's go over to the Committee offices, it's not far, on the other side of the market-place.'

'All right.'

They crossed the market-place in silence. In the doorway they passed some militia armed with sub-machine-guns.

On the first floor, Podgorski took Kossecki across several large, lofty rooms. They were crowded with people, and the noise of typewriters mingled with the sound of voices. Only the last room, also large, was empty. It contained hardly any furniture, merely a desk and some chairs. The windows overlooked the market-place.

'What was here before the war?' Kossecki asked, unable to recollect.

Podgorski closed an open window.

'The town Museum. The Germans used it for their police headquarters.'

'Of course,' Kossecki nodded. 'I suppose the collections have been destroyed?'

'Yes.'

Kossécki pulled a chair up to the desk, sat down and looked inquiringly at Podgorski, who was standing by the window. He looked tired and depressed.

'Well, what is it?'

'I expect you can guess what I want to talk to you about.'

'Of course,' Kossecki replied calmly, ' I not only guess, I know.'

'Well, then?'

'What did Szczuka tell you?'

'Everything about you.'

'What does that mean?'

Podgorski made a violent gesture.

'Don't you know what it means? Do you want me to explain? To think you dare look people in the face . . . You! It's monstrous!'

Silence lasted a while. Suddenly Podgorski came closer.

'Anyhow, that's your affair,' he said, more calmly. 'As far as I'm concerned, all I have to say is that, using Comrade Szczuka's statement, I'm going to put your case before the Security office.'

Kossecki said nothing.

' Is that all?' he asked finally.

'That's all.'

He turned and went back to the window.

'So you haven't anything more to say to me?' Kossecki inquired.

The other did not answer. Kossecki got up.

'All right, then. Perhaps you'll let me say something?'

' Go ahead,' Podgorski muttered.

' Do you really have to look out of the window? I'm not accustomed to talking to people's backs.'

Podgorski turned round.

' But you're used to beating backs, aren't you?'

Kossecki met his gaze.

' Yes,' he replied calmly, ' you simply can't believe what a man can get used to. It looks as though you either can't or won't understand anything. A war, and particularly one like the war we've been living through, brings all kinds of things out in people. It makes some into heroes, others into criminals. Isn't that so?'

Podgorski said nothing. He was standing behind the desk, both hands on it, stooping a little.

' Don't you want to answer?' asked Kossecki.

The other looked up.

' It looks as though you still don't realize,' he said in a stifled voice, 'why I brought you here. It wasn't to argue with you about who was a hero during the war. Get me?'

Kossecki bowed slightly.

'Perfectly. But I should also explain that you've misunderstood me. I had no intention of arguing with you. All I want is for you to see my point of view, knowing certain facts about me as you do.'

'You can tell that to the judge.'

'But haven't you already judged me?' Kossecki exclaimed.

'You must listen to me. I don't want to refer to our old friendship, but you must let me speak, as a man.'

Podgorski hesitated a moment.

'All right,' he said at last, 'but keep it short.'

'I'll try,' Kossecki said. 'Now I've claimed that under certain specific wartime conditions, all kinds of instincts are brought out in men. But now the war is over. There's no war. I consider, therefore, that now we've got back to normal human relationships, it's the time for new, normal estimates of society. Certain people broke down in one way or another during the war. They couldn't endure the nightmare. I'm not going to analyse at the moment whose fault was the greater: those who were forced to commit crimes or those who committed the crimes. The fact remains that crimes were committed. But is that to mean that under normal conditions many of these people cannot become honest and useful citizens again? Do you think that X, who stole from his friends in a camp, will go on stealing now that he has returned to his job and is no longer hungry? Or that Y, who became a passive tool in the hands of criminals, will now be a monster to society? Just a minute,' he interrupted Podgorski's impatient gesture, 'I've been speaking theoretically so far, considering the question *per se*. Now, as far as I myself am concerned . . . I don't know what Mr Szczuka told you. He may have oversimplified certain facts. Never mind, I deny nothing. You've known me long enough, surely, to know what I think of responsibility. Of course, I've made a number of grave mistakes. But do you think I'm any different now from before? That I can't go on being the useful and respected individual I was before the war? And who, after all, will be any better off if I get involved in a trial? I won't refer to the purely formal aspects of such a trial at present. Your charges aren't enough. There must be eye-witnesses. Suppose some are found. Suppose I am sentenced. What of it? What advantage will that have? Simply there'll be precisely one man less, now, when men are short. And what else? Some dozens of people, who knew me well, will say: if such a man can stoop so low, what can be expected from others? I assure you it won't be an elevating trial. And it won't help anyone strengthen his or her belief in mankind. So what social advantage is to be gained from such a trial? No, Frank,' he lifted one hand in a rhetorical gesture, 'you know as well as I, that while deserving condemnation in the camp – which I admit – now that the war is over I can give society just as much as I used to before the war, if not even more. And there's something else I must tell you: I'm speaking now as an individual. But it's in precisely this and no other way that intelligent and politically experienced nations reason. There's war and peace, with an abyss in between. There's one set of values for wartime, and another for peace. The first day of war strikes out peace, and the first day of peace strikes out war. What was significant during the war may not count in peacetime and vice versa. Yesterday's enemy may be today's friend. That's life, my dear sir. Two different faces of life: the face of war and the face of peace. They should not be superimposed on one another. And neither should two different people be placed side by side. The genuine man is he who, at a given moment, under certain circumstances, is socially useful. That's all.'

He took out his cigarette-case and offered it to Podgorski.

'No thanks,' the other declined.

So he lit one for himself, inhaled the smoke and sat down.

'And now you can do as you see fit, I have nothing more to say.'

Podgorski was silent for a long time. So this was the man he had once respected and looked up to as a citizen of unblemished honesty? The poverty of spirit of the man was horrifying. He could be the camp executioner, an obedient tool in the hands of criminals, he could also be a decent man. All he wanted was to save his own life at any price: at the price of good or of evil. If life required degradation – he was degraded. If it required civic virtues – he had them. Who was he, really? Who had

enslaved him? What was it Szczuka had said about the bankruptcy of the petty bourgeoisie?

For a moment Podgorski felt so tired that all he wanted was to
end this conversation immediately and have nothing more to do
with this disgusting affair. Instinctively he passed one hand over his forehead and felt
cold sweat. What was he to do? Let the man go free? Let his
crime be forgotten? Not touch filth? 'What was I going to do?' he
thought, amazed, 'to become the silent accomplice of a criminal?
Agree to his lying, cowardly arguments? Me?'

Calm came over him at once. He reached decisively for the
telephone and began dialling the number of the Security Office.
Kossecki, sitting at the other side of the desk, watched him
tensely. Wrona lifted his telephone as soon as the bell rang.

'It's me,' said Podgorski, 'hullo! Can you spare me a few
minutes?'

'When?' asked Wrona, 'now?'

'If possible.'

'In my office?'

'Of course. It's a matter that concerns you.'

'I'll be waiting for you,' Wrona hung up.

Podgorski replaced the telephone and turned to Kossecki at
last. They eyed one another in silence for a time. The sound of
voices and of typewriters came from the next room. But as the
silence in the large, deserted room continued, Kossecki's face
grew paler, as though all the blood were ebbing away, until it
became earthy.

'Let's go then,' said Podgorski.

Kossecki did not move. He could not grasp what had happened during the last minute. All he knew was that he must get
up, and that from the moment he did so, he would begin slowly,
step by step, to fall into an abyss. 'I've lost,' he thought. But at
the same time, he realized this vague phrase as though the im-
mensity of his defeat was still far outside him, as though it were
someone else's, not his own. 'I suppose they won't be able to
refuse me sleeping tablets,' he thought, rather to his own surprise.

At this moment Michael sighed deeply and woke up sure he
had slept for many hours and that it was night. He came to at

once. It was grey in the room but still day outside. He glanced at his watch: nearly half past seven. He jumped off the bed quickly, wiped his sweaty face with the towel, combed his hair and began packing: pyjamas, towel, soap, toothbrush, a dirty shirt, then he put on his overcoat and hat. That was all.

The porter was surprised to hear he was vacating his room. 'There's still time. The Cracow train doesn't leave till midnight.'

'Never mind,' Chelmicki replied, 'I've still got several things to see to.'

The old man straightened his spectacles and started making out the bill.

'Three days,' he reckoned.

Chelmicki nodded.

'Three days.'

And it seemed to him that whole years divided him from the moment when he had come in here for the first time to get a room. The porter wrote slowly and added up still more slowly. Chelmicki could scarcely control his impatience. Finally the bill was ready. He paid and gave the old man a large tip.

'Oh yes,' he remembered, 'let me have some cigarettes, too. Got any Hungarian?'

He had: they were the same brand he had smoked that first night with Christina.

He put the packet away. The porter said good-bye expansively:

'And remember,' he said, pressing Chelmicki's hand, 'as long as I'm here, you can always count on getting the best room in the Monopole.'

'Good!' Chelmicki smiled.

He was already in the doorway when the other called after him:

'And when you get back to Warsaw, say hullo to the Ujazdowskie Boulevard from me . . .'

In the market-place, his feverish haste left him. He stood undecided for a time, then began walking slowly along the pavement. The entrance to the Monopole restaurant was already lit, with people going in. A group of people listening to announcements stood under the loudspeaker. The voice of the same announcer as before resounded loudly. Red and white flags were hanging over the houses. In the middle of the market-place, men were putting up a platform. High flag-poles were being driven into the ground alongside.

He walked to the corner and suddenly turned back. Two lorries were standing on the far side of the market-place, where the passenger buses started. He went up to the timetable. The last bus to Kalinowska left in an hour. The first one in the morning left at seven. He asked the drivers which way they were going: one was not going anywhere, the other to Warsaw.

'And where do you want to go?' the first asked.

Chelmicki mentioned the name of the first large town beyond Kalinowska. The driver shrugged.

'Ah, look here now ... Driving through those woods at night?'

He was about to reply when he caught sight of a patrol of two soldiers walking along the pavement. It looked to him as though they were about to turn into the square so he tipped his hat and walked off slowly in the opposite direction. At the far end of the square, near the people listening to the wireless, he caught sight of a patrol standing on the corner. And this time he set off in the opposite direction. Presently he found himself in a narrow side-street.

There were only a few passers-by and silence all round. He followed this little street for some distance, then turned into another, equally narrow and quiet. Then he halted. What did he want here, after all? Had he really decided to go to Kalinowska? The railway station was in an entirely different part of the town. He had an hour before the train left but Christina might already be waiting for him. He was seized with apprehension lest he be late. He turned back hastily, reached the corner, turned it quickly and suddenly, a few dozen paces away, was confronted by three soldiers armed with sub-machine-guns walking along the middle of the road. He shuddered and turned back like lightning as he heard a voice behind him shouting: Stop! Only a step separated him from the corner. Clutching his brief-case more firmly, he reached into his pocket for the revolver but at once realized the gun was not there, then a strong blow in the back cut off his breath. He could hear flat, muffled firing, as if through a fog as, letting the brief-case go, he fell down. He caught sight of a great red and white banner overhead, with the blue, very distant sky, beyond it 'What's that banner doing?' he wondered, 'what's happened?'

One of the soldiers picked up the brief-case. Another knelt by the dying man and began hastily searching his pockets. Then he unfastened the overcoat.

'Well?' asked the third, standing nearby with his sub-machine-gun.

The kneeling soldier brought a card out of a pocket and had handed it to his colleague. The latter glanced at it and put it in his pocket. The first soldier was meanwhile emptying the contents of the brief-case into the gutter: pyjamas, a soiled shirt, soap . . . All three glanced at one another.

'Oh Hell!' muttered the kneeling one.

He leaned over the recumbent man. He was still alive, his eyes open, but they were already passing into the depths, shrouded with mist.

'Here, you!' he exclaimed unhappily, 'what made you run away?'

European Classics

Jerzy Andrzejewski
Ashes and Diamonds

Honoré de Balzac
The Bureaucrats

Heinrich Böll
Absent without Leave
And Never Said a Word
And Where Were You, Adam?
The Bread of Those Early Years
End of a Mission
Irish Journal
Missing Persons and Other Essays
The Safety Net
A Soldier's Legacy
The Stories of Heinrich Böll
Tomorrow and Yesterday
The Train Was on Time
What's to Become of the Boy?
Women in a River Landscape

Madeleine Bourdouxhe
La Femme de Gilles

Karel Čapek
Nine Fairy Tales
War with the Newts

Lydia Chukovskaya
Sofia Petrovna

Grazia Deledda
After the Divorce
Elias Portolu

Yury Dombrovsky
The Keeper of Antiquities

Aleksandr Druzhinin
*Polinka Saks • The Story
of Aleksei Dmitrich*

Venedikt Erofeev
Moscow to the End of the Line

Konstantin Fedin
Cities and Years

Fyodor Vasilievich Gladkov
Cement

I. Grekova
The Ship of Widows

Marek Hlasko
The Eighth Day of the Week

Bohumil Hrabal
Closely Watched Trains

Erich Kästner
Fabian: The Story of a Moralist

Valentine Kataev
Time, Forward!

Ignacy Krasicki
The Adventures of Mr. Nicholas Wisdom

Miroslav Krleza
The Return of Philip Latinowicz

Curzio Malaparte
Kaputt

Karin Michaëlis
The Dangerous Age

Andrey Platonov
The Foundation Pit

Bolesław Prus
*The Sins of Childhood and
Other Stories*

Valentin Rasputin
Farewell to Matyora